More advance praise for Amy Conner and *The Right Thing*!

"Amy Connor's *The Right Thing* takes you on a galloping ride through the lives, loves, and loyalties of two women from a small Southern town. When their childhood friendship reignites, Annie and Starr tear off on an adventure in a Thelma-and-Louise fashion that will keep you turning pages, laughing out loud, and phoning your best friend."

—Nancy Thayer, *New York Times* bestselling author of *Nantucket Sisters*

"Before you read this book, make some coffee, grab the chocolate, sit down in front of the fire, and don't plan on getting up for a long, lovely time."

—Cathy Lamb, author of *What I Remember Most*

"Told with natural Southern lyricism, and full of surprises both quirky and heartfelt, *The Right Thing* is a compassionate reminder about how every choice at every fork in the road has the power to change the rest of our lives—sometimes far better than we ever could have imagined."

—Kaya McLaren, author of *How I Came to Sparkle Again*

The Right Thing

AMY CONNER

KENSINGTON BOOKS
www.kensingtonbooks.com

KENSINGTON BOOKS are published by

Kensington Publishing Corp.
119 West 40th Street
New York, NY 10018

All Kensington titles, imprints, and distributed lines are available at special quantity discounts for bulk purchases for sales promotion, premiums, fund-raising, educational, or institutional use.

Special book excerpts or customized printings can also be created to fit specific needs. For details, write or phone the office of the Kensington Special Sales Manager: Kensington Publishing Corp., 119 West 40th Street, New York, NY 10018. Attn. Special Sales Department. Phone: 1-800-221-2647.

ISBN-13: 978-0-7582-9512-5
ISBN-10: 0-7582-9512-X
First Kensington Trade Paperback Printing: June 2014

eISBN-13: 978-0-7582-9513-2
eISBN-10: 0-7582-9513-8
First Kensington Electronic Edition: June 2014

10 9 8 7 6 5 4 3 2

Printed in the United States of America

To Mom and Dads—
For all the afternoons of the best conversation,
the uncomfortable chairs, and the love

Acknowledgments

I wish I could convey my gratitude to everyone who contributed to *The Right Thing,* but I suspect that some would rightly prefer to remain anonymous. Consequently, it's an incomplete list, but one that in part reflects the kind and generous friends of the book.

Many thanks to James Nolan, Carolyn Perry, and Maurice Ruffin: none of y'all ever let me get away with a damned thing. Also, here's a heartfelt thanks to the Nolan Group for the great reads, great minds, and encouraging words over all the Mondays.

Marian Young, agent, and John Scognamiglio, editor—thanks again for taking a chance and for the wise advice to a first-time author. You guys are the best ever.

Finally, thanks and all my heart to Fionn and Rue Casey, Zac Casey, and the ever-faithful Weasel and Baggage for the love and support. I couldn't have done it without you.

The Right Thing

CHAPTER 1

Jackson, Mississippi, 1990

I am thirty-five years old and running out of time.

It's Wednesday morning, the day before Thanksgiving. I'm tiptoeing across the kitchen's Mexican tiles like a sneak thief in my own home while this thing in my bathrobe pocket feels as though it's burning a hole through the white silk. Thank the Lord Myrtistine's broad, wide-shouldered back is to me, her big arms busy rolling out the dough for tomorrow's pumpkin pie. I'm going to take a chance and try to slip out into the backyard while she's not looking.

But be damned if my luck isn't running true to form this morning. The screen door screeches like I poked it with a needle, and then, to make matters worse, the north wind snatches the handle away from me, and *wham!* The door hits the frame with an offended bang as soon as I step foot outside.

"Oh, hell," I hiss under my breath, hurrying down the back steps into the garden. Overhead the sky is a flat gray, the color of wet sidewalks and tears, while the frigid flagstones sting my bare feet like shards of glass. It seems to take forever to reach the ornamental rose beds in the back of the garden even though I'm almost running. Yanking my robe free of what was a magnificent Peace hybrid tea this past summer, I weave between the thorns to the back corner of the bed, kneel, brush the mulch aside, and dig a hole as deeply as I can. The dirt is like crumbling cement: it hasn't rained since September, and the earth tells the story. The small, plastic object hidden in my robe's pocket goes into the ground.

For an instant, the slender white wand—plus for yes, minus for no—wavers because my eyes are wet. Stop it, I think with a swipe to my eyes, and the home pregnancy test resting in the dirt swims back into view in implacable sterility. I am not pregnant. This little grave is sister to those of at least twenty-five other EPT tests, all announcing that I'm not going to be a mother, nor will Du, my long-suffering husband of thirteen years, be father to a long-awaited child.

Well, to hell with it. This is the day I give up, I swear. I should stick to rosebushes and other, less painful things.

The wind picks up, blowing my hair into my eyes. Behind me, from across the garden, the screen door screeches open. "Miss Annie? Where you at?" It's Myrtistine, calling from the back steps. I hurry to fill in the hole, brushing the dust from my hands.

"Miss Annie!" She sounds cold and a little put out.

"Coming," I answer, even though I'm pretty sure she can't hear me. It's a big backyard. Getting to my feet, I scuff the loose mulch back under the Peace rose with my bare foot and trot to the house through the dying garden.

Myrtistine holds the door open for me, the warm air from inside the kitchen a humid veil around my face as I mount the back steps. The kitchen smells of baking cornbread, a hen simmering on the back of the stove, and Clorox. Today, the day before Thanksgiving, Myrtistine is making her famous cornbread-and-oyster dressing and bleaching the linens for the table tomorrow. I don't want to think what I'd do without her.

Seriously—I'm hopeless when it comes to all things domestic, and I can't cook worth a damn. The only thing I'm allowed to do on Thanksgiving morning is turn on the oven for the turkey because I burn everything.

"It Mr. Duane on the phone. You crazy, going outside in your nightdress? That wind blowing pee-neumonyer germs all the way from Canada," Myrtistine scolds. "And what you doing down by them rosebushes?"

"They need mulch," I improvise. It's not quite a lie and probably as harmless as burying the pregnancy tests instead of just dropping them into the wastebasket, but as months have turned into years without the hope of a child, the regular bad news has become an intensely private hell. I mean to keep it that way because here in Jackson, Mississippi, all my acquaintance knows they're entitled to a fresh misery report at least once a week. I swear, it's nobody's business but my own and I don't want *anyone* to know. Not Du, please God, and not my so-called friends: those relationships are about as deep as Saran wrap. Myrtistine especially can't know. She works for my mother on the days she doesn't come to our house, and my mother's the last person on earth I want to find out that I hadn't quit trying. Not until today.

Taking the cordless phone from Myrtistine's damp, brown hand, smelling of bleach, I'm still shivering. She pours me a cup of coffee.

"Drink this and warm your cold self up," she says. "Mulch, my foot."

"Thanks," I say, feeling obscurely guilty about the almost-lie. "I'll go upstairs with this."

I take the back staircase up to my bedroom, dusty white silk trailing behind me. "Hey!" I chirp into the phone, trying to sound upbeat. Du's little woman needs to be as cheerful as a thousand acres of Kansas sunflowers. It's part of the deal.

"Mornin', sugar pie," my husband answers. "How's my

gal?" At least, I'm pretty sure that's what he says. On the phone Du usually sounds like he's talking around a mouthful of butter beans. In 1975 when he was pursuing me around the Ole Miss campus with the nigh-insane persistence of a rabbit-bound beagle, I hadn't given it much thought. It seemed everyone talked like that back then, a sort of good-ole-boy camouflage, but now it's 1990, Du's older, and the drawl's gotten so much worse it's like trying to simultaneously translate when I can't read his lips.

"Good." Not good, actually, but I'm not going to admit to anything else this morning. "I was just outside. The roses need mulching," I add before he can ask why.

"Aww, hon—we got a man for that," he says. I hear the snap of his Dunhill lighter. Du's just lit his second cigar of the day.

"I know, but . . ."

"Glad you take such a hint'rest in them thangs, but baby, it's damn *cold* outside." Du chuckles. He puffs a long, satisfied-sounding stream of expensive smoke and commences to remind me about the law firm's partners' dinner tonight at the Petroleum Club. Putting the coffee on the bedside table untasted, I climb up onto our king-sized four-poster, back into bed. While he stresses again what an important night this is for him, I slowly drag the goose-down duvet to myself and wrap it around my shoulders. I'm not looking forward to the partners' dinner.

"You need to look good, darlin'. 'Member? Judge Shapley's gonna be there?"

Du's voice is lugging around a big briefcase stuffed with anxiety. Judge Otto Shapley is the undisputed Word of God around the law offices that have sprung up like mushrooms in a cow pasture around here in Jackson, and so Duane Sizemore's wife must be above reproach or even lifted eyebrows. Poor Du. Heaven knows I haven't been much of a success in this rendering-unto-Caesar department, although I never quit trying.

Du's still rambling on about the Judge and tonight. Half listening, with a loathing-filled glance at the open door of my room-sized, walk-in closet, I know in my bones that despite the armloads of designer ready-to-wear, the racks of shoes and boots, the unbelievable accumulation of crap that lives inside that treacherous space, I won't be able to find a single dress that'll work for tonight. The very thought of poking around in there gives me what my Great-Aunt Too-Tai would call the fantods, so I'm just going to have to go shopping at Maison-Dit this morning. Something new and different for me today—except that's not true. Shopping is what I do best, and I know it.

"Okay, Du. See you tonight," I say, pressing the "end" button. Then I fling the duvet over my head and burrow under it to the end of the bed. I'm in a goose-down cavern now, the hiding place of my childhood. Methyl Ivory, our old maid, would climb up the stairs, panting and swearing under her breath, to roust me out of bed on school days, and I'd scoot under the blankets, hoping nobody would find me there. Bless her, Methyl Ivory is long since departed, and now Myrtistine does for the family, but the years between have taught me you can't hide for long.

So how would I fill up my days if it weren't for shopping? That's a question I don't want to think about, but without a child in my life, having all this free time is a real chore. Even though it's sweetly painful, I fill up Tuesdays and Thursdays doing Ladies' League charity work, rocking those poor babies at the University Hospital while their drug-addicted mothers are in detox. I entertain when the backlog of unreciprocated invitations piles up in an embarrassingly large heap. Oh, and I pretend to garden when the weather's nice, but right now all I want to do is hide under the duvet to have a good cry, and honestly? That's too self-indulgent, even for me.

I'd better get a move on. It must be almost eleven. Emerging from under the covers, I light a cigarette and head into the bathroom for a shower, planning to wear what I had on yesterday and thereby avoid the closet. I won't bother with the armor-plate of makeup either since I'm sure that on the day before Thanksgiving, Maison-Dit will be deserted and I won't run into anyone I know there.

And so the rose garden's burial party is partially eclipsed by today's mission: an acceptable cocktail dress for Du's big night. Dressed at last, I regard my reflection in the bathroom's full-length mirror. Moss-green cashmere sweater: check. Jeans, high-heeled boots: check. Mink parka: check. Down to the five-carat diamond ring on my wedding finger, the diamond studs at my ears, I am both locked and loaded.

Maison-Dit is decorated for Christmas but hasn't turned the carols on yet. True to my expectations, I'm practically alone in the store with the massive silver poinsettias, cascading rhinestone icicles, and a mannequin wearing gold harem pants, a Madonna-inspired leather corset, and a vacant pout.

But Dolly, my saleswoman, seems glad to see me—at least, I think she is. Usually her face has all the expression of a bathroom sink thanks to this latest, less-than-optimal lift job, but today her big, yellow-tinged teeth and gums are showing. That's a sign she's in a good mood.

"I need something dressy, but not too formal," I announce. Dolly's been dressing me for years, ever since my sophomore year's debut parties. After my mother and Du weigh in, Dolly gets the final word on what I wear and how I wear it.

"Annie Sizemore, sweet peaches! We just got the new Ralph Lauren collection in yesterday, and it's divine," she flutes. "You were made to wear Ralph, honey." Her voice seems to come from somewhere underneath the silk twill scarf at her throat that's supposed to be hiding her turkey neck. It's uncanny, like watching a bad ventriloquist perform sans dummy, but Dolly's older than God and maintains she can't afford to retire, not unless she wants to give up plastic surgery. Since she's not going to give up breathing either, that's out of the question.

"Oh goody," I say. "Ralph Lauren." My lack of enthusiasm must be abundantly obvious, but Dolly plucks the sleeve of my mink and steers me past the shoe department toward the dressing rooms with a pat on my rump—a sheep to the shearing shed.

"I'll just bring some little numbers in for you to try on. You get undressed, and I'll send Ardelia over with coffee." Dolly's angular yardstick figure has already about-faced and is stalking to the Collections Room with the intensity of a hungry heron.

"I don't want any." My call to her is halfhearted because I know it won't do any good. There are no exceptions, not even for me: you always get coffee at Maison-Dit, want it or not. It's an Amenity.

But at least the dressing rooms are blessedly soothing. The lush, rosy lighting angled upward from the baseboards makes everyone's skin glow like a peach—a good thing, too, with that unforgiving expanse of mirrors lining the silk-covered walls. I drop my mink on the brocade divan and struggle out of my boots. Too late, I wish I'd thought to wear panty hose and not the striped Hot Sox. Invisible speakers are playing a piano-and-strings version of "Eleanor Rigby," a perfect song for a gray day.

On an impulse, I wad the parka into a ball and cram it under my loose-fitting sweater, turning to look at my profile in the mirrors. With that, *voilà*. I'm transformed, pregnant with five thousand dollars' worth of dead minks. I look stupid. Unwadding the fake baby, I drop it back on the divan just before Ardelia knocks on the door with the coffee.

"Come on in." I wave at the coffee service she carries in on a silver tray. "Hey, Ardelia—I don't really want that. I've had four cups already, and I'm about to jump out of my own skin."

Ardelia sets the tray down on the gilt French Empire table in the corner anyway. "Enjoy your coffee, Miss Annie." The smile on her dark face is set on automatic and vanishes as she pulls the door closed. She isn't gone thirty seconds before Dolly knocks and rolls in a miniature clothes rack on wheels that's bulging with dresses, none of which are going to be what I've made up my mind I need for tonight.

"We're in luck," Dolly crows, pulling a velvet slipcover in an aggressive shade of green from the crush of outrageously expensive fabric. "You'll be divine. We can adjust the shoulder pads before you leave. The alteration girl's on call until six for the whole holiday season."

"Umm," I reply. With a sigh I strip off the rest of my clothes—damn, why didn't I wear the good underwear?—and pile them on the divan. The mirrors' reflection of me in an antifreeze-green velvet dress with sagging shoulder pads seems all of a piece with the weather, the partners' dinner, and Eleanor Rigby.

And the rosebushes, something inside me whispers. *Don't forget the rosebushes.*

Shut up, I say to the something, knowing full well it'll be back. Like morning. Like breathing. Still, harking to childhood's oft-repeated instruction, I stand up straight and look at myself in the mirror with the detachment of the semipro shopper.

"I hate it. This one hangs on me like the curtains at Tara—if Scarlett had lived in some tacky subdivision—and shoulder pads only make the mess wider." I point at the other dresses crammed on their silk hangers. "I hate all of it. I want something with . . . a little more under the hood. In black, maybe."

"Oh, no. Honey, you can't." Dolly disapproves, the authority of my mother's say-so backing her up. Black is for funerals. Period. On any other occasion, black makes women look hard, or fast, or something else We Don't Do. "Besides, you know black's not your color—it washes you right out," she reminds me.

And the hell of it is, I know she's right. Since my first grays, I've bleached my previously blondish, shoulder-length hair to an unnatural shade of platinum and my once-apricot skin has faded to ivory. Catherine Deneuve was right: after a certain point in a woman's life, you have to choose between your face and your ass. I've chosen my ass, dieting myself into a size zero, keeping the status quo of five foot three and ninety-nine pounds of Annie by virtue of living on black coffee and Marlboro Lights. The hollows under my cheekbones will only look deeper, hovering above a black neckline. I'm about to give in like always, but suddenly I see myself in the mirror, slipcovered alive in this humongous swathe of fabric, and I just can't do it. After this morning, plus the trial of the partners' dinner tonight, I *need* a black dress.

"I'll wear lots of blush." Let the partners' wives think what they want of Du's other half in black. If I'm not pregnant (*you'll never be pregnant*), I'm going for sophisticated and edgy, if Dolly will let me. "C'mon," I wheedle. "At least let me try something on."

"Oh, all right. We just got a Calvin Klein in." Dolly's capitulation is grudging at best. "I'll go to the back and get it. You want me to have Ardelia bring you a robe to wear while you're waiting?" she asks.

"No," I say. "I'll be fine. Please, just go get the dress." She wheels out the rejects with a pained air, off to hunt down a size zero in black. *Ah, look at all the lonely people.* The Muzak sobs in saccharine counterpoint to my chronically deprived stomach's grumbling.

Dolly has left the door to the dressing room open a crack. Sitting in a discouraged heap on the divan, craving a cigarette, I succumb and am pouring myself a demitasse cup of coffee (no cream, no sugar) when I hear a raised voice out in the hallway.

"I said that account's been *closed,* ma'am." The saleswoman's voice has an edge to it, like her back teeth are chewing on tinfoil.

"But it just can't be. I know the bill's been paid up, and I hardly never use the store charge anymore." It's a sweet-pitched bell of a reply, although infected with the nasal twang of trailer park. I stifle a yawn, thinking, There they go again. The Maison-Dit sales staff is nothing if not ultrapicky about who they want traipsing around the store, and the little voice's accent, the grammar—or the lack of it—belongs precisely to the kind of person these dismissive women in last season's markdowns will want to send right out the door and back to shopping at JCPenney, where that person belongs.

"I'm sorry." The saleswoman's tone is even snippier now.

"But what am I going to wear? I don't have nothing that fits, not anymore." Trailer Park's voice is gravid with tears.

"Perhaps you should go elsewhere, like the outlet mall in Gulfport?"

"Gulfport?" Those nascent tears evaporate like an August shower on a blacktop road. In fact, Trailer Park's starting to sound mad. "Look, lady—I *walked* here from my house. They came and got the car yesterday." Well, I'll be damned. Even after getting her car repoed, Trailer Park doesn't sound like she's going to lie down for the full Maison-Dit treatment, and that spirit makes me want to cheer her on, even though she's shopping in the wrong part of town.

"So unfortunate," the saleswoman says, an audible sneer pasted across that word, *unfortunate*. "You'll just have to take everything off and leave it in the dressing room."

"Well, I should of known better than to come in here," Trailer Park grates, "even though you all couldn't have been no sweeter before, back when it suited you to take my money!"

She had money before? What's she talking about? I sneak the door open an inch or so wider. Her back to me, Trailer Park's really short, shorter than I am and that's saying something. With a furious toss of canary-diamond curls over those diminutive shoulders, she advances on the beefy saleswoman like she means to smack her silly.

"Ma'am, there's no need . . ." the saleswoman begins to say, backing down the length of the brightly lit hallway. It's Veronica. I've never liked Veronica. She sucks up to my mother.

"Oh, there most surely is a need! You got eyes, don't you, you big ol' heifer?"

"Heifer?" Pale and perspiring with the messiness of it all, Veronica might as well be carved out of Crisco. A single, perfect bead of sweat tracks a rut through her foundation and her eyes bulge just like a spooked Holstein's—if a cow's eyes could be rimmed in bright blue shadow and thick mascara. I can't help but snicker, I'm so tickled at the nerve of this tiny woman.

This tiny pregnant woman. When she turns away from Veronica, the swell of her belly is unmistakable. Price tag dangling from one fluttering sleeve, Trailer Park turns and sweeps past my door on stockinged feet, the flame-red dress hanging almost to the carpet.

Then, without even glancing in my direction, she snaps, "And what the hell do *you* think you're looking at?"

What? I gasp in midgiggle. Trailer Park stops, fists planted on her scarlet hips. Through the crack in the door, she slaps me with this *look*. Her light-colored eyes are stony, her mouth as pink as a child's, but no child ever wore a smile like this one. Too white and even to be natural, Trailer Park's teeth are bared in a humorless grin when she says, "Go on. Tell all your tight-ass friends how you saw me here." She enters the dressing room two doors down from mine like a queen going into exile, shutting the door behind her with a muted slam.

My jaw is hanging around somewhere near my collar-bones. I'm flushed all over, despite being in only my under-wear. Who the hell is this woman? Who the hell does she think she is? Unnerved, I get up to close the door and knock my knee against the rickety table. The coffee service slides to the floor in a slow-motion avalanche of dainty silver-plate, and suddenly there's coffee everywhere. I can only stare at the umber puddle seeping into the white carpet in a kind of fasci-nated shame, familiar to me but now somehow oddly con-nected to the pregnant woman. Troubled and confused, I look for something to clean up the mess, but there's nothing.

Dolly's found the black dress, though, slipping into the dressing room with it just as I'm retrieving the coffee pot.

"Leave that, Annie." She pokes her head out into the hall. "Ardelia!" She hands me the black dress. "Did you hear all that?" Dolly loves a drama. "Lord, honey, I'm hoping we've seen the last of *her*." I don't even have to ask what that scene in the hall was all about since Dolly fills me in while Ardelia is mopping the coffee up off the carpet with paper towels.

Dolly says, "She's the . . . well, I can't say a word like that to you, Annie, but she's the round-heels you-know-what who's been shacked up in the Burnside Tower with Bobby Shapley for the last six months, and honey, Julie Shapley was in here yesterday—looking like she's aged twenty years overnight, poor thing, and who can blame her, even though I always say you should always look your best no matter what, you never know who you'll run into—and she never said a thing about it, but of course everybody just knew that affair was going to burn itself out sooner or later, a tramp like that always thinking she's going to land a man in the bedroom, and *now* Miss No-Better-Than-a-Slut has gone and gotten herself in the family way, and when Bobby told her to get rid of it, that low creature said she'd die first, and oh, poor Julie!—I know it's already been H-E-double-L for her even before there was a baby involved, believe me, your husband being seen all over Jackson with that little home-wrecker—absolutely terrible, just a mess, and now an illegitimate *baby* on the way, for heaven's sake, and I was told Julie took to her bed when it got so bad her parents took the children and were going to commit her to St. Dominic's for observation, but now the word is Judge Shapley has stepped in and told Bobby to get home to his wife and family and to leave that little, that little . . ." Dolly runs out of both breath and euphemisms.

"But who is she?" Ever since this purported Jezebel shot me that look in the hall, I've felt as though I ought to know her. Something about her eyes, pale as blue ice, fierce as a feral cat facing down a pack of dogs. "Where did she come from?"

"Everyone says," Dolly yaps, happy to be of service, "Bobby met her at a Bar convention in New Orleans, where she was dancing in some night club. Well, we all know what that really means." She lowers her voice to a conspiratorial whisper, as if she doesn't want Ardelia, scrubbing away at the carpet on her hands and knees, to overhear. "She's no spring chicken, but she must have lit some kind of fire in Bobby Shapley's basement, if you know what I mean, since Julie Shapley is nobody you *ever* want to cross, honey, much less the Judge."

"I've known Julie since before kindergarten," I say, my tone carefully neutral. Julie Shapley has grown up to be the same kind of friend she was when she was still a Posey and I was still a Banks—the kind you never turn your back on because she might decide to stab you there. "So you're not telling me anything I don't already know."

At this, Dolly pauses, purses her lips, and almost lets the subject drop, but provided with both an ear and a story, she can't stop herself. "Well, that little bleach-blond money-grubber used to come in here with Bobby, buying shoes and underwear and outfits and I don't know what all else, anything she wanted, all she had to do was point," she says, hissing with indignation on Julie's behalf. "Bobby put her up in the penthouse over at the Burnside Tower, and when the board kicked up a fuss, it didn't do any good because you know how the Shapleys are when they're set on something and so he got his way. Anyhow, I don't care what wide spot in the road she came from—she's not from here."

And that, as they say, is that. "Not from here" is a hanging offense, even without the wrecking-ball-to-the-family-home part.

Ardelia gets to her feet, a clutch of damp paper towels in her hand. "I got all I could, Miss Dolly," she says. "We gone have to get the man in here with the Shop-Vac to get the rest of this up."

I glance at the peach silk wall with its Rorschach splatter of coffee and realize it's most likely ruined. "I'm sorry," I say. "I hope this comes out okay."

Ten minutes later, I'm dressed, have signed the store charge, and am walking through the big front doors. Outside on the sidewalk, I pause before going to my car. The long plastic dress bag rattles in the wind that's tearing across the parking lot like a hungry dog. My new low-cut black silk faille cocktail dress doesn't seem as daring as I thought it would, but it sure beats the hell out of curtains and slipcovers. And then as I dig in my purse to find the keys to the BMW, I remember I'm fresh out of home pregnancy tests. Sometimes I go all the way out on Old Canton Road to the discount drug store to buy them since I won't run into anyone I know there, but thanks to the god-awful partners' dinner tonight, I don't have the time today. Before I belatedly remember that I'm not going to do this anymore—the trump of doom is going to sound before I'll need an EPT test ever again—I turn to go to the Walgreens, and she's there on the sidewalk, facing me.

Trailer Park. Her pale eyes meet mine, and the wind lifts that hair, the color of good champagne, in a foamy tangle. I know this woman. I'm sure of it even before she speaks my name.

"Annie Banks," she says. She folds her arms above her belly. Even in my confusion, I notice her coat's grown too small, the buttons not able to meet. I'm speechless. Who the *hell* is she? I wonder.

"Yes," I manage. She knows me? I used to be a Banks before I married Du and became a Sizemore. Without thinking, the rite pertaining to social awkwardnesses comes to my lips and I say, "Do I know you?" Immediately I realize I've said the wrong thing—even though under these circumstances, of course it's the right thing to say—because her face closes like a prayer book at the end of a funeral.

"I'm Starr Dukes," she says. The look she gives me is as cold as the wind. "It's sure been a long time."

The Jackson liturgy fails me. There's no rite conforming to this situation, no magic incantation at my disposal to turn this into a casual encounter. I'm stunned. Before I can stop myself, I reach out to take the freezing, ringless hand of my once-best friend.

"Oh, Starr," I breathe.

It's been twenty-seven years.

CHAPTER 2

I met her in the summer of 1963.

"I hear he's a preacher," my father said, looking worn out. The end of August had been a big week for his pediatric practice, what with immunizations, back-to-school physicals, screaming toddlers with ear infections, and the day wasn't even over yet. My parents still had a cocktail party to attend after we finished eating, but this was *news:* a family had moved into the rental on the back of the block, next door to the Allens' big white Victorian house over on Gray Street, and my mother and father were talking about this development over dinner.

"What kind?" my mother asked. Her green eyes were watchful. "What kind" was an important distinction because preachers weren't the same as pastors or priests or even reverends. Preachers' sermons were characterized by unseemly physical exertion, gross quantities of sweat, hollering in unknown tongues, falling out in the aisles, and occasional snakes, so "what kind" was a serious question.

"The wandering kind," Daddy answered. "What's for dessert?"

I was seven years old and an only child, so to me, my parents, especially my mother, were still the most extraordinary people in the world. Sneaking worshipful glances at her during the course of the meal, I was almost unable to eat my chicken à la king on toast points, my throat was so backed up with inexpressible admiration. My mother, Colleen O'Shaunessy Banks, "Collie" to her friends, was never anything but enviably dressed, and that night she glowed in an emerald-green, off-the-shoulder sheath, gleaming pearls about her long neck. A real beauty, her skin had that classic Black Irish, pore-less luminosity, set off with hair as dark as crow feathers. Because her people had worked the Georgia linen mills, her past was a nightmare of hand-me-downs and cheap shoes, and so she spent a scandalous amount of money on her clothes at Maison-Dit, the most exclusive department store in Jackson. To me, my mother was always, always beautiful, and tonight she was heart-stopping.

"What are you staring at, Annie Banks?" my mother said irritably. "Eat your peas."

I swallowed and asked, "Do you *have* to go out tonight?"

"Lord, we're only going down the block to Dottie Bledsoe's for cocktails. It's not the end of the world, Annie. Wade, could you hurry up? We're going to be late."

And so, being under her thrall, I ate my peas instead of hiding them in my housecoat pocket when no one was looking like I usually did. After dessert, my parents slipped off into the warm August evening like released exotic birds, and our maid, Methyl Ivory, let me put off bedtime half an hour. I think she meant to make it up to me somehow—my mother's being out so much—but even I knew that her staying at home was a hopeless proposition since my mother would've cut her own leg off rather than miss an engagement. Her bridge club, cocktail soirees, costume parties, Ladies' League charity teas—it didn't matter. The newly prosperous, social-diamond life of a small-town doctor's wife was the manifestation of a dream that had sustained her for more years than I'd been alive.

The next afternoon, my mother was at yet another bridge party and I was in the backyard. It was the end of summer vacation, and the last scorching days of August were cooking down to Labor Day and the start of school. I was spending my life outside, for the most part, having caused a fair amount of trouble that summer. I was forbidden my preferred associates—Joel Donahoe, the boy from next door, and the rest of the Bad Kids on the block—and my mother had relegated my playdates to the company of well-behaved children like prissy Lisa Treeby, or Julie Posey, or even Laddie Buchanan, who still used floaties even though he was already eight and peed in the pool. In any case, Joel Donahoe was rumored to have been sent to a work farm for boys in Pelahatchie, and the Bad Kids had been down at the old garage by the railroad tracks on the other side of Fortification Street all that summer. So in lieu of better options, I kept to the yard, waiting for school to begin in two weeks, a high-water mark of how low my spirits had sunk.

That afternoon I was moping around the backyard, smacking the blowsy heads off the rosebushes with one of my daddy's golf clubs. Soon I would be reduced to playing with a bunch of sissies. I was in a bad way.

"Hidey!"

This shout came from the Allens' backyard, from a long ways past the boxwood maze, from the very edge of our lawn. Startled from a wistful reverie wherein my mother might come home today with a pony for me in the Buick's back seat, I turned to see who was calling. Behind the Paige wire fence waved what looked like a miniature mop draped in a slick pink shower curtain. The afternoon sun glittered on a sparkly something snagged in the mop's strings.

"Yoo-hoo."

Company! I barreled past the boxwood maze down to the

fence to see what was what. Close up, the mop turned into a girl about two inches shorter than I and therefore a midget, wearing a rhinestone crown and a long gown, the grass-stained hem a carnation-pink puddle around her dirty bare feet. This must be a kid from the rental house.

"Hey," I said. "How old are you?"

"Seven."

"Me too." I curled my fingers in the fence's mesh and poked my nose into Mrs. Allen's backyard to get a good look at this new girl on the block. She was thin as a ligustrum switch, with white-lashed, watery-blue eyes that blinked a lot, as though it had been a long time since they'd seen daylight. Her mouth seemed awfully wide in that narrow freckled face, the kind of face my mother always attributed to poor nutrition and worse genetics. Her teeth were a tannish color.

I introduced myself. "I'm Annie Banks."

"I'm Starr Dukes," the new girl said. "I got two *r*'s in my name." She pointed at the tiara snagged in her limp yellow curls. "I'm Little Miss Princess Anne Look-Alike for 1963."

"You are not." I was instantly on fire with envy and certain it was a lie. The universal Fairmont Street dare phrase was ready on my tongue. "Prove it," I added, folding my arms across my chest.

"I got a crown, don't I?"

I had to admit it was so.

"And can't you tell this is a pageant dress? I got lots of pageant dresses. The Princess Anne sash's back to the house," Starr Dukes added. "My momma's making all my sashes what I won into a quilt. We're gonna stick it in my hope chest for when I meet Mr. Right."

"Huh," I managed, impressed in spite of myself. A princess with a hope chest! "Well," I said, "that's nothing much. Last week I drove our car and ran it into the garage."

"All by yourself?" Starr asked, eyes wide.

"Sure," I said. "I stepped on the clutch instead of the brake. Mr. Tate had to fix up the front of the garage, and the car had to go to the shop."

Starr looked awed, and I decided in that instant she was my kind of people. "Want to play?" I asked hopefully. "We've got air-conditioning."

"My poppa says air-conditioning is the Devil's work. He says summer is God's fiery time to remind us of the flames in you-know-where. Jesus cries when somebody turns on the television, you know. Television's the Devil's work, too." Starr scratched at a mosquito bite on her bone-thin upper arm. "We don't have a television set anymore. I surely miss it." There were a lot of things missing at the Dukes house, Starr told me: lamps, the record player, a brand-new recliner, dishes, most of Starr's mother's clothes, and her sewing machine.

"We had to leave without our stuff 'cause it wouldn't all fit in the car." It seemed the folks at the last outpost of Christianity in Dry Prong, Louisiana, hadn't truly appreciated the quality of Mr. Dukes's preaching, so the family had made a decision to relocate in the middle of the night. "They're all going straight to you-know-where," Starr announced with conviction. "Momma brang my hope chest, though, and my pageant dresses."

"You want some Kool-Aid?" I asked. It was getting on to the middle of the afternoon, and the sun was a steam iron on top of my head. Somehow we managed to get Starr over the fence in her pageant dress and trudged up the sloping lawn to the back door. The air in the glassed-in sunporch running across the back of the house—the conservatory, as my Grandmother Banks styled it—was almost as hot as the backyard. All the ferns and bromeliads slumped in a sullen bid for water and attention, the white wicker settees dusty from the summer's long disuse.

"Y'all got a mighty big house," Starr said, looking around. "Where's the air-conditioning?"

"It gets cooler in the kitchen. Come on."

Methyl Ivory was across the wide center hall in the living room, pretending to iron while she watched television. "Methyl Ivory, can we have some Kool-Aid?" I yelled, already getting the big frosted pitcher out of the refrigerator. Starr had wandered into the living room with her hands clasped behind her back, the long dress a crumpled tide in her wake.

"Don't you touch nothing," Methyl Ivory said to my new friend. "You be careful with that Kool-Aid," she called to me. I slopped violently purple liquid into two glasses and carried them into the living room. Methyl Ivory warned me with a look that said I'd better not spill any.

"Oh, my!" Starr squealed. Her fingers entwined under her chin in delight, she was so entranced with the program on the television. "It's *Queen for a Day*. That's my most favoritest show." Without so much as a glance at Methyl Ivory, she folded up in wrinkles of dirty sateen onto the Oriental rug in front of the ironing board, taking the glass of grape Kool-Aid out of my hand without even looking.

"Mmm-mmm." Methyl Ivory cursorily ran the iron over a sheet, her eyes likewise glued to the small black-and-white screen. "That po' woman." I'd never seen the show, but with a shrug I sat down and watched, too.

It turned out that *Queen for a Day* was lots more interesting than Methyl Ivory's usual soap operas. Instead of people lounging around fireplaces talking about who loved who and who didn't, this show had some action. Three contestants, all depressed-looking, lumpy women in black dresses, sat behind boxes on a stage and told the sad stories of their lives, each woman's story more scarifying than the one before. Hospital bills, lost jobs, runaway children, disfigurements, dead husbands, unspeakable diseases, turned-off utilities, backbreaking labor at truck stops to make ends meet—these were only a few of the terrible things these women had to endure. Their tears overflowed like leaf-choked gutters. The last woman related her story about how the very evening her sick ("He got the lung-rot *bad*") husband had lost his job, that same night the family dog had been run over in the street. Oh, we were transported with schadenfreude, a term I didn't know then but was thrilled to experience.

The announcer, an oily man in a double-breasted suit with slicked-back hair and eyeglasses, sniffed theatrically and dabbed at his eyes with an outsized handkerchief.

"Oh, Missus Swank, that was just about the saddest thing I ever did hear," he said. "But it's good to know your children are healthy, even if the dog's not! Now it's time for our audience to vote on whose story pulls at our heartstrings the very most." He looked straight into the camera. "Your applause will tell the world which of these little ladies here deserves to be Queen for a Day!" A glamorous woman with a towering beehive hairdo and a long, sequined gown tripped out on the stage behind the sniveling contestants and held up her arms under a big dial with an arrow pinned to it—the Applause-O-Meter.

"Contestant Number One, Missus Rita Mae MacRevus!" The audience clapped enthusiastically, and the arrow moved halfway up the dial. The camera moved on to the next woman, a doughy lady with a fascinating wen under her left eye. She put her head down on the box and sobbed her guts out. "Contestant Number Two, Missus Geraldine Pettit!" This time the applause was thunderous, and the arrow went past halfway, dipped, and then shot to the three-quarter mark. Contestant Number Three, Missus Pam Swank, didn't stand a chance, not even with the dead family dog story. Missus Pettit was Queen for a Day.

Immediately, both the other contestants were herded off the stage, still crying, while the glamorous lady draped a velvet cape with an ermine collar over Missus Pettit's big heaving shoulders. The announcer placed a crown on her wiry gray bun. The theme music rose to a crescendo. A bouquet of long-stemmed American Beauty roses ended up in Missus Pettit's arms, and the audience clapped like mad things.

The rest of the show boiled down to a bunch of relatively uninteresting prizes, like the washing machine the beehived lady rolled out from behind a curtain and the year's supply of Duz detergent Missus Pettit was going to receive since she had eight children and no way to get to the Laundromat. The show ended with a close-up of Missus Geraldine Pettit's face wearing a brave, gap-toothed smile, waving at her loyal supporters in the audience. "Queen for a Day!"

The list of sponsors scrolled across the screen. I announced, "That was *great*. I want to be Queen for a Day."

"You can't," Starr said practically. "You got to be married, with children. It says so, right on the entry form."

"How come you know that?"

"You can get one off the back of any box of Duz detergent," Starr said with authority. From the floor, she looked up over the ironing board, catching Methyl Ivory's eye. "Isn't that right? If you're married and got kids, you can be on the show?"

Methyl Ivory shook her head. "I never seen no colored folks on *Queen for a Day*." She stretched the ironed white cotton between her strong arms, bringing them together with a disgusted sigh to put a crisp fold in the sheet. "I know I got a lot a ironing to do 'fore you momma get home, Annie Banks. Y'all git now. I got things to do."

Well, air-conditioning might have been the work of the Devil, but Starr and I were willing to risk eternal damnation. We decided to go play upstairs instead of back outside in the stifling yard. In my bedroom, Starr surveyed my collection of toys and clothes. She touched everything, seeming to figure up how much each party dress, each deck of Old Maid cards, even the worn-out pair of Keds under the bed, had cost. I began to feel a little disgruntled at this silent appraisal. When were we going to get around to playing?

"Look!" My new friend pounced on a pile of dolls on the floor, holding up one of the tribe of Barbies I'd accumulated for birthday and Christmas presents over the last couple of years. "See what you've done to them!"

I looked away, feeling uncomfortable. It was true: my Barbies were in a deplorable state. They were all naked as only plastic dolls with breasts could be since I'd carelessly mislaid their clothes, and their Dynel ponytails and bouffant hairdos were in ruins of fused plastic strands. I'd attained a rudimentary understanding of chemistry when I'd taken them to the kitchen sink so they could get shampoos and sets. A vinegar rinse was what my mother used on her lovely dark hair to give it shine, but the ammonia treatment I'd improvised had turned the Barbies' hair into frizzy, globular masses that no amount of combing would restore.

"It's just terrible, what you done to their hair." Starr was aghast, picking up each one of my naked dolls tenderly and stroking its plastic mat. "Poor things," she said. "We oughta do something nice for them."

I had an idea. "What if we made them Queen for a Day?"

"You mean, like on the TV?" Starr seemed to think it over. "We got to make them some clothes first. You can't be on TV *nekkid*."

With that, we got busy. It seemed Starr had a genius for making clothes for Barbies. We tiptoed across the hall into my parents' huge bedroom and raided my daddy's drawers for the long black silk socks he wore with his good shoes. Then, we cut off the foot ends with my mother's scissors (she'd forgotten a previous incident involving the living room curtains and returned them to her sewing basket) and poked weeny little holes in the long black tubes for the dolls' arms. When the Barbies were slid into their new dresses, we folded down the excess material at the top and ta-da! Sheath dresses, like the sophisticated, cocktail-sipping ladies wore on *As the World Turns*. Next, Starr insisted they needed underpants, so we made black panties with the socks' leftover toes and used rubber bands to hold them up.

"They need hats, too," she said. "Their hair is a dis-grace, I mean to tell you." It was 1963, and everyone was wearing the pillbox hat that Mrs. John Kennedy, the president's wife, had made popular, so we foraged in my parents' bathroom cabinet until we found enough pill bottle tops. There were a lot of pill bottles in the old-fashioned cabinet: my daddy was always bringing home samples from the pharmaceutical reps for my mother that promised to combat weight gain and insomnia and to give her some pep. The round tops to the bottles kept falling off the Barbies' misshapen heads, so we glued them on. Finally, our attention was drawn to the dolls' feet. "They can't be on TV barefooted." I was completely stumped, but not Starr. While I distracted Methyl Ivory down in the living room, she ransacked the kitchen for the roll of tin foil. Back upstairs, Starr molded sheets of it into cunning little high-heeled shoes for the Barbies.

"Now," she said. "Now, they can be on the TV." The Barbies looked like some weird religious sect—long black dresses, white plastic hats, and silver shoes—but at least their blue-lidded eyes no longer seemed to accuse me of doll atrocities.

But now it was time for Starr to go home. "My poppa wants his dinner on the table at five pee-em every day. If I'm late, he gives me a whuppin'," she told me. I realized that while I was pretty sure I wouldn't be whupped, my mother would be home soon and I had better return to the backyard since I hadn't been explicitly told I could come inside to play, much less have a friend over.

At the fence, I helped boost Starr over the wire. Landing with a kitten bounce in the grass on the other side of the fence, she hiked up the hem of her dress in both hands, scampering across the Allens' manicured St. Augustine lawn for the next yard over, where the grass was high and weedy behind the rental house.

"See you tomorrow," she called over her shoulder.

Starr was back at the fence the next morning and every morning after that for the rest of the week. She wore a different pageant dress each time, but after the first day she left the crown at home. "Don't want to lose it." We never went to her house to play, but that didn't seem odd to me. The rental house had a forbidding look—the sheet-covered windows shrouded a blank white, the eaves rotting, and the grass grown as high as your waist. My daddy called it an eyesore, but I didn't know or care what that meant. It was where my new best friend lived.

And after that first afternoon together, that's what we were. Best friends. I don't know why I didn't tell my parents about Starr, except that I had a dim but strong suspicion that my mother wouldn't approve (that wandering-preacher thing again) and I didn't want to run even a smidgen of a risk that she'd forbid me my new best friend, too. Besides, my mother was never home, and Methyl Ivory didn't seem to mind. The only time she had us underfoot was when we were literally in front of her big white nurse's shoes, clutching ourselves in high anticipation of the *Queen for a Day* Wurlitzer's theme music.

Once the camera closed on the winner's rictus of haggard ecstasy, we'd take off. The Barbies were a de facto pool of contestants clutched under our arms as we flung ourselves out the screen door to the backyard. We couldn't get enough of playing Queen for a Day, especially after we scrambled up our reenactments with tips Starr had accumulated over the course of her pageant career.

"Before they tell their stories, they got to walk down the runway and smile big at everybody." Starr daubed the dolls' permanently lipsticked mouths with Vaseline purloined from my parents' bathroom cabinet to give them some sex appeal.

"But that's not the way they do it on the show," I objected. I wasn't sure about the way the Barbies' severe black dresses had begun to show so much leg and cleavage either: they looked a lot less like Mennonites and more like showgirls, but Starr had control of the scissors and was the final arbiter of taste.

"That's 'cause on the show they haven't thought on any of this yet," she told me. "Don't these gals deserve to look pretty? My momma says she used to look pretty and now she can't hardly stand to look at herself in the mirror anymore." Put that way, I was on board with the beautification and strutting, for after all, I'd been the one who'd tied them to the oak tree like Druid sacrifices when playing kidnappers with Joel Donahoe. I'd sent them boating, naked, down the drainage ditch on a collapsing shoe-box raft when they were *Titanic* passengers, and scotch-taped them to roller skates so they could die in fiery car crashes. Sure, I agreed: let the Barbies live a little.

We got better at the stories, too. I admit, my first attempts at manufactured pitiful were feeble. Mostly I mimicked what we watched on the television every afternoon, the usual miserable litany of poverty and plain bad luck that afflicted the po', po' women on *Queen for a Day*. Starr juiced these stories up a lot, and soon I just let her be in charge. She must have heard plenty of harrowing tales firsthand, being the only child of the wandering kind of preacher.

"And then I come home from working in the laundrymat, folding other people's clothes and whatnot, until I look like a wrinkled pillowcase myself, and caught him in the bed with that Vonda from the Tote-Sum!"

"What happened next, Missus Bledsoe?" In my role as announcer, I'd taken to calling the Barbies by the names of my mother's friends from around the neighborhood. It was easier than coming up with new names every day.

"Why, then I picked up a grease gun and passed it across his lying mouth—he barefaced lied to me, right there with that hoor beside him in our Broyhill bed what's not been paid for yet—and now my Cubert's in the hospital needing twenty-five stitches and I don't know where the money's coming from anymore. I'm so tore up I can't go back to the laundry-mat," Starr wailed. We clapped until our palms were burning for that one.

Sometimes, as the announcer, I would've been hard put to decide which one of the silent dolls propped up under the sunporch windows was going to win the crown made of my mother's borrowed topaz cocktail ring. All the stories were enthralling in their utter dreadfulness, and besides, it wasn't up to me anyway. Since Starr wore the pageant dresses, she got to be the lady with the beehive hairdo and the Applause-O-Meter. She usually decided who was going to get a vacation in Hawaii—no washing machines for *this* Queen for a Day.

And so we passed that week's afternoons until the sun fell below the tall top of the live oak tree in the backyard, until the cicadas shrilled dry vespers to day's end, until Starr would go home so her poppa could have his dinner on the table at five pee-em.

Until the day of my mother's bridge club party.

I should have known something was up because Methyl Ivory had been making party food for what seemed like forever: flaky puff-pastry shells filled with canned smoked oysters in cream sauce, molded tomato aspic with olives, and her special tiny mint-fondant calla lilies to go with the demitasse cups of strong coffee my mother would be serving after dessert. The sunporch had been relentlessly cleaned, the tablecloths and embroidered napkins starched and ironed. Still, I didn't figure it out until I saw the folding chairs come up from the basement that morning. My mother was at the florist's, picking up the flower arrangements for the card tables.

"You got to stay outside," Methyl Ivory said with a grunt. She wiped her face with the sleeve of her white maid's uniform and unfolded a chair. "Can't even go to your grammaw's house. Ol' Miz Banks say you cut up too much without you parents bein' there for keepin' an eye out, and I got to serve the white ladies they luncheon." She adjusted the placement of the tablecloth and frowned at me. "Listen here, Annie Banks, you play nice in the backyard. I'll save you a few of them lily candies. Y'all can have a lil party out there."

I didn't care at all about missing an afternoon at my grandmother's house. Though it was even bigger than ours, the rooms there were dark, full of breakable knickknacks, smelling of floor heaters and paste wax. There wasn't a thing to do at my grandmother's except to ferry her obese dachshund, Pumpernickel, up- and downstairs in the elevator until my grandmother's maid, Easter Mae, made me stop. Besides, the heat had abated in the last few days as it used to do in Mississippi toward the end of August. My father had cut off the air-conditioning units to save money, and all the windows were open again to let the cool breezes inside the house, so not minding banishment, I banged through the screen door to meet Starr down by the fence. Today she was wearing fringed gauntlets and a knee-length dress liberally decorated in red, white, and blue sequins.

"Help me get up over this here fence," she said. "I don't want to poke a hole in my tap outfit."

While we were setting up, my mother's bridge club began

arriving. I stood on my tiptoes and peeked inside the open sunporch windows. Eight ladies in hats were taking off their gloves and putting down their pocketbooks. Their perfume, a light and powdery-floral mix of Chanel No. 5, Shalimar, and Joy, floated through the window outside into the yard. My mother had returned from the florist's in the nick of time, and the card tables were elegant with their low bouquets of daisies and sweetheart roses, the decks of cards and bridge tallies, the company ashtrays.

"How nice everything looks!" said one of the ladies, a stout woman in a big hat stuffed with yellow tulips around the brim. That was Mrs. Bledsoe, from around the block. Methyl Ivory was making her way around the sunporch like a barge in a white uniform, carrying a silver tray full of glasses of sherry.

"Oooh," shrilled Squeaky Posey, one of the Ladies' League's more prominent members and prissy Julie's mother. Her bright pink face beamed from under a red straw hat crowned with a cockade of rooster feathers. "I'd love one of those."

"Me too," another lady cried. It seemed my mother's bridge party was off to a good start. Soon the sounds of their bidding ("One, no trump," "Three spades," "To you, Dottie") murmured overhead. Cigarette smoke filtered outside through the screens. Bored with spying on the bridge party by now, I sat down in the grass under the windows, ready to begin my role as announcer.

The Barbies were in fine fashion today, too. Starr had made the dolls big sashes from my hair ribbons with their names printed on them in straggling black Magic Marker. By the time the Barbies had finished their parade down the runway, inside the house Methyl Ivory had already been through the sunporch with the sherry tray twice. The bidding got louder, so we had to speak up when it came time for the stories.

"Tell me, Missus Dottie Bledsoe, why are you here today?" I boomed, holding the golf club to my mouth like a real microphone.

Starr cleared her throat importantly. "Well. I'm a-hopin' you folks can help me out with my fuh-ham-i-ly." She sounded a lot like Mrs. Bledsoe, a loud lady with a Jackson accent thick as roofing tar. "My husband's run off with his secketary, but before he left, he gave me a disease what I can't tell you about on the television, 'cept it's give me the dry itch so bad it keeps me up at night scratchin' like a dog with fleas in my lady parts. Got to where I can't even leave the house, I itch so bad. Don't know how I made it here today, God's my witness."

"We're so sorry to hear about your trouble, Missus Bledsoe." I held the golf club microphone closer to the Missus Bledsoe doll.

"I can't hardly keep the lights on anymore, so I borrowed some money from the church plate, only the pastor don't see it that way and now he says if I don't put out he's calling the police to put me in jail. Now who's going to feed my children if I'm locked up in the pokey?" Starr shouted, swinging Missus Bledsoe's rigid plastic arms over her head in complete mystification as to what to do next.

For some time I hadn't paid attention to the bridge party going on behind the open windows overhead, which is why I didn't notice how deathly silent the sunporch had become.

"And how can we help you, Missus Squeaky Posey?"

"I mean to tell you, I got to get me some relief from the drink!" The Missus Posey Barbie hopped across the grass to the microphone. "Lord Jesus," Starr hollered. "If it weren't for the drink, I wouldn't beat my children with their daddy's belt. He's been laid up for years with a broke back from falling off a ladder. Sometimes Heber yells for the bottle, but I can't bring myself to give it to him because being a drunk is one thing—at least I can get to work at the nursing home when I got to—but being a bedridden drunk is just a waste of good booze."

"You po', po' woman," I said with a gusty sigh.

At that moment the screen door crashed open with the screech of rusted springs, and there on the top of the wide cement steps were my mother and Mrs. Bledsoe herself.

"I'm telling you I heard what I heard, Collie Banks," Mrs. Bledsoe said, her voice frosty as an engine block in January. "My Duh-honald wouldn't duh-ream of leaving me for his secretary, and the very i-yuh-dee-a of me stealing from the church!" The tulips on her hat were shaking with scarcely contained rage. She pointed a fat finger at the Barbies. "Look! There's my name on that, that . . . doll dressed like a stuh-reetwalker! I simply can't stay another minute." She turned her back with a loud sniff and stomped inside the house.

"I'll deal with you later, Mercy Anne Banks," my mother hissed, and her face was as wrathful and dire as God's. In a whirl of rose-colored polished cotton skirts, she was gone. "Wait, Dottie—this is all a terrible misunderstanding!" Starr and I looked at each other, round-eyed. I realized I didn't have time to cry: the scene was just littered with incriminating evidence.

"Run, Starr!" I whispered urgently. "Go home! My mother's using my whole name!" Beginning with the scissors, I scooped up all our props. Starr ran for the fence. I heaved everything under the ligustrum hedge by the armful, hoping without much hope that my mother wouldn't remember what the Barbies had been wearing. It hadn't occurred to me that stolen socks and pill bottle tops were going to be the least of my troubles, not yet.

That was the prelude to the End of the World, or at least the end of Queen for a Day. It was a measure of the social disaster Starr and I had wreaked that a whole foursome departed our house that very afternoon and subsequently formed their own bridge club. My mother took to her bed for half a week. Once she finally ventured out, she was snubbed at the Jitney Jungle in the frozen food aisle by women who hadn't even been invited to join the bridge club. Worse, when her friends from the Ladies' League tried to ease her way back into polite company, speaking to Dottie Bledsoe and Squeaky Posey on her behalf, they were met with that impenetrable, blank mask of social punctilio. My mother was almost ruined. If it hadn't been for the president's assassination giving breath to a fresh topic of conversation in Jackson, Mississippi, it's possible her excommunication would've lasted for years.

But for me, it meant Starr Dukes was forbidden. School started and even though our desks were just a few feet apart, even though we were best friends, Starr and I were Not Allowed.

CHAPTER 3

"I flat do not *believe* that you didn't know who the hell I was." It's the first thing Starr's said since we got in my car ten minutes ago. In fact, it's the first thing either of us has said, but then she was always braver than I am.

The Burnside Tower is just a jumped-up high-rise apartment building, in my opinion, but that's where we're headed. My brain scurrying like a hamster in a hailstorm, I cannot think where else we can go. Coffee? Someone would be bound to see us together, and that would be purely nuclear in this town. And not to my house, God forbid: Du would find out. I swerve left against oncoming traffic, just missing the massive brick pillars of the Burnside's entrance, and drive through the tall iron gates onto the long, curving drive lined with severely trimmed boxwoods and bare-branched redbud trees.

I pull into the big, dark garage before I say anything. Parking in a deserted corner, I leave the Beemer running so we can stay warm. Only then do I unsnap my seat belt and turn to her across the caramel-leather-covered console. Starr's staring out the window at the cinder block wall of the garage, her face turned away from me.

"I'm sorry," I say humbly. She doesn't answer. "At first I thought you were familiar, but—"

Starr interrupts. "No, I meant just what I said. You were going to pretend you didn't know who I was." She turns to look at me then. It's plain the recent past hasn't been good to her by the lavender shadows under her eyes, the weary set of her mouth, and yet now that I really look, I can't imagine why I didn't know her the moment she turned around in the hallway at Maison-Dit. It's really her.

"No, Starr," I plead. Staring at my reflection in the side mirror because I can't face that accusing gaze, I say, "No, please believe me—I honestly didn't recognize you. It's been such a long time!" I swipe at my eyes since I'm beginning to cry now. "Why didn't you ever write me? Why didn't you call me as soon as you got to town?"

Starr reaches into her coat pocket and silently hands me a tissue. "You always did tear up easy," she mutters moodily. She turns away from me again and blows on the passenger window, making a small frosted patch of condensed breath on the glass. With the tip of her finger, she draws a pair of stick figures in the mist: two little girls.

"Why do you think I didn't call?" Starr asks at last. Her voice is tired-sounding. She rubs out the stick figures. "I mean, look where we are—parked in the back of the damned garage! You don't even want to be seen with me in public, do you." It's not a question.

A silence falls in the car, broken by the faint squeal of someone's car tires making the turn into the garage on the other end of the building. How do I answer her? If Dolly hadn't told me the juicy story of Starr and Bobby Shapley, I'm sure someone else would have eventually. Jackson is social flypaper, all those little scandal corpses stuck fast to a much-handed-around broadsheet. What's happened to her is so incredibly messy, I'm amazed that I'm only just hearing about it, even though I'm usually out of the fresh-gossip loop. Like I said, I have my own issues. I don't hang around much with people who know these things, and when I do, we don't spend a lot of time chatting about the latest whispered news around town.

But I realize that Starr's hand is on the door. She pushes it open, and the November wind whips around the corner, bullying its way inside the car in a freezing gust. "You know," she says, sounding wistful, "I had an Audi, before." Her bee-stung lip curls. "Listen to me, talking about *before*. Before was a lie." She starts to get out. "Bye, Annie Banks. Thanks for the ride."

"Starr, wait. Don't go," I say, putting my hand on her sleeve. "That last day I saw you back in second grade, you never said a word about leaving. On Saturday you were there, Monday you weren't. It tore me up. Whatever happened to you?"

Starr laughs shortly. "That's a whole 'nother story, honey. A long one."

"Look," I say, frantic because she's leaving and I don't know how to fix this. "Let's go upstairs and have a cup of coffee." For emphasis, I turn off the engine and pull the keys out of the ignition. I dab at my eyes one last time. "Come on, please? I've never been in the Tower penthouse before. You can show me the view."

Starr shrugs, as if it doesn't matter to her at all.

Luckily, we don't run into a soul in the elevator that smells so powerfully of floral aerosol that when the door opens on the penthouse floor, I trade the reek of English lavender for a deep, grateful breath of unfreshened air. Up here the spacious foyer area is furnished with a demilune table and a gilt mirror, flanked with two oversized doors. Starr unlocks the door to the right-hand condo, and we walk inside.

Up here on the ninth floor, the view is a vista of roofing

shingles, exhaust vents, and oak treetops bisected by eight lanes of traffic howling along on the I-55 below. I turn from the plateglass windows and sit on one of the matching white leather sofas while Starr is in the stainless steel kitchen, making espresso in an Italian machine the size of a Ford Fiesta. Alone in this sterile space, I'm snow-blind from the expanse of chalky Berber carpet, the stark white walls, the chrome lamps like intergalactic telescopes, and the collection of artfully underexposed black-and-white photographs of desert landscapes hung around the Carrara marble fireplace. The only color in here is a bright paperback on the Lucite coffee table. *A Thousand and One Names for Your Baby*. I haven't taken off my mink. I'm shivering, and not just because the thermostat's turned down to a frigid sixty degrees to save money: according to Starr, Bobby quit paying the electric bill a month ago. I'd light a cigarette for at least an illusion of warmth, except there's a conspicuous absence of ashtrays on all these oppressively gleaming surfaces.

"Bobby redid the whole place before he even brought me here."

Walking in from the kitchen, Starr sets a teensy cup of frothy espresso next to me on a silver-lacquered table that looks as if it wants to take off for Mars. "I know," she says with a glance around the room. "Like a cross between a morgue and Cape Canaveral." Grimacing, she tosses me a white alpaca throw, one of a pair. "Bundle up in this. You want the story of Starr Dukes, you may as well set a spell. A person could purely freeze to death in here." She wraps herself in the other blanket, sits across from me on the opposite sofa, and curls up like an alpaca-wearing pregnant kitten. She folds her hands around the steaming cup. "Here goes."

"That last Saturday night," Starr begins, "Poppa got himself a calling to preach in another town. He was always 'getting a calling'—usually after the church was missing collection-basket money, or somebody's husband figured out that 'counseling' meant sharing his wife with the preacher. We were always leaving in the middle of the night, and this wasn't any different. He come in my room and told me to wake up, saying we were leaving before daylight. I was too sleepy and confused to argue with him, and oh, Annie, I was only seven years old. He handed me two brown paper grocery sacks and I tried to jam my clothes in there, but most of them wouldn't fit. The pageant dresses my momma had made for me, I had to leave them, too.

" 'What about Momma's stuff? We're going to take it, right?' I asked him, trying not to cry. 'She's coming back, won't she?' I'd been praying she'd come home for over two months.

"His Sunday voice was all hard-boiled lightning, and he was for sure using it that dark morning. 'Stop your whining,' he said. 'That whore's not your mother anymore. Don't mention her again in my presence, not unless you want a whuppin'.'

" 'What about my hope chest?' I wanted to ask, but he hadn't said I could bring it, so I had to leave that, too. That hurt so bad, but when Poppa said git, I got. Always. And I was afraid, so I did like he said when he told me to hurry, that I could put my shoes on in the car. The front door was open, and our old DeSoto was running in the driveway. I remember it was so cold, like it was going to snow. I thought my bare feet were going to freeze right off.

" 'Go back inside and get the quilt,' Poppa said. So before I got in the car, I ran and grabbed the quilt my momma's momma had sewn for her wedding present. That was the only thing of hers I had anymore, except for her string of pearl beads I slipped into the pocket of my dress when he wasn't looking.

"We rode for hours through the Delta until the sun came up, Poppa not saying anything, smoking cigarette after cigarette, until we got to Batesville and he stopped for gas. That was when I realized I'd left without knowing your address or your phone number, even. It was like being on a ship, knowing that the dry land was a powerful ways behind me, that the captain of the ship was sailing without even having him some stars to steer by. I cried then, quiet as I could, because I knew you and my momma were both lost to me, probably forever." Starr takes a deep breath, puts her coffee cup down, and wraps the alpaca throw closer. She's silent for a moment, her mouth pensive, and then she continues.

"Well, after another day on those little two-lane roads, Poppa and me fetched up in a bitter, run-down place—Fogg's Notch—outside of Nashville, away up in the hills. Those were sure some backward folks. The women wore long, prairie-style dresses and weren't allowed to cut their hair, and the menfolk all had jobs in a machinery plant down the road in the next town, but nobody ever went there, not except to work and buy groceries. Being from the Notch meant keepin' yourself to yourself. Oh, and Poppa's new church? The Tabernacle of Forever Zion was a bunch of snake handlers, people falling out in the aisle, speaking in tongues and suchlike. But they loved my poppa's preaching—at least, at first they did. They turned on us later, after Poppa bought a new TV and the collection basket figured up light two weeks running. Then we were on the road again and again. I can't think of how many pissant towns we lit in.

"Soon a woman started in traveling with us. Miss Hulda. She said she was my poppa's wife now and my new momma. Wherever we were, I wasn't ever allowed to go to school without Miss Hulda walking me there and waiting for me to come out in the afternoons. When I cried and said I missed you, Poppa said I didn't need friends. He said my only friend was Jesus, and I'd better get used to it if I knew what was good for me."

Starr's story sounds a whole lot like the explanation Daddy tried to offer me when I came home from school that Monday to find her gone, the rental house locked and empty. I was heartbroken and bewildered, crying and asking, "Why?"

"Because wandering preachers wander for a reason, Annie. I'm so sorry, honey." Daddy put his arm around my shoulders and hugged me close, but that only felt like permission to cut loose and bawl like a baby with a bad case of colic. Even my mother couldn't make me stop until I finally fell asleep under my covers that night from sheer exhaustion. Every afternoon for weeks after that Monday, I wandered over to Starr's old house, hoping she'd somehow come back while I'd been at school. She was never there. Six weeks into this, my mother made me quit hanging around the rental house when the landlord called and complained that I'd tried to break inside. Mrs. Allen had seen me perched on an old box, prying at the screen to the window of Starr's old room, and told on me.

"I was only trying to find some clues," I argued.

"Clues to what?" My mother sounded exasperated.

"Where Starr went! I'm going to be a detective and find her, like Dick Tracy."

That night my daddy told me in no uncertain terms that I was to cease and desist any and all sleuthing activities. "She's not coming back, Annie. You'll have to get used to missing her." Probably Daddy meant well: certainly he was right about them not coming back, but for me it was as though my seven-year-old world had been broken into shards and would never be whole again.

And truthfully, it seems as though it never really was after that.

I put down my cup, caught up in memory's net. When you're in the second grade, you don't know what the world can do to you yet. That's the big lie of innocence—that it's a happy state. In childhood all of the feelings you'll ever experience in your life come at you with the suddenness and ferocity of mudslides, burying you up to your neck in feelings so overwhelming that you can barely draw a breath from the power of them. My mourning for Starr had been childhood's first and greatest betrayal. Grown-ups forget that, probably because we'd all go mad if we had to experience what life throws at you every day with the same shock and wailing intensity of just-born emotions.

"Oh, Starr," I say, remembering that day. "At first, when you didn't come to school that Monday, I thought you'd for sure be there for the Christmas pageant on Tuesday. You were going to be the Virgin Mary, remember? But when you didn't show up, that overachiever Lisa Treeby got to have your part instead of being a shepherd because she'd memorized everybody else's lines. She was such a moose, your costume came up way above her knees and was so tight Lisa had to walk around Bethlehem sideways until it was time for her to sit in the straw and hold the baby. Then those seams ripped right up the sides, almost to her waist. She didn't dare stand up after that, not even at the end when the Three Kings gave their gifts and everybody clapped."

"And you were going to be the Angel Gabriel," Starr says with a half-smile. "Poor ol' Lisa, having to be head shepherd 'cause she was the tallest in the class. I'm glad she got my part."

"Julie Posey just about busted a gut, she was so jealous." Since she's Bobby Shapley's wife, I bet she's miles beyond jealous now. I don't tell Starr about how Miss Bufkin almost recast me in the play because I kept insisting—loudly—that Lisa couldn't be Mary, that Starr would be there any minute and we should hold the show.

"But how did you end up here again, in Jackson?" I ask. What I want to ask is, with the wide world to choose from, what possessed you to come back?

"Oh, Annie—that's a story for another time," Starr says,

waving dismissal. Squaring her shoulders, she gazes out the window at the gray day. "Right now, all I can say is I'm in a heap of trouble." Her hand goes to her belly protectively.

"Bobby Shapley's a . . ." I begin, but cannot seem to get the words out. Like a dry worm, dislike catches in my throat. The sacred chains of Annie-be-nice restrain me from saying what I really think of Bobby Shapley, that mean, golden boy two classes ahead of me, Du's frat brother who cheated his way through college because he couldn't be bothered to study, the up-and-coming trial lawyer with a wild streak who never lets anything go—not a case, not a grudge, not even a hand of cards—not until he's done with it. Now he's done with Starr. Thinking about Bobby Shapley makes me really crave a cigarette because my hand is itching to slap the face right off his head.

"You're right," I finally say. "He's trouble."

Big trouble. Bobby could get her arrested for any piddly-ass thing he can dream up, make sure she has nowhere to live and no job to put food on the table. Even if Starr tries to take him to court in a paternity suit, she'll lose: the Judge will see to it. Not a lawyer in town will take her case for fear of Judge Otto Shapley, a retired widower with stone mountains of time and oceans of influence. The Judge won't let one of his son's ex-girlfriends drag the family name into the paper, not him, but make no mistake, the old man is a real dog, too. One memorable night at a country club banquet, the Judge followed me outside when I went onto the terrace to have a smoke and made the most startlingly graphic proposition I've ever been unlucky enough to receive. Since I couldn't slap him either, after he was done, I said, "No thanks."

"You'll come around," the old bastard said before he threw his cigar in the boxwoods and went back inside. No, Otto Shapley will crush Starr because she has the audacity to still be here in town, because she hasn't just given up and gone away.

But both those men are traveling Mormon boys compared to Bobby's wife, Julie Shapley, née Posey, who in kindergarten was already destined to become the girl with the widest, deepest streak of mean in my sorority pledge class. Freshman year, only once I'd made the mistake of telling her the truth—that her Laura Ashley outfit made her look like an ironing board wrapped in calico—and found myself sitting in the nose-bleed section of the Ole Miss–'Bama game with the geeks from the herpetology department instead of with the other Chi Omegas on the forty-yard line. To this day, when I can, I avoid working with her on the one Ladies' League committee they let me be on. I shudder to think of what Julie must plan on doing to Starr if she gets a chance.

"And now," Starr says, "Bobby means to put me out of the condo by the end of the week." She gives herself a little shake. With an air of bravado, she raises her cup to me, a question in her eyes. "I can make some more."

"Sure," I say. I don't want any more coffee, but it'll buy me time with Starr and I need this. I can't believe how badly I need this. "Where's the ladies' room?" I ask.

Down a long, white-carpeted hallway I find the powder room, another icebox, albeit one with guest soap and a three-hundred-and-sixty-degree panorama of mirror tiles. They're even on the ceiling. As I'm washing my hands, I look at my reflections and wonder what I think I'm doing besides trying to commit social suicide, having coffee with Bobby Shapley's shack-job. Du's going to *kill* me if he finds out.

"Shut up," I say to the reflections, but I'm really talking to the voice in my head, the one that won't quit about the rosebushes and their secret. Listen, I argue, Starr's *pregnant* and even Bobby Shapley couldn't make her have an abortion. I can be brave enough to have another cup of coffee with her, right? And looking into my own troubled eyes, I'm floored by the melancholy, bone-deep realization that Starr Dukes is truly the first and last best friend I ever had in my life. Hell, the *only* best friend I've ever had in my life. There've been other friends, but they weren't her. Get a grip, Annie, I tell myself and my eyes in the mirrors return the gaze with a dubious resolve.

In the kitchen, Starr's just finished with the espresso. "Mine's mostly milk," she says. "I've got to think of the baby." She pats her belly. "I made you a latte, too."

"I can't remember the last time I had coffee that wasn't black," I say. The steamed milk is so comforting my taste buds are delirious with the richness of it. This is truly a day for kicking over the traces.

"You're too thin." One eyebrow raised, Starr looks me up and down like I'm a starving cat hanging around the back door. "Hold on." She opens a cupboard and gets a package of Pepperidge Farm cookies down from the shelf. "Have a couple of these."

My mouth waters at the sight of the white paper bag, but I shake my head. "No thanks," I say. I've got to draw the line at cookies. She shrugs and takes one.

"I love these," Starr says. " 'Sides Dr Pepper, they were the only thing I could keep down most mornings, not until about a month ago."

"When are you due?" The Chessmen cookies are calling my name. I imagine I can smell them from here, buttery sweet with that tantalizing hint of vanilla.

"April sometime. She's going to be a little Aries." Starr, finished with one cookie, takes another. "I know she's a girl," she says with her mouth full, " 'cause I had a dream about it. Sure you don't want one?"

I do. Oh, Lord, I do and I'm going to have one and damn the calories. She holds the bag out to me, and I'm careful not to let myself grab it out of her hand. After ages of serial dieting, I'm going to have my first cookie in what I think is about fifteen years.

And I don't have just one. By the time I've finished my latte, I have three. Starr takes another, and we're at that point of no return with Pepperidge Farm cookies, the part where you're through one layer and meet the frilled paper cup between the six you just ate and the six waiting for you underneath it.

"Go on ahead, have another one," Starr says. "You're company. You want the grand tour?"

Taking the cookies with us, we wander down the pristine hallway, past some more mostly white paintings and statuary, and end up in the bedroom that's an answer to a decorator's heartfelt prayer for getting rid of the pieces she can't move because they're too obnoxious for a normal house's sense of what's right and what's just wrong. If the living room is a snowed-in spaceport, then the master bedroom is a big-game safari. Under a billowing cumulus of mosquito netting, the mammoth posts on the king-sized bed are faux-ivory elephant tusks, the bedside lamps ostrich eggs sporting stitched ostrich-skin shades. There's a leopard-print velvet chaise longue, a giant clay urn of peacock feathers, and a fur coverlet on the bed that looks an awful lot like bear. The rest of the furniture is pretty much Zimbabwe rustic with zebra-skin rugs and stuffed animal heads—a gnu, an ibex, a Cape buffalo, and about five trophy bucks—gazing down at us with dusty, glassy-eyed indifference.

"Takes a whole lot of dead animals to make Bobby Shapley feel like a man, I guess." The words are out of my mouth before I can stop them. It's the kind of thing I always think but most of the time can keep to myself. Mortified, I turn to Starr, an abject apology ready on my tongue, and I realize she's laughing.

"Annie Banks, I knew that was you behind that Ladies' League bullshit!" she says with a delighted smile. "Of course it's all clear as can be *now,* but when Bobby talked me into coming back here, I was so in love with his lying self the dead animals didn't bother me enough to think on them much. Now I tell everyone good night and promise we'll all get even one day." She holds out her hand for a cookie. "Laughing makes me hungry," she says. "It's good to be hungry."

I reach into the bag and realize it's the last Chessman. "Here," I say, handing it to Starr. She breaks it in two, hands me half.

"Seems like I've been hungry forever," I say around the mouthful of cookie. "It's nothing to get wound up over."

"That's because you grew up on Fairmont Street." Starr's tone is matter-of-fact. "When you're trash, growing up in the back seat of an old DeSoto, hungry means you're still alive."

CHAPTER 4

Not Allowed was a terrible thing. It had been over two weeks since I'd talked to Starr, it was a Friday afternoon, and I was skulking past Grandmother Banks's tall iron-spiked fence by myself with all the stealth of a soldier behind enemy lines. I'd had a trying day at school, and I particularly wanted to avoid my grandmother's notice. She had the habit of hanging around the front yard in her wheelchair, pretending to supervise Wash, her manservant, waiting for the very moment I would have to pass the front gate. As soon as she caught sight of me and my book bag, she was sure to beckon one palsied, be-ringed finger in an unavoidable summons. This Friday was no different.

"Mercy Anne!"

My grandmother Isabelle Gooch Banks was an imperious creature given to edicts, fiats, and death sentences from the rolling throne of her wheelchair. Served faithfully in all things by her two lifelong servants—Easter Mae, who kept the house and did the cooking, and Wash, who drove the Packard, worked in the yard, and toted my grandmother up the stairs whenever the geriatric elevator went on the fritz—she ruled her empire with a vein-corded fist and a single telephone.

After being released from the day's enforced idleness, also known as second grade, I had to walk past Grandmother Banks's State Street house on the way home. The old Banks mansion was something of a local landmark, a moldering three-storied Greek Revival pile complete with formal gardens and a grand porte cochere, *garçonnière,* servants' wing, and dank, leak-sprung carp pond. Wash had his work cut out for him, as did Easter Mae, since the house and grounds were designed for Staff, and the Banks family fortunes had dwindled somewhat since the Crash. If my father hadn't become a pediatrician and had instead followed the family business—doing nothing with style, essentially—my parents would've been reduced to living with my grandmother. Our own house, a smaller, much less grand version of the one on State Street, was burden enough. Being a child, I never noticed the constant repairs and economies that afforded my parents their Fairmont address.

"Mercy Anne *Banks!* Do you hear me?" It was a screech that would've shamed a macaw. With a sigh, I swung open the rusted iron gate and trudged up the walk to meet my grandmother, dragging my book bag behind me. Her wheelchair was parked under the shade of an ancient Japanese magnolia, its leaves yellowing and curl-edged after the long, hot summer. The cool spell had dissipated in the last week, just in time for school to start. I was sweating in my red plaid dress, my starched petticoats wilted and white ankle socks bedraggled. My shiny patent leather Mary Janes were covered in dust from the playground.

"I hear tell," Grandma said with a lifted eyebrow, "that you punched Laddie Buchanan in the stomach yesterday. I know you're aware that he suffered rheumatic fever when he was an infant and that his heart is weak." She folded her hands in her lap, eyes sharp in her wrinkled pudding face. "I can't imagine why you'd do such a terrible thing."

I scuffed my shoe in the grass, unwilling to look at her. "Laddie's mean."

"Mean?" Her voice was deceptively mild. "Why, I've known his people all my life. Laddie's a nice child. Give me an explanation this minute, young lady," she commanded. Grandmother Banks settled back into her wheelchair for what was bound to be her favorite part of the day: the inquisition. It would be pointless to dissemble in any way because she had a nose for lies. I'd learned that the hard way when I'd tried to blame a broken mandarin figurine on Pumpernickel, her dachshund.

"Laddie's not *nice,*" I insisted. "He smells funny, like an old raincoat. Laddie said Starr was trash, right to her face. She's my friend, and I know it hurt her feelings." I stuck out my chin. "If that's not mean, I don't care what is."

"It's truthful, is what it is," my grandmother said acidly. "That preacher's child is nothing but trash. Those kind of people move into a neighborhood, and before you know it, nice children are turning up with hookworms and pellagra. Your father says there's *mumps* going around on the other side of State Street. Besides, you'll pick up bad habits. Sassing your elders, eating paste. Your mother"—and here my grandmother sniffed—"did right for a change, forbidding you that little guttersnipe."

I glared at the ground, stricken silent with the injustice of it all. I didn't know what pellagra was, much less a guttersnipe, but neither Starr nor I ate paste. Laddie was the paste eater.

"So." Grandma cocked her head like a malevolent pigeon wearing gold ear bobs. "If you need someone to play with, I'll speak to Lollie Treeby this very afternoon. You'll go to their house tomorrow and spend your Saturday with little Lisa." And with that, I was dismissed.

Wash jerked his white-haired head up from the bed of spider lilies he was tending when I slammed the rusted iron gate on my way out. "Don't you go shutting the gate like that, Miss Annie," he reproached me. I kept walking as if I hadn't heard him, teeth clenched on words unsaid. "That old gate so po'," Wash advised my retreating back, "I can't fix it, you go breaking them hinges."

My grandmother was lightning on the telephone and true to her word. By the time I got home, Methyl Ivory was waiting for me in the kitchen. Wiping her dark, capable hands on a dish towel, she said, "You grammaw called. You going to the Treebys' tomorrow to play." From the apparatus assembled on the kitchen table and the bowl of blood-colored batter, it was apparent Methyl Ivory was in the middle of baking a red velvet cake. I dropped my book bag in a despicable heap of homework just inside the back door and flung myself into a kitchen chair.

"I hate her," I said dismally. The day had seemed like to kill my spirit for good with a whole ream of math pages first thing in the morning; then having to sit next to the acknowledged baron of booger mining, Roger Fleck, at lunch in the cafeteria; plus the agony of no talking to Starr and now a whole Saturday ruined. I propped my chin in my hands, my elbows on the table.

"Who you hate?" Methyl Ivory trolled the eggbeater through the cake batter. "Not that big ol' Treeby gal—she don't got three words to say to nobody."

I stuck my finger in the batter bowl. Methyl Ivory smacked my hand. "No, not Lisa," I said. "She's just . . . *boring*. I hate Grandmother Banks. She said Starr would give me pellagra, that I'd start eating paste and get into trouble. That's why I have to go to stupid Lisa's house tomorrow."

"Mmm-hmm." Pouring the batter into two greased cake

pans, Methyl Ivory gave me a look from under her eyebrows. "Seem to me you don't need to borrow trouble on you own account. Trouble seem to find you just fine. Here." She pushed the scraped bowl toward me. "Have that."

The next morning my mother unceremoniously hauled me out of bed.

"Wake up, Annie Banks." She jerked the curtains open to a gray morning. "I'm walking you down to the Treebys' in half an hour." My mother tossed some clothes onto the bed. "Put these on."

I yawned and scratched, eyes at half-mast and hair frowsy, looking with distaste at the inoffensive yellow shorts and blouse. I took as long as I dared getting dressed. Later, in the bathroom, the black and white tiles were cool under my bare feet, the old-fashioned toilet dripping while I stared at my reflection in the wavy mirror over the pedestal sink. As I brushed my teeth, it came to me with a dawning horror that my eyes were the very same color as my awful grandmother's—the deep blue of autumn thunderclouds—and though hers were silver and mine were blond, I had her eyebrows, too. In a fascinated kind of dread, I was examining my nose, my chin, my toothpaste-whitened mouth for further resemblance when my mother burst into the bathroom.

"What are you doing up here?" she demanded crossly. Rough in her haste, she wiped my face with a damp washcloth and ran a brush over my hair. "Come downstairs this minute and eat your breakfast. We'll be late."

And if I'd had my way, we'd have been very late indeed. My mother's heels sounded a brisk, martial rat-tat on the sidewalk ahead of me. I lagged behind, feeling as though I were headed to an appointment with a firing squad. Overnight the weather had turned cooler, and I was uncomfortably aware of my bare arms and legs in the misty air. A vermilion crape myrtle leaf fluttered to the damp sidewalk, and I stopped, bending over to examine it, my hair falling around my face. In the tree overhead a crow jeered raucous advice. *Run away, run away!*

"Annie!"

"Coming."

And so, fifteen minutes after eleven o'clock, I was deposited in the Treebys' gloomy, tiled entryway with only an assortment of umbrellas packed in a purple elephant majolica stand for company. Lisa didn't count. I'd commenced ignoring her while our mothers said good-bye at the door.

"Just send Annie home before five," my mother was saying. "Wade and I are going to the Ole Miss game, but the maid will be there." Everybody who was anybody would be at the Ole Miss–Alabama game. We'd passed the Bledsoe house on the way over, Mrs. Bledsoe decked out in an intense red-and-blue ensemble of shattering school-spiritedness, Mr. Bledsoe toting a bulging picnic basket to their station wagon. Mrs. Bledsoe had ignored my mother, even though it would've been impossible for her to have missed us. After that petty humiliation, my mother's color was up, but she carried her head high.

"Thank you again for having Annie over," she said.

Tall Mrs. Treeby, wide as a boxcar in the hip region, smiled her big, square-toothed smile. "It's so nice, having Annie to play. Lisa gets quite lonely, you know." With a wave, she shut the door as my mother tap-tap-tapped her way down the sidewalk in her scarlet heels, on her way to a football game where no one would speak to her.

"Be quiet now, girls," Mrs. Treeby said to us, her voice and expression vague. "And play nicely together. I've got one of my headaches." She promptly vanished somewhere upstairs, her hand to her forehead. Lisa's mother got bad headaches, a lot of them. I'd overheard my mother's friends—back when she still had friends—gossiping about how that skinflint Jerome Treeby wouldn't allow poor Lollie a maid, how he was such a tyrant around the house, and wasn't that just a scandal?

Lisa and I stood in the entryway looking at each other with not much to say.

"Want to play in my playhouse?" Lisa finally asked. She was a husky, adenoidal girl, tall for her age, with an oversized head round as a bushel basket.

Now, I knew from previous visits that the Kenmore playhouse in the Treebys' basement was about it as far as entertainment went over there. Lisa's allergies made playing outside impossible since weeds, leaves, and dust made her moon face swell to alarming proportions and then she couldn't breathe. We weren't allowed to play upstairs either because Mr. Treeby, an accountant, worked at home and any child-related racket resulted in a fearsome display of temper. Poor Mrs. Treeby would flutter and wring her hands when he ranted like a wrathful Old Testament patriarch and then tearfully beg him to calm down. No, it was the playhouse or nothing, so down to the basement we went.

Kenmore playhouses were never made to withstand the combined assaults of mildew, damp basements, and kids who'd grown bigger than they used to be. Each was made of middleweight cardboard fastened together with tabs and plastic snaps into a top-heavy box roughly the size of a kitchen stove—Sears sold a ton of them. Lisa's playhouse had been threatening to collapse for as long as I'd known it and was pieced together with masking tape. There wasn't room for both of us to be inside the playhouse at the same time.

"You want to go first?" Lisa was a polite child with the kind of manners parents universally applauded. As a consequence, the other kids didn't like her very much.

"No, you go ahead," I said. "I need to use the bathroom,

though." I didn't really, but I was already bored to death with the basement.

"Okay," Lisa said. She squeezed through the door opening. Hunkering down inside the playhouse, she turned around like a dog in a too-small crate while the playhouse threatened to tip over. Lisa tried to look out the window, but her head wouldn't fit. She stuck her arm through the opening instead and wagged a finger of caution at me. "Watch out—don't bother my daddy."

I didn't know my way around the Treebys' house very well, but I knew where the powder room was. Upstairs in the dark hallway, the door to the half-bath was shut. The door across the hall was cracked open, though, and a strange, low hooting was going on inside the room behind it. The noise sounded like a morose beagle. I knew the Treebys didn't have a dog, thanks to Lisa's allergies.

Curious, I tiptoed across the hall to peek through the long strip of light between the door and the frame. The rhythmic moaning grew louder as I sneaked the solid oak door open an inch wider, then another inch. I peered into the dim room. Long olive-colored curtains were drawn over the window, the bright banker's lamp on the big mahogany desk the only illumination. To the right, just inside the door, was a Chesterfield sofa with a large photograph book balanced on the end of its rolled leather arm. The moaning had turned to gasping and ran rough and fast now. Cautiously, I stuck my nose inside the door for a better look.

Planted on top of the tufted cushions of the Chesterfield were two oxblood leather men's shoes and a pair of gray serge pants bunched loosely around a pair of skinny white shins holstered in gartered socks. Wide-eyed, I slid the door open another inch and saw naked hairy thighs spread wide, an astonishing thatch of wolverine-like fur, and in the middle of the fur was a hand gripping something wrapped in a large white handkerchief.

"Gah!" It was Mr. Treeby's voice, explosive as a burst gas main. His bare hips bucked in a furious spasm. "Gah!"

In a wide-eyed, disbelieving panic, I dropped to my knees to hide. The picture book slid off the arm of the Chesterfield to the floor, falling open. Through the now-open door, I could just make out an old-fashioned black-and-white photograph of three young women in maids' uniforms, bent over at the waist. Full skirts rucked up, three sets of bare buttocks waited for the thin cane brandished by a mustachioed man in a top hat. The young women's faces looked really happy, even though they were obviously in line for what Starr's father called a whuppin'. This picture shocked my intelligence to a thunderous vacancy.

Then the gasping stopped.

Mr. Treeby barked, *"Who's there!"*

Silently backing away from that photograph, I crawled backward in a perfect terror down the dark hall along the cheap runner, my hands and knees stinging with rug burns. Mr. Treeby shouted again. "Who's there, dammit!" It sounded like he was putting on his pants in a hurry—a zipper rasping, coins falling to the floor.

"Goddammit, Lollie, get down here!"

I backed around the corner to the entryway, fast. In my haste to get to my feet, I knocked over the majolica umbrella stand. The elephant broke in two when it hit the tile, and clattering umbrellas rolled across the floor like timbers released from a logjam. My hand was on the doorknob when Mrs. Treeby trundled headlong down the stairs in a flapping brown dressing gown, her brow furrowed.

"Why, Annie—where are you going?" she asked. She was out of breath.

"Home. I, I don't feel good," I improvised. Before she

could reply, I yanked the door open to the bracing air. A wind skittered through the poplars outside, driving yellow leaves before it.

"Lollie, what's the meaning of this?" Mr. Treeby strode around the corner into the entryway, his hair wild, his pinstriped shirt only half tucked in. His eyes narrowed when he saw me.

"What's wrong, dear?" Mrs. Treeby was lumbering toward me, stepping over the umbrellas with her arms outstretched, her kindly horse face concerned. I leapt down the steps to the sidewalk and landed running.

"Pellagra!" I shouted over my shoulder. "I've got pellagra!"

I ran and ran until I couldn't run anymore. The four blocks to the Treebys' house—miles long this morning when I was walking to my date with the playhouse in the basement—were a blur. I slowed to a trot and then walked, holding my ribs against the throb of the stitch in my side. I had to stop to catch my breath. The crow was still perched in the top of the crape myrtle tree. It hopped to a lower branch, and bright, bold eyes seemed to ask, *What happened to you?*

I shuddered against the memory of Mr. Treeby's study and what I'd seen there, sharp as scissors, greasy and sickening as the taste of soapsuds on my tongue. There was no possibility of going home now, no doubt in my mind that within seconds of my escape Lisa's mother had telephoned both Methyl Ivory and my grandmother. What Mrs. Treeby would say to them was beyond my imagination, but once again my natural badness had undone my best efforts to be good. Big slow tears ran into the corners of my mouth, and I yearned then to be the crow overhead, to spread shining black wings and fly home to my ragged nest in the top of the live oak tree, where crow brothers and sisters would want to hear about my adventures and tell me their own.

There was no home for me. Instead of turning onto Fairmont, I ran north, around the corner, and down the long block to the end of Gray Street. When I saw the little asbestos-sided rental house, it seemed that I'd been running there all along. It never occurred to me that Starr wouldn't be home as I punched the doorbell and waited on the cracked cement stoop. My breath returned to normal, my flushed cheeks cooled, and I realized the temperature had dropped again. There was a front pushing through, and I was cold. Rubbing my bare arms' goose bumps, I rang the doorbell again. Overhead, low clouds scudded across the sky, and a dog barked somewhere, harsh and insistent.

And then, just as I was ready to give up and walk around the block, back home to the certain doom awaiting me, the door to Starr's house cracked open.

"Who is it?" a thin, scared-sounding voice asked.

"Starr!" I said, hugging my arms to my chest. "It's me, Annie. Can I come in?"

The door opened wider. I was enveloped in the thick, stale aroma of boiled cabbage and cigarette smoke, with something unpleasant and unidentifiable lurking underneath. Starr peeked around the edge of the door.

"Get inside," she said. "Somebody might see. My poppa said don't let anybody in the house while he's to the church."

I slipped inside the doorway. Despite the smell, it was warm in the Dukes house. Starr, barefoot, was wearing a pilled yellow nylon nightgown with a limp collar. "Come on in," she said. I followed her down a short, dark hall into a bedroom not much bigger than our pantry, lit only by the listless light filtering through a small, sheet-covered window. On the bare wooden floor, there was just room for the single mattress heaped with a patchwork quilt and a battered cardboard suitcase covered in tweed-patterned cloth in the corner. A drift of spangled white tulle spilled from the suitcase's overstuffed sides. Starr's pageant dresses were hanging on nails driven into the pockmarked walls.

"Set," she said. "How come you're here? I thought we weren't allowed anymore."

I collapsed onto the mattress, drawing my knees under my chin. "I'm running away," I said, wiping my nose. "Please, Starr—won't you come with me? We can be friends again." I had only conceived the idea in the last instant.

Starr shook her head. "I can't." She sat next to me on the mattress and put her thin arm around my shoulders. "See, my momma went away last week. Poppa says I've got to look after him now since she's not gonna come back, not this time." Her pale eyes were huge in her narrow, pointed face. "I was fixing to get ready to make him some dinner 'cause he'll be coming home at five pee-em. He'll be *real* hungry, Annie. A man's got to eat," she said uncertainly. "Right?"

Starr's mother's desertion fought for precedence with the day's disaster. My spirits plummeted as she stroked my back. "But I can't go home, Starr," I said. Voice shaking, I told her about the Treebys' house. It was hard to confess what I'd seen through the cracked door, harder still to explain my consummate dread of my mother's lashing disappointment at my failure—once again—to stay out of trouble. This was the biggest trouble yet of my short life, and I was sure I would not survive it.

When I had finished, Starr shook her head and said, "Poppa says this world's nothing but sin, woe, and sorrowful torment, and we only get through it with the healing from Jesus. I surely miss my momma, Annie."

"And I'm scared to death of mine."

We sat quiet for a minute.

"Hold on." Starr stuck her hand underneath the mattress and fished around on the floor for something, a picture in a cheap frame. "This's my momma on her honeymoon with my poppa. They went to Biloxi."

I took the faded black-and-white photograph from her, looking intently at the slight woman, her arms folded tightly across a shirtwaist dress, standing on the flat sands of the Mississippi Gulf Coast. She looked worn out, as though she'd been up for days on end, her shoulders tensed, unsmiling. I couldn't help but compare her to my own mother, Collie Banks, the beauty. How would I feel if she were to disappear into thin air like Starr's momma had done? I shivered, wondering if my latest descent into bad behavior would make her leave me, too.

"She's sure pretty, huh?" Starr asked.

I nodded, although I was thinking that Mrs. Dukes was anything but pretty. Her face with its long upper lip and protruding teeth bore a strong resemblance to the pet rabbit Joel Donahoe kept in a cage in the backyard.

"After she left, Poppa threw this picture away, but I fished it out of the garbage can." Starr took the photograph from me and kissed her mother through the glass. "My momma used to be the Soybean Queen of Avoyelles Parish, you know. After we come here, sometimes she'd put makeup on me and her when Poppa wasn't home so's we could be pretty together. She always said everything looks better when you got your best face on. But Poppa didn't like it. He came home early that last time and made us wash it all off. He gave me a whuppin', then he made her put every bit of her makeup in the trash and she cried." With another kiss, Starr shoved the picture under her mattress again. "I wonder where she's at all the time, Annie. I surely wish she'd come home again, but Poppa says she's not gonna."

"I'm sorry." It was all I could think of to say, but Starr nodded.

"I know," she said.

Wrapped in each other's misery, we sat on Starr's bed for at least another minute before we realized that for the first time in nearly three weeks, we were together again. We looked at each other shyly. I couldn't help but smile then.

"Want to see what I got in my hope chest?" Starr jumped up off the mattress and opened the suitcase. Crammed inside it was a long net veil spangled in silver sequins, Starr's Little Miss Princess Anne Look-Alike tiara wrapped in tissue paper, a gold-flowered porcelain bonbon dish, six cheap violet sachets, a pair of scuffed ivory satin pumps ("Momma says maybe I'll grow into 'em"), a stiffly crumpled bouquet of pink plastic roses, a white leather Bible with a stain on the cover, shiny pearl pop beads, a yellowed *Vogue* wedding dress pattern, and the earnest beginnings of a quilt made from Starr's pageant sashes.

Starr carefully lined these items up on the mattress with pride. I stroked the quilt made of satin sashes as she rewrapped the tiara in tissue paper. "Starr, can I stay here with you?" I asked, feeling hopeful. At that moment, even the thought of her father's return was preferable to what I was sure I'd be facing at home.

"You can stay while I make dinner, but you've got to go home after," Starr said. "Your momma will worry about you."

"No, she won't," I said, the knowing like an icefall in my heart. "She'll be glad if I never come back. I can't do anything right, *never,* no matter how hard I try. Look at what happened at Lisa's house!" In my mind I was certain—however confused that certainty—that my natural wickedness was somehow at the epicenter of my mother's endless anxiety. And then there was my grandmother. How was I ever to explain myself to that terrible old woman now? I couldn't say why, but as surely as I knew my own name, I knew that even from her wheelchair over on State Street, she used me to feed a rapacious appetite for domination. Without the words to express them, these were all feelings, merely, but feelings that rivaled the dark malignity of certain fairy tales, the ones I read with a stirring of recognition and fear.

"Huh. All mommas worry about their little girls," Starr said, sounding practical. She picked up the sash quilt and folded it. "That's how come I know my momma's coming back someday. She just needs a vacation." She was changing into a too-big sweatshirt and a pair of old corduroy pants that looked like they'd once belonged to a boy twice her size.

I shivered. My throat was scratchy from crying, and I was so tired. "Can I have a glass of water?"

"Surely," Starr said. "Come on in the kitchen. I'm cooking supper."

During that long afternoon my throat grew steadily worse, my joints aching in time with my throbbing head. I shivered under the long, grubby pink cardigan Starr gave me to wear over my shorts and sleeveless shirt. Like the rest of the few, tired clothes in the closet, it had been left behind when her mother had fled the house.

And so I sat at the kitchen table, trying to swallow past the burning lump in my throat, racked with the chills of a high fever, while I watched Starr drag pots and a bag of potatoes out from under the sink. Her straggling blond curls tied up in an old scarf, she got a pound of ground meat, an egg, and a bottle of milk from the refrigerator. She was making mashed potatoes, Starr said, and a meatloaf with ketchup on top. In spite of my body's increasing wretchedness, I stirred the instant butterscotch pudding for dessert, and it felt good, knowing I couldn't get into trouble there.

Too soon, according to the clock on the stove, Mr. Dukes's dinner was ready and it was time for me to go home. In the gray light of the fading day, Starr walked with me next door, across the Allens' sloping lawn, down to the fence dividing their property and our backyard. I tried to climb over the wire, but my legs crumpled like Play-Doh and refused to do their job. No matter how urgently Starr pushed my bottom upward, I couldn't get to the top of the fence, much less climb over it. Yellow rectangles of light from my house shone through the sunporch windows down across the lawn. I could see the large, white-uniformed figure of Methyl Ivory passing like a ship of state in the center hall between the kitchen and the living room, and falling to my knees, I rolled into a miserable ball on the ground.

Starr knelt next to me in the cold grass. Her face was pinched and nervous in the gathering dark. "Annie," she said. She shook my shoulder. "Hey. Get up. You can't lay here. I got to get home—it's almost time for my poppa to come back." I couldn't answer her around the blaze of pain in my throat.

"Wait." Limber as a cat, Starr scaled the fence, landing with a soft thud on the other side, in my backyard. "I'll be right back, okay?" The whisper of her bare feet running across the lawn faded into the chill dusk, and the slow rumble of occasional cars over on Gray Street, crickets, the call of a night bird, and the rasp of my own hot breath kept me company instead. The stars came out, one by one. I slept, I think, at last.

Later I woke in my own bed, in my pajamas. In the soft glow of the lamp, my mother and father were sitting on the edge of the mattress. My daddy had his stethoscope around his neck, and my mother's lovely face wore a worried frown.

"I'm sorry." That's what I tried to say, but my throat was a hot hornet's nest. My mother reached across my father and took my hand in hers. Her fingers were cool, soft, and fragrant with Pond's hand cream.

"Shh," she said. "Don't try to talk, Annie. You're sick." Her fingertips touched my cheek. "Poor thing, I remember when I had the mumps. It was awful."

Daddy smiled down at me. "Now take this paregoric. It'll help with that sore throat." Paregoric was nasty stuff, but I was too sick to put up much of a fight. The bitter, banana-flavored thickness slid past my lips, and within minutes, I felt the tidal pull of the liquid's narcotic undertow. Kissing me good night, my parents turned off the lamp by my bedside, leaving the door cracked open to the bright light in the hall outside.

It was a severe case of the mumps, and all day Sunday I slept, except for one memorable trip to the bathroom where my swollen face in the mirror looked *nothing* like my grandmother's. Monday morning Methyl Ivory came huffing upstairs with a glass of ginger ale for breakfast, all I was up to swallowing. I halfway sat up in the bed, feeling like I was going to die of thirst.

"You doing better?" she asked. I nodded as I sipped, my face buried in the tall glass. Cool ginger bubbles popped against my flushed cheeks and inside my nose. "You looking better. Good thing—whole house turn up crazy Saturday night. When Dr. Banks carry you in here, I thought you mama gone fall out, she so overset with you being sick and all."

"Really?" I croaked. I settled back into my pillows.

"Child," Methyl Ivory said with a sigh. "I told you daddy and mama how Miz Treeby call and say you run off feeling poorly, and then when you didn't come home—well, all's I got to say, Annie Banks, is you mama went just 'bout out a her mind callin' the po-lice, the neighbors, even callin' ole Miz Banks. She was fixin' to go look for you herself when that little gal come knocking at the back door. Look like a scairt rabbit, but she spoke right up, say you run away to her house. She say you was layin' down sick in the Allens' backyard and couldn't get over the fence." She held out her hand. "Now give me that glass. You get back to sleep."

That evening, after a day of paregoric-induced drowse and slumber, my mother came upstairs with some cream of tomato soup for me. Placing the steaming teacup on my bedside table, she fluffed my pillows so I could sit up. She shook the glass thermometer, and when I'd put it under my tongue, my mother said, "If your fever's down, I think you might have some company tomorrow."

"Company?" I said suspiciously, the word muffled around the thermometer. I was feeling grumpy, although the soup smelled really good.

"Close your mouth and keep that under your tongue. Yes, I was thinking of Starr," my mother said.

I nearly bit the thermometer in two.

"Not Lisa," she said. "Not after Saturday. Lollie was horrified when you told her you had pellagra—honestly, Annie, what gets into you?—and I thought Jerome Treeby's head was going to explode, he was so angry. He acted as though you'd set the house on fire instead of just breaking that ugly old umbrella stand. I guess we'll have to pay for another one, although where we'll find one to match it I can't imagine."

At the mention of the Treebys, I was suddenly queasy. What else might they have said to my mother? Did she know about the study? My anxiety must have showed in my face, for she stroked my hair.

"Oh, Annie." My mother sighed. "I don't know why you didn't come home, but I don't want you to run away." Her eyes were misty. "Never think I don't love you with all my heart, because I do. A long time ago, I had a friend just like Starr Dukes." She fished in her skirt pocket for a handkerchief and blew her nose. "Little girls need friends. Even though she's not the sort of child that I'd choose for you, still . . . I think you could see her every so often." Taking the thermometer from under my tongue, she read it in the light. "One hundred and some change. That's good news. Your fever's down."

I took a cautious sip of my soup. "What about Grandmother Banks?" I asked. "She says Starr's trash."

"Then you'll play with trash. Besides, Starr said she'd already had the mumps, so you won't be infecting anybody else. Here. Have some more of this soup."

CHAPTER 5

"So," Starr says, "this town being what it is, you must have heard all about me and my situation since before I ran into you." She switches on one of the ostrich-egg bedside lamps, and in its muted glow the room's atmosphere softens to a kinder, gentler grisly theme park. "I mean, you came straight here, didn't even have to ask where I was living."

"I heard some of it," I venture, feeling my way here. I don't want Starr to think I've been gossiping about her. I'll blame it on Dolly.

"Dolly's mouth flaps at both ends," I say. "How in the world did you get mixed up with Bobby?" I sink onto the leopard-print chaise. Starr sits on the edge of the monster California king–sized mattress, her legs dangling, looking like a child in an African whorehouse. Her eyes drop to her folded hands, pink nails bitten to the quick.

"It sure felt like the real thing this time." Her voice is so quiet I strain to hear her. "And I'd been looking for Mr. Right for seeming like forever. Remember Mr. Right? The man my momma told me was going to carry me off, love me forever, and get me whatever my heart desired? Well, Bobby does the best Mr. Right of any man I ever did know." She glances at me quickly, and if I didn't know her better, I'd swear her eyes are crystalline with tears. "It was so good in the beginning, Annie. Back then, things were the best—at least till I told him I was expecting a baby."

I bet. Nothing puts a monkey wrench in the works of a perfectly good thing-on-the-side like a pregnancy.

"Oh, Starr," I say. "I'm so sorry."

"Don't be," she says. "I'm not." She mashes the heels of her hands into her eyes, rubbing them. "Not so much."

"Dolly said you told him you'd rather die than have an abortion," I say without thinking.

"She said that?" Starr looks at me without expression and is silent for a moment. "Amazing to me how word gets around in Jackson. Well"—she sighs—"that's one thing I told him. I mean, I couldn't understand how he would ask me to do that when he'd been swearing up one side and down the other he was going to leave Julie just as soon as she got back on her feet again, that we'd get married any day now." Her mouth turns down, bitter with betrayal. "After I told him I was expecting, the truth came out in about five seconds flat. Bobby never meant to marry me at all, he wasn't ever going to leave her, and wasn't even going to help me after the baby came. 'I've already got two kids—I'm not going to get held up by some white trash at their expense' was his exact words." Starr looks out the window and bites her lip.

My face reddens, remembering the overheard conversation at Maison-Dit. After all, "trailer park" was my first impression before I knew the woman in the hallway was Starr. "He's a sorry piece of shit," I say with heartfelt venom.

"Oh, but Annie." Starr's eyes have turned dreamy now, her lips curved in a half-smile. "In the beginning, in New Orleans, it was all so . . . *special.* Early last April, over to the racetrack where I was cocktail waitressing, he came in one night with a bunch of liquored-up lawyers who'd decided to blow all their folding money on the ponies after the convention was over. They were your usual brand of jackass, the kind I'd been dealing with since I was fourteen years old. After I ran away the third time, I got my first job by lying to a motorcycle bar outside of Pigeon Forge, telling the manager I was sixteen, the manager lying to the Board of Health and telling them I was eighteen. When a mess of bikers comes through the door with a load of home-cooked speed on, looking to mellow down with some beer drinking, pool playing, and hitting on the help, you catch on fast.

"But that night at the Fair Grounds, Bobby was different. He told all his drunk friends to leave me alone, to quit playing grab-ass when I served them their margaritas. I remember he was drinking top-shelf whiskey—'just one ice cube, honey'—and he let it sit in front of him, sipping it slow, just like a gentleman. So good-looking, too, what with his black, black hair and that five o'clock shadow he gets even though he shaves twice a day, the way he wears his clothes like they're made for him."

"They are," I mutter. By some little old man over in Hong Kong. Bobby brags about it all the time. Du's mentioned more than once that he'd like to get some shirts from the Shapleys' tailor.

"I know," Starr says. "Vainest man I ever did meet. Well, Bobby took most of his shit with him after I said I'd throw everything he owned in the bathtub and set it on fire," she says with a tight smile. "Anyway, after the races were done for the night, his asshole buddies left and I was closing out my shift when he came up and asked real nice, 'Won't you have a drink with me? I promise not to break anything.' His eyes were so sweet, oh—I could of fell into them and melted, just like a dab of butter in hot chocolate sauce. I'd had a long night on my feet, and having a drink with this good-looking man seemed like just the ticket. It was a warm evening for April, and the air like a live thing, wrapping itself 'round my bare shoulders. Bobby didn't ask me where to go. With the top down on that Corvette of his, we drove to the Fairmont Hotel and drank until close at the Sazerac Bar, talking about this and that, but we both knew we were going to end upstairs in his room on the fifteenth floor."

"You slept with him the first night you met him?" I don't mean to sound judgmental, but that's the way it comes out.

Starr doesn't seem to mind, for she says, "I did check to see if he was wearing a ring, Annie. He wasn't. If that makes me a slut, okay, I'm a slut."

"You are not!" I say fiercely.

"Stupid, then," Starr says with a sigh. "I should have known better, but like I said, it'd been a long time since the last Mr. Right and he didn't mention his wife and kids until after we'd already done the deed. The next morning, he ordered up champagne and orange juice from the room service and we stayed in bed for three days straight 'fore we came up for air. He was the best I ever had, and that's damn good, believe me. Never misunderestimate the power of great sex, honey. It'll make your best intentions into orphan dogs."

I'm almost blushing, impressed and more than a little envious. I've never known lovemaking like that. Du was my first, and he's still the only man I've ever slept with. For years, I've found myself in bed with a man who snores like a grand piano dragged across a terrazzo floor, who hogs the covers and complains about how cold my feet are, so I have no basis for comparison. In fact, in the last few years, we've rarely done it at all, and when we do, it's mainly on the nights when I'm ovulating and hope to make a baby. Then, it's all up to me to get the ball rolling. After years of temperature taking, charts, and planned sex, Du complains about the lack of spontaneity. He wouldn't even go in for a sperm count. He swears that all the men in his family have more kids than they know what to do with, so it must be me who's got the problem.

Starr, on the other hand, sounds as though her romantic past has had all the heat and electricity of a summer lightning storm. "Poppa," she says, a half-smile on her lips, "always used to say that the wages of sin was death, but I'm still here. I've made me some mistakes, but I can't say I'd do anything different."

"I wish I could say the same," I blurt. "Sometimes I wonder what would have happened if . . ."

But I don't finish the thought because I rarely let myself indulge in what-ifs. They're like cookies that way. You have one, and before you know it, you've had a dozen and regret every last bite. Instead, I look down at my Rolex. It's four o'clock. The afternoon is suddenly gone, vanished as if I fell down a rabbit hole. I have got to get home before Du does. I need time to get my act together, to get ready to lie to my husband about how I really spent my afternoon, to be dressed and braced for dinner tonight with Starr's number-one problem—although she doesn't seem to realize it yet—Judge Otto Shapley.

At this moment, the phone on the bedside table explodes with a series of demanding trills while at the same time another one shrieks from somewhere else in the condo. I expect Starr to reach for the phone, but she says, "I'll take this up front. Wait here, okay?" Gathering her skirt, she hops off the bed and trots down the hall to the insistent summons of the telephones. I'm left in Bobby country with the stuffed animals, nibbling at a hangnail and dying for a cigarette. I've really got to go home.

Five minutes later, knowing I'm really going to be late

now, I'm rehearsing my reasons for leaving when Starr walks back in the room. From her compressed lips and distracted expression there's no question about it. This wasn't a happy call.

"So," she says, her eyes cast down on the carpet. "I guess that's that."

"That's what?"

"That was the reason I was trying to get a new dress at Maison-Dit. Before he canceled on me, I sort of had a . . . meeting, an appointment with someone for later on tonight, and needed to be at my best. None of my winter clothes fit me right anymore, and I can't afford to be looking desperate, not now." Starr runs her fingers through her curls, pacing. "It was a long shot, anyhow." She stops and looks over just in time to see me glancing at my watch again.

"Got to go, huh?" Starr asks.

I nod, hoping I don't look as helpless and guilty as I feel.

"That's okay," Starr says. "It's been good catching up—except we never talked about you, did we?" She leans against the elephant tusk bedpost and folds her arms expectantly. I don't say anything because I don't know how to begin, not without a load of self-serving explanations. The room is quiet. You could drop a city bus into the well of deepening silence.

"Guess that talk's probably not going to happen, is it," Starr finally says. It's another one of her nonquestions.

There's no probably about it. I try to imagine another Ladies' Leaguer caught up in this mess, like . . . What Would Kendall Do? Kendall Carberry is a walking billboard of the big Southern gal with a big Southern smile, an ace on the tennis court and a crackerjack chairman of the baby-rocking committee. *Kendall wouldn't be caught dead in this situation,* the rosebush voice whispers. Kendall would've disposed of Starr like junk mail the instant she was approached in front of the Walgreens. Kendall would've pretended amnesia of her entire childhood if it came down to that or acknowledging a once-friend who's sunk herself as deep as Starr has. No, Kendall Carberry is no help to me now.

"Oh," I manage weakly. With damp hands I crush the empty Pepperidge Farm bag into a crumpled paper ball. "I mean, it's really not like that."

It is like that.

"I'd love to get together again soon," I rattle on, "but I need to dash home and get fixed up for this god-awful law partners' dinner I've got to go to tonight." With a nervous laugh, I get to my feet.

"Law partners?" Starr arches her delicate eyebrows in inquiry. "That's a surprise. What kind are you?" She waits a long beat for me to answer.

"Oh!" In a head-clap of understanding, I get it. "I'm not the lawyer. My husband, Du. He's a partner in his law firm."

Starr nods slowly. "Your husband's a lawyer? Lord, I surely need to get one of them *now*. Bobby says I can't prove this baby's his and if I say otherwise he'll sue my ass to kingdom come, drag up every last man I ever slept with and brand me a whore."

Oh, God, I think. Please don't let her ask.

"You think your husband would take my case?" she asks, sounding hopeful.

I can't look at her. Instead, I gaze upward at an immense palm-leaf ceiling fan planted in the middle of an acre of pleated batik fabric, as if the patron saint of cowards is going to open up the penthouse roof and deliver me from this impossible request. When I finally make myself look back at Starr, her eyes are full of questions. Now that same damned silence between us ripples outward in a steep wave, freighted with the weight of those questions. Before I break on the crest of it, Starr saves me.

"I bet he's not the kind of lawyer I need," she says. Her voice is cool and composed. "I bet he only does wills and contracts, or criminal de-fense. I bet he's too busy, anyhow. No, I'm definitely going to need me a shark, a real man-eater for what I've got in mind." She briskly straightens the bearskin coverlet on the bed and takes the balled-up paper bag from my nerveless hand. "I'll just put this in the trash. I know you've got to be on your way." Her proud back to me, she's walking down the hall toward the kitchen.

"It was good of you to have coffee with me, Annie. So nice to see you again," she says without turning around. Oh, I should be grateful to Starr for this polite dismissal. I should make my own polite noises and go, but instead, I follow her to the kitchen. She's got to understand what she's up against since an explanation is all I can do for her.

"Look, Starr." I plant my hands on the cold marble countertop, determined to see this through. "You *know* Bobby and his family. Even if I could make Du represent you—which I can't—you don't have a bug's chance in a hurricane of getting anywhere with this, not in Jackson. Nobody's going to take on the Shapleys. Nobody. You know that, don't you?"

Starr slams the garbage compressor shut with a *thwack* of rubber gaskets.

"So I'm supposed to just take it?" Her eyes are narrow pale-blue fires. "Isn't that what everybody expects me to do? I'm supposed to quit, cry quiet-like, and go away?" Arms folded, she slowly shakes her head. "Dammit, Annie, I'm not about to do that. Me and my baby are going to see that lying nickel son-of-a-bitch pays for every damn box of Pampers, every pair of soccer shoes, every trip to the orthodontist, and anything else I can think up. I've got the money for the kind of lawyer I need, I just can't get my hands on it, not right yet. New Orleans has got more lawyers than goddamn cockroaches, and one of them is going to take my case even if nobody up here will."

She's walking back into the white living room, across the tundra of snowy Berber carpet to the front door. "So don't tell me what I know or don't know, Annie Banks," she flings over her shoulder. "The life I've led, I know a thing or two about trouble and how to kick its ass 'round the front yard."

Starr is at the front door now, opening it to the entryway. All I have to do now is walk through that door, push the button for the elevator, and this is all over.

"Maybe after the holiday, we can get together," I offer, floundering in another meaningless social reflex.

But Starr's pointed little face is a study in detachment, seemingly engaged in battle elsewhere. Her hand on the doorknob, she says, "Bobby and those old bitches over to Maison-Dit might have won this round, but I'm not near done for yet. I just got to get to New Orleans."

"New Orleans? Why?"

"Somebody's holding onto my money for me down there," she says grimly. "I mean to get it."

"But New Orleans!" I exclaim. "Starr, that's three hours from here, and you don't have a car."

As the words leave my lips, somewhere on the penthouse floor of the Tower, a dog commences a low, miseried howling. It must be in the other condo, and it sounds as desperate as I feel. "How in the hell are you going to get there?" I argue.

"I'll work something out," Starr says, waving a dismissive hand. "I always do. I can hitchhike if I got to." Standing in the doorway with her sweater riding up over the bulge of her belly, the gaping waist of her skirt fastened with safety pins, Starr positively swaggers. But then, she never did back away from much of anything.

Now, like the soundtrack to a Swedish melodrama, the howling next door climbs a scale of dog angst from a basso profundo of loneliness to the mountaintop region of I-need-to-pee. And then, it's only then, that I finally understand that I can't walk out of this hideous penthouse leaving her alone and without a prayer of help.

"I, I could give you the money to take the train," I stammer, wishing I could put my fingers in my ears.

The howling doesn't faze Starr. "I thought on the train already," she says. "Amtrak's booked until after Saturday. So is Greyhound, and I've got to get this done before tomorrow afternoon."

"Why the rush?" I ask, frustrated. Why won't that dog shut up? Raising my voice to be heard over the howling, I demand, "Seriously, Starr—why don't you wait until after Thanksgiving?"

"I can't," Starr says loudly. "They mean to put me out of the condo by Friday, and my money's at the Fair Grounds."

"You couldn't keep your money in the bank like the rest of America?" I'm practically shouting. And then, as if the sound of our voices comforts it, the dog stops howling. Instead, it whimpers at the base of the other penthouse's door, snuffling against the jamb to fetch up our scent.

"Look." I sag against the door frame, half in and half out. "I'd drive you, but today's just impossible. Like I said, I have to be at this partners' dinner tonight, and tomorrow's Thanksgiving, for God's sake. I couldn't do it until Friday at the earliest." Maybe I can get away with a day trip to New Orleans after Thursday, maybe nobody will figure it out—if I'm careful. And lucky.

But Starr shakes her head in resolute denial. "Friday's too late."

And so it comes down to this: I have a new black dress hanging in the back of the Beemer. I have a husband who'll be home in less than an hour, expecting me to be in that dress and putting on my makeup for an evening of too much chardonnay and sanitized chitchat with Jackson's rich and powerful. I have a million reasons why I should get my ass home and away from this evolving catastrophe. I have no reason at all for what I say next.

"All right! I'll drive you to New Orleans. Be ready by six thirty." Like punctuation, the dog barks once and then goes quiet, silent as the space between us.

What else can I do? I won't deny her again.

CHAPTER 6

"Because President Kennedy wants you to, that's why."

Miss Bufkin, my pretty second-grade teacher whom I usually adored, said this to me with a layer of exasperation over her habitual cheerfulness. The President's Council on Physical Fitness had sent out a directive for all of us schoolchildren to live our lives with vigor. John F. Kennedy himself had walked fifty miles to inspire the American public, and today our class was doing its part by running the fifty-yard dash.

"Yes'm," I muttered, and got back into the line of kids waiting their turn.

I didn't see the point of sprinting the length of the softball field while Miss Bufkin timed me with a shiny stopwatch, certainly not more than once. The bright, cold October afternoon was perfect for kickball, a sport I was really good at. Besides, the time tests were humiliating since I was slow, slower than everybody else except for Laddie Buchanan and the girl with the back brace. Even lumbering Lisa Treeby was faster than I was, for Pete's sake, and that was just plain insulting.

Starr, however, had outrun Roger Fleck, the fastest boy in

our class, and what's more, she was handicapped by her shoes. Looking as though they had come out of a Goodwill bin, those brown lace-ups, with their thick soles and clunky heels, must have weighed a pound apiece. If she'd owned a pair of Keds like mine, she probably would have been able to fly.

Not so me. After what seemed like my fifty-fifth trip up the softball field, I was finally allowed to collapse in a panting, disgusted heap under the pine tree behind the wire-mesh backstop. Starr was still speeding down the field, now in contention for the fastest kid in the whole second grade, not just Miss Bufkin's class. I watched with a dawning envy as she proceeded to trounce the other class's finalist.

"Running is for boys," said Julie Posey, sitting next to me under the pine tree. The most popular, and therefore powerful, girl in the second grade, Julie adjusted the full skirt of her pink dress and made a face. "That girl"—she pointed at Starr—"thinks she's so great, running with the boys. Well, she's not."

Nearly two months into the school year, Starr was not fitting in. Her clothes showed the unmistakable stigmata of her mother's absence: unironed, petticoat-less dresses and a telling lack of hair ribbons. And as if that wasn't bad enough, her sorghum-thick accent marked her as surely as if she had "hick" mimeographed across her forehead in purple ink. Even lovely Miss Bufkin didn't seem to care for her much. Starr was never asked to clap erasers or carry notes to the principal's office. She wasn't called on in class, nor had her artwork been displayed on the classroom walls. Basically, it was like her desk was an empty one. Julie, Lisa, and I got our names written on the chalkboard for being good students, but Starr, whose grades were identical to mine and who was always quiet and well behaved, hadn't had her name up there once this year and it was almost Halloween.

This injustice rankled since it was the first time I'd ever had a front-row seat witnessing an adult's unfairness—other than my grandmother's, that is—and even though I very much wanted to take Miss Bufkin to task for her discrimination, I knew better. It was just a matter of time before my name was in her slim green ledger-book with the rest of the problem kids. The miracle was that I'd masqueraded for nearly two months as a model second-grader. Sooner or later, Miss Bufkin would find me out and any leverage I might have accumulated would vanish faster than Starr could run, so I kept my thoughts on justice to myself, hoarding my spurious capital.

"Hey," Starr called. She was trotting across the patchy grass of the softball field, victorious from her rout of the entire second grade. Reaching the backstop, she threw herself to the ground beside me. "I guess I won," she said with a satisfied grin.

Julie sniffed and made a big point of looking away. I had a hard time returning Starr's smile myself. Up until today, in the country of our friendship we'd been equal citizens, with me being a little more equal than she when it came to clothes, other stuff, and an assured place in the second grade's ruling class. With Starr's newfound celebrity, the status quo had shifted, and I was far from comfortable with this development.

Starr didn't seem to notice. She fell backward on the thick, fragrant carpet of brown pine needles, arms clasped behind her head, a blissful smile on her face. "Yep," she sighed in contentment. "I whupped everybody."

"Show-off," Julie sneered.

Now, Julie Posey was the biggest show-off ever. She already had a boyfriend in her Sunday school class at the First Baptist Church, brought a purse to school, and boasted about sleeping in hair rollers so her mouse-brown ponytails would hang in bouncy ringlets. Last year, Julie's mother, Squeaky Posey, put her daughter's picture in the Jackson paper, the *Clarion-Ledger,* for her piano recital. Julie even brought her Shetland pony to show-and-tell and gave a favored few rides around the softball field. Having been one of those kids clutching the horn of Socks's miniature Western saddle, I knew from show-offs and Starr wasn't one of them.

Still, I didn't say anything, but idly scratched my name in the red dust with a twig while nascent envy poked its head into the light like a sly Johnson weed in a rose bed.

Already wise to the Julies of the world, Starr shrugged her thin shoulders. "Want to go get a ball and practice kicking?" she asked me. "Miss Bufkin said we could since the time tests are done." I didn't answer, but Julie did.

"Let's go get a drink of water." She put her hand on mine. "I'm thirsty." All three of us got up, brushing the dust from our skirts, but Julie said, "No show-offs allowed." She smiled an unpleasant smile. "Only Annie and me are going."

Starr's face fell. She looked at the ground, stricken. "Oh." Her voice was small, and she looked even smaller in her faded blue dress and clodhopper shoes.

"C'mon, Annie," Julie said loftily. And for my everlasting shame, I went. To this day, drinking-fountain water—lukewarm, flat, and metallic—tastes like a mouthful of guilt to me.

But envy, that robust weed, shot up another rank inch or two when, after recess, Miss Bufkin announced Starr was the president's winner in front of the whole class. Everybody clapped, except for Julie and her circle of carefully blank-faced friends.

And me.

After the ban was lifted, Starr and I had walked home together every day after school, but that afternoon I was yanked into Julie Posey's orbit forthwith. For six blocks she talked of nothing but what a show-off Starr was, how she was just downright trashy, and anyway *real* girls didn't run as fast as boys.

For my part, I was mostly silent, wishing I had never fallen in with Julie's assumption that I'd walk home with her. I kept thinking of how hurt Starr had looked, and how it was I who had done the hurting. It wasn't even worth the effort of trying to lay the blame on Julie Posey because ever since kindergarten she'd been like a tornado that way—destructive by nature, impervious to the damage she wreaked. Before Starr, I'd been a mere bystander observing the hurt feelings, the petty horriblenesses she left in her wake like smashed cars and flattened houses. By denying Starr, however, I'd become another member of Julie's flock of sycophantic parakeets.

"See you tomorrow," she said when we reached my house.

"Yeah," I said in a low voice, my hand on the gate. "See you tomorrow."

For once, my mother was home when I let myself inside the big front door and came into the entryway. Wearing a nubby Harris Tweed suit, she was sitting in the Queen Anne chair in the living room and talking on the telephone. Her crocodile pumps were kicked under the coffee table, her stockinged feet resting on the old-fashioned, fringed hassock. In front of the fireplace, she was backlit by the early fire that was crackling on the hearth. As I passed in the hallway, she waved a hand distractedly, indicating that I should come in and sit down. I slouched over to the camelback sofa and threw myself into its down-filled cushions, dropping my book bag at my feet.

"The Snow Ball?" My mother's face glowed with an animation I hadn't seen for quite a while. "Of course, Squeaky. I'd love to!" In the last week or so, there'd been a thaw in the winter of her exile from Jackson society, the phone had rung often, and she'd been lots more cheerful. Today, the loud person on the other end of the line, Julie's mother, yodeled on at length while my mother listened, twisting the phone cord in her slim fingers. I leafed through my health book. The drawings of boys and girls dutifully brushing their teeth and making wise choices from the food pyramid did nothing for my tortured conscience.

At last, my mother put the phone down in its black cradle. She lit a cigarette with the cut-crystal lighter on the table beside her. "Well," she said, "that was Squeaky Posey. I'm back on the Ball committee."

I grunted.

"I saw you walked home with Julie. That's nice."

I didn't answer, but closed my health book with a loud sigh.

"You certainly seem to be crossways with the world this afternoon." My mother began to slip into her high-heeled pumps, then stopped. Her green eyes narrowed, and she inhaled a drag on her cigarette. "Annie Banks," she said, "are you in trouble?"

"No, ma'am," I mumbled.

"Then what on earth is the matter?" Her tone was impatient as she exhaled a long ribbon of smoke.

"I did something mean today," I said, not able to look at her.

"Mean? Did you punch Laddie Buchanan again?" She sounded alarmed. If my grandmother got wind of any further Laddie assaults, there'd be hell to pay.

"No." I shook my head. "I was mean to Starr, but it wasn't fair—she's going to get a medal and I didn't get *anything*. And, and . . . Julie said Starr was a show-off. I didn't say it." I was defiantly miserable, seeking the solace of confession but unable to force myself to get around to it.

"So what did you say?" my mother asked. She mashed her cigarette out in the ashtray.

"Nothing." I swallowed. "But that was the mean part." I hugged my health book to my chest. "I shouldn't have not walked home with her either. That was mean, too. Starr had to walk by herself."

My mother's face was thoughtful. She must have seen the opportunity lying there like a twenty-dollar bill in the street: she must have understood that there wouldn't be a better time to sever my undesirable connection to Starr once and for all.

But instead, she said, "That doesn't sound like you, Annie. Are you ashamed?"

I nodded, relieved to get the whole awful business out in the open. "I want to make it better, but I don't know how." My mother motioned to me to come to her. I put my health book down, slowly got up, and walked over to the chair beside the fire.

"Sit in my lap," she said. When I was comfortable, my head resting against her soft tweed bosom, she said, "When you do something mean, you should apologize."

"I can't." I hid my face in her shoulder. "Starr'll be so mad at me."

"I bet she's not," my mother said. "I bet if you run over there, she'll be glad to see you." She stroked my hair and kissed the top of my head. "I know you'll do the right thing, Annie."

I could have sat in her lap forever, peacefully breathing in the combined scents of her perfume and fire-warmed tweed, but with a brisk pat on my leg my mother eased me to my feet.

"Go on." She smiled. "The right thing's always easier if you get to it straight away."

Outside on the front steps, the air smelled of wood smoke from our chimney. I passed through the front gate with dragging feet, dawdling in an aimless way toward the end of the block. Somehow, it didn't seem right to go to Starr's house through the backyard, over the Allens' fence. Instead, I intended to turn left and go the long way around the block, turning down Poplar and then over to Gray Street. The days were getting shorter now, and the afternoon's shallow light was sinking fast into the west's cold blue sky. It would be Halloween soon.

Somewhere far away across Fortification Street, the raised voices of what might have been a particularly physical touch-football game rose and fell in the chill October evening. I recognized a stentorian bellow of bloody intent: Buddy Bledsoe, the fourth-grade terror of Fairmont Street. Even Joel Donahoe avoided Buddy, the biggest kid in the neighborhood who wasn't in junior high. Back before the calamitous bridge party, back when our mothers had been on speaking terms, Mrs. Bledsoe had referred to her son as "husky," an inapt expression for an oversized troglodyte with a pit bull temper. This past summer, he and his cohorts had been at Boy Scout camp, but now it was fall and they were back to slaughtering the kids unfortunate enough to fall afoul of them. Yes, Buddy and his gang were feared and loathed, but it didn't do any good telling grown-ups. Buddy wore a different face to them, a guileless face of pie-eyed boyish charm, but behind their backs, the approach of Buddy Bledsoe was like witnessing an Illinois Central locomotive come to juddering life, a locomotive with savage fists and feet. *Nobody* messed with Buddy Bledsoe.

Still, focused upon my apology, I didn't give the boys and whatever they might be up to much thought as I turned the corner onto Gray Street to walk the long stretch before Starr's house. In passing the Bledsoes' three-story brick Colonial, though, I crossed the street to give their yardman, Tate, a wide berth. Tate Barlow, Methyl Ivory's grandson, also worked for my parents sometimes, doing odd jobs like cleaning out the gutters, mowing the lawn in the summertime, and hammering the garage back together after I'd run the Buick into it. A tall, taciturn man, his wide shoulders straining the faded blue straps of his bib overalls, Tate intimidated me with his black, closed face, even though he'd never had two words to say to me. He reminded me of the shadows living in my closet, the ones who claimed the corners of my room after the lights were out, the ones that scared me witless even though I was too big to be afraid of the dark.

Tate had raked the Bledsoes' fallen leaves and pine straw into the gutter and heaped everything into a pile. As I passed by, he picked up a long-tined pitchfork and began hefting leaves into the high-sided, homemade trailer hitched behind his truck, never once turning his head in my direction. Starr's house was in sight now, however, and Tate Barlow abruptly was replaced with my real worry. What if Starr was too mad at me to accept my apology?

Walking past the Allens' big white Victorian, a tiered wedding cake of dormers, turrets, and string work towering over the rental house next door, I almost turned around and went home. I imagined ringing the bell, Starr coming to the door and then slamming it in my face. Still, I kept putting one foot in front of the other, remembering my mother saying, *Do the right thing, Annie.* And even though I was practically walking backward, too soon I was at the rental house, standing on the cracked front step with my finger on the doorbell. The pack-like howls of the boys were growing closer. I hesitated. Buddy Bledsoe's voice was braying something. It sounded like, *"Get her!"*

More apprehensive than ever now, I rang the doorbell anyway. It buzzed with a dusty clatter. After waiting a moment, I pressed the bell again. The driveway was empty except for a big oil stain and an overflowing garbage can. No one came to the door. I'd turned away and was ready to head home, apology unuttered, when Starr rounded the corner of the house, sprinting pell-mell into the weedy front yard.

"Annie!" she cried. "Run!" She grabbed my hand on the fly, and we ran like scalded cats.

I didn't ask her why we were running—I didn't have to.

Buddy Bledsoe's shouts and those of the gang were closing in; they were almost upon us. We bolted down the hill between Starr's house and the Allens' sloping backyard, down to the end of their lawn, to the fence. Behind us on the other side of Starr's house, the boys bayed like coyotes with the quarry almost in view.

"C'mon!" Starr panted. We didn't have time to scale the fence, but doubled back and ran up the slope into the Allens' front yard and down Gray Street faster than ever I ran the fifty-yard dash. The boys still hadn't caught sight of us, but when they did, we'd be done for. In front of the Bledsoes' house, Tate's leaf-burdened trailer sagged on its old axles. Tate himself was nowhere to be seen. The street was deserted, but now the boy's voices were in the Allens' backyard. Thinking fast, I tugged Starr's hand and pulled her toward the trailer.

"Quick!" I gasped. "Get in." Like squirrels we clambered over its high sides, diving into the leaves, burrowing under the big pile. We were barely covered and didn't dare even to sneeze as the gang of boys exploded around the corner of the Allens' house. In a hooting pack, they chased our trail up Gray Street. Starr's hand trembled in mine. I squeezed it back and closed my eyes, praying to the infant Jesus that they'd pass Tate's trailer by.

There's rarely an adult experience like the thump-in-the-guts terror constantly lurking beneath the still-water ordinariness of a kid's life. Hidden under a heap of pine straw and musty-smelling oak leaves, Starr and I knew down to the soles of our feet we were going to be killed outright if we were caught. That knowledge didn't ease when the gang pounded to a stop at the Bledsoes' house, massed on the sidewalk right beside Tate's trailer.

"Where'd the little bitch go?" That snarl was Buddy Bledsoe's. I was positive I could smell the animal reek of his sweat, like a hog gone bad and murderous.

"She must've run up this way," another boy offered, sounding out of breath. "Sure was fast."

"Yeah," Buddy's voice agreed. "She shouldn't've spied on us. We'll get her, and then we'll stick cherry bombs up her bagina." The other boys reacted with muffled guffaws.

"Then we'll—" Buddy's plans for further violence were cut off when the front door of the Bledsoes' house opened.

"Boys?" High-heeled shoes clacked down the brick path, and Mrs. Bledsoe's happy, drawling voice said, "Buddy! How nice you've brought your fuh-riends over to play. Y'all want to come inside, have a Co-cola and some tater chips?"

The pack shuffled its collective feet. "No'm," Buddy said. "We're going to . . . uh, play some more football. Thanks anyway, Mom."

"Oh, all right." Mrs. Bledsoe sounded disappointed. "Well, if y'all change your minds, there's puh-lenty of snacks in the kitchen. Don't be too late now—it's almost dark." And Starr and I listened with sinking spirits as our one faint hope of a reprieve clacked its way up the front steps and shut the door.

"So where'd they go?" somebody asked.

Before Buddy could issue new search-and-destroy orders, heavy footsteps shuffled across the desiccated lawn and onto the sidewalk. Starr and I clung to each other's hands, exhausted with fright. I wondered who the new arrival was but couldn't risk breaking cover to find out. Maybe another boy, maybe another indifferent adult, the situation was the same: we were trapped.

"Hey, nigger," Buddy said. The other boys chimed in.

"Nigger, you get home."

"Yeah, nigger."

Tate had returned to his truck and trailer. Without a word to the taunting boys, he tossed the pitchfork into the bed of the truck with a thud and a clang. The truck's door opened, rusted hinges groaning. The trailer settled as Tate got inside the cab. He cranked the engine with a series of gagging coughs, and a dense, fuel-rich fog of burning oil and gasoline filled the air, competing with the smell of the leaves, the pine straw, and Buddy.

"Get out, nigger!"

The boy's harsh voices faded as the truck and trailer loaded with dry leaves and two terrified girls pulled away from the Bledsoes' house. Too soon, the truck was chugging down the street, too fast for us to jump out. It seemed we were out of the frying pan and into the Hinds County dump. A layer of leaves swirled upward into the cold rush of wind.

The trailer slewed right as the truck turned the corner, and Starr rolled through the pine straw until she was next to me. "Where's he going, Annie?" she whispered in my ear.

"I don't know," I whispered back. Tate's truck turned right again and after a short distance slowed to a stop. The scratchy-sounding radio was playing over the truck's sputtering engine, someone singing about a love that wouldn't die. I thought my heart would leap out of my chest it was pounding so hard. Cautiously, I parted the leaves over my face to the deep-violet dusk shot through with wood smoke. As I sat up, Starr poked her head up out of the pile, too, her curls wreathed with brown oak leaves and pine straw. The truck idled as we peeped over the high plywood side of the trailer.

We were in front of my house.

"Hurry," I whispered. "He might come back." We climbed out of the trailer and down to the sidewalk, brushing the leaves out of each other's hair and off our clothes. Still trembling with the aftershock of our near-death experience, I jumped when the trailer began to pull away from the curb. Behind the wheel of the truck loomed a great shadow: Tate.

But he'd saved us. Impulsively, I ran down the middle of Fairmont to catch up with the truck. It slowed, rolling to a shuddering stop. On tiptoe I looked through the open window into the cab, into the mild brown eyes of Tate Barlow. His face betrayed nothing except a stolid weariness.

"Thank you, Mr. Tate," I faltered. "Thanks for the ride home."

He nodded once and shifted the truck into first gear. Then he drove away.

Back on the sidewalk in front of my house, Starr and I walked through the gate. We sat down on the cold limestone front steps, our shoulders touching.

"I'm sorry," I began. "I shouldn't have . . ." My voice trailed off.

She brushed away a stubborn oak leaf caught in the laces of her shoe.

"It's okay, Annie," Starr said simply.

And with that, it was. Everything was okay again. When you're seven, an apology is a magical potion, a prince's kiss, a shiny golden lamp with three whole wishes in it.

The long day was nearly done, a fat half-moon hanging low in the evening sky. My daddy was home from work, his car in the driveway. Starr and I trotted down the side of the house, past the boxwood maze to the Allens' fence.

"What did you see?" I asked after I helped her over the wire. "I heard what Buddy said, that you'd been spying on them."

"Oh," Starr said, her eyes round as silver coins in the dusk. "The boys were lighting farts in the old garage down by the railroad tracks! I went for a walk and came up by 'em on accident."

"Lighting farts?" I was mystified. How could anyone manage such a thing, and why would you want to?

"I'll tell you about it tomorrow," Starr promised. "I've got to go now. G'night, Annie."

" 'Night, Starr."

★ ★ ★

That afternoon I learned that I could run almost as fast as Starr—given sufficient motivation—and that my mother had told me the truth, that doing the right thing is always easier when you get around to it straight away.

The next day, I learned that methane gas is flammable.

CHAPTER 7

I park the car around the corner and hurry through the deepening dusk, trotting up the lamplit street to my house. These high-heeled boots aren't made for anything faster than a stroll, but surely nobody sees me racing past in the dark on my tiptoes. The neighboring families should be inside by now, gathered together in their big, warm kitchens, getting ready for Thanksgiving tomorrow.

And Du's Mercedes isn't in the garage yet, thank God. With any luck at all, Myrtistine will have left for the day, too. Pinned to the screen door, the note addressed to me in her sprawling backhand confirms her absence.

Turky 325 oven 8 a.m. Take it out before it burn.

I rip the note off the door and toss it in the garbage. My luck is holding. I don't need any witnesses for what I'm getting ready to do next.

In the kitchen I throw some milk, bottled lemon juice, yellow mustard, and Kraft Parmesan cheese in a mug and stir. The mixture promptly curdles and smells just like vomit, a trick I've used since I was nine for playing sick. Grabbing the mug, I take the back stairs two at a time and run through my bedroom to the bathroom. With a grimace at my wild-eyed reflection in the mirror, I force myself to take a bare sip of the disgusting mess in the mug, swish, spit it out in the pink marble sink, and almost vomit for real. Swallowing my gorge, I pour the rest of the malodorous concoction into the toilet.

Lord help me, Du's Mercedes is purring up the driveway. To add a visual, I rub a light dab of blusher under my eyes to approximate a fever. In my hurry to toss the mug into the laundry hamper, I almost forget to flush the toilet.

There's no time to lose. Leaving the light in the bathroom on, I yank my mink parka and sweater over my head, dump the clothes onto the closet floor, and grab my bathrobe. Myrtistine's made up the bed earlier today, carefully arranging the eyelet-embroidered boudoir pillows in an artful scatter. I heave all that preciousness across the room onto the window seat and throw back the duvet. With no time to remove my jeans and boots, I belt my silk bathrobe on over them, leap into the bed, boots and all, and am pulling the covers up to my chin at the exact moment Du's heavy tread on the back stairs reaches the landing.

He stops in the doorway. "You in bed, honey?" Du sounds confused. Why wouldn't he be? The last time we spoke, I was all on board with the partners' dinner, as bright as ever I am before my fourth cup of coffee.

In what I hope sounds like pure pitifulness, I moan. My husband tiptoes across the carpet, as absurdly light on his feet as one of those pink elephants from *Fantasia*. Did I mention that Du's a big man? Six foot four, he weighs nearly three hundred pounds, and though a fair amount of that weight is situated over his belt like a French Quarter balcony, if I squint I can still see the defensive lineman he used to be. As he nears forty, Du's taken to arranging his dark hair sideways to cover a growing bald spot, but when you subtract the excess poundage and the comb-over, he's still a good looking man with a passing resemblance to Elvis Presley. Since Du's originally from Tupelo, Elvis's birthplace, it seems fitting.

"Hey, sugar, whassa matter?" His voice is more than a little slurred. I can smell the bourbon on his breath from here. Getting a jump on Thanksgiving with the other guys at the firm, sharing the bottle he keeps in his credenza, I gather. It wouldn't be the first time he's knocked back a few before coming home, and while he usually just passes out in front of the television before dinner, this time I might can use the leverage.

"Oh, Du—I feel so stinky," I whimper. With luck, I look as flat-out ill as I manage to sound. "It got so bad at Maison-Dit, I had to leave the car in the parking lot and take a taxi home."

The bedsprings groan as he sits beside me and pats the duvet somewhere in the vicinity of my left hip. "You sick?" He blinks owlishly in the darkened bedroom, lit only by the glow from the bathroom. "Aw, hon. I'm sorry. Want me to stay with you?"

My eyelashes flutter at the thought. "No, sweetheart," I whisper. "Judge Shapley's expecting you tonight. Go on ahead without me. I'll be okay—this is just some twenty-four-hour bug."

Du flinches at my breath, which is sure to be dreadful. His hand on my perspiring forehead is like a boxer's glove filled with sand. "You sure?" He sounds dubious. "I could probably get ol' Myrtistine to come over and sit up with you. What if you're sick again?"

"I already threw up a bunch," I murmur, hoping my olfactory ruse backs me up. "But I think if I just rest, it'll pass. Go on, honey—you need to be getting ready. Sorry about the smell in the bathroom." Du gets up with a protesting pop of knee joints, the price of all those tackles and goal-line stands.

"Guess I'm going to have to get along without you tonight," he says, and I feel a quick rush of relief. He sounds regretful, although I can't imagine why since I know he walks on the thinnest layer of ice around the Judge anyway and having me on his arm only adds to Du's worries. He must be repressing all those occasions when I've had a glass of chardonnay too many—it's not easy to gauge how much social lubricant I can hold, seeing as how I usually don't eat—and that fatal glass leads to saying and doing things even the most liberal soul could only term as peculiar. Like, last year when I wandered outside the country club during the Snow Ball "for some air" and didn't come back but went and smoked a whole pack of cigarettes with the parking valets instead, or how when I can't recall any one of Du's partners' names I'll invariably call the poor man Steve, or the time I asked old Dottie Bledsoe how Buddy was getting along in his new life. Buddy grew up to have a few peculiarities himself, although the sex-reassignment surgery was supposed to have been a success.

"We can pick up the car tomorrow," Du says. He strips off his coat and tie, drops everything on the chintz chair in front of the fireplace, and kicks his shoes off with a one-two thump on the carpet. His big, slope-shouldered silhouette fills the brightly lit bathroom doorway. "Lord, Annie," he says before he shuts the door. "You sure are sick." Soon the muted thunder of the shower affords me a tiny bit of room to breathe and plot.

I can just make out my watch in the gloom of the bedroom. It's 5:30. Du will be gone by 6:00 so he can be at the Petroleum Club in time for cocktails. I can pick Starr up for 6:15 if I hustle. It takes two and a half hours to drive the two hundred miles to New Orleans if I push the BMW to eighty-five and don't get nailed for speeding. Figure a maximum of an hour for Starr to get her act together with her money, two and a half hours back. No matter how I do the math, it's still going to take six hours. Du will be at the partners' dinner until 11:00, 11:30 at the latest. I need to buy time—about an hour and a half, to be exact.

Inspiration strikes. Our house is way too big for us: five bedrooms, four and a half baths, great room, dining room, formal living room, study, and a kitchen that only Myrtistine has ever mapped completely. When we bought forty-five hundred square feet of imitation Tara on a hill, we were thinking of the children we were going to have and Du insisted that all the potential children have their own bedrooms. Growing up on a red-dirt cattle farm down the road from a gas station, he had to share a room with two brothers until he got his scholarship to Ole Miss, and after that he lived in a suite with three other football players. Du's a big fan of privacy, and in this house that's something we have in abundance.

He comes out of the bathroom, a billow of steam preceding him. Toweling off his hair, he says, "Sugar, anything a-tall I can do for you 'fore I go?"

"Well," I say with a wan smile, "I think I'll go sleep in the guest bedroom tonight. That way I won't keep you awake, honey, and we can both get some rest."

"Shoot, darlin'," Du says. He's in the closet now, getting dressed. "I'll go down the hall. You rest up, get to feeling better. I'll just kiss you good night now and not bother you when I come in." He emerges backlit by the light in the closet, his suit coat on his arm, tie loose around his neck. "You seen my shoes?"

"They're on the floor by the chair." It's almost as if Du's in on this conspiracy with me: I can't hope for more. "That would be great—you letting me sleep. I'll be much better for Thanksgiving tomorrow." And I can sneak into the house around 1:45 Thanksgiving morning and no one will ever know. I hate lying to him, mostly because it's so easy, but sometimes it's the only way.

"Your mom still coming?" he asks, knotting his tie.

"Mmm-hmm," I murmur. "And Aunt Too-Tai's still planning to come up from Chunky. Myrtistine's done everything but put the turkey in the oven. I'll do that around eight tomorrow morning, and we'll have Thanksgiving dinner by one."

Du leans over the bed and kisses me on the forehead. He smells of sandalwood soap, bourbon, and aftershave. "Well, you get some shut-eye and I'll let everyone know you're under the weather." Am I hearing the faintest note of relief in his voice? "See you in the ay-em, sugar." Du shuts the door gently on his way out.

It's all I can do to stay in the bed until the sound of his car leaving the driveway fades, but after what seems like an hour, he's finally gone. I throw back the duvet and rush into the bathroom to brush my teeth. In my closet, there's no time to get picky about what to wear: it's the green cashmere and the mink parka one more time. Dressed again and ready to go, I turn off the lights in the closet. Then I turn them back on because I need cash.

You should know that I have my own money, sort of. Days after my debut, Grandmother Banks finally achieved her expiration date (done in by her own meanness, in my opinion, although the coroner pronounced it complications from shingles) inside the elevator of her house on State Street. It took the Jackson Fire Department, two policemen, and the Jaws of Life nearly a whole day to remove her body and the wheelchair from that gilt birdcage: they built elevators to last back in the twenties.

When her will was read downtown at the attorney's dark, old-fashioned office, in a quavering rumble of faintly disguised disapproval, elderly Mr. Billy Spotswood Sr. informed me that, after endowing an annuity for Pumpernickel and leaving the bulk of her estate to my father, my grandmother had also engineered an inheritance for me, her only grandchild, to be administered by Daddy. The trust fund came to a respectable amount of cash and bank stocks, plus her collection of unfashionable, exceedingly filthy diamonds. My grandmother's housekeeper, Easter Mae, received a half-dozen sterling-silver pickle forks and Wash, her manservant, got the ancient Packard, which was at death's door itself. Conspicuous in its absence was any bequest to my mother. Nonetheless, both my parents enjoyed the boost to their standard of living after Grandmother Banks's demise, and they never said a word about it. In fact, I don't think I've ever heard my mother say anything even remotely disparaging about her vicious mother-in-law, not even after Daddy passed five years ago and nobody was left to give a damn.

Now we come to the "sort of" part of my own money. After Daddy's death, my mother became the trustee of my inheritance by default. It was a convoluted trust instrument that Mr. Spotswood Sr. had crafted, one that illustrated what Grandmother Banks must have thought of my ability ever to manage my own money. I can have as much as I want or need from the estate—so long as I run it past my mother first and she agrees to it. Grandmother would surely disapprove of this development, but that's too bad: if she wanted to rule her empire forever, she shouldn't have died.

In any case, my mother's cooperation has insured that Du and I can live like we do. If we had to get by on his salary (which is by no means a small one), we'd be up to our ears in debt, but having the old trust fund to fall back on has made all the difference. So tonight, in light of the "sort of" provision, it's a good thing I've kept nearly five thousand dollars in cash inside the dreaded walk-in closet, behind our ski boots, tucked underneath my extra shoulder pads in a cedar-lined box. I call it my "running money," and no one knows a thing about it but me. Since Du can never learn about tonight's adventure, I can't use my credit cards, and Starr and I may have need of cash, so

I stuff a handful of hundred-dollar bills in the pocket of my parka. Then I arrange the heap of eyelet pillows under the duvet to stand in for stomach-virus-afflicted, sleeping Annie—just in case.

Then I run.

The wind has stopped and the air is crystal cold, but the night sky overhead is full of stars as I pull the car into the parking garage at the Burnside Tower. I punch the "up" button for the elevator and wait, praying there won't be someone riding it up to their condo from the lobby downstairs at the same time. The seconds crawl by. I'm beginning to think about taking the stairs, and then the doors slide open at last.

As it happens, I'm not going to be alone on my trip up to Starr's penthouse.

There's a hairy little dog in the elevator, a black-and-tan creature resembling a miniature, flop-eared version of a German shepherd. It can't weigh more than ten pounds. With a shrug, I step inside. The doors close, and the smell in the elevator assaults my nose like a slap, ripe with a warm, familiar stink. The source is a pile in the corner, surprisingly large for such a small dog. He looks up at me with an air of depression, seemingly embarrassed about the mess, and so to be polite, I avoid looking at the small mountain of shit. The dog sighs as the elevator travels in a smooth, uninterrupted climb up the seven stories to the penthouse floor.

When the door opens, the dog—it's some obscure breed of terrier, I think—gets out with me. He follows me to Starr's door and sits by my feet when I knock, just as if he's at home there.

The door opens and Starr steps out into the foyer. She's changed into a pair of baggy acid-washed jeans and what looks like a man's Arran-knit sweater, the heavy, cabled sleeves hanging past her fingertips, the hem falling halfway to her knees. In spite of wearing what must be the last of Bobby's clothes, Starr looks beautiful: her color is high, and her pale eyes are bright as, well, stars.

"I'm ready," she says. She reaches down to pat the dog. "Hey, Troy Smoot." He looks up at her with recognition, tail wagging, his grin full of sharp white teeth. "You meet Troy in the elevator?" she asks.

"I met him and his shit," I say. "What the hell's that about? Is he yours?"

She ruffles the wild hair sprouting behind the terrier's ears. "Jesus wept, no. Troy here lives next door with ol' Jerome and Lollie Treeby. Remember Lisa's parents? Lollie can't even recall her own name anymore, and he can't be bothered to walk a dog, so three times a day ol' Jerome just sticks Troy in the elevator and lets him ride up and down until he's done his business. Then he phones down and tells Mr. Jarbo, the maintenance man, to clean it up and spray some Glade around. Bobby said Mr. Treeby's been doing it for years."

I can't believe what I'm hearing. "You mean to tell me he keeps a dog up here and doesn't even walk it?" It explains the howling earlier and the atomic cloud of air freshener on my previous trip up in the elevator this afternoon. "That's cruel. Not to mention disgusting."

"Honey," Starr says patiently, "people think this place is the last word on gracious living, but let me tell you what, the Burnside is full of mean old folks who're used to getting their own way. When they say 'shit,' they mean for somebody to drop their drawers. If Mr. Jarbo wants to keep his job in this crappy building, he'll keep on cleaning up after all of them, not just the Treebys. You ready to go?" Starr slings her purse over her shoulder and locks the door behind her.

"Someone should report this to the Humane Society." I've known that after Lisa grew up to become a geneticist and went to work bioengineering soybeans for ConAgra in Dubuque,

Mr. and Mrs. Treeby sold their old place and moved to the Burnside. I had no idea that they'd gotten themselves a dog, but with Lisa and her allergies gone, there wasn't any reason not to, I guess, and Mr. Treeby must have missed having someone to boss around. In her old age, Mrs. Treeby has become increasingly dim, so I'm betting he takes it out on the dog instead of her these days. And knowing Jerome Treeby, he must have been as appalled by Starr's presence next door for the last six months as I am about him making his dog shit in the elevator.

The doors to the elevator slide open again, and the little terrier trots inside. "Does he just ride up and down until they let him out?" I ask as we walk in after him.

"That's right," Starr says. The elevator descends. "That's how come Troy and me got to know each other. I call him Troy Smoot after a boy I knew what got ten years at Parchman prison for a crime he didn't even do. Poor thing. It isn't his fault." Troy looks stoically away from the mound in the corner.

The door opens onto the parking garage and the clean, cold November night smells like freedom. Starr and I get out of the elevator. The dog stays behind, intelligent brown eyes mournful, head cocked in wistful farewell as the doors begin to close.

"Wait!" I shove my arm between the closing doors to hold them open. "C'mon, Troy."

Troy trots out of the elevator, his stub tail wagging. "What're you doing?" Starr asks. Her voice echoes in the cavernous garage. "We're going to New Orleans, right?"

"That's the plan," I say. "And Troy's coming with us." Not content with being a liar and a coward, I'm a dog thief now. I open the door to the BMW, and he jumps into the front seat.

"What're we going to do with a dog?" Starr sounds confused. "Annie, I thought we were going to travel light." She gets in the passenger's side and pats Troy's head. The dog leans into her hand and exhales a gusty sigh. "Don't get me wrong—me and Troy are good to go, if that's what you want."

It's like this morning's black silk dress, still hanging in the back seat of the car; it's like this furtive trip to New Orleans in the dark. Taking this poor bastard away from his miserable life with the Treebys is something I'm going to do because I just know it's the right thing to do, even if I can't explain why.

"Get in the back, Troy," I say, pointing behind me. The dog hops across the console and sits up on the back seat, ears pricked and ready for a ride in the car.

"Time to get this show on the road, then," Starr says. "And no smoking 'round the baby."

My grandmother would just die if she weren't already dead.

CHAPTER 8

My grandmother was only one reason why I'd never liked Thanksgiving.

At my house, the morning always began with a frantic dash to get to church for the early service. My Sunday clothes were uncomfortable in the extreme. Starched petticoats, stiff patent leather shoes, my Sunday coat's blue wool collar scratching the back of my neck, and a tight black velvet, wide-brimmed hat—by the time Daddy pulled the Buick up to the Gothic palace that was St. Andrew's Episcopal Cathedral, I was already surly and wanted to get the hell out of there before we even walked in the doors. "Thankful" was the last thing on my mind, believe me.

This Thanksgiving, after an hour of sermonizing and hymn singing, scribbling pictures on all the tithe cards and in the back of the prayer book with the pew's little pencil, wriggling and sighing in discomfort until my mother had given me a swat on my leg, I'd come to a gloomy reappraisal of the benefits of going to heaven. If church was any indication of what I could expect for eternity as a reward for good behavior, I was ready to be my usual bad self and take my chances with the place Starr called you-know-where.

Needless to say, when we arrived at home on Fairmont Street, I bolted out of the back seat of the Buick.

"Annie Banks!" my mother called. "Keep your good clothes clean."

And Thanksgiving dinner, the whole point of this obnoxious day, was still a good three hours away. Upstairs, I threw the blue wool coat with its scratchy collar onto my bed and sailed the hat after it. The petticoats and shoes I could do nothing about, so I resigned myself to a long day of irritation, boredom, and interrogation. Grandmother Banks was coming for dinner around one, and her arrival would put an effective end to any hopes I had of enjoying the day. For a pallid little bright spot, Aunt Too-Tai was coming, too.

Younger sister to my awful grandmother, Aunt Too-Tai was old—at least sixty—a chalk cliff of a woman in bib overalls. She lived in a poky, run-down house in the Mississippi countryside, out from Chunky, off the highway to Meridian, which had an attic fan and no television. When she came to Thanksgiving dinner at our house, her rump-sprung tweed suit always smelled like motor oil and a whopping dose of mothballs. By the time the turkey was on the table, my aunt would smell even more powerfully of bourbon, for even though Hinds County was ostensibly dry in 1963, my daddy could buy package liquor at the bootlegger's drive-through down the road in Pearl. He and Aunt Too-Tai could put away nearly a whole fifth between them whenever they got together on Thanksgiving Day, talking politics and Ole Miss football. Watching the grown-ups get plastered made for a break in the long tedium of the holiday, a small measure of cheer in an otherwise cheerless day.

Downstairs in the kitchen, Methyl Ivory was busy basting the turkey, the big, golden bird glistening under the oven's bright light. Pumpkin and mince pies were cooling on the kitchen table. Nobody would notice if I broke off a little piece of crust, I thought, so I sidled up to the table to sneak a bite of something to eat.

"Git," Methyl Ivory ordered, not even turning around.

"Fine!" I flounced through the door into the hall. In the living room, my daddy was watching a bowl game by the fire, while my mother was in the dining room, making sure that the table was set perfectly so that her mother-in-law would have one less thing to criticize. And me, I was set adrift on the day with nothing to do, held hostage to my clothes.

It seemed that my parents wouldn't care if I took myself outside for a walk around the backyard as long as I stayed clean, so naturally I went down by the fence even though I hadn't any expectation that I'd see Starr. After all, her father was a preacher and today would be a big day in the little Pentecostal church over on the other side of Fortification Street. I comforted myself with the thought that likely Starr would be bored to death and wearing uncomfortable clothes, too.

The day was crisp as good stationery, a seamless cold with a deckle edge, and full of starlings. Overhead the massive cloud of birds swirled in an impossible earthbound arc, at the last instant breaking free of gravity, rushing upward with an explosion of wings. I hung my fingers in the wire mesh and looked across the Allens' backyard at the rental house with longing. To my delighted surprise, Starr was sitting on the back steps with her head in her hands.

"Hey!" I pitched my voice over the starlings' mad whirr. "Hey, Starr!"

Starr's margarine-yellow head lifted, and she raised her

hand in a listless wave. It seemed to take forever for her to walk down through the Allens' backyard to the fence.

Starr wasn't dressed up for Thanksgiving. She was wearing the boy's corduroy pants and her old sweatshirt. Her feet were bare.

"Hey, Annie," she said. Up close, her eyes were red-rimmed.

"What's the matter?" I asked.

Starr looked at the ground. "Nothing."

"Oh."

She looked up and swallowed hard. "See, it's just my poppa won't get up out of the bed this morning to go to the church. I tried and tried, really I did, and the phone just kept on a-ringing. I know it was folks from the church, wanting to find out where he was at."

I had no idea how to respond to this. "D'you think he's sick?" I finally asked.

Starr laughed without humor, sounding shockingly adult. "No, Annie. He's not sick. My momma used to get him up when he goes like this, make him drink a pot of coffee and see he made it to the church, but I couldn't do it." She wrapped her thin arms around herself and shivered. "No turkey either. He forgot, I guess."

"But it's Thanksgiving," I said, round-eyed. Much as I disliked this holiday, it seemed to me that there were *rules* about this sort of thing, and here was Starr's poppa, breaking a lot of them. "What are you going to eat?"

Starr shrugged. "There's a can of hash and some eggs. I can make that, hash and eggs. We're out of whatever else."

This was just plain wrong. "C'mon," I said. "You can come to my house for dinner, if you want." Of course she could. Hadn't Bishop Thwaite said just this morning that we needed to feed the hungry on this special day?

"I better not, Annie," Starr said. "Look at me—I bet your family gets all dressed up."

"Well," I said, "go home, change into your Sunday clothes, and come back!"

Starr's face brightened ever so slightly. "Really?"

"Sure," I said. "Hurry up. I'll go tell my mother."

"You did *what?*" my mother demanded.

"Asked Starr to come to Thanksgiving dinner?" My voice was small. "I had to—her father's in the bed and he won't get up." I hung my head. It hadn't occurred to me that feeding the hungry was a Christian duty only so long as it wasn't at our table.

"Well, you'll just have to uninvite her." My mother leaned across the snowy Irish linen tablecloth set with the Haviland dinner plates and good silver, straightening a candle that was just out of true in a way only she could discern. "Thanksgiving is a *family* holiday, Annie. Besides, you never ask someone to dinner without getting permission first."

"But what about Bishop Thwaite?" I asked defensively. "He came last year, and he's not family."

"That's different," my mother said, sounding as though she was keeping her temper on a short leash.

"But why?" I insisted. "Why can't Starr come?"

Before my mother could answer, Methyl Ivory poked her head in the dining room.

"Miz Collie?" she said. "That child from 'cross the way's at the back door. She say Annie ask her to Thanksgiving dinner." Methyl Ivory's broad, dark face was expressionless, bland as unsalted rice.

"Well, I'll just have to explain to Starr that Annie was wrong, inviting her without asking first." Her cheeks flushed, my mother was untying her apron as she stalked around the dining table to go to the sunporch through the kitchen.

"But we've got tons of food!" I stomped my foot in its uncomfortable Sunday shoe. How could she be so mean?

"Absolutely not."

"Aunt Too-Tai won't care," I argued, following her through the swinging door into the kitchen.

Just inside the doors to the sunporch, Starr was standing with her hands clasped together at her waist. She'd changed into a dress that I knew was her favorite—pink candy stripes on pale-blue cotton—and her cracked-leather pair of school shoes. But the wrinkled dress looked tired to death, the sash hanging unevenly where she'd had to tie it herself. She'd forgotten to brush her hair, too, the yellow curls drooping around her downcast face. Now, I can look with memory's eye and see Starr as my mother must have seen her: an undernourished, untended child standing on the doorstep of poverty, wearing a worn-out dress and cheap shoes.

But that Thanksgiving morning on the sunporch, I didn't notice how my mother had fallen silent, too caught up in arguing my case.

"Starr's daddy didn't even get a turkey!" I howled in righteous indignation. "It's Thanksgiving and he forgot the turkey. Starr's going to be hungry!" I'd played my trump card.

My mother turned her head and frowned down at me. "That's enough from you, Mercy Anne Banks," she said coldly. I shut up, looking at the red-tiled floor with tears in my eyes, biting my lip. When my mother used my whole given name, all hope was lost.

In her blue wool challis dress with the white silk cuffs and collar, her pearl necklace and black suede pumps, my mother slowly crossed the sunporch. She sat on her heels in front of Starr, put her fingertip under Starr's chin, and lifted it so that she looked at her face.

"Come with me," she said. Taking Starr's hand in hers, she led her through the kitchen, then out to the front hall's staircase. I followed behind them. "You wait down here, Annie Banks." They vanished up to the second floor, Starr with one perplexed look at me over her shoulder. After a minute of looking up the empty staircase in complete mystification, I went back to the kitchen.

"What's my mother doing?" I asked Methyl Ivory. "Why'd she take Starr upstairs?"

"That you mama's business, I 'spect." She stirred the saucepan of bubbling giblet gravy. "Here." Methyl Ivory handed me my mother's discarded apron. "Make you self useful," she said, pointing at the sink full of pots and pans. With a long-suffering sigh, I dragged the step stool to the sink and began washing.

It seemed to be taking forever for my mother and Starr to return. Not knowing what was going on up on the second floor strung out the time like a dangling fly on a spider's silken strand. I finished washing the pots and pans and dried them, even. Methyl Ivory took the turkey out of the oven. The kitchen clock's hands ticked the long minutes off until it was one, and then the doorbell rang.

"I'll get it," my daddy called from the living room.

"Quick, child," Methyl Ivory said. "Take off that apron and go kiss you grammaw."

"Do I have to?"

"Git!"

In the entryway by the front door, Daddy was helping Grandmother Banks out of her coat and mink scarf, the one with the stuffed minks' tiny jaws biting each other's hindquarters in a gruesome chain of fur. The coat-removal operation was fairly complicated. Wash stood behind Grandmother Banks's wheelchair, looking as though he were waiting for a bus that was a long time in coming.

My grandmother's sharp, faded blue eyes caught mine the instant I walked around the corner into the long center hall. "Come here, Annie Banks," she said sharply, "and give me a kiss." With dragging feet, I walked toward her wheelchair, dreading the tribute I knew had to be paid on arrival. Like always, she smelled of attar of roses and Vick's VapoRub. I felt like wiping my mouth as soon as I delivered the ritual kiss on her powdered, withered cheek, but knowing better, instead I backed away and hid behind my daddy.

"Wash," Grandmother Banks ordered, "go wait in the car." She folded her liver-spotted hands, knuckles ringed in old diamonds, over the pocketbook in her lap.

"Yes'm," said Wash. He opened the door, whistling as he walked down the sidewalk to the Packard, tossing the keys in the air and catching them. Daddy shut the door and rubbed his hands together.

"Can I get you a little glass of sherry, Mother?" he asked. He took the handles of her wheelchair and began to push it down the hall to the living room, where the fire crackled on the hearth.

"Oh, I don't know, Wade." My grandmother bridled like a spoiled flirt. "You wouldn't be trying to get me tipsy, would you?" I was surprised to hear my daddy laugh in what sounded like embarrassment, and then at that moment my mother and Starr came down the stairs. My mouth fell wide open.

Starr had changed clothes. She was wearing one of my Sunday dresses—the red plaid taffeta with its white bell of crinoline and black velvet sash—clean socks and my second-best pair of patent leather Mary Janes. Her curls were caught back with a black velvet hair ribbon, and her scrubbed cheeks were as pink as if she'd just come in from out of doors.

"Mother Banks," my mother said smoothly, reaching the bottom of the stairs. "Happy Thanksgiving to you." She took Starr's hand. "This is Starr Dukes, one of Annie's friends. She'll be having dinner with us today because her father's feeling poorly. Starr, meet Annie's grandmother Mrs. Banks."

Starr's smile was shy. "Pleased to meet you, ma'am," she said politely.

Grandmother Banks lifted one imperious, sparse eyebrow. "Dukes?" she said, sounding as though someone were trying to sell her an inferior brand of mayonnaise. "I don't believe I know that family." Grandmother Banks turned in her chair and lifted her chin to look up at my father. "Surely she must have someone else at home, Wade. We'll have Wash drive her back to her house."

Before my father could say anything to this, however, my mother said, "Starr's our guest today, Mother Banks. Just as you are." And with that, she took the handles of the wheelchair from my father and pushed her now stone-silent dragon of a mother-in-law into the living room to the place of honor beside the fire.

"Wade," my mother said, and her voice was like music, "why don't you pour us a glass of sherry? I know I could certainly use one."

Thanksgiving that year was anything but tedious, especially after Aunt Too-Tai arrived twenty minutes later and Daddy broke out the bourbon. My grandmother was more than rude, speaking only to my father, except for once when she asked Aunt Too-Tai about someone who turned out to be dead.

And then, after we'd sat down to dinner, Daddy had carved the turkey, and we'd all said grace, Starr dropped her fork. The heavy silver striking the floor rang like the bells at St. Andrew's. Everyone at the table looked up from their plates. Conversation stopped. Starr's face was as red as her borrowed dress.

" 'Scuse me," she mumbled, looking as though she wanted to vanish under the Irish linen tablecloth.

My grandmother gave a loud sniff of disdain and cleared her throat, obviously about to render a fatal judgment from on high, but before she opened her mouth, Aunt Too-Tai had picked up her knife and dropped it on the floor next to her chair. That knife really clattered because she'd put a good spin on it.

"Whoops," she said, her voice bright. She gave my thigh a poke under the table. "Now, Annie," Aunt Too-Tai muttered. "Drop something."

With a startled glance at her, I dropped my fork on the floor, too. *Clang.*

"Really, Wade," my horrible grandmother began, sounding vastly annoyed.

With a grin, my daddy dropped his knife, and my mother laughed and dropped her spoon, too. Looking at my mother from down the table, Starr's eyes shone with what could have been worship. When everyone had collected their silverware from off the floor, Thanksgiving dinner resumed. My grandmother didn't even talk to Daddy after that.

That year was a better-than-usual Thanksgiving, and better yet, at the conclusion of dinner, instead of joining everybody by the fire, Grandmother Banks made Daddy go out and wake Wash up from his doze in the front seat of the Packard to take her back to State Street. It was as though the dragon sulking in its wheelchair had decided to roll on to a location farther south, taking the oppressive atmosphere with it. My parents and Aunt Too-Tai raised their after-dinner glasses of bourbon in a silent toast while Starr and I stretched out on the rug and played Old Maid in the firelight.

At last, Thanksgiving Day ended, Aunt Too-Tai left to make the drive back to Chunky, and it was time for Starr to go home.

"Wade," my mother said. "Let's drive her. It's dark."

Gathering the cards, I got up from beside the fire to go, too.

"No, Annie," my mother said. "You'd better go on upstairs

and have a bath. Methyl Ivory will stay with you until we come back. Say good-bye to Starr, now."

They were gone what seemed a long time, much longer than it should have taken just to drive around the block. I was in my flannel pajamas and robe, sitting at the kitchen table with Methyl Ivory and having a last slice of pumpkin pie and a glass of milk, when my parents came in the front door.

". . . disgraceful," my father was saying. "Tighter than Dick's hatband, no better than a drunk."

"Shhh, Wade." It was my mother's lowered voice. "Let's not talk about it now." You know, I can still remember the way they looked as I ran to meet them in the hall—tall and handsome, somehow bright around the edges—like princes of the earth.

I have never loved them more.

Later that same night, I was reading *The Secret Garden,* snug under the covers. My mother came in my room to kiss me good night. She sank down on the bed beside me.

"Annie, she said, "I need you to listen to me." I sat up, and she took my hands in her own. "Starr's father isn't a well man." My mother pinched her red lips together, as though remembering something nasty. "Your daddy and I had a word with him this evening when we took Starr home. We told him he has to take better care of himself, but I don't know how much good that'll do. Now if you hear that he's . . . sick . . . again, I want you to tell me right away. Starr can come stay with us for a while, just until he's better."

"He's not really sick, is he?" I remembered what my daddy had said. Drunk. My only experience with drunks was watching Red Skelton's Willy Lump-Lump staggering around the light pole on the television, but I knew what drunk meant. "But how come he's tighter than Dick's hatband? Did somebody tie him up?"

"Never mind that." She didn't say anything for a moment; then my mother burst out, "No child should have to endure what that little girl is going through!" Her eyes were fierce, her hands tightening on mine. "And if I have anything to say about it, she won't have to, not anymore. We can at least go through your closet tomorrow and find some nice things for her to wear. Good night, Annie."

" 'Night."

She kissed my forehead, turned out the light, and I fell almost instantly fast asleep, full of pie and Thanksgiving.

Chapter 9

Even though I began this frantic race to New Orleans with a mostly full tank, we have to stop for gasoline at the Fernwood Travel Plaza, just outside of McComb. The Beemer is a great car for a road trip, but a V-8 eats up the fuel exactly like it devours the road.

It's just as well. Starr, being in her second trimester, has needed to find a restroom since we passed the Jackson city limits eighty miles ago. I give her a hundred-dollar bill from the wad in my parka's pocket and ask her to pay the cashier while I pump the gas. In the back seat, Troy Smoot is whining and pawing at the window. I'm guessing he probably needs a quick whiz himself, so, finished pumping, I hang up the hose and open the door to let him out of the car before I remember he isn't wearing a leash.

I don't have a lot of experience with dogs, obviously.

At our house, we never had pets at all, not even a goldfish, much less a dog. I think it was a mutual decision for my parents—Daddy having grown up with a series of ill-tempered dachshunds and my mother unwilling to have a four-legged nuisance underfoot in addition to her two-legged one. If I wanted to play with an animal, she'd say, I could go next door and visit with King, Dr. Thigpen's German shepherd. Like Dr. Thigpen, King was retired and only wanted to laze underneath the live oak tree in the peace and quiet of his own front yard. Once, when I was really little, I tied myself to the oak with a clothesline and tried to convince King to bite the rope in two like Rin Tin Tin did when rescuing Rusty from the Comanches. The mailman gave me an odd look, shaking his head as he passed on his rounds. Dr. Thigpen came outside and asked me what in tarnation I was up to now. I wasn't yet discouraged, but after a long half hour of commanding a snoring King to spring into action, I finally untied myself.

Troy Smoot the terrier may look like a ten-pound version of King, but as soon as he bounds out of the car and hits the oil-spotted pavement, he's off—sprinting into the darkness like he's got a hot date with a small, crunchy mammal. I'm ready to panic until I realize he's made straight for the parched grass at the dark edge of the parking lot, just beside a row of big semis idling with their low beams on. I keep an anxious eye on him as he lifts his leg on a mud flap, then noses around the gravel perimeter while I'm waiting on Starr to come back from her trip to the ladies' room.

Which she does at last, carrying two big Styrofoam cups of steaming coffee. "Whew," she says, lowering herself into the front seat. "That surely was a relief. Here's your change."

Stuffing the fistful of bills into my parka's pocket, I whistle an uncertain summons to Troy. To my utter relief, right away he comes belting across the lot under the sodium vapor lights, wearing a doggy grin and a high-held tail. He springs into the back seat and curls up with a contented wriggle, clearly pleased with his new, elevator-free circumstances.

Then, as I get in the driver's side, a whistle shrills from somewhere in the darkness by the rank of idling semis. I squint in the whistle's direction, feeling confused. Is someone else calling the dog?

"Hey, babe!" somebody hoots. It's a greasy-haired guy in a gimme cap, hanging out the window of his tractor-trailer's cab and waving at me. I shut the door, quick, and hit the lock button.

"Somebody thinks that scrawny ass of yours is mighty fine," Starr says as she hands me my coffee. I snort.

"Oh, right." I back out of the truck stop's circle of lights and head the car toward the black on-ramp, onto the I-55. "Ronald Reagan still had most of his mind the last time anyone looked at my ass, let alone made a comment about it." I glance at her in the glow from the instrument panel. "Except for you, that is. How come you keep calling me scrawny?"

" 'Cause you're the size of a Bic ballpoint." Starr gives a snort of her own, holding her thumb and forefinger about half an inch apart. "You don't know anything about what men *really* like, but they surely appreciate a woman with a little meat on her bones. You," she says with authority, "probably have no idea how men look at you—like they want to buy you a ham sandwich, then take you home."

I can't imagine why she'd think that. Except for the Judge and his obscene proposition two years ago, no one's expressed that kind of interest in me since I was in college, really not since Du started dating me. Maybe it's because I'm so dismally inept at flirting I usually end up embarrassing myself and don't even bother with it anymore. Maybe Du scares them off. Anyway, feeling a little uncomfortable at Starr's observation, I take a sip of my coffee and practically spit it out. It's loaded with artificial creamer and sugar.

"Hey," I sputter. "This shit is—"

"Fattening? Oh, please." Starr sounds bored. "Go on, honey. A little Cremora and a couple of packs of sugar never killed anybody yet."

I take another begrudging sip. Okay, it's not bad, and I can certainly use the caffeine. The highway stretches before us, dark and deserted on this night before Thanksgiving. Out here in the country night, all I can find on the radio is that terminally nasal brand of down-and-out hillbilly music and some backwoods preacher hollering into his lonely microphone about huma-seck-shu-als among us. I turn it off. During the twenty miles since the truck stop, conversation's been in short supply so I venture a question.

"Hey," I say. "Tell me about this person who's got your money."

"There's not a lot to tell," Starr replies, her nose buried in her coffee cup. "She's . . . an old friend, from my racetrack days, mostly. She did me a favor a couple of months ago, before me and Bobby hit the wall. 'Round about Labor Day, Bobby gave me a thousand bucks mad money from his poker winnings, she put that thousand bucks down on a sure thing for me, and don't you know that bangtail came in at twenty-to-one! Since Bobby was paying for everything at the time, I asked her to hold on to the money till I could come and get it."

"Oh." This woman must be a hell of a good friend, holding on to Starr's twenty thousand dollars. That's a lot of money, even though twice that amount probably won't be enough to see her through the legal Armageddon she's going to be facing with Bobby and Judge Shapley. I keep this discouraging fact to myself, though, and drive another ten miles before I ask her another question, one that's been in the back of my mind ever since earlier this afternoon at the condo.

"So who was it you were supposed to be meeting tonight?" I ask, feeling playful. "You know—the guy on the phone?"

"Nobody," Starr answers. There's a tone in her voice warning me not to push this.

I do anyway. "Nobody?" I repeat. "Oh, come on, Starr. You can tell me."

"Okay," she says. "Since you're so damn nosy, it was somebody who told me he maybe could help me out with my situation. He sure doesn't want his name dragged into it, though." Her profile in the dashboard's glow is sullen. "Look, Annie—don't make a big deal, 'kay? It's not like he's going to do anything for me anyways. Let's not talk about it."

I digest this cryptic explanation. Who could it be? And why is Starr acting like this is some Vatican state secret? I'm never going to tell anyone *anything*. Once we pick up her money and get back to Jackson, I'm praying my part in this midnight expedition never sees the light of day, so it's not as though I'm dying to go around town gossiping about this mystery man of hers. This just seems . . . off, somehow, maybe even sort of insulting that Starr doesn't trust me with his name. I wish I could smoke a cigarette. I always think better with a cigarette, and I'm not sure what to think about all this secrecy.

As I mull this over, Starr reaches for her purse and rummages around inside it. With a rustle of plastic, she unearths a jumbo pack of Slim Jims. Troy perks up and sticks his head between the front seats. I think he's drooling an unobtrusive, little-dog inquiry.

"Here." She opens the package and tries to hand me one of those meat sticks. "I bet you didn't eat before you came to get me."

"I can't have Slim Jims!" I say, even though my nose twitches at the rich, greasy aroma. Get thee behind me, Satan, I think with a shudder. "Do you know how many calories are in that thing?" I complain. "*Junk* food. Besides, eating those cookies this afternoon means I can't have anything but vitamins and lettuce until Friday."

"You serious?" Starr's voice is aghast. "There's something bad, bad wrong with that, sugar. What're you supposed to do tomorrow? Sit around with an empty plate while the normal folks load theirs up with turkey and all the fixings? Doesn't anybody ever tell you to eat?"

"Du likes me fine the way I am," I say defensively. "And my mother's never said a word to me about my weight. I bet she's happy I can still fit into my deb dress. Anyway, so long as I put some food on my plate, I can push it around for an hour and nobody really notices."

"I can't believe it. That's terrible." Starr shakes her head. "It's like you're starving yourself so you'll look like a twelve-year-old or something. What size are you, a two?"

"A zero."

Starr makes a disgusted noise. "A zero. So you're trying to disappear, then."

"I just like to fit in my clothes, that's all," I say quickly. "And I've seen what happens if you let yourself go." *If you can't be pregnant, you sure can't be fat,* says the rosebush voice. *Who'd want you then?* "So if you don't mind, I'll pass on the Slim Jims."

"Huh." Starr's mouth twists in wry concession. "Then I guess you won't want the Reese's cup either. Here, Troy, have some yummy grease."

With a genteel snap of his jaws, the dog takes my Slim Jim and nearly swallows it whole.

We crossed the state line an hour ago, trading the gentle hills of Mississippi for the flatlands of southeastern Louisiana. The miles fly by now. At a quarter to nine, we're crossing over the Bonnet Carré Spillway with ten miles to go before we hit the city limits.

New Orleans appears to the southeast as a golden arc on

the black horizon, its skyline floating above banked clouds of fog and light, and in spite of my nagging suspicion that this trip is going to turn out to be a really bad idea, I can't help but feel my spirits lift at the sight of the city.

I've always loved this town. I love its improbable, tattered buoyancy, its insatiable appetite for all good things and more than a few bad ones. Ever since I was a child, I've loved wandering the shadowed, mysterious streets of the French Quarter, loved sitting by the Mississippi River and watching the great ships of the world cleave those terrible, fathomless currents. The challenging grace note of a solitary jazz trumpet flung like a dare against the evening sky; a long, cold drink in a short, dark bar while the rain courses silver tears down the face of the marble dryad on a hidden courtyard—oh, Lord, if I was ever going to run away from my life for real, I might run to New Orleans. It'd be a sight more effective than hiding underneath the duvet and a whole lot more fun.

We're crossing the last elevated mile over the marsh before we get to the city limits, and I ask Starr, "Where do we find this friend of yours with the money?"

Starr thinks for a moment; then she says, "Get off at the exit at St. Bernard Avenue. I'll tell you how to get to the racetrack from there." She shifts uncomfortably in her seat. "I can't hardly wait. I need a bathroom."

I glance at her in the flat glare from the interstate's rows of lamps. "You really have to go again?" Here's an aspect of pregnancy I've never imagined, being at the mercy of your own bladder. For me, being with child has been on a par with walking through the gates of Mecca in holy ecstasy, the culmination of an endless pilgrimage through the desert wastes. I haven't given much thought to what Mecca would be like if I ever got there.

"It's chronic." Starr winces. "Like I said before, I wouldn't do anything different, but I wish someone had told me about this part when I forgot to take my pills. I'd have bought stock in Charmin."

We're coming up on the exit. I brake the car and glide down the ramp to the stoplight on St. Bernard. The neighborhood is dark, the streetlights' hazed glow muted by the fog and the massive oaks' heavy-leafed limbs. I check again to make sure the doors are locked. I've never been to this part of the city before, and this doesn't look like a good neighborhood. It's a far cry from the Quarter, for sure.

"Where next?" I ask, trying not to sound apprehensive and almost succeeding.

"Turn right." Starr guides me down St. Bernard to Gentilly Boulevard, then from there into an even more poorly lit rabbit warren of narrow one-way streets with exotic names like Crete and Trafalgar. The small shotgun houses here are crowded shoulder-to-shoulder in the darkness as though they're keeping an eye out for trouble, and a couple of times Starr tells me to reverse the car and go back because we missed a turn. I'm starting to freak out when, finally, rows of cinder block and sheet metal buildings appear to our left. Starr points to a gate up ahead in the high, barbed-wire-topped chain-link fence.

"We'll go in here." In the back seat, Troy puts his feet up on the window and whines at an alley cat slinking under a dilapidated house. "Shit, I forgot," Starr says, dismayed. "The dog. The guard's not going to let us bring the dog onto the backstretch. Quick—stop the car."

I pull over to the right-hand side of the street, in front of a house with foil-covered windows and a cement shrine to the Virgin hunkered down next to a junked car on cinder blocks. "He's a little dog," I say. "Maybe the guard won't see him."

"Can't take that chance." Starr shakes her head. "Take your coat off and cover him up with that. Let me do the talking." I struggle out of the mink, and Starr drapes it over the dog. "Be good, Troy Smoot," she warns. "Lay still."

I drive the car through the gates onto the river-sand road leading to the backstretch. A tall, black man in a khaki uniform steps out of the guard booth, shining a flashlight inside the front seat. I roll the window down. The night air, substantially warmer and more humid than that of the freezing truck stop back in Mississippi, fills the interior of the car with smells of wet dirt and horse.

"Evenin', ladies," the guard says. His security badge gleams in the glow of the flashlight. "Little late for visitin', ain't it?"

"Hey, Bone Man," Starr says, bright as a rhinestone tiara, flashing him that too-white smile. "Remember me?" She leans across the console into the light. The heavy cabled sweater stretches taut across her breasts and with that single move Starr manages to transform herself from a pregnant woman who desperately needs a bathroom into a sexy chick in a BMW.

"It's Starr, honey. I'm back!"

The guard, Bone Man, chuckles. "Well, well. So you are." He tips his hat back on his head and gives her the once-over, the smile never leaving his face, but I don't think much gets by this man. "Heard you were marrying a rich Mississippi lawyer, wasn't going to have time for us working folk anymore."

Starr flashes that smile again. "Now, Boney, you know I never, ever forget my friends," she purrs. "Speaking of friends, this here's my oldest friend in the world—Annie. Annie, say hey to the Bone Man."

"Hey," I manage. In the back seat under my parka, Troy thumps his tail and the guard shines the light over my shoulder. I say hastily, "Nice to meet you."

"Likewise, ma'am." The look the security guard gives me makes me feel like he knows exactly how I look in my underwear. I feel the hot blush spreading upward from my collarbones and have to force myself not to shrink out of the light.

"Always good to meet one of Starr's friends," Bone Man says, clearly enjoying this.

"We're here to see Bette," Starr interjects.

Bone Man cocks his head to one side. "What you wantin' with Bette? Ever since that little spic she shack up with went and took that spill, broke his leg, and gone back home to Miami, she been in a bad way—just 'bout murderize a person, you so much as say good mornin'. Not like Bette ever easy, nohow. All them hormoneys she take."

"Oh, Annie and me, we got some catching up to do with ol' Bette," Starr says. "I already called and let her know we're coming by for a visit."

Of course, I've never met this woman before in my life, but I smile up at Bone Man, too, nodding like an idiot while inside I'm ready to strangle Starr. I thought my sole responsibility was to chauffeur her to New Orleans and back again, and now I'm supposed to "catch up" with murderous Bette, she of the out-of-whack hormones? Starr didn't care to share this information beforehand, I seethe to myself. Why? More secrets?

"Well, Bette's trailer be where it always be," the Bone Man says with an affable smile, "just behind the cafeteria. Y'all pass a good night." With a wave to us, he steps back inside the guardhouse.

I roll up the window and pull the BMW through the gates before I turn to Starr and demand, "Honestly, why'd you tell him that? I'm not going to talk with *anybody* in a trailer tonight. I'm going to wait in the car while you get your money and then we're hightailing it back to Jackson!"

"Hush," Starr says, sounding like she's preoccupied. "Just turn here and park behind that semi." She points into the dark at a big, battered horse van with Virginia plates. Beside it, a good-sized Airstream trailer is backed up to the eight-foot fence surrounding the Fair Grounds. To the left of the Airstream is a low cinder block building with yellow-lit windows. It must be the cafeteria because the trailer's practically on top of it.

"You can wait here if you want to," Starr says. "But you should come on in. I, I . . . think you and Bette would have an awful lot to talk about."

"I can't imagine," I say, feeling mulish. I slam the car into park, turn it off, and fold my arms. With a shrug, Starr gets out.

"Think on it," she says, her hand on the door frame. "She's kind of . . . well, somebody you should meet." She waits for me to answer. When I don't say anything, she shrugs again and walks away into the night.

I can't go in there, I think, watching Starr climb up the steps of Bette's Airstream. There's no telling what kind of person lives in a place like this. Hell, there's no telling what you might *catch* in a place like this. The wide, old-fashioned travel trailer is lit up like an oil rig, decorated with strings of multicolored Christmas lights and Japanese lanterns draped across its aluminum roof and curved sides. Silk palm trees in pots flank the fold-down steps: it's hard to tell in the dark, but I think they're hung with plush monkeys and plastic parrots. A healthy pile of black garbage bags spills pink silk magnolia blossoms on the ground around the lacquered Chinese-red bench positioned underneath a window that's tastefully curtained with a Confederate flag. It appears the Airstream decoration process is a work in progress.

Starr knocks and waits for a minute. The door opens, and a Myrtistine-sized woman wearing a bathrobe stands backlit, hair in rollers, her fists on her considerable hips. There's an excited exchange, Starr goes inside the trailer, and I'm alone out here in the dark. I lock the doors again. Minutes pass. Emerging from under my mink, Troy Smoot pokes his nose under my arm. I can't imagine what he could want, but after my scare at the truck stop, I'm sure not going to take the chance of letting him run around loose behind the racetrack. Maybe he just wants out of the car. I decide I can handle it, if I'm careful.

"C'mon, dog. Let's go have a smoke while we're waiting." I pick Troy up, unlock the door, and get out, holding him in my arms. He doesn't weigh much and licks me under my chin. "Yeah, I like you, too, but don't get any big ideas. We're not going to be here long."

Across the night, a light east wind carries the nearby music of guitars and a happy, loud chorus singing some kind of repetitive Mexican song. This fiesta is coming from inside the cafeteria next door. Troy's nose twitches at the smells of frying meat, cumin, and onions on the wind. It sure sounds like they're having a good time in there, whoever they are. I glance around in the darkness, lit only by the Christmas-light-festooned Airstream, but Troy and I are alone out here.

What's keeping Starr? Shifting the dog in my arms, I try to read my watch: I think it's 9:15. If we leave in the next ten minutes, I could almost beat Du home. I mean, how long can it take to collect twenty thousand dollars, say good-bye, and go? And if Starr and Bette are such old friends, then why didn't she tell me about this damned special relationship when I asked before? Secrets again, Starr and her secrets.

But Troy's getting heavy. I'm going to go sit on the spindly red bench under the Airstream's Stars-and-Bars-hung window and smoke a cigarette. Nudging a garbage bag of magnolia blossoms out of the way with my boot, I plop down with a sigh.

Damnation. I remember I left my purse in the car. I debate going back to get it so I can have that cigarette, then decide it's probably better if I don't. What if I dropped an ash on one of these plastic bags of silk flowers and set the whole tacky mess on fire? The guitars across the way finish with a flourish, in one of the nearby barns a horse whinnies a coda, and in the lull I realize there's a conversation going on behind the window overhead—Starr's voice and a husky contralto that sounds weirdly familiar. She's in there "catching up" with Bette, I think irritably. Starr's been gone a long time, and I really do need a smoke: it's been hours since I had one.

"Come on, Troy, I'm going to go get that cigarette." I go to stand up and find that I *can't*. To my disbelief, my ass is stuck to the bench like it was glued to it.

"What the . . . ?" I exclaim to Troy. I turn to look over my shoulder and smell the flat plastic smell of wet paint. Ol' Bette or somebody else must have just painted this bench and the night's humidity has kept it from drying. My entire backside and sweater have to be covered in Chinese-red lacquer, and now I'm one with Bette's bench.

Furious now, I try to get up again and for an unbelievable moment the bench gets up *with* me before it tears free of my paint-covered behind in a ripping sound. The bench lands upended with a thud on top of the bags of magnolia blossoms. I'm cussing a blue streak and holding a now-wriggling Troy and simultaneously trying to get a look at the seat of my jeans to see how bad things are when the trailer door bangs wide open.

A mountain of a woman descends the rickety stairs in an avalanche, her arms swinging. "Who the fuck're you, vandalizing my property?" Each metal step screams for mercy under her enormous bunny slippers.

"Hey, I only sat on your bench . . ." I begin, stupefied at this vision of trailer doom advancing upon me. This is Starr's *friend?*

"Who said you could sit on my goddamned bench?" the mountain bawls as she closes the distance.

I back up a step—who wouldn't?—and my feet get caught up in one of those damned garbage bags. I fall over backward in the dirt like a load of spilled gravel. Troy Smoot jumps out of my arms and dashes up the steps into the trailer between Starr's legs as she appears in the doorway.

"Hold up, Bette!" Starr cries. At her feet the dog is barking a lunatic chorus.

"Shut up," Bette snarls over her shoulder. She looms over my sprawled body and announces, "Now you're gonna get it." Pushing the sleeves of her bathrobe higher on her tattooed arms, she bends down and grabs the front of my cashmere sweater, and even with the acre of makeup covering that brutal face, oh my God—I know who this is, I do.

"Buddy Bledsoe?" I squeak, shielding my face with my arms. "It's me, Annie Banks. Please don't hit me!"

Chapter 10

At school on the Monday after Thanksgiving, Miss Bufkin began assigning roles in the second grade's holiday pageant. Her class would be performing the Christmas Story, while the other one would provide carols and the stage setting, she told us.

"Now I know all you children want to be good little boys and girls, so there'll be no talking amongst yourselves while I assign everybody's parts." Miss Bufkin waited a moment for our excited whispering to cease.

Mine was one of the first names Miss Bufkin read. I'd be playing the Archangel Gabriel, an unlikely bit of casting by any yardstick. I knew it would be a small part, but at least I wasn't going to have to be a shepherd like Lisa Treeby: Miss Bufkin's class was low on boys compared to the other one, and so some of the girls were going to have to stand in for the male roles. Lisa, the tallest kid, was a natural for head shepherd. Roger Fleck, the booger miner, was to be the mean innkeeper who wouldn't let Mary and Joseph inside the inn before Baby Jesus was born. Joel Donahoe, still deeply tanned from the Pelahatchie work farm, was Balthazar, the black Wise Man, and Laddie Buchanan was a weak-chested Joseph.

Starr was the Virgin Mary.

I was flabbergasted. Why on earth had Miss Bufkin given her the starring role? Ever since school began, our teacher had shown no interest in Starr whatsoever and this was a plum of a part. Still, I reached across the aisle and squeezed Starr's hand when Miss Bufkin's attention was elsewhere. Starr looked so happy, but just as amazed as I was because Mary was a big role: she'd be on stage for nearly the whole play. We even had a scene together, when I as Gabriel came to Mary and announced that she was going to have a baby. In her desk behind me, Julie Posey savagely whined to one of her friends that it wasn't *fair*. That show-off Julie was the innkeeper's wife, a practically nonexistent part with no lines except for "They can go sleep in the stable!"

But fair or not, our class was put to work that afternoon rehearsing while the other class got to paint sets, make props, and practice Christmas carols. Outside the cold rains of late November fell on the dead grass, the leaves falling to the ground in wet drifts under the sweet gums and cedars, but inside the classroom was warm and nobody worked on their health booklets but practiced their lines instead. Starr was amazing. It seemed she had only to look at the mimeographed sheets a couple of times and she knew her part cold. In fact, the only other kid who learned their part better was Lisa Treeby. Lisa was so good at memorizing that in two days she knew everybody else's lines as well as her own, promptly supplying them whenever someone was even a little bit slow remembering their part.

By the end of the week, it came time to try on our costumes. The terror of Fairmont Street, Buddy Bledsoe, and another big fourth-grade boy, Bobby Shapley, hauled the dusty cardboard boxes in from Miss Bufkin's station wagon, dropping them on the floor in scarcely concealed disdain. Their second-grade Christmas pageant was decades behind them. All of us crowded around the boxes as soon as the big boys swaggered out of the room.

When Miss Bufkin pulled Mary's blue gown from the heap of costumes, the mystery of Starr's casting was revealed. The sky-colored robe was made for someone her size—that is, the smallest girl in the class. The white veil looked good over her blond curls, too. Laddie's long, brown costume kept getting hung up on the wooden donkey's wheels and making him trip, so Miss Bufkin had to tuck the hem with safety pins: last year's Joseph must have been a giant. Gabriel's gold-painted cardboard halo kept falling off my head, and the chicken-feather wings were fairly moth-eaten, but they were still big and fluffy, so for the most part I was content with what I was going to wear. Poor Lisa's tunic looked like it had been made from a gunnysack. Julie's dress wasn't much better, but at least she didn't have to wear a beard like Lisa did.

The next week, we moved our rehearsals to the school's auditorium. Pretty Miss Bufkin took to tying a scarf around her throat and wearing a dashing beret like a real director, and in the girls' bathroom the conversation was of nothing but the makeup we'd be allowed to wear for the play. Being a bunch of seven-year-old girls, we were fascinated with makeup—powder, eye shadow, rouge—but what had us all in a whispering fever of anticipation was *lipstick*. Lipstick was the flashbulb-popping, red-carpeted threshold between little girls and real teenagers. Our mothers wore it every single day without exception, wouldn't leave the house without doing up their mouths. We had all been madly impatient for our own tubes of grown-upness even before the pageant had consumed us, and now we were practically on fire.

Of course, Julie Posey already had a pink lipstick in a baby-blue case. Since we weren't allowed to wear it at school, she didn't put any on in the girls' bathroom, but only showed it off to everyone when we went in there before lunch to wash our hands.

"It's called Pixie Pink," Julie announced. All of us were crowded around her, ready to throw up with envy.

"But this one isn't for the play. It's kind of babyish." She dropped the lipstick into her purse and closed it with a snap. "My mom's going to buy me a red one—Revlon's Fire and Ice." Julie shrugged off her loyal hangers-on and surveyed her reflection in the mirror over the dripping sink. "We're going to Beemon's Drugs this afternoon." She fluffed her ringlets and squared her hair ribbon's bow. With a flounce of her skirts, Julie pushed through the big swinging door and left the bathroom.

Starr and I washed our hands in silence as the other girls filed out after her. I caught her eyes in the mirror and made a face.

"Show-off," we both said at the same time. Linking arms, we left the bathroom, giggling.

Saturday morning came, a day that couldn't make up its mind whether to storm or merely rain. I'd spent a restless morning inside. After Methyl Ivory fixed me a bologna sandwich for lunch, I sat with it under the sunporch windows on a wicker settee, watching for Starr while I nibbled the sandwich around the edges. Methyl Ivory was running the Bissell Sweeper over the sunporch's tiles and humming to herself. I was hoping she'd hurry up and leave, for I was on fire to put my scheme into action.

My mother's purse sat on the kitchen table, just off the sunporch.

Inside that purse was a lipstick.

If Methyl Ivory would only finish her floor sweeping and go away, I planned to borrow my mother's bright red lipstick, maybe her compact, too. Then Starr could show me how to make up my face for the Christmas play since she already had plenty of pageant experience. I was sure my mother would never realize the lipstick had been out of her purse for a couple of hours because she was upstairs in her bedroom this afternoon, her hair covered in a bandanna, wearing no makeup at all. Engaged in Ladies' League Snow Ball business, she was making giant snowflakes out of white poster-board sheets, silver glitter, and Elmer's glue. In fact, I didn't expect her to come downstairs this afternoon for anything, not until it was time for dinner.

"Mary had a baby, hmm-mmm," Methyl Ivory sang under her breath. *Brump, brump* went the Bissell Sweeper as she finally moved her floor cleaning to the front hallway. "She call the baby Jesus, mmm-hmm."

I eased off the settee with a cautious glance down the hall, then tiptoed in my sock feet across the sunporch into the kitchen. Carefully, I eased open my mother's black alligator pocketbook. There it was, beside her keys, cigarettes, and lighter: her makeup bag. I slid the brass clasp open, and lying on top of her powder compact was a lipstick in a golden case. It was in my hand when I was startled by my mother's voice.

"Methyl Ivory?" she called. She was descending the stairs. "Can you bring that up here to the bedroom? There's glitter everywhere."

I snapped the makeup bag closed, abandoning the compact. Like lightning, I skidded across the newly swept red tiles of the sunporch to the settee, where I plunged the lipstick under a throw pillow. Picking up my discarded sandwich, I hastily took a bite the instant my mother walked through the door from the hallway.

"What are you up to this afternoon, Annie?" she asked me. Flushing with guilt, I nearly choked on my bologna and Wonder bread, but then she said, "Today's such a gloomy day, I know. It's starting to rain again. Are you and Starr going to play here?"

I gulped the bite of sandwich before I lied. "We're going to Lisa's house."

My mother frowned. "Is Mr. Treeby going to be home?" she asked. "I'm sure he's not going to want you girls disturbing him while he's working."

I blushed, remembering the last time I'd been at the Treebys' house: Lisa's father hadn't been working then, but I had no doubt I'd disturbed him as much as he had disturbed me with his picture book.

"Oh, we'll be real quiet," I assured her. "We're going to read Bible stories. Starr's got a big book of 'em, with lots of pictures and the words of Jesus in red letters. We'll go by her house to get it before we go to Lisa's."

"Well, that's all right then. You won't go inside the Dukes house, though, will you?" My mother gave me a stern look. She didn't have to say anything more. Starr's house might well have a drunken Mr. Dukes in it.

"No, ma'am."

"Have a nice afternoon, then, and take an umbrella," she said. "Remember to be home before dark, Annie. I think I'll go make myself a cup of coffee." With a smile for me, my mother went in the kitchen. Quick as a snake, I palmed the lipstick, shoved it into my pants pocket, and went back to looking through the window for Starr.

"Methyl Ivory? Are we out of coffee?" my mother called from the kitchen.

Where was Starr? Down by the Allens' fence, something big and black finally caught my eye—an umbrella with a somewhat bedraggled Starr waving from underneath it. She was wearing a yellow raincoat that was so long it dragged behind her on the brown grass.

"There she is—I've got to go." I shoved my feet into my

waiting Keds, shrugged into my own raincoat, and grabbed an umbrella from the stand by the back door. "Bye." The screen door banged shut behind me. Hurriedly, I squelched down the hill to the fence. The rain was falling slowly, but by the time I got there, my shoes and pants cuffs were soaked through.

"That's a really big raincoat," I observed while climbing over the fence.

"It's Momma's—she left it, too." Starr's voice was muffled underneath her umbrella. "Did you get the lipstick?"

Thrilled with my successful "borrowing," I nodded. "It's a *red* one."

We trudged up the Allens' backyard and angled in the direction of the rental house in case anyone was watching. This subterfuge was necessary to keep my mother from figuring out we had no intention of going to Lisa's but were headed in the opposite direction. We didn't dare use the lipstick at my house, and Starr's poppa was at home and working on his sermon. Starr didn't have to remind me that he would take a more than dim view of little girls playing with makeup. It was grounds for another whuppin', I was sure, so we planned to cross Fortification Street and go down to the abandoned garage by the railroad tracks for some privacy.

It was a well-used place, the old garage. Kids from every grade for blocks around the neighborhood congregated there. Perched on the hillside above the railroad tracks like a shabby mockingbird nest on a sumac branch, the rotting wooden structure smelled of the long-collapsed privy in the back, the ghosts of engines and motor oil. It had once been part of a larger establishment, a house probably built back in the days before Jackson's zoning laws would have rendered a place without indoor plumbing impossible. The old foundation of the house was a great place to play war, though, with its bunker-like, fieldstone sides, the ground littered deep with blackjack oak mast. The garage itself had been spared whatever cataclysmic event—a fire, a tornado, or the family falling on hard times and forced to abandon their house—had transpired. As far as I knew, nobody's parents had a whisper of a clue as to the garage's existence, but occasionally there'd be signs some wandering bum had stopped for the night: an empty pint whiskey bottle, the remains of a campfire, a sooty Castleberry's beef stew can in the middle of the ashes.

That afternoon Starr and I sneaked away from her house and turned onto Devine Street, where we walked to the woods at the dead end. Looking over our shoulders, we slipped between the two huge old live oaks standing sentinel at the slender opening in the trees. The hillside path to the garage was treacherous today, with sodden leaves piled underfoot, the hard-packed earth slippery beneath our shoes. Starr and I tried to make our way through the woods by holding onto bare-branched saplings, but the umbrellas kept snagging on their spiky limbs, and she kept stumbling on the bottom of her yellow raincoat. Finally, we gave it up, slid downhill, and walked the railroad tracks winding through the bottom instead.

"I don't hear anybody, do you?" My breath misted in the cold. As we approached the garage, the woods were silent. No other kids had claimed it for their own on this rainy Saturday afternoon.

"Nope," Starr said. "I think we're the only ones today. C'mon." We furled the umbrellas and, bending almost to all fours and using the umbrellas like ski poles, we struggled up the steep hillside. The three-sided structure welcomed us out of the gently falling rain. It was darker inside the garage than out, but still there was plenty of light to see the old International truck crouched on its axles atop four cement blocks. Long ago, somebody had removed its doors, too.

We dropped our umbrellas into the bed of the pickup. Starr and I climbed up onto the seat, avoiding the rusty springs poking out of the rotted upholstery, and huddled together in front of the cracked rearview mirror. Outside in the woods, the rain began to fall harder, pelting the leaves and the old tin roof overhead.

"Can I see it?" Starr asked. I fished my mother's lipstick out of my pocket and handed it to her. "Oooh," she breathed. "It's so *pretty*." In the dim light, the lipstick shone in Starr's hand like a piece of pirate's treasure, smooth and golden. She held the end of the tube higher in an effort to catch the light and make out the name. "It says, 'Vixen,' Annie. What's a vixen?"

"It's a girl fox, I think." Starr handed it back to me, and I took the cap off. The fiery red of the lipstick was every bit as warm and lush as a vixen's brush. I held it under my nose and closed my eyes, the fragrance conjuring my mother in the musty, slightly spoiled air of the garage. Putting the cap back on, I handed the lipstick to Starr. "Here," I said. "Put some on me first?"

"Sure." She took it from me with a smile and adjusted the rearview mirror. "Now hold still. You don't want to mess it up." I made a pout and closed my eyes.

"What d'you morphadikes think you're doing?"

The loud, angry growl came from behind us, just inside the garage, as though a rabid dog had snuck up on Starr and me and was ready to bite. With a jolt of alarm, I knew that voice even before I turned my head.

The terror of Fairmont Street was wearing a raincoat, too—a camouflage one like the big boys in the sixth grade wore. In the dark of the garage, Buddy Bledsoe's shadowed outline loomed as huge as one of the blackjack oaks outside.

"No girls allowed!" He punched his fist into his palm with a meaty smack.

I wanted to scream, and Starr's face was white. We scrambled out of the front seat, nearly ripping our raincoats on the rusted springs in our haste, but Buddy advanced on the truck with his fists clenched and swinging. Cornered, we retreated until our backs were against the splintered wall of the garage.

Upon us now, Buddy's face was red and twisted. My sight grew blurry, my breath running fast as a rabbit through the tall grass. Beside me, Starr's hand groped for mine.

"What's that you got there?" Buddy demanded. Eyes narrowing, he poked Starr's shoulder so hard she staggered. "Give it!"

Her voice was quavering, but she spoke right up. "It's a lipstick. Boys don't wear lipstick." My mouth went dry. I couldn't believe she'd talked back to Buddy Bledsoe like that, but she wasn't done. "Why do you want it, anyways?" Starr asked reasonably.

"Shut up! Give it to me," Buddy said, "or I'll beat the shit out of you." He grabbed Starr's left hand, squeezing her wrist. With a small squeak of pain, she let go of my mother's lipstick and it fell at his feet. Grunting, Buddy leaned over and picked it up. The sight of the golden cylinder vanishing in his big, dirty hand brought tears to my eyes: my mother was going to kill me even if by some miracle Buddy Bledsoe didn't do it.

But Starr folded her arms, tossed her straggling blond curls, and said, "You're nothing but a big ol' bully—picking on girls."

"Shut up," Buddy roared and shoved her up against the wall.

Even then Starr didn't fold. "Stop it!" She pushed back, and when I saw his fist lifted to punch her, I finally found my courage and did something previously unimaginable. I kicked Buddy Bledsoe in the knee as hard as I could, which was considerable since I really was good at kickball.

"Yeah!" I shouted, sounding braver than I had any right to be. "You're a big old bully. Give it back!"

And in that next instant it was like we were a pack of two. Starr and I fell upon Buddy, swinging and kicking, shouting at him to give it back, give it back *right now*. Standing up for once was so exhilarating I wasn't afraid of getting hit at all. Oh, Buddy got in an awkward punch or two, but the close quarters were to our advantage and adrenaline drove us like a gasoline-fueled house fire. I smacked him a good one across his ear, and when he turned to pound his fist on my head, Starr got in a lucky kick to his groin. He fell to his knees on the dirt floor of the garage.

"Aagh," he moaned.

And then I saw the lipstick. It had fallen out of Buddy's hand and was lying next to the old truck's cement block standing in for a front tire. I swooped upon the golden cylinder as Buddy collapsed on his side with an agonized expulsion of breath, his hands cupping his testicles.

"Cheaters," he gasped. "Two against one."

"Run, Starr!" I cried. "I got it!"

Her long raincoat flapping like a loose yellow tarpaulin in a monsoon, Starr leapt over Buddy, who was now groaning and rolling around in the dirt. Without a backward look, we ran, leaving our umbrellas and the terror of Fairmont Street behind us. Starr and I slid downhill through the leaves and charged down the railroad tracks in our muddy shoes. Giddy and breathless with victory, we turned uphill, clawing from tree to tree to the edge of the woods on Devine Street. The rain had slowed again, cold silver droplets falling from the bare branches overhead as we emerged from the trees onto the pavement.

Starr and I began to walk homeward in the rain, trying to catch our breaths, before I said, "D'you think he's going to come after us?"

"Nope," Starr said. "We whupped him good." She kicked a rock down a storm drain and grinned.

"What if he goes and gets his gang?" I worried. "What if he tells?"

Starr gave me a sideways look from under her wet hair and didn't say anything for a long beat. Finally, she said, "Don't you get it, Annie? Buddy Bledsoe can't ever say anything about this to anybody. He was trying to take a *lipstick* away from two little girls, little girls who beat the tar out of him."

I thought about it for a minute. "You're right. And we can't tell either. We were supposed to be at Lisa's house, reading Bible stories."

Starr nodded. "I'm going to get into trouble anyways, for losing the umberella."

Pushing my drenched bangs out of my eyes, I thought for a minute. "Let's say we gave them to some poor people." I warmed to my imaginary pair of umbrella-less beggars. "Let's say they were cold and wet and it was the Christian thing to do."

"Maybe your folks'll buy that," Starr said, "but my poppa won't." By now we were at the corner of Gray Street where the rental house stood. We trudged down through the Allens' backyard, not speaking. The fence seemed higher than usual when I climbed over the wire.

"See you Monday." I was shivering, ready to go indoors, return my mother's lipstick, and put this adventure behind me.

"See you Monday," Starr said. She turned to go home, a little girl lost in a grown woman's long, yellow raincoat.

That was the last time I saw her.

When I got home, I was cold and wet, dirty and tired. I sneaked in the back door and slipped out of my muddy shoes. Methyl Ivory must have been busy in another part of the house because no one answered my subdued "Hello?" With a weary relief, I went into the kitchen. A pot roast simmered on the stove, filling the air with its good smell. There were snap beans in a colander by the sink, a paring knife and a bowl of red potatoes on the table.

My mother's purse wasn't there.

She must have gone out today after all. However was I going to get the lipstick back in her purse now? My stomach plummeted to the linoleum. The lost umbrella suddenly seemed like nothing compared to the trouble I was going to be in when my mother came home. I was too wrung out to cry, so I bit my lip, thinking hard.

The only idea I could come up with was to sneak into her bedroom, leave the lipstick on her dressing table, and hope she never found out I took it. It was a feeble idea—she never went anywhere without making up her face and so was bound to have missed it already—but it was the only idea I had. Lipstick in hand, I plodded up the stairs and down the long, dark hall to my parents' bedroom.

Their door was shut. I eased it open and poked my head into the room to the sound of someone singing in the adjoining bathroom behind the closed door. My parents must have been going out that evening because draped across the end of their massive half-tester bed was a Christmas-red chiffon gown and a black velvet wrap.

Next to the dress was my mother's purse.

Holding my breath, praying for grace, I tiptoed across the floor to the bed.

But in the bathroom, the singing stopped. There was the splash of water sloshing, the glug of the bathtub draining. Catching a glimpse of my face in the marble-topped bureau's mirror, white and dirt-smeared but determined, I opened my mother's purse and dropped the lipstick inside her makeup bag. I had just snapped the pocketbook shut when the bathroom door opened. My mother came out in a cloud of steam, her hair in a towel, belting her bathrobe.

"Annie!" she exclaimed. "You gave me a fright—and what are you doing in here? You're soaking wet and filthy. However did you get so dirty reading Bible stories?"

* * *

We had an early dinner that evening since my parents were going to attend a holiday cocktail party at the country club later on. While Methyl Ivory served the pot roast and mashed potatoes, Daddy asked me about my afternoon.

"What was your favorite Bible story, Annie?"

I told him I liked the one where Eve took the apple from the Tree of Knowledge without God's permission.

I could just see her—breaking the shiny red fruit from the hanging branch, knowing it was wrong but doing it anyway, biting into the crisp flesh, the juice running down her chin.

At least Eve got to eat the apple.

CHAPTER 11

"Look on the bright side: you didn't get any of that paint in your hair. Bleachy like you got it, you'd of had to cut the red straight out."

Starr and I are crammed into Buddy's—I mean Bette's—prehistoric-pink little bathroom in the Airstream, trying to get me out of my clothes without smearing paint everywhere. My jeans are in a garbage bag on the pink bath rug, and my boots are outside in the cramped hallway. I'm shivering on the fuzzy pink toilet seat cover, crouched under a gilt filigreed shelf just over my head. There's even a pink crocheted toilet paper cozy on the extra roll of pink paper up there. Somebody likes pink. A lot.

"Bright side, my scrawny ass," I mutter as Starr carefully peels me out of four hundred dollars' worth of red-stained, dirty green cashmere. Some of the paint has soaked through the sweater, and so my bra's ruined, too. I catch a glimpse of myself in the bathroom's dollhouse-sized mirror, and a fright looks back. In the yellow glare of the overhead light, my hair is sticking up all over my head, my winter-white skin is broken out in goose bumps as big as mosquito bites, and I'm sitting here in my oldest underwear and ratty Hot Sox.

"The bright side," I complain, "is Buddy Bledsoe not beating the crap out of me. And I'm *freezing*."

Starr grabs a pink towel embroidered with swans and drapes it over my shoulders. "Buddy's Bette now, honey," she reminds me. "Try to remember—it means a lot to her. Think on what it's been like. Year in, year out, knowing she was a woman on the inside but having to act all macho because she had the wrong plumbing!" The bra and sweater join my jeans inside the black garbage bag. "That's why Bette was so hateful, back before she got the surgery."

"Like he's not hateful now?" I snipe, running my fingers through my hair to make it lie down.

There's a timid knock at the bathroom door. "I got it, Starr," Buddy says in a muffled voice.

Starr slides the door open a crack and trades the garbage bag for my new black dress that was previously hanging in the back of the Beemer, taking it from the hot-roller-wearing former terror of Fairmont Street.

"Here, Bette," Starr says. "Take this. Just put the keys in my purse. You might as well stick that garbage bag right in the dumpster. Annie's clothes are toast." She shuts the door and, with a little difficulty, turns around to face me again. This bathroom's not really meant to hold two people at the same time, especially not if one of them is pregnant. I don't like the way she's looking at me, as though I'm the one who's done something awful.

"What?" I demand.

Starr's mouth is determined. She says, "Look. Bette's real sorry, Annie, for tonight and all the trouble she gave us back when we were kids." She strips the plastic bag off my low-cut, off-the-shoulder dress. "You want some help getting done up?"

I take the dress from her. "I think I can handle this by myself, thanks." Then, knowing I sound snotty but unable to stop myself, I say, "Why don't you get back to 'catching up' with your old friend out there in Trailer Land." I can't look at Starr after that, so I fuss with getting the dress off its hanger instead.

"What the hell's the matter with you?" Starr asks. She tries to put her hands on her hips and bangs her elbows into the plastic shower door and the plastic wall of the bathroom. "Ow." She rubs her arms.

I finally get the dress off the hanger. "Why didn't you tell me who *Bette* really was when I asked you?" I demand in a lowered voice. "I'm the one who's just driven to New Orleans, lied to Du, and risked an ass-load of trouble! You couldn't tell me the truth? That Buddy Bledsoe is your best friend?"

Starr raises an eyebrow. "She's not my best friend, Annie. You are, or were. Okay, so I've been knowing Bette was really Buddy ever since she and Jesús—that's Bette's boyfriend, Jesús Ortega, he's a jockey—started in to living here year-round. They go to visit Jesús's family in Miami for the summer while the Fair Grounds is closed. Bette put the money on that horse for me at Gulfstream Park. We both made out pretty good."

"How nice for you. And Buddy."

Starr goes on like I haven't said a word. "Me and Bette first met up when I was working the Clubhouse, cocktail waitressing. I recognized who she was when she and Jesús got into it after he started flirting with me—not that he meant anything by it, those Latinos, they'll come on to a bucket of spackle if it's wearing a skirt—but Bette got mad as a snakebit hog. Seeing that red face and those eyes going squinty, it all came back to me then. 'Buddy?' I asked. She drank down her mai tai in one gulp and busted into tears. I felt so sorry for that big ol' gal, Annie. Bette asked me not to tell anyone about how she used to be Buddy Bledsoe. She's an equine acupuncturist now, calls herself Bette Swann."

There's that timid knock at the bathroom door again.

Oh, please. "Little girls, little girls, let me come in or I'll huff and I'll puff and I'll beat your brains in," I say under my breath. Starr gives me another exasperated look, and I feel like a jerk.

On the other side of the door Buddy says, "Annie? You want some coffee? I've got some whole-bean Jamaica Blue Mountain and a French press. It won't take but a jiffy to make you a cup . . ." This is going to drive me crazy: that wistful voice still reminds me of somebody. I can almost put my finger on who it is.

"Go ahead, Bette—she'd love some coffee," Starr says loudly to the closed door. Then, turning to me, she hisses, "You going to act nice, or you want to go back to waiting in the car? Look, if you'd have come in when I asked the first time, you'd have never sat in that paint. You and Bette could have had a chance to get reacquainted."

I think this over while I'm maneuvering myself into the black dress. It's tricky because the dress is so tight and the bathroom's so small. With a fair amount of difficulty, I manage to get it over my head, banging my own elbow into the shower, almost upending the little gilt shelf with the toilet paper cozy and assorted bottles of lotions and gels. However does the lummox lurking outside ever get in that shower? I wonder. With a crowbar and a vat of Vaseline?

"Zip me, will you?" I ask, lifting my hair off the back of my neck. Without a word, Starr zips up my dress. "Okay." I sigh as our eyes meet in the mirror. "It's not like I'm going to tell him to go to hell because of what happened over twenty years ago. Sometimes I used to wonder where he ended up, and now I know."

"You sure do," Starr says. "It's kind of a big deal."

Knock, knock.

"You girls need anything?"

I finally realize who Bette's voice reminds me of: Cher, with a honking head cold.

"We'll be right out," Starr answers. Without waiting for me, she opens the door and steps out. Reluctantly, I follow her into the cabin of the Airstream and tug my high-heeled boots on over my Hot Sox. I feel skanky, got up in the short black dress and boots, but that's what I've got to wear if I don't want red paint all over the Beemer's upholstery. I sure can't do eighty-five on the way home now: if I get pulled over dressed like this, I might get mistaken for a working girl.

While we were busy in the bathroom, Bette has removed the curlers, applied fire-engine-red lip gloss, sprinkled some Shalimar in her cleavage, and changed into a teal velour sweat suit. Except for the bunny slippers, she looks really pulled together, like she could go shopping at Wal-Mart. As Dolly, my saleswoman at Maison-Dit, says, you should always look your best because you never know who you're going to run into.

Earlier this evening when I stumbled inside the trailer howling about the paint and near-assault, I didn't exactly take the time to have a good look around. Now I see that the Airstream's kind of homey, with armfuls of crocheted afghans covering the built-in sofa. The lightbulbs in the Tiffany-shaded lamps are pink—the better to see your complexion in, my dear—and every surface that isn't covered by tatted doilies has a swan on it: a whole flock of porcelain swans, glittering swans of Swarovski crystal, carved wooden swans, swans in snow globes, framed holograms of swans in flight, swan wind chimes, swans painted on velvet, plush stuffed baby swans, and a life-sized, painted cement swan standing guard at the door.

Now before you think I'm being judgmental, you should know that, much against her family's wishes, Du's grandmother lives in a double-wide and her trailer décor is strikingly similar to Bette's. Old Mrs. Sizemore's icon of choice is bullfrogs. Every available space is cluttered with green amphibians in various weird vignettes, but my favorite is the bullfrog got up like a matador, swirling his cape before a pawing bullfrog wearing a big old pair of horns. When it's our turn to go to Tupelo for Christmas, I always get a bang out of stopping off at Miz Estelle's trailer down in Noxubee and getting the lowdown on the latest additions to her collection, so I'm not a trailer snob, okay? I'm just not used to them.

And I'm glad to see Troy Smoot hasn't run off while I was occupied in the bathroom. He's sitting on the sofa amid a pile of swan-embroidered throw pillows, looking little, lost, and hairy. At the sight of me, Troy wags his whole body in recognition, so I think he's happy to see me, too.

"How do you like it?" Bette asks, throwing her arms wide in an encompassing gesture that just misses a swan mobile.

"You, ah . . . certainly have made the place . . . ," I begin and then stop, stuck for words.

"It's as sweet as can be." Starr gives me a discreet poke in the back, pushing me toward the dinette, where three coffee cups and saucers have been laid on scalloped rose-colored placemats. The china pattern is, naturally, swans on a pale-blue background. I really don't want to believe I'm going to sit down and have coffee, but I slide into the booth anyway. This black dress is so much shorter than I'm used to that I have to tug it down my thighs or risk having it climb up around my waist. Starr sits next to me on the outside so I can't bolt, and Bette joins us. I can't help but stare at her in a kind of sick fascination as she squeezes into the opposite side of the booth, the banquette's plywood groaning.

Oh, if anyone ever finds out about this, you are finished, do you hear me? It's the rosebush voice weighing in. *Get out* now.

Another helpful observation. Listen up, Annie, I remind myself. You've sat down at barbeques and Ladies' League meetings with Bobby Shapley's uranium-plated bitch of a wife,

Julie Posey Shapley, and you can get through this, too, hear? And besides, Julie's mean little eyes never betrayed a desperate need for acceptance into the girls' club. She didn't pour me a cup of coffee with hands that shake ever so slightly, setting the cup and saucer to a dainty jangle of bone china. I feel myself thawing like ice cubes in a pitcher of just-brewed tea, and taking a sip of the very good coffee, I tell that stupid rosebush voice to shut up and go wait in the car if it can't act like a lady.

"Can I get you gals anything to eat?" Bette asks. "I've got a batch of cookies that just came out of the oven." She smiles, an awful hope glowing in those bearlike brown eyes. Oh, Lord, those have got to be false eyelashes and she's *fluttering* them at me.

"No thanks," I say hastily, looking down at my cup. "This coffee's perfect. We've got a long way to go tonight." I give Starr's foot a kick under the table.

But Starr ignores me and kicks me back. "Did you make your snickerdoodles? You know I just love them. I could eat your snickerdoodles all night long."

Bette's toothy smile is as big and bright as a lit-up carnival ride. "I'll go get us some. Y'all just hold on." Prying herself out of the dinette, she lumbers to the spotless countertop and grabs one of several gaily decorated cookie tins. "Let me see," she says. "I think they're in this one." She opens it and shakes her head. "No, that's the brownies. *Here's* the snickerdoodles." She rummages in a cabinet, pulls down a plate, and arranges some cookies on it.

"Bette's a big baker," Starr tells me, her pale eyes wide and guileless. "She makes a sinful pan of brownies."

Bette giggles delightedly, shrugging an oh-shucks gesture. "I made the special fudge brownies last night 'cause I just had to have 'em," she confides. "I get so down these days, and baking's about the only thing I've got to look forward to when I get home from sticking horses all day. I'm all on my lonesome until Jesús comes back from Miami, so I've got nobody to cook for." She brings the cookie-filled plate over to the dinette and the snickerdoodles look scrumptious indeed. Starr reaches for one, but I sip my coffee instead.

"Y'all dig in!" Bette beams.

"Mmm-hmm." Starr's mouth is full of cookie. I'm not going to succumb to temptation, not this time, not again. "Annie says she's not eating anything until Friday," Starr informs Bette. She takes another cookie. "Annie's got issues with food, big time."

Before I can tell her to knock it off, Bette says, "Now Starr, don't pick on her, honey." She smiles at me from across the table, her eyes glowing in that thicket of false eyelashes. "You look *fabulous,* but then you've always been a china doll. I used to envy you the most, Annie." She pops a whole cookie into her red, glossy mouth and chews enthusiastically. I can't take my eyes off her because I would really love a snickerdoodle right now, but I tell myself to forget it and have another sip of coffee.

"I was there," Bette reminds me, "when you made your debut at the Snow Ball, remember?" She licks her fingers one by one and takes another cookie off the plate.

"Um, not really," I say. I force myself to look away at a porcelain swan tissue dispenser sporting a Kleenex tail on top of the television set behind her.

"Oh, honey—you remember. I know you do. I was Lisa Treeby's escort, and you were there with that big ol' fella you married right out of college. Isn't his name Duane? I'll testify that you were definitely the belle of *that* ball. I always wondered why you ran off the stage and didn't come back until after the Presentation was done with and the dancing began, but I couldn't get over how perfect your dress was, and your hair—sugar! It was divine . . ." Absentmindedly, Bette extends the tip of her kielbasa-sized pinky to catch a crumb stuck in her lip gloss, lost in her reverie of me and my debutante ball of sixteen years ago, an occasion I'd prefer not to revisit right now with the vision across from me. It's a little creepy.

Starr brings Bette back to the table, placing a small hand on top of Bette's pork-roast-sized one. "Babe, this has been heaven and I expect you and Annie must have a lot of catching up to do, but we've got to get back on the road."

"I haven't seen you in months." Bette pouts, those red lips drooping.

"I know," Starr says, "and I thank you from the very bottom of my heart, putting that thousand bucks down for me. It's an answer to a prayer, and I'm going to need every cent." Starr pats the Winn-Dixie bag full of cash next to her on the banquette seat. I give it a glance, but my eyes return to the last snickerdoodle on the plate. Be strong, Annie, I tell myself as Starr tucks the plastic grocery bag in her purse.

Somewhere in the trailer's back half, behind the folding door, a telephone loudly whoops.

"Goddammit!" Bette explodes, her eyes narrowing to burning, fringed slits. "If it's not one fucking thing, it's another. Asshole trainers wait until the last minute, think I'm gonna drop everything to acupuncture some poor nag in the middle of the night—like its back wasn't sore this *afternoon*—but no-o-o, Mr. Big Shot from Churchill Downs thinks I'm just sitting here, hoping for the phone to ring, like I don't have a *life*. Those arrogant pieces of shit, I could smack their heads together just to hear the splat!" She's breathing hard; her massive fists pounding the table hard enough to make the coffee slop out of my cup.

My eyes widen. There's still an awful lot of Buddy underneath all that Bette, and right now I'm feeling sorry for that poor arrogant piece of shit, Mr. Big Shot. Better him than me, though.

Bette gets to her feet with a poisonous look toward the

ringing phone. "Y'all hold on while I take care of this bullshit, hear?" Like a semi in low gear, she heads to the bedroom in the back of the trailer, squeezes through the opening, and slides the door shut with a slam that makes the trailer shake.

I turn to Starr. "She's really an acupuncturist? They actually do that to horses?"

"She is, and they do," Starr replies.

"You're right, you know," I concede. "She's changed a lot—I mean, it's still *Buddy,* but she's kind of sweet now, in this WrestleMania kind of way. I'm sorry, I didn't mean to be so bitchy."

"Look, Annie . . ." Starr hesitates. "Bette's been a good friend." She looks down at her hands on the table. "But I meant what I said before. You're my *best* friend, always have been, no matter what. When things got bad—and they got that way a lot—I used to tell myself stories about what you might be doing. I could see you, going to school, having dinner with your folks, playing with other girls, then growing up and starting to go out with boys. You know, a normal life? Those stories I'd think up would keep me going. I could almost forget about the lights getting turned off again, or that Miss Hulda had found Momma's picture and tossed it out." Starr looks at me then, her eyes grave. "Sometimes I wondered if you missed me, too. Every time Poppa drove us off into the night, I told myself that somehow we'd find each other again, someday. . . ."

I nod, the back of my throat heavy with tears. It was the same thing for me even years after she was gone. "We went through so much together, especially for a pair of second-graders. Nothing was the same anymore, not after you left."

Starr says slowly, "I can't ever let myself . . . *care* . . . that way about anybody anymore, Annie. Never. You know what I mean?"

Again, I nod. I do.

We're quiet for a moment while in the back of the trailer Bette's giving someone a loud, unintelligible, but profanity-laced piece of her mind. With a sigh, Starr finishes her coffee and wipes her lips with a paper napkin from the swimming swan caddy.

"That Bette," she says with a shake of her head. "Anyhow, we found each other now, didn't we? That's got to mean something, like maybe we was supposed to be together again for some reason."

"Maybe so," I say.

Starr grimaces. "Damn. I got to go visit the little girl's room, sugar. Wait here for me and try not to eat anything." With a smile that belies that last dig, she gets up, goes into the bathroom and shuts the door.

I sit for a minute, wondering how the hell I'm going to pull off being Starr's friend when we return to Jackson. Tonight's mission is one thing, but sooner or later we'll be chin-deep in Jackson politics again. Do I have the courage to stand by her? I think of what Du will say, about the fallout in the Ladies' League and all over town.

"So grow up, Annie," I mutter.

Oh, that'll solve everything, the rosebush voice jeers. I shift uncomfortably on the bench seat, hating the fact that for once it's probably right.

But then, out of nowhere, my stomach grumbles, loudly, and I find myself grateful for the distraction from my self-loathing. Maybe those Chessmen from earlier today have set my long-denied appetite into relentless motion, but ever since the sight of those snickerdoodles earlier, it's been in the back of my mind, whether I could afford to eat one of Bette's cookies. I need the comfort of something sweet, and don't I deserve it? This has been one hell of a night, and the taste of those cookies in Starr's condo is fading fast.

Now that I'm allowing myself to consider jumping the

traces again, though, I know what I really want is a *brownie,* not a snickerdoodle. Bette mentioned she'd made brownies. Surely she won't mind if I have one? Before I agonize anymore, I slide out of the dinette, sidle over to the counter, and open the tin Bette picked up earlier. Furtively, I part the wax paper, grab a brownie off the top, and cram it into my mouth.

It tastes a little strange, as though Bette's recipe is a foreign one, maybe a kind of . . . Mexican brownie? She does have a Latin boyfriend, so that might explain it, but this isn't really how I remember fudge brownies and a bit of a disappointment. I chew thoughtfully for a minute and can almost identify the herby aftertaste, and then there's Starr's muffled voice coming from the bathroom. I shut the lid on the tin, chewing as fast as I can because I don't want to listen to Starr's ragging me about my weight. This brownie is between me, my out-of-control appetite, and no one else. So what if it's lettuce and vitamins until Friday?

"Annie?"

I swallow the rest of the brownie with difficulty because it's kind of dry and extra chewy. Really, I think, that was hardly worth it. This indiscriminate eating has got to stop, or I'm going to wind up the size of Bette, having to go through doors sideways.

"Yes?" I manage, brownie swallowed at last.

"I might be in here a while. You want to take Troy for a quick walk before we get on the road?"

Even though I'm coming to dread the idea of returning to Jackson, I'm ready to do anything that'll get us gone faster. It's nearly eleven, and we really ought to leave in the next ten minutes. Troy, half hidden in the throw pillows, is sound asleep on the afghan-covered sofa. He looks okay to me, but maybe she's right—what do I know about dogs?—and then it occurs to me that I need a leash, or something like one. Looking around the trailer, I don't see anything useful I could borrow and Lord knows I don't want to disturb Bette. She must have put the fear of God into Mr. Big Shot because even here in the front of the Airstream I hear her slam down the phone so loudly it seems there ought to be shards of plastic flying through the door. Bye-bye, arrogant shit head.

Or not. The phone whoops again almost immediately. "Oh, *now* you've done it!" Bette yells. Maybe it'd be a good idea to just grab Troy and get out of here until she puts paid to this latest interruption of her girls' night.

"Wake-y, wake-y, baby," I croon to the terrier as I lift him up off the sofa. "Let's find you a leash." Troy stretches with a big yawn. "I'll be right back," I call softly to Starr, and walk outside into the night with the dog in my arms.

Pausing on the top step for a moment, I think, wow. The night is so, so . . . *beautiful.* The foggy canopy over New Orleans is an opalescent dome of light high, high, high above me. Over by the cafeteria, a door opens, spilling hot yellow light and mariachi guitars into the quiet. I barely notice, being so enthralled with the crazy-beautiful sky that I stumble going down the steps and almost fall. Catching my balance in my high-heeled boots only to reel into one of the silk palm trees, I'm breathlessly proud that I've managed not to drop the dog and that I'm still on my feet.

"Whoops," I sputter as I fight my way out of the silk fronds. I've got a thing for those palm trees, don't I? But now my heels are trapped in the black garbage bags piled around the bench. My balance is going again. *"Shit,"* I exclaim.

"Hey, watch yourself." Out of the darkness, it's a man's voice. A strong, warm hand catches my elbow, another solid-feeling hand across the small of my back, steadying me. "You've conquered the steps, don't take a tumble now."

"Eek!" It's a small, involuntary squeak of surprise. I'm startled, but the world's mad orbit slows and I'm caught before I even begin to fall, as though I'm paired with a really good dance partner. In the orangey glow of Bette's trailer's Christmas lights, I have to look up at the man who's just saved Troy and me from tumping over on our asses once again in the magnolia blossoms.

He's not too tall, maybe a hair over six feet, but that's still a lot taller than I am, his face worn around the eyes with the kind of lines you get from working outside in all weathers, squinting into the sun, the dust, the rain, timing the horses as they battle gravity around a hundred racetracks. It's a face as open as an Oklahoma horizon with a jaw as solid as Ozark bedrock. It's a good face, and he's smiling down at me in a way that makes me want to smile back. Like a flamenco dancer, with a certain élan I kick the black garbage bag wrapped around the heel of my boot onto the overturned red bench. Olé!

What in the hell do you think you're doing? You have no idea *who he is!*

I don't care. To hell with the rosebush voice. "Thanks," I say, feeling grateful. "That was close."

"You new in town?" the man asks. "I haven't seen you around here before, have I?" Taking those wonderfully steady hands away, he gestures at the dark backstretch around us.

"I doubt it. I'm not from here," I say. "I'm Annie."

"I'm Ted." That smile broadens, his longish dark hair lifting in the light breeze from the east. "So, Annie not-from-here—you want to introduce me to your friend?"

I look around. There's nobody here but me. I'm feeling confused until I realize he means the dog in my arms. "Oh!" I'm laughing. "Troy Smoot. I liberated him tonight from an elevator. He needs a leash so he can have a pee without getting lost." This strikes me as one of the funniest things I've ever said in my life. I mean, I'm laughing so hard the nice man in the jean jacket, faded Levi's, and dusty cowboy boots has to take me by the arm again when I turn around and walk smack into the Beemer.

"Crap, that's pitiful. I just ran into my own car." I giggle.

"Nice car. Well, I believe I can help you with a leash, at least," Ted—his name is Ted, I remind myself so I won't call him Steve by accident—says with that same *great* smile. "I just happen to have a quantity of hay rope over in Barn Nine, down at the other end of the backstretch. Want to take a stroll and get it? Shape you're in, I hate to leave you by yourself."

This sounds like a fantastic idea to me, so I say, "Lead on!" Grabbing his arm, I lean into his shoulder because suddenly the ground seems very far away and I need to concentrate on it. Wait—where's Troy? I don't remember putting him down, but he's got to be around here somewhere, right?

"Umm, Ted?"

"Yes?" Ted says.

"Have you seen Troy?" I'm panicking.

"I'm holding him, lady."

That's certainly a relief. Now I can work at getting across the treacherous, uneven dirt beneath my boots without falling down anymore. We're walking what seems a long way from the Airstream, past a lot of darkened barns, and the night air is cool on my arms, my neck. I remember Starr telling me how the air here in New Orleans was like a live thing, and so it is, a silken creature purring around my bare knees and thighs, and I laugh again because it feels so good that I can't imagine air ever feeling like anything else.

"Isn't air wonderful?" I almost trip over my own feet.

"You okay?" Ted's face seems concerned as he steers me into a dim, half-lit stable. Suddenly, the world slips a gear, a tilt on its axis, and again I'm glad for his arm.

"Sure!" I say brightly, looking around. There's nobody here except for Ted, Troy, me, and some horses, but I'm fine with that. Somewhere a radio is playing country music, the volume turned down low. The horses, bay, gray, and chestnut, come to the front of their stalls, blinking with sleepy interest at us.

"The rope's right here," Ted says. Opening a half-door, he steps inside a stall where grass bales are neatly stacked in a golden-green tower, loose hay piled in sweet-smelling drifts on the hard-packed clay floor. I want to lie down in that hay, it looks so clean and soft. I'd be in a good place if the world tilts sideways again, and suddenly I'm afraid it's going to. I'm beginning to feel as though I'm surfing the night, that there's a huge wave building underneath my boots, making my every move a little tricky.

"Okay, big guy," Ted says to Troy. "Let's get you fixed up."

I lean against the dust-covered cinder block wall without a care for my black dress and try to catch my breath. My heart is pounding as though I just ran here all the way from Jackson. Whatever is wrong with me? Why am I so flushed? And I'm thirsty. Really, really thirsty—like I'd trade my BMW for a glass of water, and there's that *wave* again.

"Here you go." Ted hands me a length of rough twine with Troy on the end of it. He bends down and ruffles the terrier's fur. "Good dog you've got there."

"He's really a Treeby," I say faintly, swaying on my feet. "But thanks anyway."

"You're welcome," Ted says, his voice grave. "My hay rope is your hay rope." He sketches a bow, and before I realize what he's doing, he takes my hand, brushing his lips over my fingers. "It's not often I get the chance to do a lady a favor."

"Could you please do me another one?" I blurt. The words stumble out of the desert that is my mouth. My fingers are burning where his lips just were. "I could really use something to drink."

"A drink?" Ted says, looking uneasy. "Don't you think you've had enough?"

"What do you mean? I haven't had anything to drink tonight but coffee, and all I want is a glass of water!" I'm sincerely indignant, at least until he smiles that smile again.

"Water it is then, Miss Annie. Come with me." Ted's saying I can have some water is a huge relief. I'm ready to deal with that damned wave beneath my feet now because everything's going to be okay, water's on the way and I'm with a nice man instead of all alone in a strange place.

Without thinking I stretch up on my tiptoes to give him a kiss on his stubble-covered jaw for being such a nice man, but at the same time Ted turns his face down to mine like he wants to ask me a question, and even though I don't intend for it to do that, my mouth folds into his mouth and oh Lord I think I'm going to pass out he feels so wonderful so amazing so bone-deep *right* that I drop the hay rope and my arms are around his neck and his hands are on my waist I breathe him he smells of leather and night and cologne I do not dare let go I will fall and all the while Troy Smoot that good dog sits at my feet patient as a saint with all the time in the world to wait for this kiss to end.

Chapter 12

It was a week and a day before the Snow Ball and my debut. For better than forty years, Miss Pettie Gompert had made debutante dresses for girls all over Mississippi, from the Delta to Natchez, from Jackson to the Gulf Coast, and she was thoroughly out of patience with me this Friday afternoon in early December.

"If you don't hold still," she gritted through the mouthful of straight pins held in her teeth, "I'll call Miz Isabelle." That was a threat and a half: my grandmother might be castled in her house over on State Street this afternoon with an attack of the shingles, but that didn't mean she couldn't lay down the law in this cramped sewing room all the way across town in west Jackson. Grandmother Banks and Miss Pettie knew each other of old. The State Street mansion being one of the last houses in town where Miss Pettie still made house calls, she sewed all of my grandmother's clothes, including her foundation garments and underwear.

The sewing room was so crammed with debutante dresses it resembled a bakery where the icer had lost control of the frosting gun, spraying the low-ceilinged, dress-filled space with mounds and rosettes of sugar-leavened lard, spandrels and ribbons of white ganache. There were twenty-five of us debs that year, and Miss Pettie was swamped. I was tired and cranky myself, having just driven down from Oxford after taking a sociology final that morning that had left me with a pounding headache. The last thing I wanted was to be standing in my four-and-a-half-inch, high-heeled satin pumps under the brilliant lights of Miss Pettie's workroom, getting my deb dress hemmed. My feet hurt.

"Yoo-hoo?" The bell over the front door tinkled while a blast of frigid air set the white dresses to swaying on their racks. Julie Posey and her mother, Squeaky, had arrived for Julie's last fitting, too. "We brought the shoes."

"Close up that pneumonia hole!" Miss Pettie commanded, jerking her tightly permed gray head from around the back of my skirt. Unless you wanted to drive all the way to New Orleans or Atlanta for fittings, Miss Pettie's was the only game in town for custom-made dresses, so she could say anything she pleased. "Hurry up and get changed, Julie Posey," she snapped. "Your gown's on the rack next to the changing room. Miz Posey, you can sit down over there and wait." Under her breath, Miss Pettie muttered, "Ninnies. Heat costs money."

"Hey, Annie," Julie sang out as she passed me on her way to the changing room. Mrs. Posey, a stout woman done up like always with thick foundation the color of cotton candy, collapsed onto one of the folding chairs arranged along the single free wall. Her feet must have hurt, too.

"Oooh," Julie said. "I like your dress." Her eyes told me she didn't, no matter what her mouth said.

"Hey, Julie," I said. "Thanks." I couldn't very well tell her I liked her dress because I wasn't sure which one of the fabric ice floes was hers, and besides, since second grade, our mutual understanding had progressed to the point where we heartily hated each other and pretended we didn't. It was a social survival skill I was still struggling to master.

"Miss Pettie, it's too tight," I complained, tugging at the fabric around my waist. "This dress is trying to strangle me."

"Don't touch," Miss Pettie ordered with a swat of her pincushion to my plucking fingers. "You'll smudge it. You've gained weight since your last fitting," she said matter-of-factly. "It's that time of year—finals. All the girls do it. That's why I always leave an extra inch or two in everyone's waistlines so I can let 'em out." Round-shouldered Miss Pettie sat back on her little house-slippered heels, looking discouraged. "I hate finals," she said. "More work for me."

"More French fries for Annie, you mean." Julie's observation carried from behind the curtain. Her mother smirked but didn't look up from her magazine. "Most everyone loses their freshman ten by sophomore year, but not Annie," Julie trilled. "But then, Annie's so little an extra ten pounds looks like fifty on her." It took my last ounce of self-control not to retort that at least I had breasts, unlike *some* girls who threw up on a regular basis so they could resemble extension ladders in platform heels.

Unfortunately, though, my dress told the whole story. It was daringly different from all the others—a sleeveless sheath of plain and unadorned silk peau-de-soie with a short fishtail train—and I loved it. The dress glowed with a lambent, hammered sheen, and in the highest pair of heels I could find I'd imagined looking almost tall and elegant. Now I surreptitiously peeked in the floor-to-ceiling mirror, at my backside packed in straining peau-de-soie like Spam in a can, and wanted to cry. Well, I'd be damned if I let Julie know her barb had hit home. We were both Chi Omegas, which in theory should have made us friends, but Julie and I got on like hair and gum. Worse, my big sister in Chi O had appointed Julie my "Diet Buddy" to help keep me on track since my most recent weight gain and Julie never lost an opportunity to twist the knife.

Well, two could play that game. "Hey Julie," I said, sounding perfectly innocent. "Who's your escort again?" This was going to be so satisfying, better than a big plate of salty French fries.

My Diet Buddy didn't answer right away. There were sounds of fabric rustling in the dressing room, but it appeared she was pretending not to have heard me. Squeaky Posey jumped right in, though, on her daughter's behalf.

"Julie's going with Laddie Buchanan," she said, a definite frost overlaying her usual fan-belt squeal of a voice. She licked her index finger and turned the page of her magazine. "And you, Annie?" Mrs. Posey looked up then, accusation in her eyes.

"Oh, Du's my escort." I was only just able to mask the triumph in my reply. Wide-shouldered, good-looking, six foot four and two hundred pounds of to-die-for muscle, Duane Sizemore was a starter for the Ole Miss Rebels' football team, a senior, my first real conquest and the ex-boyfriend of Julie Posey. Having had the misfortune of being broken up with exactly eight weeks ago and now without a new boyfriend lined up in time for the Snow Ball, Julie was reduced to going with that perennial loser Laddie Buchanan. Laddie might still have a weak chest, but he was in regular demand as the last-minute, all-players-on-the-field variety of escort.

And Du and I had been going together for exactly eight weeks, ever since Homecoming. Julie had made a legendary scene in a library carrel when he broke the news to her during their last study date. Du wouldn't talk about it. Word was, however, she stabbed him in the jaw with a pencil before she threw his books out in the hall, then lobbed herself on him like a grenade and sobbed into the blood trickling down his neck.

Anyway, that was a long time ago and by now Du and I were an established couple. My sorority sisters hadn't warmed up to the idea right away, though, and I suspected that they'd inflicted Julie on me as a punishment. It didn't matter. What mattered was that I had an escort to the Snow Ball who was universally recognized as a catch, and that fact gave me a shot of badly needed confidence. Standing up in public on display to a bunch of people I barely even knew and in the company of girls like Julie to boot—the prospect of making my debut was giving me regular fits of high anxiety and foreboding. If it hadn't been for the unlikely and historical alliance of my mother and Grandmother Banks ganging up on me, I'd have refused this honor in a flash. My weight gain hadn't helped either, but it seemed that the more anxious I became, the more I ate—and it showed.

"You're done, missy," Miss Pettie said to me, finished pinning the hem of my dress. "Now go take that off and don't touch it!" Wondering how I was going to accomplish that, I stepped down from the dressmaker's stagelike drum. Julie emerged from behind the curtain in her dress, a classic antebellum battleship of silk chiffon, bugle beads, and looping alençon lace. Julie's thin, sallow face was waspish, her eyes a yellow jacket on the back of my neck. It was bound to be payback time for the Laddie question.

"Don't forget, Annie," she remarked, stepping up onto Miss Pettie's drum. "You're supposed to lose ten pounds by next Saturday."

"She better not," Miss Pettie announced, sounding dire. "That dress is *done*. No last-minute alterations."

Only the thought of my mother kept me from remarking that even if Julie *gained* ten pounds, her chest would still be flat as a popped balloon. I left Miss Pettie's as soon as I got out of my dress and wrestled into my jeans, burning with the humiliation of it all.

★ ★ ★

Home for the holidays. My mother had a wreath on the door, but she wouldn't be putting the tree up until a few days before Christmas. All her formidable powers of concentration were currently fixed upon my debut, undoubtedly fueled by Grandmother Banks's telling anyone who would listen that my mother was certain to prove to be unequal to the task of launching me into society since she had no background herself whatsoever.

Sitting in my car outside on the driveway, I fished in my purse for the pack of cigarettes and the lighter I'd bought on the way home. "Here goes," I said to myself as I lit up. With only a little over a week before the Snow Ball, I'd made up my mind: nothing was going to stop me from losing those ten pounds so I could wipe out my Diet Buddy's reason for living. And, remembering the way the white silk had pulled across my behind, I'd lose them just so my beautiful dress wouldn't be ashamed to be seen on me.

The Marlboro Light tasted flat and hot. Determined, I took another deep drag and coughed up a gray cloud. I'd never really smoked before. Oh, I'd had a token cigarette at frat parties, but mostly I'd waved it around without inhaling. However, one of my sorority sisters, Libby Suggs, had told me that she'd lost fifteen pounds in two weeks last year by smoking a couple of Virginia Slims before she was supposed to eat.

"It flat kills your appetite, Annie," she'd confided. We'd been sitting on the front porch of the Chi O house, waiting for the rest of the girls going to the Kappa Sig mixer to finish their eternal primping and come on downstairs. Libby was having a cigarette, and I was drinking a Diet Coke. I liked Libby a lot. An upperclassman, she drank with a sophistication, style, and dedication that I found inspiring and wished to emulate. No throwing up in the shrubbery for Libby, no waking up horrified and naked in the wrong bed like some girls. If she said smoking was the way to lose weight, I could take that to the bank.

It was getting cold inside the car. I stubbed my cigarette out in the ashtray. Sure enough, I felt queasy. Food was the last thing I wanted, and a good thing, too, because every principle Methyl Ivory stood for demanded huge pots of fattening stuff simmering on the stove inside the kitchen, just lying in wait to assault my hips.

That evening at the table, I pushed my meal around on my plate and drank water.

"Annie," my mother asked, "are you feeling all right? You've hardly touched a thing." It had been a real Southern dinner of gargantuan proportions to welcome me home: smoked ham, buttered sweet potatoes, collard greens swimming in an oil-sheened lagoon of bacon drippings, Parker House rolls, and Methyl Ivory's justly famous red velvet cake for dessert.

Expecting this shot across my bow, though, prior to dinner I'd had a couple of cigarettes out in the backyard, down by the Allens' fence in the dark. The smoke rising in a wreath around my head, I looked across their tended lawn to the rental house where Starr used to live. The lights were on. I wondered who lived there now, and for a moment, I curled my fingers in the wire mesh, remembering the afternoon I'd tried to break in through Starr's window, looking for clues. Sometimes I'd thought about it: if I'd succeeded in getting into her house, would I have been able to find her?

If only. In all the years since that terrible day I learned she was gone, I'd never had another friend like Starr. Oh, I'd learned how to get along with the other girls and pretend that we were close, but deep down where it counted I'd always kept them at a distance. Their frothy chatter about hair, makeup, and boys and all the other things that matter so much to teenagers were like cartoon thought balloons in Japanese to me, disconnected and beside the point to the life I was living inside. My social survival skills, rudimentary and unreliable as they were, had somehow become a wall, an invisible perimeter defense that kept everyone out of Annie Land. My sorority sisters, those madly self-involved butterflies, probably never suspected a thing. Why should they? Likely the time for that kind of profound attachment had passed for us all. We were too assured of our exalted place in the grand order of the world; we all knew the rules by now. Like migratory birds, we flocked without our wings touching, each traveling the instinctive routes and flyways of our kind. The other Chi O's tolerated my peculiarities and gaffes because I was a Banks from Jackson, never noticing the high-wire act I performed so that I could pass as one of them.

But what if Starr had never moved away? Would our friendship have survived high school and the sniper wars of who was who and who was nobody? My debut? Would she be here now at the fence, smoking with me? I smiled to myself. She probably would have been. We could have laughed at the small-town rituals that Jackson took in such deadly seriousness, and that would've been like water in the desert to me—sustaining, clean, and life-giving.

I tugged at the wire mesh, rusted now. I could still climb over, I thought, but then my daddy called from the back door that dinner was on the table. I took a drag and threw my cigarette to the ground, grinding it into the grass with my tennis shoe, but not without a last, lingering glance at the discouraged-looking rental house. Where was she now?

"Annie, aren't you hungry?" Above her empty plate, my mother's face was concerned.

I looked at my own nearly full plate with satisfaction. "I had a burger at McDonald's. I'm still stuffed," I lied, feeling thinner already. Oh, I was in control at last. Later that Friday night, I drank two big glasses of water and smoked another cigarette right before I went upstairs to bed and never had the slightest urge to eat.

The next morning saw only me at the kitchen table. Methyl Ivory was engaged in making deviled ham salad for lunch with the leftovers from last night's prodigal spread.

"You want some eggs, Miss Annie?" she asked. "I could scramble you up a couple, make you some toast." Methyl Ivory's back was to me, but her tone said that she didn't approve of my having slept in until after eleven o'clock. Her wide shoulders said that they had things to do and cooking me breakfast right before lunch was not supposed to be on the list.

"Oh, I'll just make myself some coffee," I said, yawning. A cup of steaming black coffee in hand, my pack of cigarettes in the pocket of my Ole Miss sweatshirt, I went outside and sat on the front steps. It was a cold, glorious day, the gem-blue canopy of sky shining a thousand miles above me like a promise—high, wide, and handsome. This Saturday morning felt like the start of something important, and when I went inside to take my shower, I weighed myself.

I'd lost a pound.

The rest of that Saturday was even easier than the first day of my off-the-radar diet. I smoked, drank black coffee, and used another excuse at dinner (a fictitious large lunch with an equally fictitious friend), and later that night, after I'd gone out and bought another pack of cigarettes, I talked on the phone with Du in the smoky privacy of my bedroom.

"I've lost two and a half pounds!" I crowed. "It's working." I ran my finger around the waistband of my jeans, and to my delight it was noticeably looser. "And the best part of it is, I just got started."

"Aw, baby-cakes," Du said. "You're perfect already." I heard him sigh. " 'Sides, aren't you kinda asking for trouble? I mean, everbody's gotta eat, right? You're not gonna turn into one of those arexonemia girls, throwin' up all the time?"

Falling across my bed because in truth I was feeling a little tired and empty, I lit another cigarette and immediately perked up again. "I'm not *anorexic,* Du, and throwing up is just gross. I'm on a temporary, extreme diet. That's all."

"Well, if you say so." He sounded dubious, but then his voice changed, dropping into that deeper register that meant he was thinking about sex again. "I can't wait to see you, honey." I hadn't slept with him—or anybody else—yet, but knew it was only a matter of time. With a catch like Du, you either put out or you got out. I didn't want to think about that yet, though.

I rolled over onto my elbows to reach the ashtray I'd begun keeping in my room. "Just six more days, and then we'll be together," I said. Tonight Du was at home in Tupelo, but he was driving down next Saturday morning to escort me to the Snow Ball that night. It was the first time I'd ever had a boy home from school, and I wasn't sure how he and Daddy were going to get along. What if they didn't?

Trying not to think about that possibility either, I said, "I'm glad you're going to be with me. I'm scared I'm going to do something heinous, like trip on my dress, or drop my bouquet, or . . ."

"Don't you worry, sugar-bunch." Du laughed. "I'll bring somethin' to take the edge off."

We hung up twenty minutes later after a lot of sighing and I-love-yous. I wasn't sure about the "I love you" part. It seemed to me as though by saying that I was crossing the border into a country I wasn't sure I wanted to visit. All the boys—all three of them—I'd dated before had said that same thing sooner or later, but with Du I was pretty positive that this time I was going to have to do something about it. This was a disquieting thought, but that was just the way it was. Everybody assumed that life flat wasn't worth living without a presentable boyfriend, and Du wasn't just presentable, he was a *prize*.

I'd gotten myself this far, though, and with such a substantial investment already in this gratifying, high-profile relationship, I was well aware that I was going to have to work at keeping Du happy so everyone would be happy with *me*. At least I was on the right track with my new diet. I knew that if I could maintain the momentum of my weight-loss campaign, it'd be a very different Annie meeting him at the front door next Saturday morning. Good-bye, chubby sophomore; hello, slim, sophisticated new me. Take *that,* Julie Posey.

Emerging victorious from the battlefront of Sunday dinner, by midweek I'd lost seven pounds and my mother was raising her eyebrows at the plates of food I wasn't eating. Oh, I had to take a token mouthful of something when she was watching, but the rest of the time I managed to move the food around on my plate in a purposeful way. Miss Pettie grumbled at having to take in the waist of my deb dress when we went for an emergency fitting Thursday morning, but she swore she'd have it ready by two o'clock.

Later that day, after my mother and I went back to pick my dress up, she suggested we stop on the way home and have coffee together at the Olde Tyme Delicatessen. What a minefield *that* was. The Olde Tyme's bakery was renowned for its fabulous pastries: apricot Danish, chocolate croissants, éclairs, napoleons, fruit tarts, fudge brownies so good they'd make you weep. All the help, from cooks to counter help to the cashier, were round as sugar doughnuts and looked damned happy about it, too. Now, normally I could never have passed up a whack at the Olde Tyme's pastry case, but I'd had a cigarette in the car after my fitting. We ordered at the counter, and when I asked for black coffee, my mother gave me a long look and then requested the same.

We sat down at our table in the crowded, bustling deli. My mother took off her mink and gloves. I shrugged out of my coat and braced myself. Sure enough, after she took a sip of coffee, my mother put her cup down in its saucer and said, "I've noticed you've lost some weight, Annie."

I squirmed uncomfortably in my chair, rearranging sugar packets in their dispenser, before I muttered, "It was about time, don't you think? I mean, before I looked like a white Sears side-by-side in my dress."

My mother raised one eyebrow. "Surely not. You'd gained a little weight since you went to Ole Miss, but that's normal. A lot of girls do that."

The sugar packets were well sorted by now, so I finally had to look her in the face. "I was sick of it," I said. "Besides, it's only a couple of pounds."

"It looks like more than a couple, honey," she said gently. "Annie, you're smoking a lot. Your clothes are hanging on you. I've noticed you're not eating your dinner, and Methyl Ivory says you don't have breakfast or lunch anymore. You can't live on black coffee and cigarettes." She reached across the table and put her hand on mine. "Your father's concerned, too."

I sighed a long-suffering sigh. "Look—I never wanted to do this debut anyway, but you and Grandmother Banks ganged up on me. So if I've got to be a deb, at least I'm not going to look like, like some, some . . . *refrigerator* in front of half of Jackson. I'm just dieting. Don't worry. I've got it all under control, okay?"

She didn't look convinced, but let the subject drop. I was extremely grateful. My hand shook as I picked up my own cup. It had occurred to me that all the coffee I was drinking was probably contributing to my jitters, but I needed the caffeine almost as much as I needed the cigarettes: coffee and nicotine were almost the only materials my body had to work with.

Late Saturday afternoon, a day dry and warm for December, I'd already been to my mother's hairdresser, Lily, that morning for a shampoo and set. I'd insisted that my long, thick blond hair be piled high in a chignon because I was convinced that wearing it up would make me look taller and thinner. My shellacked hair felt heavy and unnatural on top of my head, but thanks to all the hairpins Lily had jammed into my chignon, at least I wasn't worried about it falling apart. My mother's pearls around my neck, my makeup applied, the dress hanging on the door of my closet in a long snowfall of purest white—for the next two hours all I had to do was hang around in my panty hose, robe, and underwear until it was time to put on the dress and go.

I couldn't sit still but paced between my bed and the window, smoking and looking down into the backyard, where Du and my daddy were sitting in lawn chairs, drinking beer and talking football. At least that seemed to be going well, thank goodness. My mother hadn't yet returned from her own appointment with Lily, and even Methyl Ivory had left to go home. My nerves shrieked for action, but there was nothing to do but wait. Finally, I couldn't take it anymore: I went into my parents' bathroom to weigh myself again.

Glory be, I'd done it. I'd lost ten pounds in eight days! Practically fizzing with glee, I opened my bathrobe to look in the full-length mirror and marveled at the delicate hollow between my prominent hip bones, the frank spareness of my ribs. My newly slender neck seemed like a flower stalk, only just able to hold up the crown of my hair.

I came back to earth with a thud, stricken again with the gnawing certainty that, ten lost pounds or not, I was sure to make a mess of tonight, that I'd do something awful, embarrass my parents and send Grandmother Banks rocketing into the stratosphere in her wheelchair, jet-propelled on I-told-you-sos. In an unexpected blessing, though, the old dragon wasn't going to be able to attend tonight, being still laid up with shingles, so whatever I did, it wasn't going to be in front of her at least.

My eye caught my flushed reflection in the wavy old mirror of the white-painted medicine cabinet. Desperate for a little relief from constant anxiety, I opened the door to see if the pharmaceutical rep-fairy had left a present there for me. A blister packet of something called Librium lay on the glass shelf, next to a bottle of the Seconal my mother took for her insomnia.

Librium. The name recalled equilibrium, a state I would do anything to achieve right now. I dropped the two capsules in their sample pack in my robe's pocket and went downstairs to get something to drink. Popping one of the pills free, I washed it down with a cup of lukewarm coffee while standing over the sink. Fifteen minutes later I felt calm enough to head out in the backyard in my robe and slippers, to sit down with Daddy and my boyfriend. Their conversation had moved on to the topic of where Du was going after he graduated this spring. He'd been accepted to Ole Miss law, but he wanted to see if he could make it in the NFL. Daddy thought law school was the better choice, and Du was politely listening. He looked so handsome, and Daddy seemed to like him well enough. That was one less thing to fret about, and maybe now I could relax. Maybe even my mother would quit worrying about me, now that I had such an indisputably suitable boyfriend.

My aimless thoughts drifted to the deepening evening sky overhead, the clean, green smell of the pine trees. A pair of crows had built their nest high in the branches of the live oak, and they were returning home with desultory, welcoming noises. I was so grateful for the sweet sense of chemically induced peace stealing through my body that my eyes closed, the heavy weight of my chignon resting against the back of the lawn chair. Du and Daddy went inside to shower and change into their tuxedos. I could've fallen asleep then, but after some time—how long, I don't know, time had lost its terrible urgency—my mother came down the steps into the backyard with a plate in her hand.

"Here," she said, holding the plate out to me. "Eat this." Her green eyes were steady on mine. I looked at the inoffensive pimento cheese sandwich with misgiving. "You need something on your stomach, Annie Banks. It's going to be a long night." I could tell she wasn't about to go away until she'd seen me eat it, so I took the plate and somehow choked the sandwich down, every last bite.

And then it was finally time to get dressed. I could have sworn I saw the outline of that pimento cheese sandwich lurking under the taut silk across my stomach. Panic rose again, so before I left my room to go downstairs, I palmed the second Librium from the sample pack and dry-swallowed it, just to be sure. Everybody loaded up in my mother's new Lincoln, and after the dreamlike drive out to the country club, I was feeling so outstandingly mellow that when we got out of the car and Du grabbed my hand, I sailed along behind him like a kite on the end of a string as he led me toward the corner of the parking lot by the overgrown gardenia bushes.

"Go on." I gaily motioned to my parents. "We'll meet you inside." My mother paused, looking at us, and for a moment it seemed she was going to follow Du and me to the outskirts of the parking lot. "Seriously!" I called. "Y'all go get some champagne and we'll be right along." With a wave, my father took my mother's hand then and they turned up the sidewalk to the front doors of the country club, the covered breezeway lit with tiki torches and lumieres in paper bags.

When they were out of sight, Du said, "Here, baby. I tole you I'd take care of you. Have some of this." He took a pint bottle out of his coat pocket and put it in my gloved hand. "Take you a few swigs of Ol' Granddad, and he'll settle you right down." I looked at the flask dubiously, wondering if I ought to be putting bourbon on top of pimento cheese and Librium, but decided it couldn't hurt. I screwed off the cap on the bottle, lifted it to my lips, and took a big swallow. Cheap bourbon cascaded in a harsh burn down my throat and ignited like a frat-party bonfire in my stomach.

"Whoa," I coughed. "You got a hankie?" I needed to wipe my mouth and didn't want to ruin my gloves. Elbow-length white kidskin fastened with twelve pearl buttons, they were emblematic deb wear. I could only imagine my grandmother's reaction if she heard I'd gotten lipstick on them.

"Here." Du gave me his pocket square, and I dabbed at my lips. "Take one more, baby," he said encouragingly. I tipped back my head and took another gulp, then another. In my stomach, the bourbon seemed to be having a one-sided discussion with the pimento cheese sandwich already in residence. It felt like the bourbon was getting its point across just fine, so I had one more pull on the pint bottle before I handed it back to Du.

"Thanksh, honey," I said. My mouth felt numb. I took Du's arm. "Thanksh. I'm glad you're here."

"Aw, Annie," Du said. "I wouldn't a missed this for the world. I'm afraid to touch you, you're so pretty."

I rested my forehead on his black wool shoulder. "Y'mean it, Du?" I was slurring my words, but only a little.

"A 'course I do," he said, putting the pint bottle back in his pocket. "Those other girls give you a hard time, but you're gonna be the best-looking gal in the place. Bet on it." I felt a surge of accomplishment: maybe all this would turn out to have been worth it if Du felt that way about me. We were walking toward the entrance to the country club now. My feet hurt, and I had to be extra careful in my four-and-a-half-inch heels, but Du's arm and the bourbon and the Librium held me up admirably.

Inside the lobby, I blearily patted Du on the cheek. "I'll shee you later, after the dancing starts."

"Where you going?" he asked. "Need me to come, too?"

Touched at this evidence of Du's devotion, I smiled. "I'm off to the ladies' room for a lipshtick check. G'on, now—get yourself a glass of champagne." With a lighthearted wave, I listed down the wide, dimly lit hallway, not really lurching at all, but when I pushed open the door to the ladies', I almost ran into Julie Posey in that aircraft carrier of a dress. She was just leaving, followed by Lisa Treeby wearing what looked like her mother's yellow-tinged wedding gown, a big lace flounce obviously added to its hem so her dress would hang all the way to the floor. This recycling was a sign that Mr. Treeby's legendary cheapness must have triumphed as usual.

"Watch out, Annie!" Julie snapped, glaring. She paused in the doorway, looking me up and down in the bathroom's bright lights. She didn't mention the fact that I was remarkably thinner, that my dress now fell in a smooth line from waist to floor, that I had rendered her services as Diet Buddy obsolete.

She didn't have to say anything because Lisa did. "Oooh, Annie!" she exclaimed. "That dress is just, just *beautiful* on you." Good ol' Lisa—we weren't ever particularly close, but she had always been nice to me. Julie sniffed, swept up her skirts, and left the ladies' room like a galleon under full sail without another word.

"Thanksh, Lisa," I said, and burped. The smell of bourbon on my breath was strong, even to me. I reddened ever so slightly, but the Librium carried the day and I managed to say, "You look wonnerful. I love your hair." Poor Lisa's hair was woolly as a sheep's. She'd tried to corral it in a lace snood and had stuck some big old rosebuds behind her ears. "Did you do it yourshelf?"

Lisa's smile was as wide as if she'd won first prize at the 4-H show. "Yes," she replied. "You really like it?" Self-consciously she touched her hair and a rosebud fell out from behind her ear and onto the floor.

I bent down to pick it up for her, and it was only then I realized that leaning over or any other move involving reaching downward was going to be a very bad idea. Still, I managed to grab the rosebud before I toppled over onto the bathroom's marble tiles.

"Here." Straightening, I held it out to her on the palm of my glove, feeling foolish.

"Thanks!" Lisa flashed me another smile, returning the rosebud to behind her ear. "I better go," she said. "It's almost time." Damned if Lisa didn't sound thrilled with anticipation. I almost envied her but decided to be happy for her instead. Good ol' Lisa. I checked my makeup in the mirror one last time. Good to go, Houston. Rocket ship Annie left the launch pad and began burning through the atmosphere of the country club in a wobbly trajectory toward the ballroom.

It all went pretty well until I had to descend the steps for the promenade.

I'd managed to present myself as they announced my name like a contestant in some bizarre game show, even managed to curtsy and not fall over in a heap. Flashbulbs popped in a galaxy of blinding light. Daddy met me on the stage, and I laid my gloved left hand on his arm with an exquisite relief. This ordeal was almost over and I hadn't outraged or embarrassed anyone yet. Clutching my bouquet of white roses and baby's breath in my right hand, I remembered to lift the skirt of my dress so I wouldn't trip over it and took the first step down the little stairs in front of the stage. My daddy patted my hand on his arm.

"You okay, honey?" he asked me under his breath. I couldn't answer because the next step was coming up, my heels were wobbling like pine trees in a high wind, and I needed to concentrate. Clutching his arm now, I prayed that I could navigate the next two steps without incident, so intent on staying on those damned heels that I never even saw the rosebud underfoot until it was too late.

I stepped squarely on it, and my ankle turned with a twist of agony that shot right up through my leg into my spine. Daddy caught me as I missed the last step, and to everyone else it might have looked as though we were just sharing a quick hug before we made the circuit of Jackson's biggest ballroom. If it hadn't been for Daddy, I would have fallen. If it hadn't been for his steady arm, I could never have made it around the circuit of that throng of clapping, champagne-guzzling strangers.

But if it hadn't been for catching a glimpse of my mother's face—so proud, so very proud of me—I couldn't have done it without limping like a three-legged horse. For her, I gritted my teeth in a rictus of a smile and stayed on that ankle until we finally got back to the stage.

Racehorses who run even when they're hurting are said to be "game." Well, I guess I was only half-game that evening because while I was standing on one foot up there on the stage, waiting for the other girls to make their own debuts, I could lean on Daddy's arm and tell myself that I'd pulled it off. But halfway through the presentations, I felt a delicate sheen of perspiration break on my upper lip while a strong message issued from my stomach from the pimento cheese sandwich, which had apparently won out over the bourbon and Librium. Thank goodness I was on the far end of the stage.

"Be right back," I managed to gasp to Daddy before I slipped off into the wings, elbowing my way through the last half of 1975's crop of debs. Bracing myself on the wall, I hobbled pell-mell down the long hallway to the bathroom. I almost made it to the toilet, but Julie Posey was coming out as I was going in, and while I didn't precisely ruin her dress, an orange-ish portion of bourbon and that pimento cheese sandwich splashed on the hem. My own dress I missed completely. As I staggered past her into the bathroom stall to finish the miserable business of throwing up, I could hear Julie outside the door, shrieking that I had *destroyed* her debut.

I, on the other hand, now felt much better, so much better in fact that after I'd sponged my face with a damp paper towel and rinsed out my mouth, I decided that it was time to go out and enjoy the rest of the Snow Ball. Dancing was likely going to be out of the question—my ankle still felt like it was broken and was about to fall off—but after all, I did look fabulous.

And it seemed dancing wasn't entirely out of the question. My daddy, looking relieved, claimed me as soon as I limped into the noise and big-band music of the ballroom. We were able to have an abbreviated, careful dance together along with all the other debs and dads.

"Nerves got your stomach going?" he asked me. I nodded vigorously because it was better than the truth. Then, with a hug, Daddy handed me off to Du so he could go dance with my mother. From across the ballroom her eyes asked me if I was all right. I gave her a thumbs-up and an exaggerated wink. I didn't want to get too close, not wanting to spoil her triumph with even a whiff of whiskey on my breath. She and Daddy looked so perfect together—she in her long apple-green velvet and diamonds, he in his white tie and tails—as they swung into the dance with the grace of long years as partners. I think the band was playing "Pretty Baby." Du basically held me up in his linebacker arms, my weight entirely on my left foot, my right one dangling in its four-and-a-half-inch heel as we swayed in place to the music.

"Gonna marry you, Duane Sizemore," I mumbled into the front of Du's tux. If I could pull this night off, I could do anything in the world I had to do.

"Say what, baby?" Du looked down at me, his big, handsome face smiling.

I tipped my head back to look him in the eye. "I said," I enunciated carefully, "I am going to marry you."

Du laughed, but that laugh sounded perplexed. "Hon, I haven't asked you yet," he said.

"You will." In that moment, I was sure of it. And rocking in his arms in the darkness, under the fractured reflections of the mirror ball, in the midst of a thousand perspiring people smelling of warm wool tuxedos, mothballs, and too much perfume, I could see it all. The next white dress, my ten sorority-sister bridesmaids, Libby Suggs catching my bouquet, a shower of rice and a honeymoon in Mexico, my mother relieved and vindicated at last in her heretofore doomed quest to see me doing what everybody else was doing for a change. I could see it all, that promise—high, wide, and handsome.

Thin, married, and safe.

CHAPTER 13

"Wow—that's a first."

His forehead pressed to mine, Ted's low-voiced comment is shaky, and it's in that instant I realize what a terrible thing I've just done. I stiffen in his arms, and immediately he lets go of me as if I'm radioactive. I'm only just able to stay upright in the aftershock. I stagger backward away from him, reaching for the relative safety of the cinder block wall.

"Me too," I manage to say. What I don't say is that I'm *married,* for God's sake. I don't say that kiss was so out of character for me I might as well be in the throes of some cerebral event, what the old-timers used to call a brainstorm. Like I said, there's never been anybody else but Du, not really. Still, thinking of Ted's kiss, I wouldn't take it back—not for anything—and that astounding realization is something I keep to myself, too. Feeling the way I do right now, I'm not even sure what's going to come out of my mouth will sound like English anyway. I sway on my feet, blinking and trying to lick my dry lips with my dry tongue.

Ted's face is flushed, and I imagine mine is as well. "You all right?" he asks. He reaches down and picks up Troy's makeshift leash, obviously avoiding my eyes.

"No." The edges of my vision are darkening, and the barn rotates in a steep, ominous spiral. Swaying in the aisle, I know that this time I'm going down. "Christ," I moan.

"Okay, okay," Ted says. He takes my elbow, steadying me. "Easy, now. Can you hold on here a minute while I go get that water?" When all I can do is nod, he puts Troy's leash in my limp hand and with quick, easy strides heads down the aisle, turning inside a door at the end of the shed row. I want to sit down in the dirt, but I've got to stay on my feet, however unsteady they are, since I'm sure that once I sit, then I'll lie down, then all the blood will rush to my head, and then I'll pass out. The longest minute later, Ted's coming back with a Dixie cup in his hand and a concerned look on his face, probably wondering what he's gotten himself into. He gives the cup to me, and I take a long, cool drink of what is undoubtedly the best water on the planet. God, that's good. When I've finished, Ted takes the paper cup from me and drops it in a nearby garbage can. I close my eyes and return to my new friend, the cinder block wall.

"If you haven't been drinking, then what the hell's wrong with you?" Ted asks. He sounds concerned.

"Don't know," I mumble, opening my burning eyes and trying to stand up straight.

"Have you eaten anything today?" Without making a big deal out of it, Ted brushes my hair off my face, a gesture that both warms and alarms me. His fingertips are calloused, slightly rough on my cheek.

"Some Chessmen." I try to take a step forward and promptly bang up against the stall door of the really big horse who's been giving me the stink-eye for quite a while now. Ears flattened, the massive chestnut head rears backward in terror as if I'd come after the damned thing with an assault rifle.

"And a brownie," I add.

"One of Bette's brownies?" Ted shakes his head. "Honey, you're high."

Even in my addled state, "high" gets through to what's passing for my brain. That's almost exactly what this feels like, but my abortive experiments in college with marijuana and other drugs are so far in my past I'd purely forgotten all about them. Back then, it seemed like everybody except for ol' Just-Say-No Julie Posey was smoking dope, but I usually faked it, passing the joint without taking a hit. Marijuana made me sleepy—and hungry, a state I'd begun to avoid whenever possible.

"That brownie did taste funny," I admit, remembering the herby aftertaste.

"Bette's brownies are notorious. You'll do better walking it off," Ted says. I have misgivings about leaving the wall beside the sulking chestnut horse's stall, but he sounds serious. "C'mon. I'll introduce you to some friends of mine. Here." He wraps my hand in his own and encourages me forward. "You can do it."

And like that, Ted, Troy, and I are walking down the aisle of the barn. I'm slow like an old lady, unsteady as a grandmother without her walker, but I do find that with each step I get a little better and Ted only has to catch me once or twice when I go crashing into the wall. Still, I'm grateful when we stop in front of the next stall and a tall gray horse pokes his head out, chewing a wad of hay. Ted strokes the horse's long neck, sleek and smooth as dappled marble.

"This is Triton, one of my stakes horses," Ted says, his voice affectionate. "Seven years old and sound as a Swiss bank. Won over eight hundred thousand bucks and the monster still runs like he's three. Go ahead, you can touch him."

The tall gray horse noses the front of my dress inquisitively, leaving a few white hairs on the black silk. Feeling timid, I slide my hand down the undercurve of his neck, mesmerized with the strong, slow heartbeat under my fingertips. "One of your horses?" I ask. "Do you own a herd of them?"

"I *train* ten," Ted answers. "No herds, though. I can't afford to own any horses myself. Damned things eat their heads off. Triton here belongs to a couple of really nice gay guys from New York, Ray and Stu. Great clients, pay their bills on time, and love to watch their horse run. He's on the card for the Thanksgiving Classic tomorrow so they'll be in town." He takes my hand again, and we walk next door to meet another horse, a bay beauty with a blaze face and tiny ears like quotation marks. This one's not nearly as intimidating, being a lot smaller than the gray.

"Say hi to Helen Wheels," Ted says. "Filly's fast as a lightning strike, so she's a sprinter—needs a short race where her speed can make up for her lack of size." The little filly arches her neck when Ted fondles her ears, her half-closed, liquid eyes glazed with contentment. "If I could own a horse, she'd be the one. I like her style." Ted's smile at me is intimate. "I like little women with guts."

Blushing, I pet this one, too, loving the satin-like feel of her skin sliding easily over the exquisite crest of her neck. And Ted's right: walking is helping, and so is the reassuring solidity of his hand holding mine. Taking our time, we move down the length of the aisle, meeting the horses he trains, getting to know them. When we reach the end of the shed row, I feel as though I'd remember these friends of Ted's wherever I saw them, and slowly, the clean smells of hay and sleepy horses, Troy Smoot's curious snuffling, and the papery rustle of pigeons overhead in the dusty rafters quiet my overshot senses. This peaceful company has helped bring me back to myself, enough so that it's hard to believe I have just kissed a man who isn't Du.

What got into me? I peek sidelong at Ted. Accident or not,

once that kiss began I didn't exactly back away. Ted steps into the last horse's stall to rearrange an off-kilter blanket, and I lean my arms on the half-door, watching him seem to magically create order out of a tangle of mysterious straps and buckles while the horse nibbles from a hay net.

"Thanks." I have to make myself say it, embarrassed now for being such a mess. And for that kiss. "Thanks for not taking advantage, for sticking around to make sure I'm all right."

Ted straightens, brushing a loose straw from his jeans. "If you ate a pot brownie, might be a while before you're really all right. Could take hours to wear off."

"I feel a lot better," I say, "just a little floaty, like I could walk off the edge of the world at any moment, you know?" Ted steps out into the aisle and shuts the latch on the door to the stall. "Look, I'm, uh, sorry for what happened before," I say. Pausing, my cheeks hot, I'm determined to soldier on in my apology, even though I'd rather be in a midnight fire at sea than talk about it because I'm sure I need to say *something* about it. "That was really . . ."

Turning to face me, Ted takes both my hands in his own and smiles that great smile down at me. Before I lose my nerve, I rattle on doggedly. "I mean, it's not like I go around kissing strange men all the time."

"Yeah, that ring's kind of hard to miss."

"I used to have a little one," I blurt. "Du—he's my husband—thought I needed a big ring once he started making money."

"Got it." Ted nods but doesn't say anything else, and for a long moment I'm belatedly dumbfounded to discover that, with no effort whatsoever, I can dismiss that five-carat rock and what it's supposed to mean from my mind because I want to kiss him again. I want to put my fingers in that dark, a-little-too-long hair, gently pull his mouth to mine so I can feel that smile against my lips just one more time. Amazed at my thoughts,

I tilt my head and really *look* at him, this nice man who's just showed me his horses, inviting me in as though I have every right to be a part of this world of his.

There's a strange, comfortable quiet between us, and in that growing quiet I begin to hear things I thought were done, the sounds of possibility, of change. If I can kiss someone besides Du, maybe I can muster a backbone and stick it out with Starr after we get home. Besides, that amazing kiss and this good silence have shut up even the rosebush voice—probably shocked to smithereens at the widening rift, seemingly as broad as the Gulf of Mexico, between the me of this morning and Annie tonight. I could get used to this silence, I think.

"Well, Annie not-from-here," Ted finally says. "You okay to head back to Bette's? It's a ways." He lets go of my hands. "I could go get the golf cart if you want."

Reflexively, I look down at my watch. In the dim light of the shed row I can barely make out the time, but even so it's plain that I've been gone a lot longer than the ten-minute walk I'd promised Troy when we left Bette's trailer. More like an hour has passed, and now it's well after midnight. If Starr and I can leave in the next fifteen minutes, I can still get home before I get into real trouble, but the thought of home elicits a stirring of apprehension, as though there's something I've forgotten and need to remember before it's too late. It's probably the dope making me paranoid, but in any case, I really do need to get back.

"I can make it. That Airstream ought to still be where it was an hour ago," I say, hugging my arms with a shiver. Without warning, it feels as though the temperature in the barn has dropped twenty degrees and it's not like this dress is made for traipsing around in the damp New Orleans fog anyway. Seeing me shiver, Ted shrugs out of his jean jacket and drapes it around my shoulders, body-warm and smelling of him. Lord, he looks good in his white T-shirt, that broad chest, those smooth-muscled arms. I blink and look away while Troy Smoot sits at my feet, all business now after having thoroughly smelled everything he could get his nose into and lifted his leg on the garbage can.

"Thanks for the water," I say, hugging myself tighter so I'll be sure to keep my hands to myself because Ted looks so good. Then the nice man in the white T-shirt puts a finger under my chin, lifting it so my eyes meet his. He's smiling, and in spite of my growing apprehension, I find myself helplessly smiling back at him. "And thanks for the hay rope."

"Thanks for the kiss," Ted says mildly. "I'll walk you back to Bette's place."

My car's missing.

It's gone. Vanished. No longer there. I shut my eyes and open them again, sure that this time it'll be where I parked sixty thousand dollars' worth of German luxury engineering, behind the big semi with the Virginia plates. No—in the damp dirt the tire tracks are unmistakable, but the BMW is gone.

"Hey, Annie?" Ted asks. "Where's your car?"

I don't answer. I can't. I stand in the space where my car used to be, my mouth open wide as one of the semi's tires. Unbelieving, I stumble away, leaving Ted and the dog behind me. I run between the silk palm trees, up the steps of Bette's Airstream, and bang on the door with both fists.

"Starr!"

The Confederate flag covering the window twitches, but it's Bette who opens the door, her false eyelashes removed, a smear of night cream on her big-pored face.

"Oh, Lord, Annie," she says, looking nervous. "You better come on in, sweetheart. Ted, that you?"

"I'll wait out here," he says.

I fall inside the door, fending off Bette's attempt at a wide-armed embrace. The trailer, smelling of stale coffee and Shalimar, feels way too warm, entirely too bright after the cool, foggy night. All those swans stare at me with beady-eyed smugness from every corner of the room.

"My car's been stolen! I've got to talk to Starr," I say wildly, looking around the Airstream's cabin. "Starr?"

Starr doesn't answer. Her purse isn't on the Formica countertop either.

"Bette? Where's Starr?" My voice is trembling on the edge of the kind of panic that sends people out screaming into the streets. I have a very bad and altogether too familiar feeling about this. Somehow, I've screwed up again. *Serves you right,* the rosebush voice says, *for kissing that man,* and the swans seem to nod in agreement.

Bette wraps her hand around my arm, her big, greasy face concerned. "You better sit down, honey. I'll pour us some coffee."

"No!" I whirl away from her and stick my head outside the open door, shouting, "Starr Dukes, where the hell are you?" Ted, who's now leaning against the side of the battered semi with his arms folded, looks up at me. His face is expressionless until he lifts an eyebrow.

"She's not out here," he says.

It's a long beat before I realize Ted knows who I'm shouting for, that he knows Starr. I can only stare at him in dumbfounded vacancy. Behind me, Bette tugs at the jean jacket hanging from my shoulders, and I just restrain myself from slapping her. Where's Starr? Where's my car? Has she taken it to get gas or something? She has to be coming back, she has to. I'm shaking like I have a high fever, my heart pounds like the surf in a storm, and the trailer's linoleum seems to lift under my feet with a sideways tilt.

"Sit down, Annie." Bette pats my shoulder as she guides

me to the dinette. Like an obedient dog, I sit in a stunned heap. She leans out through the Airstream's door, into the foggy night. "You can c'mon in, Ted," she hollers. "I'll pour us all a cup of coffee."

My hands are knotted together on top of the table when Ted ducks his head to walk in the trailer. He pauses and looks around, seems nonplussed by all the swans, and then slides in across from me on the dinette's other bench. I can't look at him.

I can't look at anyone.

"Bette," I say, my voice low and dangerous. "Tell me where Starr is this minute. Tell me she didn't just take off in my car."

Bette's back is turned to me as she pours out the coffee I don't want. Her wide shoulders slump. With a sigh, she pushes up the velour sleeves of her sweat suit like she's got a tough job ahead of her and turns around to face me.

"Well, she did, Annie. Starr took your car and went back to Jackson. You were gone for so long, over an hour, and we didn't even know where you'd gone." Bette folds her tattooed arms across her bosom, her face worried. "I'm so sorry. She said to tell you she couldn't wait."

My mouth falls open again, and nobody says anything. "What?" I falter, finally. *Jackson?* Starr left me here, in New Orleans, in the middle of the night without a way to get home? "What?" I say again, still unable to believe this is really happening to me.

Like a dancing bear in teal velour, Bette trundles over to the dinette with two steaming cups, putting one in front of Ted, the other in front of me. "Here you go, honey." She squeezes in next to Ted and pats my clenched hands. "Oh, Annie—I got another call, and it wasn't an asshole trainer with a sore horse this time, it wasn't for me. That call was for Starr."

I jerk my hands away, clutching Ted's jacket to my bare shoulders. *"So?"* I demand, panic turning to dread.

Bette's naked little eyes are guarded. She looks down at the table. "So after that call she had to leave. Right away. She wouldn't wait."

"I heard that part already. What was so goddamned important that she'd strand me in New Orleans," I say, my voice rising to an almost-shout, "when she knows how much trouble I'm going to be in *when I can't get home tonight?*"

And with that outburst I'm exhausted, collapsing against the leatherette back of the bench seat, dully appraising the disaster Starr's landed me in. Across the table, Ted takes a sip of his coffee, his eyes watching me with what looks like compassion. I'm numb inside, but my thoughts are racing: even if I could get a rental car on the night before Thanksgiving, my driver's license, my credit cards, and the money in the pocket of my parka—they're all in the BMW. I'm broke and alone in New Orleans in the middle of the night. How could Starr do this to me? My eyes fill with tears.

"Didn't she know?" My whisper sounds broken. "Didn't she know what's going to happen to me now?"

Bette sighs. "Oh, honey," she says gently. With a grunt, she gets up to get me a Kleenex from the swan-shaped dispenser on top of the television. "Starr knew it was going to be a problem, but she had to do it. She said to tell you it was Mr. Right who called."

Remember Mr. Right? The man my momma told me was going to carry me off, love me forever, and get me whatever my heart desired?

Bette goes on. "It was her chance to get together with her baby's father, to go get married and get shut of the world of hurt she's been in, but she was afraid he might have second thoughts. She didn't dare waste any time."

"But *tonight?*" This horror is making less sense by the minute. Starr? Going back to Bobby? "Why tonight?"

"I don't know, sugar," Bette says, shaking her head.

"Eight hours ago she had to be in New Orleans tonight!"

I want to put my head down on the table and sob, but I can't summon the energy even for that. "She's going back to Jackson to marry Bobby? After all he put her through, Starr's going back to Bobby Shapley? Has she lost her mind, thinking he can marry her just like that? Last I heard, he wasn't even divorced! He's still with Julie."

I can't seem to take this in, my mind shrieking *no*. Please, please tell me I'm not going to be ruined because Bobby Shapley changed his fucking mind.

Bette sits down again, and the bench groans under her weight. Her husky contralto is loaded with a galling commiseration when she says, "I know it's a shock, sugar."

"No, it's not." Ted says.

I turn from Bette's heavy-jowled face to meet his steady, brown-eyed gaze. "What do you mean, it's not a shock?" I ask. "What the hell are you saying?"

Ted's eyes don't waver. "You've known her—how long?"

Without thinking I say, "Since I was seven years old. What about it?"

Ted shrugs. "Then how can you be shocked when Starr Dukes runs off with your car?"

This hits like a baseball bat to the gut. I stare at him, hoping I heard wrong.

"So you do know her," I say. "In fact, you seem to know Starr better than I do." Could Ted be one of the men in her past? Starr, sitting on that god-awful ugly bed, clasping her hands in her lap and looking dreamy. *Poppa said that the wages of sin is death. I've made me some mistakes, but I can't say I'd do anything different.* Not knowing why I should care, I swallow hard and have to ask, "So . . . how well do you know her?"

Ted doesn't say anything right away. He takes a sip of coffee and puts the cup down before he says, "It's not what you think, Annie. Starr's like a lot of people—comes from nothing, wants a lot. I'd say that if taking your car and leaving you behind was the one way for her to get over, she'd drive off with your BMW in a heartbeat and never look back." He idly turns his cup in its saucer. "Starr and I were friends once, sort of. That's all." His tone tells me to take his word for it.

Bette runs her fingers through her tight brown curls, working them into a loopy, corkscrew halo. She looks tired, too. "And that's the way it is with me and Starr," she says, sounding subdued. "She only tells me what she thinks I need to know, so I can't answer all your questions, Annie. She hadn't even told me about being pregnant, and wasn't that a surprise when she walked in the door! But I'll tell you what, once Starr's made up her mind, she's like a round from a thirty-aught shotgun—whatever she's aiming at, she's gonna take it *out*."

Eyes cast down at her wide lap, Bette gulps, obviously steeling herself for what she says next. "And Annie"—she lowers her voice—"this isn't the first time Starr's been pregnant, but she swears it's going to be the last, said that phone call meant she wasn't going to have to fight anymore, she'd never be broke again. Starr's going to be set for life."

I'm reeling with humiliation. I want to crawl into a hole and die. I want to wake up in my bed at home to find that this has been a wicked, wicked dream. Ted's face is carefully without expression, but the terrible sympathy in Bette's eyes tells me I've been a fool. What have I done to myself now?

Finally, I locate my voice. "I still have to find a way home," I say, defeated and thin as tap water. "All my money, my driver's license, everything's in the car. I have the clothes I'm standing up in. And a dog."

"Well, the dress looks fabulous on you." Bette narrows her eyes and gives me the once-over. "I'd lose the boots, though. You need a killer pair of Ferragamo sling-backs."

"And he's a good dog," Ted offers.

"Where is he?" I ask. In the midst of all this sickening revelation, have I lost Troy Smoot, too?

"He's in my truck," Ted says. "There's a pile of clean horse blankets in the back seat, fresh from the Laundromat. He's warm and comfortable."

"Why'd you do that?" I rub my eyes, put my face in my hands.

Ted reaches across the table and gently pushes a thick sheaf of hair off my face. I look at him through my fingers. "I'm going to drive you both home," he says. "You ready to leave?"

This offer is as surreal as everything else. "Why are you being so nice to me?" I ask.

"You liked my horses, and I don't have another date for tonight." His voice is easy, but his eyes tell me that he means it. "I can get you home and be back here before my first horse runs tomorrow."

Looking relieved, Bette nods her approval. "Ted's one of the good guys, honey," she says. "Go on home, Annie. Things will look better in the morning."

It's already morning.

Ted's truck is humongous, an older black four-door Ford diesel with an extra pair of tires on the rear axle. Ted calls it a dually. There's a welter of fast-food bags, gas station receipts, road maps, a couple of shiny aluminum horseshoes, a tattered paperback copy of *To Kill a Mockingbird,* and a claw hammer underneath my feet on the passenger's side. I'm shivering on the frigid bench seat that's as cold under my bare thighs as only vinyl can be, waiting for the big engine block finally to warm up so we can have some heat.

"Somebody stole the radio back in Virginia," Ted says. "I could sing, if you want. My ex-wife used to say I sound okay for a guy whose only musical experience is hymns from when I was an altar boy. Sometimes I sing Van Halen in the truck, just because it feels good."

"I'm not really in the mood for music, thanks."

It's a quarter of two o'clock in the morning, black as the underside of a crow's wing except for the brief pools of efflorescence surrounding the deserted interstate's lamps. Just as the truck begins to lose its chill, we pass the last exit and leave New Orleans, plunging into the darkness of the spillway, going back the way I came, across the marsh and up the I-55. Slipping off my boots, I curl my feet underneath me and lean my head against the window, looking through the bug-splattered windshield at indistinct stands of cypress trees, the hummocks of switch grass and reeds spread under the scattered stars. Troy Smoot snores softly in the back seat, ensconced in his pile of horse blankets.

I glance over at Ted. He drives like a guy accustomed to the thousand-mile distances between racetracks, forearm resting on top of the wheel, one long leg bent, the other stretched to the pedal. His profile in the greenish light of the instrument panel is cut from the cloth of the night.

"You hungry yet?" he asks.

"No." I can't imagine eating anything. Hell, I don't even want a cigarette—which is unusual, although just as well because the pack's in my purse in the BMW. I wish I hadn't thought of that. *Damn* her. "I'm not hungry."

"You're going to be. Bette packed up some cookies for later, for when you want them." He pauses. "I told her about the brownie while you were in the bathroom."

Cookies. If I hadn't eaten those Chessmen, I probably wouldn't be in the mess I'm in. If I hadn't eaten the damned brownie, Starr, Troy, and I would be almost to Jackson by now. The truck hums along the elevated miles of the spillway, its diesel engine a constant drone, and the silence, so alive before, is thick and lifeless between Ted and me. What can I possibly say? I don't deserve his kindness—a silly, vacuous woman who deceived her husband, ran off to New Orleans, and got stranded there.

Finally, I clear my throat. "I'm sorry," I say. "I'm sorry you have to drive me two hundred miles back to Jackson."

"I'm not," Ted says. "Sorry, I mean. It's a good excuse for spending more time with you. I'd like to know you when you're sober, Annie." He turns and glances at me briefly before he puts his eyes back on the road again. "Besides, driving's half of what my job's about. I'm good at it—better than singing anyway."

"Still," I persist, "you shouldn't have to—"

Ted interrupts. "Why don't you just say thank you and let it go?"

I swallow my apologies. "Thank you," I whisper. But letting it go is going to be a lot harder.

Still, after that the mood in the truck lifts. As if by mutual agreement, Ted and I don't talk about Starr. I can't even think of her without crying, and he seems to know this.

Instead, we head directly to all those places you're never supposed to go with an acquaintance: politics (he's a nonvoting Republican, I'm a blue-dog Democrat), religion (he's a Christmas Catholic, I'm a lapsed Episcopalian), and money (both of us agree that while it doesn't buy happiness, it sure makes miserable a lot easier to take). I find myself laughing at Ted's absurd stories of the backstretch, especially the ones about Bette and her temper, something of a small miracle since I was sure it would be years before I laughed again. Even so, from time to time there's a sense of black ships on my horizon, the foreknowledge of what might be waiting for me at home. It's a disturbing disconnect with a whiplash effect. I'll be laughing, talking, and then out of the blue I'm besieged by sharp-edged, wince-worthy memories of a tribe of Barbies in sock-dresses, a broken majolica umbrella stand, a burning tractor, a four-and-a-half-inch heel and an empty pint bottle left under a gardenia bush. Disapproving faces around the dining table. My mother's perpetual disappointment with me. Du's wary eyes watching me maneuver myself into yet another corner at a law firm cocktail party.

He trusts *you*. It's an ambush. The rosebush voice has been lying in wait for this opportunity. *Look what you've gone and done to Du. He* trusts *you.*

Trusts me to screw everything up, you mean. The realization presents itself like an old diary, my private thoughts misplaced and found in a box in the attic many years after the fact.

I've known this a long time, it seems. I shift uncomfortably in my seat, the unwelcome understanding coming home to roost like pigeons on a ridgepole at sunset: one at a time, each with a soft thud of inevitability. I'm cringing as I think about how we live together, thoughts I usually avoid. Of course Du never would have agreed to let me take this trip—he barely lets me go shopping on my own. It's Du who supervises the dinner menus, signs off on the gardening, consults Myrtistine on every damned little thing around the house, keeps me on his radar whenever we're at a function or even just out for drinks with another couple. No, I think, Du Sizemore doesn't trust me at all.

What's most disturbing about this knowledge is the fact that I already knew it.

More subdued now, I let Ted talk and drive, two things he really is good at. He keeps it all light and humorous, thank God, because I'm sorely distracted. After another sixty miles, we've crossed the state line and I find I'm hungry—no, ravenous—only to discover that Troy Smoot has surreptitiously nosed open Bette's bag of snickerdoodles and eaten them all, every crumb.

"It's okay," I say. Another random eating episode averted. I know I ought to feel relieved, but instead, I'm ready to hunt through the jumble on the truck's floor for anything, even just a leftover pack of Wendy's saltines. I don't think I've ever been this hungry in my life.

"You sure?" Ted asks. "I can stop."

"I've had plenty already today. I'll live."

"Not if you don't start eating," Ted says. "Seriously. You're one beautiful lady, but you're way too skinny. If you were a horse, I'd worm you. There's a truck stop at the Fernwood exit. I'm going to buy you a ham sandwich and then take you on to Jackson."

And like that I hear Starr, in the passenger seat of the BMW. *You probably have no idea how men look at you—like they want to buy you a ham sandwich, then take you home.*

Starr. All over again, I experience the gash in my utterly unfounded trust. I lose it then, bursting into loud messy sobs that seem to rip their way out of my chest. I can't stop them either because, like seeds, these tears were planted this morning in the rose garden when I gave up on the baby, they took root when Starr rubbed out the two little girls drawn in her breath on the car's window, and they've been waiting for their chance to explode into the light ever since I learned she'd abandoned me. I *trusted* her. She was my best friend once, a long time ago, but how could I have been so gullible? Tears are all I have left.

And it appears these upstart tears mean to have their way with me, and so they do, all the way to the off-ramp, all the way to the dark edge of the parking lot behind the Fernwood Travel Plaza, all the way—inevitably it seems—to Ted's arms again.

"Hey, baby," he murmurs into my hair. "Hey, now. It's going to be okay." He strokes my back, soothing me as he might a nervous horse or a worn-out child. I'm getting the front of his T-shirt wet, but I can't quit crying.

"You'll be home before you know it, sweetheart," Ted says.

I sob. "That's the worst part of this—home."

Ted tucks my head into the hollow between his neck and broad shoulder. "Well," he says lightly, "isn't that the place where they have to take you in?"

"You have no idea. You have no idea how awful it is, how awful I am. All my life, I've tried to do the right thing, but the right thing always seems to turn into the wrong thing somehow." The words pour from my mouth like a busted faucet in my rush to get it out. "If I can't get back in time tonight, everyone is going to be giving me that *look* again and I can't stand it, I can't take being a fuck-up of the highest order anymore. It's always been that way for me. Why is it so damned hard? Why am I always such a mess?"

Feeling emptied out, I come up for air at last, wiping my eyes, but Ted is warm, Ted smells wonderful. Ted feels too good for me to move back to my side of the front seat, so I rest my head on his shoulder and come closer.

He kisses the top of my head, his lips just barely brushing my hair, but I feel it. "You seem just fine to me, Annie," he says. "For what it's worth, I think you did the right thing by a friend and she let you down. You can't be responsible for the whole world, honey."

That's when I really cut loose crying. It's that word. *Responsible.*

Ted scoops me up like a load of caterwauling laundry, and I instinctively wind my arms around his neck. He opens the door, carrying me the short distance to the back seat of the truck and gently sets me down in the heap of horse blankets with Troy Smoot. Alarmed at this noisy interruption of his nap, the dog shakes himself and leaps into the front seat. I roll to my side and curl up in a miserable ball in the midst of the blankets, still warm from Troy, crying myself into hysterics. The rosebush voice, strangely on the same team as I am for once, is crying, too. Then the slick fabric of the horse blankets rustles as Ted climbs in the back, shuts the door, lies across the seat and takes me in his arms again. Ah, I breathe. That's better. Gradually the tears slow. I catch my breath while he holds me close.

"Hush, baby," Ted says softly. "I've got you." I'm quieting now, aware of his body pressed against my own. I wipe my eyes and look up at him.

"Ted?" I ask. "What are we doing?"

He sighs, shifting so that there's the barest space between us. "Getting to know each other better, I think," Ted says, his voice thoughtful. "I've been doing most of the talking so far. Tell me something about you, Annie," he says. "Tell me about something that's important to you." His hand is on my hip, just resting there, but I feel the warm weight of every finger, the solid breadth of his palm, and for the first time that I can recall, for once I come to understand. This time, in this place, I already know what's important. I know what's important to *me*.

"Not yet," I whisper. "Not yet."

This time, the kiss isn't an accident. No, and this time I slide my hand to the front of his jeans, closing around the long, hard length of him. I press my lips to the surprised groan deep in his throat. Ted pulls me closer, his breath running rough.

"Are you sure, Annie?" he says, low-voiced and hoarse.

I am.

Chapter 14

After Starr left the first time, the new year of 1964 came like a cut-off notice from the electric company.

Within the first week after the Christmas holidays, my name found itself figuring prominently in Miss Bufkin's green ledger of problem students. I missed Starr so much I couldn't bring myself to play with Lisa Treeby or any of the other, more tractable children my grandmother tried to force upon me. I was such a consummate brat because they weren't Starr: "accidentally" sitting on Lisa's Kenmore playhouse, collapsing it beyond repair (she cried), taking Laddie's Christmas money in a game of poker with the Old Maid cards where I made up the rules and so couldn't lose (he cried), cutting the real human hair off of Julie's Madame Alexander doll (she smacked me). Among many other infractions, I was so bad that everybody's parents complained and that put a stop to that. My grandmother was livid, but for once she couldn't make everybody do her bidding and have me back over to play. No, I was anathema, and the word got around.

But the weeks passed and I eventually got used to the isolation, to having no best friend. In time, the intolerable pain of missing Starr faded but, feeling obscurely vengeful and wanting to make a point, I turned again to the forbidden company of the Bad Kids. No matter how often I was punished for my part in their exploits, I sneaked, lied, and hung out with them anyway. My mother despaired of me during the dark days of that long winter.

Like all seasons, though, the winter ended. Finally summer vacation rolled around, and true to winter's promise, life had become a slow-motion disaster epic from which I seemed to learn nothing. Even so, when Joel Donahoe tried to put my eye out that June, by then I was eight years old and should have known better. Buddy Bledsoe had been shipped off to Boy Scout camp again for the summer, and so Joel obligingly filled the miscreant vacuum to become the baddest of the Bad Kids in the neighborhood. That alone should have been proof no good could come of us playing circus together in our garage during a rare, unsupervised afternoon.

"Hold still, Annie," Joel warned. He was balanced on one foot, my mother's sewing scissors in his hand cocked and poised to let fly. My back was pressed flat against the stucco wall, arms outstretched in a classic posture of a knife thrower's girl-target. Joel let fly, and the sharp point of the scissors struck my forehead just above my left eyebrow, then fell to the garage's cement floor with a clatter.

"Ow!" A warm trickle flowed into my eye. It didn't hurt yet, but I couldn't see for the blood. "Methyl Ivory," I screamed, running for the back door and the pillowed fortress of her dark arms. "Joel Donahoe put my eye out!"

"I didn't do it." Joel's yelp was already far away, past the ligustrum hedge separating our yard from Dr. Thigpen's house next door.

That summer, my mother was playing a lot of bridge. When she got home and saw the bloody Band-Aid over my left eye, she didn't wait to hear the whole story. Her face assumed that someone's-gonna-pay-for-this expression indicating the end of that someone's life. Not even stopping to take off her hat, she marched out the wide front doors in search of Joel Donahoe, stomping down the steps, and across the St. Augustine in her spike-heeled pumps, white gloves fisted, her gray silk shantung skirts billowing gun smoke. From the homeland of Methyl Ivory's vast lap, I contemplated the death of Joel Donahoe with a self-righteousness reserved only for the young and naïve. Vengeance, I was sure, would soon be mine.

Five minutes later, my mother banged back through the front door, down the long center hall, and into the kitchen, a Fury in a pillbox hat. The hem of her skirt was covered in grass stains.

"The little hooligan got away," she snapped. "Methyl Ivory! What were you doing all day? How could you let Annie play with that, that little . . . *weasel?*"

Methyl Ivory was imperturbable before my mother's wrath, but I felt her stiffen. Her voice composed, she said, "Annie s'posed to stay in the backyard, where's I can keep an eye on her, ma'am. I plenty busy cleaning this house, cooking dinner, doin' the laundery."

Sensing things were not going my way, I commenced a noisy demonstration of sniveling victimhood. Methyl Ivory gave me a discreet push, and I slid off her lap into disgrace, my bare feet coming to rest on the cool linoleum. A tear plopped wetly on my big toe.

"That's it," my mother announced in disgust. She yanked off her gloves. Rummaging in her purse, she fished out her cigarettes and fired one up with a snap of her lighter. "If it's not one thing, Mercy Anne Banks, it's another," she said, expelling smoke in a furious stream. "Before you lose an eye or end up in the back of a police car, I'm sending you to stay with

Aunt Too-Tai in the country. You've *got* to learn to be more responsible."

"But I don't want to go to Aunt Too-Tai's," I squalled. "It's boring. And she, she . . . doesn't have air-conditioning!" Rattling window units had been installed late last summer when my father had finally saved enough money to get the house—a big old Greek Revival relic—air-conditioned. This summer, we would no longer be too embarrassed about the box-fans on the floor to invite people over for cocktails. The air-conditioning seemed like an excellent reason not to be banished.

"Too bad, missy," my mother announced, looking grim. She stabbed her cigarette out in the sink. "I'll go write her a letter right this minute." Aunt Too-Tai lived so far out in the country, she didn't have a telephone either.

My summer vacation was going to be ruined.

Awaiting Aunt Too-Tai's reply, my mother made sure that I was practically chained to the rusted swing set in the backyard for the duration. Joel and the other Bad Kids leaned over the fence, daring me to climb out and join them on expeditions of thievery and random vandalism.

"We're going down to the creek," Joel taunted. The creek was an enormously attractive drainage ditch across Fortification Street, past the old garage above the railroad tracks. It was full of interesting household debris and deformed frogs: just this past spring we'd found half a dozen wriggling tadpoles with two heads. "Too bad you can't come." Joel sniggered. Then he lobbed a brown paper bag over the fence. "Here's something to play with, crybaby." I glared at him from my perch on the top of the slide.

"Joel Donahoe, I hate you," I shouted.

After the Bad Kids left, though, I slid down the scalding metal chute and ambled over to investigate the bag. It was full of dog shit, probably the product of King, Dr. Thigpen next door's German shepherd. I dropped it in the grass in my rush to report this latest infamy to Methyl Ivory. She was in the living room, watching *As the World Turns* on the black-and-white TV while she ironed my daddy's shirts.

"Methyl Ivory, Joel Donahoe threw dog shit in our backyard," I complained. "Can't I go beat him up?" I held up my fists like Cassius Clay. "I'll teach him not to be so mean."

"Don't you say shit." Methyl Ivory tested the iron with a finger-flick of water from the tall, condensation-beaded glass on the ironing board beside her. The iron hissed.

"You said it," I pointed out.

"Talk like that why you going to the country. You best stay inside till you mama get home from the bridge party." I was speechless at her indifference. How could she not understand that this salvo couldn't be ignored? If I was going to be gone for weeks this summer, who was going to defend our home and our honor? I had a vision of stinking brown bags in heaps all over the backyard. "Go on now, read one of your books," Methyl Ivory advised me.

"But Joel Donahoe—"

"That boy gone end up in the 'formatory 'stead of the work farm, he keep at it." Serenely sure of her predictions as ever, she added, "You gone have a good time with your old auntie this summer 'fore you come home and go to third grade. All kinds of chirren'd love it out there. Didn't I hear your mama say Miss Too-Tai got a horse for you to ride?"

I folded my arms and sniffed, refusing to be mollified. It wasn't a horse; it was a mule, and Aunt Too-Tai's mule, Bob, was even more ancient than she was. Besides, the whole barn area had been off-limits to me whenever the family had made the pilgrimage to Chunky to visit: my mother wanted me to keep my company clothes clean, and Daddy worried about hookworms.

At any rate, the lingering hope of appealing to my father

for relief was utterly extinguished that evening when he went outside to light the barbeque and stepped on the paper bag.

Late in the day the next Saturday afternoon, I was spying from behind Dr. Thigpen's oak tree as a dusty black Chevrolet rolled into the driveway. My great-aunt Theodosia Imogene sat in the front seat. Long before my time, my grandmother Isabelle had nicknamed her Tootie. When their mother told her to stop it, she called her little sister Too-Tai instead. Great-Grandmother Gooch had wisely let that particular dog sleep in peace, probably knowing from experience with the awful Isabelle that things could only get worse.

Aunt Too-Tai got out of the passenger side in her bib overalls and men's work shoes. She adjusted the wide-brimmed straw hat on her head and walked up the steps to the front door. Her farm man, George, stayed with the car.

I'd seen George before, of course, but I'd never heard him say anything. He was the oddest man, taller than my daddy, with long, skinny flamingo legs that seemed like they should bend backward at the knee. Unlike a flamingo, though, George was black, a black that was almost blue. His hair was a curling, steel-wool silver, but most fascinating of all was the white-veined scar twisting his full upper lip, winding in a mysterious serpentine to his left nostril. I'd imagined he'd caught it in one of the savage-looking machines piled up in my aunt's barnyard. Sidling closer to the car in shameless voyeurism, I stared at the scar while George pretended I wasn't gawking at him. Daddy lugged my little cardboard suitcase and box of books down the steps. George unfolded like a stepladder from the front seat and arranged my worldly goods in the cavernous trunk while my parents and Aunt Too-Tai discussed the terms of my exile.

"Make her wear shoes," Daddy stated. "The hog pen is awfully close to the house."

"And keep an eye on her," my mother broke in. Her eyes met mine with a fearsome promise. "You've *got* to be more responsible, Annie."

But I was already planning on making a run for it. I eyed the Chevrolet. I could steal the car. I already knew how to drive, although after I'd run the Buick into the garage last summer I hadn't been able to practice since. I was certain I could join the French Foreign Legion once I got to Africa, but ten minutes later I was fuming in the back of the Chevrolet while George drove and Aunt Too-Tai smoked all the way to Chunky, some forty miles of two-lane road from home.

After my dreadful behavior since Starr left, responsibility was a big theme that summer. Undaunted, though, on my first day of vacation I'd conducted a scientific inquiry: I put dead houseflies in the freezer ice cube trays and filled them with water so I'd have my own personal Ice Age specimens, timing the experiment with my late grandfather's gold pocket watch. When my daddy came home and went to make old-fashioneds, he discovered the watch atop a container of ice cream. Dr. Thigpen discovered the flies when he finished his old-fashioned and rattled the ice cubes to signal my dad for another round.

The summer was young, so over the course of the next week I'd gone on to set a fire in the barbeque pit with sticks from the backyard, using my mother's silver sandwich scissors to make s'mores with pilfered marshmallows; dye the Poseys' white poodle pink in a tin-tub bath infused with scarlet crepe paper; steal the entire block's mail from the boxes to play postman and, after it began to rain, leave every scrap of it—wedding invitations, bills, letters from the government, etc.—under the ligustrums. When in desperation my mother enrolled me in an unsuspecting playgroup in another, far-off neighborhood so as to keep me out of trouble, I told all the little girls it wasn't true, babies being born under piles of cabbage leaves in a gestational truck garden. Now everybody's command of the facts of life was clinically accurate thanks to my father's commitment never to lie to his child.

And concluding with the incident involving the off-limits scissors in the garage, this was all accomplished in seven days, a span of time nothing short of biblical considering the damage I'd done. Since these were the days before time-outs, I'd received seven spankings followed by seven lectures on responsibility. I should think before I acted. I should respect my parents' wish to live a peaceful life on Fairmont Street. Did I want to grow up to be a lady, or was I going to jail? Methyl Ivory's being inconvenienced wasn't mentioned at all, but she let me know about it just the same.

"Why you want to cut up, child? Don't you know I got the heart-flops?"

Summer in the country was the price of irresponsibility. I should have been reflecting on my behavior that long afternoon in the back of the Chevrolet, but the combination of Aunt Too-Tai's Pall Malls, the road, and strenuous unrepentance put me to sleep.

George must have carried me inside the house when we arrived because I woke early the next morning on a pallet beside Aunt Too-Tai's bed. I yawned and scratched, feeling grumpy as a damp cat, unwilling to get up and explore my new surroundings. The ceiling fan creaked overhead, pushing a tepid wash of air to ruffling the lace curtains, fluttering the hem of my aunt's nightdress hanging from a hook on the bedroom door. She was already risen and gone, as evidenced by her voice coming from through the open window from outside.

"Hand me that crescent wrench." A clanging racket commenced. "Dammit, hold her steady." Some large piece of machinery struggled to life with a series of barking coughs. I wandered to the window and stuck my head out into the day through the moon vine overtaking the side of the house. Aunt Too-Tai and George were beside a coffin-like, wheeled contraption containing a mess of gears, belts, and toothed cogs. The dew-covered tractor hitched to this mystery chugged blue exhaust into the brilliant eastern sky. The engine's growl covered my aunt's voice, but she was deep in a conversation with George. His hands were planted on his thin hips, George's scarred face dubious. He shook his head, and his mouth moved. My aunt leaned in to hear his reply, putting her hand on his shoulder. So George *could* talk, I thought, if he wanted to.

By the time I went to the bathroom, put on my shorts, shirt, and shoes, and scraped my thick blond hair into a messy ponytail, Aunt Too-Tai was in the kitchen. It was a long, narrow room with an old-fashioned iron stove at one end, a deep porcelain sink, a table, three chairs, and a new refrigerator.

"I'm hungry," I declared. My stomach was rumbling.

"Here," she said. Aunt Too-Tai handed me a spoon and a bowl with some dry cornflakes in it. "Milk's in the icebox."

"Where's the sugar?"

"Rots your teeth," my aunt threw over her shoulder. She was at the sink, washing her big-knuckled hands with a cake of yellow soap. "We don't keep sugar here," Aunt Too-Tai added.

Glaring at her back, straight and tall as a white-haired telephone pole, I didn't dare argue, for it had dawned on me that my aunt was no Methyl Ivory, making sugar-butter sandwiches whenever I wanted. Instead, I ate my cereal without sweetening while Aunt Too-Tai drank black coffee. She lit a cigarette, popping the match head into a bloom of light. The sharp, sweet scent of cigarette smoke reminded me of my mother, and in that moment I missed her desperately. It would be months before I'd be allowed to go home.

"We're not going to church this morning," my aunt announced without preamble. That was good. A more useless waste of time hadn't been invented, in my experience: even school was preferable to the eternity I spent squirming on St. Andrew's varnished oak pews in my Sunday dress with its scratchy petticoats.

"We're going to the garden," Aunt Too-Tai said, "before it gets too hot. The tomatoes are covered with cutworms."

The sun was well up when we stood at the edge of the garden's long rows of growing things. Our shadows, one tall and one much smaller, stretched before us in the morning. A haze of moisture lifted off the plants, soon to evaporate in the day's coming heat.

"Take off your shoes," Aunt Too-Tai said. I piled my Keds and ankle socks beside a coiled garden hose. "Here." She handed me a large glass pickle jar. "I'll pay you a nickel for every five worms you put in this jar," my aunt said, pulling on a pair of work gloves.

"A nickel?" Even in 1964, it wasn't much.

Nodding, Aunt Too-Tai parted the towering rows of tasseled sweet corn and at once vanished from view. Her voice faded as she called, "If you're thirsty, get a drink from the hose. I'll be back in about an hour." Corn stalks rustled, and I was alone except for the conversational grunts of the hogs in the nearby pen.

The dirt was cool and damp between my toes. I eyed the tomato plants with misgiving but didn't mean to ignore my instructions—not yet, anyway. Squatting beside the row, I wondered if there would be enough worms to be worthwhile. Tomatoes hung in green-striped balloons from their staked vines, and I soon discovered that hidden underneath their leaves were armies of cutworms. I held one up for a better look: the front end and the back end both had faces. The worm writhed as I dropped it in the pickle jar, coiling into a fat bud of destruction.

"That's one." I was determined to keep count. Surely by

the time I'd captured a jarful of worms, I'd have enough money to support myself when I took the Chevrolet and drove off to join the Foreign Legion. The garden was still in the hot morning, and sweat ran down the back of my checked shirt. A mockingbird called, another answered, and the verdant aroma of the tomato plants, rich and sharp as gasoline, filled my nose while a smiling breeze tickled the back of my neck. Engrossed in cutworm removal, I was fully into plans for getting to Africa and concentrating on the best way to stow away on a freighter when two big work boots appeared beside me in the dirt.

"I got fifty-nine, Aunt Too-Tai," I said. "You owe me a bunch of nickels." I looked up, squinting in the sun. The boots belonged to George. His ruined face was serious, arms in his faded denim shirt folded across his thin chest.

"Hey, Mr. George," I mumbled. I couldn't take my eyes off that scar. Maybe he would finally say something. But no, his eyes were patient as he sighed just once and glanced in the direction my aunt had taken.

"Oh—you want Aunt Too-Tai?" I asked.

He nodded.

"She went thataway." I pointed a dirty finger at the corn where a thin plume of cigarette smoke wafted. With a nod that might have been a thank-you, George disappeared between the tall, green spears.

"Did you get the spreader going?" Several rows over, my aunt's voice was faint but clear. "Just leave it behind the barn, then. We'll fill it with that moldy hay, spread the bad stuff over the south pasture after you're done with the gear box." Shrugging, I went back to work. Sixty-one, sixty-two . . . A sibilant whisper of corn shocks meant Aunt Too-Tai's return, and I clapped the lid on the pickle jar just as I finished the row.

"You done with the worms? Good." She took the glass jar from my hands. "Looks like about, oh—sixty to me."

"I got eighty." Well, it was almost that.

"Eighty, you say? That's sixteen nickels, then. Put your shoes back on and come along." My thighs aching, I stood up, but as we walked across the backyard toward the barn, a dark, sinuous shadow slung itself in rapid *S*-curves across the mown grass.

I jumped backward in instinctive fright at the snake. I was mortally afraid of snakes. In a panic, I froze, my mouth wide open and ready to holler like I'd seen Frankenstein's green-skinned monster lurching around the yard, but Aunt Too-Tai put her hand over my lips.

Almost too low to hear, she said in my ear, "Stay put now, Annie. Don't move a muscle." The shadow had coiled under the shade of a sweet gum tree, near hidden in the tall grass around the roots. My aunt slipped away from my side and let herself into the darkened doorway of the barn.

"Aunt Too-Tai!" It was a tin-whistle whisper of a scream. "Don't leave me!"

An age ticked by. Positive I would have no choice but to stand there and burn up in a fever of terror, I practically melted in relief when Aunt Too-Tai came through the barn doorway with a garden hoe. Raising a finger to her lips, she glided across the grass to the sweet gum tree, and fast as a snake herself, she raised the hoe and struck. Divots of earth flew. A meaty hunk of snake shot skyward as she reduced the snake to its component parts in unimpassioned efficiency until it was done. I was openmouthed with admiration. The snake's dispatch was the most thrilling thing I'd ever seen that wasn't on television.

"Come on to the house, Annie," Aunt Too-Tai said. She leaned the hoe against the tree trunk. "I'll get George to bury that cottonmouth."

Back inside at the kitchen table, she lit a cigarette and poured us each a glass of ice water. "Here." She handed me a twist of paper. "Put this BC Powder on the back of your tongue." I rolled my eyes like a balky horse since I was skittish of even baby aspirin and dreaded pill taking to the point of hysteria, but Aunt Too-Tai was too forceful a presence to deny. Look at what had happened to the snake.

"Why do I have to take it?" I asked plaintively. "I don't have a headache."

"Do it. It'll calm your nerves." The powder was bitter and dry, but I managed to wash it down with the cold water. My tongue burned like I'd scrubbed it with Comet. "Now you sit here and wait for that to make you feel better. I'll go find George." She hesitated and then landed an awkward pat on my shoulder. "Be a good girl and put that snake out of your mind." The screen door banged shut. "George!" she called. "Get a shovel."

Alone again, I sat on the kitchen chair, swinging my feet and drawing faces in a puddle of water on the rock-maple table, fast becoming bored, never a desirable state. My eyes lit on the pack of Pall Malls by the sink.

Smoking. I'd always wanted to try it but knew my mother would have shaken me bald-headed if she'd ever caught me. I tiptoed to the sink, shook the pack, and a lone cigarette fell on the floor. Almost without thinking, I put it in my shirt pocket—but I was definitely planning ahead when I took the matchbook.

I had just returned to my chair when Aunt Too-Tai called to me from the yard, "You can come out now." Still, I lurked on the other side of the screen door until George had finished with the last of the cottonmouth, finally screwing up my courage to edge past the sweet gum tree. I tried not to look at the blood and ran to join my aunt at the barn.

The old wooden barn was a dim, vaulted cathedral of cobwebs and dust, where ancient birds' nests festooned the crossbeams. Arrows of sunlight pierced the tin roof high overhead, falling on sawhorses, a decrepit set of harness, bald tires, a rowboat with a hole in the bottom, tools, stacks of lumber, an engine, heavy tow chains, paint cans, bundled magazines, and a thousand other discarded, wonderful things. An orange cat stretched in the shaft of light pooling on top of a mountain of hay.

"That's last season's hay crop. It's gone to mold." Aunt Too-Tai stooped to pick up a snarled length of baling twine. "It needs out of here before we get the first cutting done next week. You can handle this—you did a fine job on those worms." My aunt smiled, and her sun-faded eyes looked at me with an unusual expression. It was a moment before I recognized it as approval, an opinion I was fairly unfamiliar with, especially recently.

"You did well before, too—being so still," she said. "I bet you didn't know that if you run from a cottonmouth, it'll chase you all the way to Memphis. You were a brave girl."

Well, I had been, hadn't I? Joel Donahoe would've run off screaming for his mommy, more than likely. My aunt handed me a pitchfork taller than I was, then pushed open a big sliding door in the back of the barn, allowing the breeze to come play inside.

"Just toss that hay into the manure spreader behind the barn over here." Aunt Too-Tai gestured at the boxy machine attached to the tractor just outside the door. That machine was the manure spreader, whatever that was. "Come on back to the house after you're done, and we'll have dinner." Then she was gone, leaving me with a pile of hay higher than my head.

I got busy right away, stoutly flinging the hay through the door into the waiting manure spreader. As I struggled with the unwieldy pitchfork, dropping more hay than I picked up, I reflected on the morning's activities and discovered I enjoyed the newfound feeling of being responsible.

At home, *responsible* meant "don't do that." Here, I'd eaten cereal without sugar. I'd made sixteen nickels and saved the tomato crop single-handed. I'd helped Aunt Too-Tai kill a dangerous snake and taken bitter medicine without complaining. Now I was in charge of moldy hay removal, and it wasn't even dinnertime yet. I was in love with this feeling until about ten minutes into the project, and then the hay began to get under my shirt collar, into the waistband of my shorts. My nose itched. The cat had moved to another patch of sunlight on top of the lumber pile. She opened one eye, blinked, and went back to sleep. I deserved a break, I decided. The breeze beckoned me out behind the barn, so I dropped the pitchfork and slipped outside.

A crow lit on the steering wheel of the tractor and cocked its head, cawing once before it flapped off to the fig trees to poke holes in the ripening fruit. Off in the distance down by the pond, Bob the white mule grazed in the water-meadow amid the purple vetch and cow parsley, his switch tail busy swatting flies. Resting against the manure spreader, I contemplated the new me with satisfaction until I remembered the cigarette in my shirt pocket.

It was time to have my first smoke.

Unaccustomed to playing with fire, I used half the matchbook before I could get the thing lit. The first puff was awful, and the second one was worse. I tried to get the hang of it with another drag and broke into a coughing fit. The cigarette had lost its charm, but I carefully stubbed it out on the edge of the manure spreader and was ready to put it back in my pocket when I heard my aunt's voice.

"Annie—dinnertime!"

I forgot about saving the cigarette for later. Tossing it over my shoulder, I ran around the back of the barn to the house, suddenly starving.

Sunday dinner was on the table, a feast of vegetables in

bowls: sliced tomatoes and cucumbers, tender corn fried in bacon drippings, snap beans with bacon, stewed okra, butter beans and bacon, biscuits, and golden summer squash, also with bacon. Three desiccated pork chops looked lonely on a platter all by themselves. I seated myself, and George walked in the back door and came in the kitchen. He washed his hands and sat down at the table.

I was more than a little surprised. I'd never eaten with a colored person before. The rare times I'd seen Methyl Ivory eat at our house, she took her meals in the laundry room and used her own plate and silverware, kept in the cabinet with the box of Tide soap and the Pledge.

But George put his napkin in his lap, just like everybody always did, so I put mine in my lap, too. After my Aunt Too-Tai's perfunctory grace ("Bless this food. Amen."), I helped myself to some fried corn and a pork chop, but I couldn't take my eyes off the scar climbing George's upper lip as his jaw worked around a mouthful of butter beans.

"Please pass the salt, Annie." My aunt generously salted everything on the table. "And don't stare—it's impolite." She speared a tomato slice on her fork.

I looked down at my plate.

"Sorry," I mumbled. Sneaking a glance at George again, I marveled at his stoic mastery of the tough, dry pork chop with his knife and fork. I'd barely made a dent in mine. He wiped the scar with his napkin and broke a biscuit, raising a piece to his mouth. There was an eyeblink of knurled red gum, a twisted knot of flesh brilliant against his dark lip.

"Annie!" My aunt put her fork down. Her look was icy. "What did I just say?"

"But Aunt Too-Tai," I said, defensive, "I can't help it. What's wrong with Mr. George's mouth?" George pushed snap beans around on the plate with a hunk of biscuit.

"Mr. George has a harelip." Aunt Too-Tai looked tired.

"What's a harelip?" I couldn't imagine how George got along with a lip made of hair.

"The roof of his mouth has a hole in it. That makes it hard for him to speak or to eat, but that's no reason for you to stare." She picked up her fork again and pointed it at the blue bowl of okra. "Now pass him some of that. We'll have no more rudeness at my table."

Chastised, I passed the okra. We ate in silence, but inside I was seething. It was George's fault, surely—Aunt Too-Tai's being so unhappy with me, the ruination of my previously wonderful morning. Everything had been fine until he sat down with us, him and that scar. I spooned fried corn into my sullen mouth. It was delicious. Why did Aunt Too-Tai let him in the house, anyway? And so my thoughts went in a hateful round-song of self-pity and blame until dinner was almost done.

Perhaps it was the breeze, suddenly shifting to the south and wafting through the screen door, or maybe up until then the omnipresent aroma of smoked pork products had overlaid the smell of something burning, but my aunt's head lifted, her eyes narrowing. She sniffed the air.

"Do you smell that?" she asked, sharp and apprehensive. George stood up from the table, knocking his chair to the floor.

"You didn't say excuse me," I accused before I remembered George didn't talk.

Aunt Too-Tai jumped up. George was already halfway across the backyard, those long flamingo legs pumping in a ground-covering stride. My aunt was running down the steps before I could speak another word.

"Wait!" I called after them from the kitchen table, my mouth full of biscuit and slack with amazement. Why were they running for the barn? In a tempest of curiosity, I ran outside, too. George and Aunt Too-Tai were nowhere to be seen, but a thin blanket of smoke lay over the backyard. Through the half-open barn door the cat streaked across the grass, an orange ghost in the hazed sunlight, its tail electric in alarm. The hogs squealed and milled in their pen. My eyes smarting, I slipped through the barn door in search of my aunt.

Inside was all choking smoke, lit with an eerie glow. The manure spreader was in flames just outside the back door of the barn.

"Aunt Too-Tai?" I tripped over the pitchfork and fell to the hay-covered floor. As I struggled to my knees, a strong arm grabbed me by the back of my shirt, yanking me upward and swinging me effortlessly over a bony shoulder. My forehead bounced on the back of my aunt's overalls as she ran with me through the barn, coughing. She banged the barn door open with her hip. My chin slammed the ground when Aunt Too-Tai flung me under the sweet gum tree.

"Stay there." My aunt was already racing back to the barn. "George!" Her scream was broken with smoke. "Don't do it!" In the next instant the tractor's engine caught with a harsh growl. Coughing, gasping like a fish on a riverbank, I sucked the smoky air deep into my lungs.

"George!" Aunt Too-Tai sounded terrified.

Then, with a screech of straining gears, the tractor hove into view from around back of the barn, pulling the flaming manure spreader behind it. High on the wooden seat of the tractor, George's face was a scarred mask as he steered the tractor in a slow arc toward the pasture, down the rutted track leading away from the barn.

"George!" my aunt called. The tractor lurched onward while the fire in the manure spreader grew huge, fed by moldy hay, smoldering tires, and engine grease. George was hunched low over the steering wheel, the sleeve of his denim shirt smoking where a spark had caught. My aunt ran behind in the tall grass, calling for him to stop, but he held the tractor to its grinding track, hauling the burning manure spreader away from the barn.

George's shirtsleeve was in flames now. At the last minute he threw himself off the tractor just before the gate to the pasture and rolled when he hit the dirt, but one of the big wheels ran over his work boot before he could yank his foot out of the way. Driverless, the tractor shuddered on and knocked the old iron gate off the hinges, crushing it to rusted ruin while rambling onward into the pasture. Bob the mule galloped to the far end of the field near the pond, honking defiance as though the flaming manure spreader had been sent by Beelzebub to come and take him to hell.

"George!" Aunt Too-Tai stumbled down the path to where he was just trying to get to his feet. When she took his arm across her shoulders to help him get off the ground, George cried a wordless moan of pain. He didn't put any weight on his right foot.

Under the sweet gum, I stood up and something fell out of my shorts pocket.

The little matchbook.

I was a dead child: even Baby Jesus couldn't help me now. I closed my trembling hand on the matchbook and stuffed it deep in my pocket. My aunt and George were almost to the backyard, and the hogs were shrieking and trying to climb out of their pen. Down in the pasture the manure spreader was a bonfire, the tractor smoking now, too. Around it a field of flames wavered glass-blue on a black plain of ash, but the barn was safe and the fire would eventually burn itself out in the water-meadow. My great-aunt and George limped past me on their way to the back door, smoke-begrimed and exhausted, and I burst into tears.

* * *

In the kitchen, Aunt Too-Tai took care of George.

She cut what was left of the denim shirt off him, washing and salving the burn. George's arm was spalled and blackened, the skin raw, the smell sickening, like nothing I'd ever known. I stood in the corner by the icebox, still crying, and tried not to draw attention. After dosing him with a BC Powder, Aunt Too-Tai helped George out to the Chevrolet and drove forty miles back to Jackson, to the closest hospital that would treat Negroes. This time, I rode in the front. George lay across the back seat, his broken ankle on a bed pillow, cradling his burned arm across his undershirt and apart from that solitary cry he never made a sound. When we got to the University Hospital, my aunt and I sat in the colored waiting room with George until a harried resident came, put him in a wheelchair, and took him away.

Deep in the pocket of my shorts, I clutched the matchbook in my sweaty palm. *You must be more responsible, Annie.* Oh, a great weight of responsible descended with giant, thundering treads on my soul until I thought I would suffocate with it. All that long Sunday night in the waiting room, my aunt didn't call my parents. She never accused me of having set the manure spreader on fire. She didn't have to, for the cast of her mouth and the fact she wouldn't look at me buried me deep in the pit of responsible. Unable to bear her silence, I pretended to read a *National Geographic* while Aunt Too-Tai watched the big double doors for George to come out. When he did—on crutches, white gauze swathing his dark arm—we drove back to the farm in Monday's dawn.

George, Aunt Too-Tai—they were responsible for each other, and I was responsible for a burned manure spreader, a dead tractor, and the new scar George would wear for the rest of his life, the limp he would have until the day he died.

I spent the rest of that summer in Aunt Too-Tai's gloomy

parlor on the spavined sofa, reading books she would hand me wordlessly before she went out to work on her farm, without the tractor and single-handed until George could come back. I read the Bible mostly, but also several severe, old-fashioned books about heedless children who came to spectacularly dreadful ends. When we had exhausted these instructional tracts, she told me to move on to the antediluvian set of encyclopedias for a little light reading. The day I got to the *O* volume, at last I was allowed outside and given various menial chores—but only under her watchful eye. Aunt Too-Tai gave up smoking.

Near the end of my visit we had a talk, Aunt Too-Tai and I. It would be time for me to return home soon, and we'd never discussed the events of that day. I had to find out if she'd forgiven me, as well as whether she was going to tell my mother.

It was late, I remember, and the air in the house was sleeping off the day's heat as though the relentless sun had beaten it half to death. Taking a deep breath to fortify myself, I knocked on the door to the room that Aunt Too-Tai and I had shared all that summer.

"Come in," she called. Wearing her old housecoat, Aunt Too-Tai was sitting on her bed and had just finishing brushing her iron-gray hair in front of her pier glass. Her faded blue eyes met mine in the mirror. "What is it?"

"I'm sorry," I muttered, dropping my gaze. "I'm so sorry about Mr. George. I didn't mean to do it."

Turning from the long mirror, Aunt Too-Tai patted the bed, inviting me to sit down on it beside her. "It's a terrible thing, Annie—doing something you know you can never take back. I know you're sorry, child."

I swallowed hard. "Are you going to tell my mother?"

Her face was grave. "Do I need to? I have a feeling that you've already learned an important lesson, maybe the most important lesson you'll ever learn. No matter how sorry we are, we still have to take responsibility for what we do. Forever. I don't think you'll forget it, will you?"

"No, ma'am." I shook my head. "But it's hard, Aunt Too-Tai." My chest burned, on fire with the longing to say something, anything, to make this right between us. I didn't realize then that Aunt Too-Tai had already forgiven me, that it would be many years before I'd forgive myself. "It's *real* hard." And it still is.

Aunt Too-Tai smiled ruefully and smoothed the hair on my bowed head. "I know, child. That part never goes away, no matter how old you get."

Later on that last week at the farm, George came back to work, but he wasn't able to get a full day in yet. I brought him a glass of ice water where he sat in the shade of the sweet gum tree, mending some arcane piece of machinery. He nodded his thanks as I approached.

"Here you go, Mr. George," I said politely, and ran to rejoin my aunt in the garden. We were picking the tail end of the pole bean crop, and she was counting on my help.

"Pay attention to me now, Annie," she said. Though my bucket was heavy and my fingers were tired, by then I knew better than to do anything but keep on picking pole beans and listen. Responsibility, Aunt Too-Tai said, is a ladder. We move up, we move down, and sometimes we miss a rung and swing out into the void, but the ladder is forgivingly endless. I was young, she said. Don't worry, she said. I'd have many chances at that ladder. She set her bucket down in the dirt and gave me a hug.

I still have the book of matches.

CHAPTER 15

"I still have the book of matches."

"Really?"

"I've always kept it in the bottom of my jewelry box, like a kind of . . . keepsake, you know?"

The truck's windows are fogged to opacity, and Troy Smoot is curled around my bare feet like a snoring fur space heater. He jumped over into the back seat a while ago and laid claim to that end of the blankets, although I didn't notice him right away, being too caught up in my story about that summer spent down on Aunt Too-Tai's farm. It's warm here in the truck, wrapped in Ted's arms, pressed skin-to-skin against his smooth chest, so different from Du's heavy pelt of hair. I never knew horse blankets could be so comfortable, even though they still smell faintly of stable and laundry detergent.

Ted's been propped on one elbow, listening to me. In the grainy half-light of the truck stop's distant arc lamps, his face is thoughtful. I run my fingertip along his stubbled jaw, tracing the line of his generous mouth.

"Tell me about that matchbook, what it means to you," he says.

I think for a long moment, and just like always, I'm right back under the sweet gum tree in Aunt Too-Tai's yard. Like always, I can still smell the smoke, hear the hogs screaming. I can see George and my great-aunt stumbling away from the burning pasture. I still feel the terrible weight falling upon my eight-year-old shoulders, the near-adult knowing that like Cain, I was indeed cursed and now would always bear the mark even if I tried to be good for the rest of my life.

"It reminds me that the shit you do comes with consequences," I say finally. "And that sometimes other people end up paying those consequences. So I try, God knows I try, to do the right thing, but sometimes—okay, a lot of the time—my best intentions amount to being irresponsible instead. Like driving Starr to New Orleans. Oh, no question about it, I knew up front it wasn't the *responsible* thing to do. I mean, *responsible* would've wished her good luck, walked out of that tacky condo, and gone to my husband's partners' dinner, but I couldn't abandon her because it wouldn't have been right. She had no one, Ted. And I knew for sure that *responsible* would've left the Treebys' dog in the elevator, but that shit was so wrong I had to do something about it."

"And," I say, looking up to meet the interest in Ted's dark eyes, "*responsible* certainly wouldn't have made love with a near-stranger. At a truck stop in the middle of the night. In the back seat of a pickup truck."

Ted laughs, stroking my bare shoulder. "Not so strange anymore, but I'm definitely with you on the innocent bystander thing, baby." His lips brush the side of my neck, a sweet wandering along my collarbone. He kisses the hollow at the base of my throat, murmuring, "You never want to hurt the innocent bystanders."

"So much of the time, the responsible thing doesn't feel like the *right* thing and I can't always tell the difference. It's like, oh, that talent some people have for finding water with a stick, whatever that's called. If there's ever a way, I'll find me some trouble and jump right into it."

Ted yawns. "Well, I don't think *this* was trouble," he says. "I'd call it damned incredible." He gathers me to himself, holding me closer. "You cold?"

"No," I say. "What time is it?" I lift my wrist to look at my watch but can't make it out. It doesn't matter: whatever o'clock it is, it's late and I need to get home.

And I need time to understand what I've just done. Like so much of my experience, having made love with Ted *feels* right, but—based on my track record to date—this may turn out to be as destructive as what my grandmother used to call the War for Southern Independence. Still, no matter how I look at it, I can't make myself believe that this wasn't a good thing, so long as no one finds out. No, not even the rosebush voice can make me believe that.

Ted suddenly rolls over onto his back with me in his arms, and now I'm on top of him, looking down into those whiskey-brown eyes. "You still want to go to Jackson?" he asks, smiling his lovely smile up at me. "Can't I convince you to turn around and head back to New Orleans with me?"

"Oh, Ted—awful as it is, Jackson's my home," I answer, trying to keep it light. "Like you said, it's where they have to take you in."

His arms around my waist, Ted's quiet for a moment, looking directly into my eyes with unsettling intensity. "So what was this?" He doesn't sound angry, I think, just as though he wants this one thing to be really clear between us. If I could make it that way, I would, but to me, what happened tonight was as profound as a parable: self-evident and bound to be diminished by explanations. Besides, here in the back seat of this truck, questions can be dangerous things, and then Ted goes and asks another one.

"Was this a . . . fling, something you do when you decide you need a little excitement in your life?" He doesn't sound happy.

"No!" I press my forehead on his chest, unable to look at him. "It was a very big deal. Lord, Ted—you're only the second man I've been with in my whole life. Hell, I don't even *flirt*. In fact, I'm always trying to cut way back on excitement."

Ted appears to think on this. "Okay," he says at last. "I guess I get that. Sort of."

I've never been much for rationalizing. I believe actions stand or fall on their own merits—mine usually falling—but at this moment I badly want to tell Ted something he wants to hear. There are women in this world so good at smoothing things over that I'm in awe of them, but since I've always been really bad at smoothing, I can only keep my mouth shut and hope: please, don't let me mess this up, too.

"You going to tell your husband?" Ted plays with a strand of my hair, slipping the heavy platinum strands through his fingers. He asks as though it's a casual question, but underneath that I hear something more. I'm scared of something more. There's only one answer I can give in any case.

"No."

Reluctantly, I roll off him, sit up, and hunt for the black dress. It's somehow ended up in the front seat and is covered in dog hair, Troy Smoot having used it for a bed when he was exiled from the back seat. With difficulty I struggle into it, remembering ruefully that it comes off a lot easier than it goes on. Where are the rest of my clothes? I can't find my underwear to save my life.

Ted has pulled on his jeans and cowboy boots and is hunting underneath the seats and between the horse blankets for my panties. "I can't find them," he says after a pretty thorough search. It's as though they've returned to the underwear mother ship with all the odd socks, but I've already got too much on my mind to obsess about panties. Offering Ted his T-shirt wordlessly, I clamber into the front seat. He pulls the white cotton over his head before he climbs into the front seat with me and gets behind the wheel.

"Why not?" he asks, slipping the key into the ignition, his voice neutral.

I know exactly what he's talking about. Telling Du. I pull on my boots while I'm thinking about how to answer him. "Because I'm not going to leave him," I say, deciding that brutal honesty is best. "Because this was between you and me, just us. Du and me, we're . . . used to each other, and I couldn't, really couldn't, live in Jackson without being married to him."

"You mean you're afraid he'd leave you?"

I think this unsettling possibility over. "There's that," I say eventually. "For one thing, for years everyone's been expecting Du to get fed up and walk out on me. My mother would literally die of shame. And I'm trying to be responsible here. Telling Du would do a lot of unnecessary damage, the kind that takes a lifetime to mend, if ever. He always forgives me, you see, and I, I . . . just can't do it."

I can't set my marriage on fire and expect Du to get over *that.*

But have I already done damage here tonight, with Ted? Surely not. My own impulsive actions aside, I'm not about to try to fathom Ted's reasons. And anyway, aren't men supposed to want uncomplicated sex more than they want a bottomless beer keg and fifty-two weeks of football? Back at the Chi Omega house that was the gospel, all of us knew it by heart, and with the exception of my father none of the men of my admittedly limited experience have seemed to think anything different.

My explanation falls into silence. Ted doesn't say anything

more, but his jaw tightens. With a sigh I'm not even sure I heard, he turns the key in the ignition and the big diesel engine fires up immediately.

I guess there's nothing left to explain.

It's a long eighty-five miles from the truck stop to Jackson.

Except for directions, Ted and I exchange very little real conversation. The more time I put between me and the Fernwood Travel Plaza, the more I'm sure what happened there probably wasn't one of my best ideas, and I don't think I can blame it all on the dope. Even the dog seems subdued. He's coiled beside me on the front seat, his nose on his paws, as though wishing his adventure could last longer.

I haven't thought about what to do with Troy either. Should I try to get him adopted into a good home, a good home far away from Jackson—somewhere out of state like, say, Manitoba? Should I threaten Jerome Treeby with a visit from the Ladies' League SPCA volunteers? They're always swooping in like World War II fighter pilots when it comes to animals in distress. Or should I just keep him myself?

Should I tell Du?

The enormity of the last fifteen hours is starting to sink in. I'm not the same Annie Sizemore who blew into Maison-Dit yesterday on the hunt for a cocktail dress. Hell, I'm not even the same woman who lied to her husband and drove to New Orleans in the middle of the night. Can I just slip inside my house tonight and pretend that none of this ever happened?

Should I tell Du?

Of course not, the rosebush voice says crossly. My watch says it's 5:20. I know that soon the dark will be lifting, the dawn a pale, ice-white rind on the horizon. Soon, I'll be sneaking into my own home, changing into my nightgown. Before Du wakes up, I'll be lying in bed, trying to figure out how to explain my missing car—God knows where Starr left it—and my new acquaintance Troy Smoot. I can't say a word to him about Ted and Starr, not if I don't want to blow a gaping hole below my own waterline. No, if all goes according to plan, this night will soon become a memory, I remind myself, a memory that belongs to me alone.

But how, I wonder, will that memory fit into the tired narrative of Annie Sizemore, the spoiled, aging child with the irresponsible streak? And what about the change I can feel inside me like an underground river, its current carving deep into bedrock? How will I feel about this next year? What about five years from now when I'm forty, childless, perhaps still balanced on the high-tension wire between what I really am and who everyone thinks I ought to be?

All these thoughts run on a treadmill in my head, and then, too soon, just as dawn purples the east, we turn into the gates of the tall iron fence that protects my paranoid neighborhood from all the undesirables plotting to gain entrance. The massive, dusty pickup rolls alongside the parked Mercedes and minivans like a professional wrestler through a day spa, rumbling past the manicured, frost-leavened lawns and sprawling, too-big houses. Before we get to the corner, I ask Ted to stop and let me out.

"I need to walk home from here," I say, knowing how it sounds but unable to think of a better way to say it. I may not have my keys, but I can sneak in anyway: there's a door key taped inside the mailbox, and Du's such a heavy sleeper. The truck idles on the street, diesel exhaust a dense white fog in the frozen air. I turn to Ted before I open the door.

"There's no way I can thank you enough." So, wanting to make this as right as I can, I say with a tentative smile, "Bette said it—you're one of the good guys."

He doesn't reply and I want to slide across the truck's bench seat to touch his face, to tell him I'll never forget him, never. Instead, Ted reaches over and ruffles the fur behind Troy

Smoot's ears. "Be good," he says to the dog. "Take care of her." Stung, I shrug out of the blue jean jacket and try to hand it to him.

Ted looks at the jacket. He looks at me. "Keep it," he says briefly. "I don't want you to be cold."

I bite my lip. "Thank you." The dawn light is powder-pale and bitter cold, a snappish cold assaulting my bare legs and face as soon as I open the door to the truck. Now I really miss my underwear. "Come on, Troy," I say to the dog. The little terrier springs out and onto the sidewalk with me, nose twitching and on the alert for matters needing his immediate attention.

I don't want Ted and me to part like this. "Hey," I say with my hand on the door, teeth already chattering. "Good luck this afternoon. At the races, I mean."

"Thanks." Without a glance in my direction, Ted's eyes look straight ahead through the windshield. "Girl," he says, "you burn like butane—clean, fast, and too bright to look at. You've messed up my head like high-octane coke. Go on home now."

No one has ever said a thing like this to me before in my life.

Not trusting myself with another word, I shut the door. I know Ted's watching me walk away from him, but I can't look back, I can't. Troy trots beside me on his leash made of hay rope, our breath icy egret plumes in the cold. We're at the corner when behind me I hear the truck turning around in a neighbor's driveway, then the quiet roar of its diesel engine drawing away.

Then it's gone.

There's a police car in front of my house.

My mother's Lincoln—a fastidiously maintained relic the color of dyed ranch mink she's driven for the past twenty years—is parked halfway on the lawn, as though the car hadn't stopped moving before she jumped out of it. The cold burns my lungs when I gasp at the sight, my boots planted to the brick walk. There's going to be no sneaking into the house now. Impulsively, I turn and look back over my shoulder, but Ted's truck is, of course, nowhere to be seen. A lone crow wings high overhead in the pitiless light of early, early morning, cawing *this way* to the rest of the flock. With the sincere dedication of a housebound dog who's not used to being outdoors, Troy pulls on his rope, barking at the bird.

"Hush up, Troy."

No running, Annie. This time's going to be bad, very bad. Maybe the worst yet, but where else do I have to go? Possibilities flood my mind—Memphis? Atlanta? Angkor Wat?

I'll have to pray that they take me in. So even though I'm shaking with the cold and the knowledge that I'm in serious trouble, I square my shoulders in Ted's jacket and tighten my grip on Troy's hay rope. Climbing the sweeping front steps to the columned porch, I discover the front door with its heavy brass knob isn't shut all the way. I slip inside, feeling as though I'm wearing an old-fashioned diving suit—lead-footed, cut off from the world above with all its air and light. At least it's warm inside the house. Troy's nails click briskly on the travertine floor as we tiptoe through the foyer.

Raised voices are coming from the living room, Du's heavy baritone drawl louder than them all.

"Cut the effin' *crap*. What's this forty-eight hours shit? You can't tell me my wife isn't a missing person!" he bellows. I wince. My mother murmurs something I can't make out before he responds angrily, "She's s'posed to be in bed, but she's not. She's gone. That makes her a got-damn missing person!"

Like a coward, I peek into the living room first. Two cops in blue uniforms—one short and ferret-faced and the other the size of a small asteroid—are parked in front of the fieldstone fireplace, my most recent portrait simpering above their heads. Like the cops have heard this same story one too many times, their body language radiates a skeptical professionalism, while my mother is slumped on the Danish linen sofa Du picked out last year, a handkerchief to her eyes. Wearing his bathrobe and slippers, my husband paces around the grand piano neither one of us knows how to play, looking like he just fell out of bed, with the back of his hair standing up in disordered spikes. Du's face is as red as I've ever seen it: he always gets mad when he's scared. Gulping past the trepidation I feel in my chest like a hot rock, I force myself to walk in the big double doorway to the living room. I clear my throat.

"Hey, y'all," I manage, my voice faint. "I'm home."

I have never wished for a pair of underwear more in my life.

"Annie!" Du's jaw drops, a look of bafflement crossing his crimson face, as though I'm an inappropriately dressed ghost of myself. I don't think he even sees the dog at my feet.

My mother's face is the pure white of paper, of snowshoe hares, of freshly laundered sheets. "Annie!" she exclaims in a low voice, getting up from the sofa.

"Where the *hail* you been?" Du crosses the football-field-sized Tabriz rug in about two furious strides, his bathrobe flapping. "Do you know how got-damn crazy I've been? You stop to think about that, huh?" he says. His mouth twisted, he grabs my shoulders in Ted's jacket and shakes me like Troy would shake a rat. "But you don't ever stop to think, do you?"

Christ, I've never seen him this mad before. What have I done?

"Du!" I squeak. For the first time in our years together, I'm scared of what he might do to me. At my feet, Troy Smoot's hackles lift like a little hedgehog's, a miniature growl thrumming in his barrel chest.

My poor mother's mouth is a shocked *O*. "Duane . . ." she begins, but the ferret-faced cop cuts her off.

"Mr. Sizemore, I know you want to get a handle on your temper." His tone is calm, but this pair of Jackson's finest is on the alert now, ready to run my husband in for getting physical with his wayward wife—even though Du would cut off his own arm before he'd ever hit me. I think. Du drops his hands from my shoulders, clenching them at his sides, and, freed, I find my voice at last.

"Honey, I'm so sorry." Gripping Troy's leash as though it were a lifeline in that midnight fire at sea I'm always saying I'd rather be in, I drop my eyes in shame, looking down at the pattern of the rug.

"And your mother!" Du's tone is like a stranger's, heavy with contempt. "I called her at four this morning when I went to look in on you, saw you weren't in bed—just a pile of fucking pillows. You could have given her a heart attack."

My mother speaks up at that. "There's nothing wrong with my heart, Duane Sizemore," she says. "We all need to calm down, now that we know Annie's safe." Her eyes are a red-rimmed, steely green, her backbone ramrod straight. Silence fills the big, overdecorated room. Du turns away from me to the officers in his house.

"Well," he says, stiff as a length of stove wood, "y'all can see she's home now. Sorry to have called you out for a false alarm."

The asteroid-sized cop closes his notebook. "Happens more often than you think, Mr. Sizemore," he says cheerfully. "We'll be on our way now. Y'all have a happy Thanksgiving."

That's guaranteed not to happen in this house, but I say anyway, "And the same to you, officers. I'm sorry again about the mix-up."

Du walks the cops to the front door, doing his best to look like he's got this situation under control. There's a low-voiced exchange outside on the porch I can't quite hear, but from the cops' guffaws I gather his good-ole-boy instincts are coming through in the clutch.

My mother crosses the room and folds me into her thin arms. Dropping Troy's hay rope so I can hug her back, I'm aware of her ribs beneath my hands, frail as swallowtail butterfly wings under her woolen dress.

"I'm so sorry," I whisper into her shoulder. "I shouldn't have worried you."

"Oh, Annie," she sighs. "What have you gone and done now?"

My throat closes around any words I might have spoken when Du stalks back into the living room, his footsteps loud as the banging of my heart. I move away from my mother's side, wondering if my marriage, the life I left behind yesterday, will survive this Thanksgiving Day.

"I'm gonna ask you one more time," Du says, his voice cold and distant as the surface of the moon. "Where you been? And where the hail did that *dog* come from?" Troy's tail is erect and quivering, his expression wary, but he holds his ground.

Taking courage from the dog, I walk across the acre of carpet toward my husband, and with every step I feel the rosebush voice howling inside me. I choose the easy question first.

"He's a rescue," I tell him, my voice shaking. "I, I found him in an elevator."

Du snorts in disgust. "I mean it. Where. You. Been." I peek at him. He folds his arms, eyes narrowed to coin slots. I look down at his fleece slippers, away from the mask of rage on Du's normally amiable face.

Here I am again.

It's time to grovel. I'm literally being called on the carpet, an all too familiar experience. For more times than I can count, Du's spoken to me as though I were a disobedient child, but this is the first time in thirteen years of marriage he's been so angry he doesn't sound like he wants to forgive me. Like always, I can't speak up because I don't know what to say, how to justify the unjustifiable.

And then, with a jolt of self-awareness like a thrown breaker, I'm amazed to discover I'm mortally tired of this. I'm sick to my soul of the carpet and my usual place on it. I'll be damned if I can stand living like this anymore, always wrong, always apologizing. For better or for worse, this is me.

I lift my chin, tilt my head back, and look my husband in the eye, defiant. "I was helping a friend."

"Which friend?" Du demands. "Where were you all night, dressed like a damned slut?"

I'm not turning back from this. If I'm going to be damned, let me be damned for the truth—at least, the parts of the truth I can tell him.

"Starr Dukes is my oldest friend, my best friend since I was seven years old. She needed a ride to New Orleans, and I drove her." With every word, I know I'm not wrong. Not this time, not about *this*. "Before you ask, I didn't tell you because I knew you'd say I couldn't do it since she's Bobby Shapley's pregnant girlfriend, the one everybody's been talking about. Starr didn't have another soul in the world to help her. It was the right thing to do, and I did it."

In this room, among the carefully curated furniture and artwork, the outward and visible manifestations of Du's success, my explanation falls like a dead bomb: nobody wants to pick it up because it might go off.

Du's blank-faced, his eyes dull. He slumps, and his big, meaty shoulders collapse inward as though he's taken a body blow from the heavyweight champion of the world. When he finally speaks, he says heavily, "You thoughtless bitch. Bobby's pregnant girlfriend. You helped that little whore, and now I'm going to have to deal with the shit that's gonna come down. *Goddamn* you, Annie. The Judge will see me tossed out of the firm and doing wills for niggers when he hears about this." Blindly, Du turns and stumbles away from me, his hands in his hair. I can only watch him leaving the living room, crossing the foyer, taking the stairs to the second floor.

"It's too much. I can't take this shit anymore. I'm gonna pack me a bag, go somewheres else and think things over." Du's voice dwindles with his footsteps, and then I hear a door quietly shutting upstairs. My mother's tired face is oblique, unreadable, but she says nothing.

I should go after him.

But I don't.

My mother and I are outside down by the rose garden, letting Troy Smoot run around in the backyard. Off the hay rope, the dog's hurling himself across the frosted brown grass like a manic Frisbee, peeing on the lawn furniture and chasing imaginary rabbits through the bushes.

The BMW turns out to be parked in the garage, the keys in the ignition. On the front seat I found my purse and parka, its pocket still stuffed with hundred-dollar bills. It's something of a relief that now I don't have to remember Starr as a thief but as an inconsiderate, lying, ex-best friend instead. I can imagine Du thought the worst after he discovered the car, after he'd found I wasn't in the house. Actually, I can't imagine what he thought and I'm not sure I want to try.

My mother's bundled up in her old mink, sitting on the cement bench beside the denuded rosebushes and smoking a cigarette. She offers me one from her pack.

As I light it, she surprises me by asking, "Where'd you get the dress? It's not your usual style."

So grateful for being able to smoke again, without thinking I say, "Maison-Dit."

She takes a ladylike drag on her Parliament. "Somehow I can't see Dolly selling it to you. And I doubt the jacket came from there." The dog sniffs inquisitively at one of the rosebushes, the Peace hybrid tea, scoping out his new surroundings. My mother smiles. "I like him," she says.

"He's a sweetheart of a dog," I say absently, wondering how I'm going to explain that I stole Troy Smoot from that perverted cheapskate Jerome Treeby. "I guess he's mine now."

"Not the dog," my mother says. "I meant the man who loaned that jacket to you—he must have been worried you'd be cold." My mouth falls open at this. She stands up and smoothes my hair behind my ear. "It's been the most dismal fall," she says, "far too chilly for Thanksgiving."

"I love you," I say, my voice breaking. "I'm sorry I did this to you, to Du."

"Mercy Anne," she says, "Duane's a grown man. He can take care of himself. And if you wanted to help Starr, I'm glad you did—although it would've been better to have told him what your plans were. He really was beside himself when he called me."

"But I knew Du wouldn't let me even have *coffee* with her. I couldn't exactly tell him I was driving Starr to New Orleans to get money for a lawyer so she could take on the Shapleys. Besides, the whole damned thing was a terrible idea, a waste of time, not worth what I may have lost here today." I bite my lip and look away. "She just . . . left me."

My mother mashes her cigarette out on the cement bench and asks casually, "How did it go so wrong between you and Starr?"

So I tell her about Starr's predicament, about her trouble with the Judge, her inexplicable decision to get back together with Bobby, how she stranded me in New Orleans. I give her an abbreviated version of how I got home, too, leaving out the truck stop part. Even now, the memories of Starr's betrayal, of Ted's face as I left him, tear through my heart like a dull knife cutting a ripe tomato.

"And so it was all for nothing," I say when I've finished. I stub my cigarette out on the sole of my boot. "I should have known Starr would act like that. It was a, a . . . trashy thing to do, just like what everyone used to say about her." I gulp, remembering my husband's reaction. "And Du's so *angry*."

My mother's mouth tightens. "That's ridiculous. I can only imagine what it's been like for you," she says. "Duane Sizemore has always meant to keep you on a pretty short leash. I could have told him that taking such a heavy-handed approach would end up, well, much the way it has." She points at Troy Smoot, who's digging in the rose bed, scattering the pine-straw mulch with furious energy. "Isn't that the Treebys' dog?"

"Yes," I confess.

"Good for you. Someone should have taken that poor thing away from Jerome a long time ago. I almost stole him myself once."

At this astounding information, I have to sit down on the cold cement bench next to her, remembering right away I really ought to go inside and put on some underwear. That's why I don't notice that the dog has unearthed a small pile of dusty EPT tests and has dropped them beside my boots like he's sharing a kill. My mother and I seem to see them at the same time.

"What's this?" she asks. She reaches down, picking up one of the wands.

Of course. Let the unraveling of my lies continue. Why ever not?

"Oh, Annie." Shaking her head, my mother's voice is sorrowful. "Why have you *buried*"—she gestures at the pregnancy tests on the ground with an air of despair—"all this? Why didn't you tell me? I'd assumed that you and Duane had decided you didn't want children after all."

Too tired to cry, I shake my head and look away, hopelessly sliding the rough length of Troy's hay rope through my fingers.

"I buried them so no one, especially not *you,* would know I was still trying to have a baby," I say with a short laugh, arid as the dirt of the rose bed. "I gave that up for good yesterday morning. After nearly thirteen years, I've finally had enough. I'm a failure at getting pregnant, just like I'm a failure at everything else."

"Darling," my mother says. "You're not a failure, not really."

"No?" I drop the EPT test on the ground. "Look, you don't have to be kind to me. I know it's true. All those goody two-shoes over at the Ladies' League act like I'm the last person on earth they want on that stupid committee, and I can't really blame them because I'm positive rocking those babies just gives them gas. Oh, and at the firm? The other partners' wives always stop talking when I come in the room and give me these *looks,* like I just ripped open a big bag of ripe garbage and dumped it on the carpet. And . . . and it seems like Du's done with me, so I guess it's sort of a blessing, me not being pregnant. A baby would only make this situation even more complicated."

I still can't believe it: after thirteen years of a maybe-not-so-bad marriage, Du's gone and perhaps not ever coming back. He left without knowing the worst of it. The hell of it is, he left because of *Starr.* Coiling the hay rope and putting it in the jean jacket's pocket, I consider the EPT tests piled like grimy finger bones on the dead grass. There're fifteen of them so far, and Troy's still digging.

"I swear to God," I mutter hopelessly. "It's always been like there was some big-ass, super-important rule book that got passed around, only I was out of town the day everybody else read it." I put my face in my hands, rubbing my eyes, gritty from lack of sleep. "And don't try to tell me I haven't been this crashing disappointment to you all my life. I already know." My joints protesting, I get up off the cement bench, wrapping Ted's jacket closer around me. It smells like him. The heady scents of night and leather and the faintest trace of cologne bring me almost, unaccountably, to tears.

My mother takes my hand. "Come on," she says. "Come with me to the house. I'm sure that dog needs to eat, even if you won't. I'm so cold I feel like a freezer-burned catfish."

"Okay," I say. She's right: her hand is like ice in mine. "I'll make coffee, and we can have some pumpkin pie, at least. Oh, and I should call Aunt Too-Tai to tell her Thanksgiving's off."

"Besides, there're some things I need to tell you."

Curious now, I whistle to the dog. We really should go back inside before we all catch pneumonia. The three of us walk across the lawn to the flagstone terrace together, silent, my mother and I thinking our own thoughts. Reaching the back steps, I open the screen door to go into the kitchen.

"I didn't love your father, you know," my mother says, looking back over her shoulder at the rose garden, shivering. "Not at first."

CHAPTER 16

"Oh, Annie," my mother begins, "your father was the bright, golden dream of a near-destitute girl growing up in Lannette, Georgia. That was me." With a sigh, she then falls silent.

We're sitting at the kitchen table, cups of steaming coffee in front of us. After all the coffee I've had in the last twenty-four hours, my cup is supremely unenticing, but I take a sip anyway. My eyes are burning with fatigue, but I need to hear this.

"You've never talked about your childhood very much," I say. "I always wondered."

She nods. "It's not hard to understand why. God knows, I've never wanted to call attention to my upbringing. You see, my parents worked in the West Point Pepperell towel mills—lint-heads, they were called. My father, a Black Irish immigrant from County Mayo, could only find work in the bleachery, and my mother was a folder on the third shift. We were tenants in the mill houses then, cheap little four-squares with no insulation but only the bare clapboard siding between us and the weather. The winter wind whistled into those cramped and drafty rooms like a southbound freight, so my father used to stuff old newspapers into the leaking window frames, but the wind found its way inside anyhow. In the wild ravine behind those houses, the mill creek ran gray and greasy with foam curds of soap and factory chemicals. My father's hands were scarred a permanent fish-belly white from the bleach, and my mother coughed all night long, a racking cough so labored that it woke me up in the dark. In those houses, the walls were thin as glass, and you could see the ground through the holes in the floors."

She takes a sip of her own coffee, watching me over the rim of her cup as if to see how I'm taking this.

Thanks to my Grandmother Banks's relentless, corrosive disdain for my mother, I always knew she came from nothing much, but this is a revelation. I mean, I never knew it was that bad. After a quiet moment, my mother goes on.

"It was a hard life. Many times, Annie, we didn't have much to eat, but my parents made sure that I had oranges, milk, and meat while they'd make do with bacon drippings on stale bread. Mother lined their own shoes with cardboard when the soles wore out, but every fall she always saw to it that I had a new pair of sturdy oxfords for school. I was a lonely, studious high school senior when my parents died within six months of each other. My father went in a machinery accident at the mill, and my mother from the emphysema—brown lung, the mill workers called it—that she'd gotten from breathing in all that lint, year after year."

"How old were you?" I ask.

She looks away. "Eighteen, just two months shy of graduating. Far away in North Carolina, all of my mother's people had turned their backs on her when she'd married a bog-trot Irishman, and my father's kinfolk were only mysterious names in the family Bible, so when I had to quit the mill house after they died, I rented a miserable little room in town with the hundred dollars Mother had managed to leave me.

"But you should know that although I was an only child, I wasn't left completely alone in the world. The women at the Reform Methodist church in the next valley got together and held pancake suppers, paper drives, and bake sales to raise money for me. Those good women. They must have known that after my mother passed I would have died, too, if I could. I only knew I wanted out of Lannette. The memories of my parents were too strong there."

This explains so much—the thundering silence about my maternal grandparents, their utter absence from my life. I've always known they died young, but not how miserably they died, how alone my mother had been. Having to rely upon the kindness of strangers must have galled like acid.

"But I thought you and Daddy met at Tulane, where you were both in school," I begin. "How . . ."

My mother looks out the window and compresses her lips. "I'm getting there. My scholarship from Newcomb College came through three days after we buried my mother. I worked in the mill myself all that summer, but in the fall, when I set my cardboard suitcase on the gleaming wooden floor of my new dorm room in New Orleans, I couldn't believe it. I'd never lived anywhere as fine as that small, unassuming space. There was a clean, bare mattress on the iron bed frame waiting for the hand-pieced quilt my mother had sewn from her old dresses, a sunny window overlooking the college's front lawn. I had my very own desk, too.

"I'd be sharing the closet, though. My roommate's wardrobe was already hanging there, and my clothes, so proudly made by the churchwomen, were shabby things compared to her beautiful frocks, walking dresses, and suits on scented, padded hangers. She had hats and pumps, court shoes and handbags, and the most darling matched set of luggage—caramel-colored leather covered with luxury liner stickers. Her bed was made up with lovely pink sheets and a matching comforter, and I was just touching the silk bathrobe thrown across the end of it when my roommate walked in the door with a friend, both of them dressed all in white. They were laughing and windblown, while I was wrinkled and worn out after the fourteen-hour bus ride from Lannette.

" 'You must be Colleen,' the tall, blond one said, holding out her hand for me to shake. 'I'm Tess. Do you play tennis?' Of course I didn't—the solitary court in Lannette was at the country club, and only the executives and their wives played there. I was so embarrassed before those two graceful girls in their tennis dresses, embarrassed that I'd been caught out touching something that wasn't mine.

"But as the semester wore on, Tess became my best friend. We were roommates for three years, and from her I learned how to make my poor clothes look their best and was thrilled to have her barely worn castoffs since we were almost exactly the same size. I bought a secondhand copy of Emily Post and copied Tess's table manners, trading my hick Lannette accent for her cultured one. And though I was pitifully shy at first, I learned soon enough how to talk to boys because they all flocked to her like bees to a branch of pear blossom. She had the knack of making everything seem so, so . . . *easy*. Tess was the best thing that had ever happened to me, until I met your father."

My tired ears perk up. I've heard at least this part of her story before. "You had a terrible cold. When you went to the infirmary, that's when you two met."

My mother smiles. "Your father was the handsomest man I'd ever seen that wasn't in a picture show—tall and slender, with thick silver-gilt hair and perfect white teeth. When he smiled and shook my hand, his cool hand was clean, with long fingers and even, trimmed nails.

" 'I'm Dr. Banks,' he said.

" 'You seem awfully young,' I blurted, and then wanted to crawl under the examining table for being so forward.

" 'Third-year resident,' Dr. Banks said. He was unwrapping a tongue depressor. 'Doing a little moonlighting before I finish my last stint in pediatrics. You just might be the last grown-up head cold I treat before I'm up to my eyeballs in diaper rash and whooping cough. Now, let's take a look at your throat.' "

My coffee cup's empty, but I don't move to get up and get another. "So it wasn't love at first sight, the way Daddy used to tell it?"

My mother shakes her head. "Oh, no, Annie. You see, back in Lannette, I'd walk to school as the sun came up. I'd cross over the railroad tracks with the folks working the second shift, but then, even though it was out of my way, I used to turn and take North Street so I could get a glimpse of all the big, beautiful houses where the mill executives, the banker, the doctor, and the owner of the car dealership lived. Their houses were built of bricks or smooth plaster, surrounded by oak trees, dogwoods, and maples, boxwoods and English ivy, set high above the street on green hills with lawns tended by armies of yardmen. I'd walk up North Street in my cheap skirts and blouses, in the awful shoes my mother had sacrificed for me to have, and clutch my books to my chest while I imagined that one day I'd own a home like this one, or that one, dreaming of having a maid and a closet full of pretty clothes to wear. I dreamed of children—well-behaved children who'd go to good schools. I dreamed of the professional man I'd marry, a banker or a lawyer, or best of all a doctor. Oh, before the end of my visit to the infirmary that afternoon, I knew your father was the one I'd been dreaming of, the man who could be the door to that life. Lord, he'd hold the door open for me, and we'd walk through it together with me on his arm."

This comes as less than the revelation I thought it was going to be, but inside I ache for the girl she was, longing for what she'd never had. My mother, however, smiles and goes on.

"The only problem," she says, "was that Dr. Banks hadn't acted like he was interested in me at all, except for having the worst head cold he'd ever treated. He even got out a fancy camera and took pictures of my red, swollen throat to show his department head.

" 'Take these pills,' he said, 'and if you don't feel better in a couple of days, come back to see me. I'll check you for strep.'

"I wasn't about to give up, not when I'd just met the man of my dreams, and so I was looking my best when I went back to the infirmary two days later. That morning, I was wearing my favorite of Tess's sweater collection—a cherry-red cashmere—and a fawn-colored wool pencil skirt, imitation lizard pumps, and had brushed my hair until it shone like black glass. My string of pearls could have passed for real unless you looked too closely. When Dr. Banks walked in the examining room, his eyes widened.

" 'You seem to be much improved, Miss O'Shaunessy,' he said.

" 'Oh, but I'm not,' I said earnestly. 'My throat's still scratchy.' He seemed unconvinced, but once again, he shone a light down my no-longer-scratchy throat.

" 'Hmm.' Dr. Banks's eyes met mine, and at once I understood that he knew I was only pretending to be sick. He turned away and threw the tongue depressor into the wastebasket. 'You're doing fine,' the man of my dreams said, sounding depressingly cheerful. 'When you get back to your dorm tonight, gargle with warm salt water. That should fix you up.' He smiled, but I shook my head in denial.

" 'Tonight? I can't go back to my classes, not feeling like

this.' I fluttered my eyelashes, pouting like Tess did when she wanted a boy to sit up and take notice of her.

"Dr. Banks's smile turned serious. 'No,' he said. 'Of course you can't. I'm taking you downtown to Tujague's for dinner and then to the Joy for the double feature. You can have that salt-water gargle after I drive you home.'

"Well, he didn't try to kiss me good night after our first date, nor on our second, but by our third date I'd realized he was a little shy when he wasn't wearing his white doctor's coat, so I kissed him instead. I still don't know what would have happened if I hadn't, but I had nothing to lose and everything to gain.

" 'Hubba, hubba,' Dr. Wade Banks said to me, his eyes wide. Then he kissed me back. Thoroughly."

Her face is soft, almost dreamy with that memory, but then she looks at me and her gaze is sharp. "We were engaged four months later."

I've never heard any of this. When Daddy talked about their meeting, he always made it sound as though he and my mother were wild about each other from the start. What bravery my mother had, risking everything to capture the man of her dreams. She was also, I realize, more than a little cold-blooded about it, and this makes me look at her with new eyes.

Coffee finished, we move to the living room, where it's more comfortable. I curl up on the sofa with Troy, and my mother goes to the window, looking out at the afternoon.

"He asked me to marry him when we were parking in his Jaguar under the oaks in City Park," she says, her expression faraway. "Your father had considered giving me a ring that had been his mother's, but he said, 'I want you to have your own, one that's never belonged to anybody but you. Let's go to Adler's on Canal Street and you can pick it out.' I was thrilled and more than a little scared of the high-wire act I had to perform now that we had wedding plans, but when I wasn't studying or waiting for envious girls to call up and say Wade was waiting for *me* downstairs, I began to let myself think about floor plans and gardens, of my three beautiful children, my doctor husband. My dream was so close I could almost taste it.

" 'You want to watch out for his mother,' Tess warned me one afternoon. We were lying on my bed, looking at her movie magazines together, leafing through the pages. 'I'll bet you a nickel she's not going to be thrilled about her darling baby boy getting hitched.' "

My mother glances at me and raises a sardonic eyebrow. For sure, I can imagine Grandmother Banks blowing a gasket at the news. "Don't I know about that!" I say, rolling my eyes.

My mother smiles grimly. "Well, at the time I didn't. It was spring in New Orleans, the window was open, and the scent of jasmine and the trill of mockingbird song floated into our dorm room on the warm breeze. That morning was too pretty for me to worry about anything except where I was going to get the money to pay for a wedding gown.

" 'Why, I'm sure we're going to get along famously,' I said to Tess, feeling confident. 'To hear Wade tell it, she's an old-fashioned southern lady with loads of friends. She's supposed to throw these great parties. In fact, Wade says she wants to meet me soon, that she's going to give us an engagement party when we visit up there after he's finished his residency.'

"Tess, wiser to the ways of the world of my dreams than I was, shook her head. 'Still, Collie. That southern charm has teeth and claws. I bet she's a mean old thing.' "

My mother sighs and turns away from the window. She walks back across the room to sit down beside me.

"When Tess said that, I wanted to put my hands over my ears," she says. "In my mind, I could see Mother Banks greeting me on the porch of her mansion with a kiss, sliding her arm around my waist and telling me how *thrilled* she was that

Wade and I had found each other. That's why when the invitation came in the mail a week later, I felt no apprehension opening the heavy, cream-colored envelope, my name written on it in an exquisite cursive. Besides the handwritten invitation—which, according to Emily Post, was the living end in refinement—inside the envelope was a short note from Wade's mother, asking me to come up to Jackson a day before the party so we could 'get acquainted.'

"For three years, I'd managed on the money the church ladies always sent me, a hundred dollars a semester, and that had been enough so that I didn't have to worry about having a job until summer vacation. It had been enough so that—if I was very careful—I could keep myself in decent clothes and have a little spending money. Tess, however, took one look at the invitation and told me there was nothing in my wardrobe that would pass muster with my future mother-in-law.

" 'Here,' she said, throwing open the door to our closet. 'Take anything you like. This dress would be fun for the party since I'm sure it's not going to be a formal affair, probably just family and her intimate friends, and this suit's perfect, I think, for when you meet the old cat.' I tried the suit on, but Tess and I were only *almost* exactly the same size. This summer suit, made of a lovely peach silk poplin, was a bit tight across my bust and derriere. I turned and tried to look at myself from every angle in our mirror, tugging at the jacket and skirt.

" 'Hmm. Wear this blouse.' Tess pulled a white linen blouse with a floppy bow from the closet. 'You can leave the jacket unbuttoned.' "

Remembering how beautifully my mother has dressed since I was a child, I can just see her in her borrowed finery. "I bet you were lovely," I say loyally, but she shakes her head.

"Oh, no, Annie. Two weeks later, when Wade and I walked up the wide front steps of the Banks mansion, that suit felt all wrong. Worse, when his mother rolled out onto the columned porch in her wheelchair, I could see reflected in her eyes a calculation that left me wanting. She smiled a faint smile, leaving me with no illusions. We were not going to have that moment I'd dreamed of.

"She dangled a diamond-ring-bedecked hand in greeting. 'Colleen, sweetheart,' she said. 'I've heard so much about you from Wade, why, I feel like I know you already. You're *exactly* as I've pictured you. Tell me everything about yourself.'

"Inside, I was cursing my damp palms as I took her hand, but your father must have only heard his mother being kind to a young girl, her beloved only son's fiancée, because he smiled and kissed the iron-haired woman in the wheelchair on the cheek.

" 'Now, Mother—hold off. Collie needs to come in and sit down, have a glass of Easter Mae's iced tea before she gives you the lowdown. It was a long drive up from New Orleans.' He squeezed her shoulder and then went out to the Jaguar to bring in our luggage. It was a sweet, disarming thing for him to have said, but old Mrs. Banks's eyes were flat and assessing, just like a cat's before it decides if it's going to eat that mouse or just play with it a while. Without saying a word, her narrow glance at Tess's peach suit informed me that she knew I was dressed in someone else's clothes, that I was an imposter.

"Face to face with a nightmare, I almost ran down the walk to the Jaguar, where Wade was unloading my poor old suitcase, to that wonderful car in which we'd shared kisses in front of my dorm. I wanted to ask him to take me back to New Orleans, but I knew he'd be mystified, maybe even think I was crazy because his mother hadn't said a thing to me that could be construed as anything other than a kindly interest, a warm southern welcome for the girl from the wrong side of the tracks who'd managed to snare her son with trashy, underhanded wiles.

"But even though I was afraid, I knew that I couldn't let

her do that to me. The dream was within my grasp if only I had the nerve to reach out and grab it. I forced myself to smile at her.

" 'Thank you for inviting me,' I murmured. 'It's so nice to meet you at last, too. Wade and I are *so* happy.' Mrs. Banks lifted an eyebrow, as if to acknowledge that the battle had been joined.

" 'Come in, do.' She turned her wheelchair around on the red tiles of the porch with a shrill shriek of rubber tires, turning her back on me. I hastened to hold the front door open for her. She didn't say thank you, and by dinner that evening, I knew what I was in for. Mrs. Banks had interrogated me mercilessly all afternoon—all under the guise of 'getting to know you, honey'—until I felt as gray and tired as the mill creek behind our old house in Lannette. Thank the Lord we weren't just the three of us when we sat down in her gloomy, high-ceilinged dining room, where those old family portraits seemed to gaze disdainfully down at the interloper in their house. Thank goodness Aunt Too-Tai joined us, having driven up from the farm down near Meridian. *Her* suit was a heavy tweed, an odd choice for May."

I smile, thinking of how Aunt Too-Tai must have appeared to my mother back then. I *know* that suit: she still has it. "I bet she was great."

"Oh, of course." My mother continues. "In fact, she was much the same as she is now. 'Collie!' Too-Tai said in a booming, happy voice, her handshake as strong as a man's. 'It's a great pleasure.' Wire-thin, gray-haired, and as tall as Wade, she towered over her thin-smiling older sister enthroned in her wheelchair at the head of the table. She said to me, 'You're pretty as a speckled pup, girl. Glad to know you.'

"Throughout dinner with its five courses, from consommé to chess pie, Too-Tai told us funny anecdotes about her life on the 'home place' while the silent maid served us all. Her friendliness was a bulwark against Mrs. Banks's constant, sweet hostility offered like poisonous bonbons on a pretty dish. Oh, and thank goodness for Emily Post, too. Before I'd devoured her book, all those forks and spoons would've looked like a silver tiger trap to me. I felt myself beginning to relax, to think that perhaps I was going to win my way through this war, and then Wade's mother casually mentioned that the help would be starting preparations for the party at six the next morning.

" 'We've a lot to do to pull this place together,' she remarked. 'The flowers, the food, the folding chairs. My friends are helping me out with a few things, but Easter Mae and her cousin Methyl Ivory are going to have to get started at the crack of dawn if we're to be ready to receive by three.'

"Wade groaned. 'This isn't going to be one of your crushes, is it, Mother? You said it was going to be a small party.'

"His mother shrugged and rolled her eyes, a picture of helpless charm. 'Oh, Wade—you know how it is. Once I invited one family, I had to invite all the families. I'm afraid it's going to be rather a big do.' Her eyes slid over to mine, and I was startled to realize that, while she sounded like she was composed and pleasantly anticipating the next afternoon's party, in reality she was more than a little apprehensive.

"Of course she was. Whether I held up to scrutiny or not was going to be her problem, too. If I was trapped, then so was Mrs. Banks because by then I knew I wasn't going *anywhere*. You may find it hard to believe, but there was a hard little part of me willing to cut up just so she'd be disgraced along with me. It wouldn't be hard. I could talk like a hick, gobble the tea sandwiches, and pretend to be ignorant, but that part was the mill girl, the lint-head, the one who resented the fine folks living on top of the hills of Lannette and everyone just like them. I squashed that part of me flat. I couldn't bear the thought of being a laughingstock even if it would embarrass this cold woman, not when I'd fought so hard for my place at this table.

"We finished dinner after much discussion of the party—the food, the flowers, who was coming and who had sent their regrets—and then Mrs. Banks kissed Wade, gave Too-Tai a pointed reminder that she needed a new dress, and rolled her chair into her elevator to go upstairs to bed. At the foot of the grand staircase, Wade and I shared a quick embrace before he went to stay in the *garçonnière* at the back of the gardens.

" 'You're not worried, are you? Why, you're going to be fine, sweetheart,' he murmured in my ear. I laid my head on his shoulder and wondered. Before I went to bed in the most intimidating of the guest bedrooms, I unpacked the dress that Tess had loaned me and realized that it, like the suit, was all wrong. The poppy-printed silk sheath was too bright, too daring, and a little too tight for this immense, gloomy old house, with its servants and family silver. As you might imagine, I didn't sleep well, dreaming of appearing on stage without having learned my lines, wearing the wrong costume—or, worse, no costume at all.

"After a restless night, early the next morning I awoke to the sounds of the rental men delivering the folding chairs, and I sat up in the big half-tester bed in a panic until I came to the grim realization that there was nothing I could do about anything, none of it. I wanted to throw the covers over my head and never come out from under them.

"But then a knock on the door startled me. 'Come in,' I said.

"Too-Tai poked her gray head into the room, wearing the same old tweed suit from the night before. 'Gracious,' she said. 'I'm always up early, but this is more noise than a baling machine in high gear. Listen, Isabelle's going to put Wade to work as soon as he has a cup of coffee. Why don't you get dressed? We'll have some breakfast and get out of here. I can show you around Jackson.'

"I couldn't imagine anything I wanted more. A couple of hours later, we were driving around the town in Too-Tai's brand-new black Chevrolet. 'I usually bring the truck,' she confided. 'But this time Isabelle swore she'd turn me away if I didn't wear my good duds and drive the car. Since I was dying to meet you, I've had to behave myself.' I giggled at that.

"Too-Tai glanced at me. 'It's good to hear you laugh,' she said. 'I was beginning to wonder if you knew how. Tell you what. Let's go do a little shopping. I've only got the one suit, and Isabelle's laid down the law—I have to wear a dress. I don't own a dress, and Maison-Dit has got loads of 'em.' I was too embarrassed to say that I hated shopping when I had no money to buy anything, so we found ourselves at Maison-Dit, being waited on hand and foot by Dolly, Aunt Too-Tai's saleswoman."

I can't help laughing, thinking of Aunt Too-Tai in Maison-Dit. "What did Dolly look like before she became a quilt?" My mother smiles faintly.

"Much as she does now," she admits. "Maybe not quite so thin. 'Meet Miss Colleen O'Shaunessy, soon to be Banks,' Too-Tai ordered the hovering staff. 'And bring us some coffee, please.' We were in the Collections Room, sitting on a velvet settee that was fearfully deep and ferociously soft. The headless mannequins showed off dresses I knew were just the thing for this afternoon's party, and thinking of my all-wrong outfit, I wanted to cry. Meanwhile the saleswoman bustled off to get Too-Tai the plain navy shirtwaist she demanded. Sipping my coffee when it came, wishing for the thousandth time I had money to buy what I needed, I resigned myself to disaster. Jackson's society folk would always remember me as the girl who wore a flashy cocktail dress to her own engagement party.

" 'Just put it in a bag,' Too-Tai told Dolly when she appeared with the shirtwaist. 'I don't need to try it on.' She must have seen my wistful expression, though, like a child at a Christmas window, for she said next, 'And I'd like you to bring Collie a few things to try on, too.'

" 'Oh, no!' I was aghast. I couldn't allow her to do that. 'I have plenty of clothes. I mean, I already brought a dress for this afternoon.' Never mind it wasn't the right kind of dress.

"But Too-Tai shook her head. 'Let me do this for you, child,' she said under her breath. 'I'm Wade's only aunt, and I want to do something nice for his bride.' She patted my hand. 'I've never had any nieces to spoil. *Please* let me do this.' "

Smiling at her memories, my mother strokes Troy Smoot's head and he wriggles with pleasure. "Oh, it was beautifully done. She'd seen the suit the night before, as well as the shoes that were too cheap to keep up with it. In a million years, Too-Tai wouldn't have dreamed of pointing out that I needed clothes. She was too kind and well-bred for that. I couldn't refuse, not after she so tactfully offered what I needed more than anything, and so that morning I walked out of Maison-Dit with the perfect dress, a full-skirted grass-green linen that took my breath away because it was so sweet, so demure, and so wickedly fashionable. Too-Tai had insisted I get green linen pumps, too, a green that was as close to dyed-to-match as could be."

My mother falls silent. Troy rolls over on his back, begging for a tummy rub now that he knows she's a soft touch. She obliges with a smile.

"So that was all you needed, right?" I ask. God bless Too-Tai.

"Oh, it was a lovely dress," she agrees, "but I still had the party to get through. Back at the Banks house, we walked in the door to a controlled chaos. Jackson's gardens must have been stripped bare for Mrs. Banks's party, for there were masses of flowers in vases wherever you looked. The immense arrangement in the middle of the dining room table was a firework display of daylilies and phlox, early roses, ferns, marguerites, the last of the Dutch irises and tulips, all of them only just contained in a silver urn the size of a laundry basket. And I've never seen so much polished silver in my life before or since—epergnes, candy dishes, sandwich trays, a magnificent tea and coffee service, a punch bowl you could take a bath in, and an amazing array of gleaming flatware and serving pieces.

" 'Looks like Isabelle's throwing a party, all right,' Too-Tai remarked. 'Good thing it's not bee season, what with all these flowers everywhere.' I shuddered at the sight of all those busy servants. It was going to be, as Wade had said, a crush. I took my new dress and shoes upstairs and tried to eat a sandwich for lunch, but couldn't manage more than a mouthful.

"And so at two thirty, in the relative calm of my room, I was dressed in my new dress and heels, had checked for the fiftieth time that the seams of my hose were straight and that I didn't have lipstick on my teeth. When there was a knock at the door, I opened it, expecting to see Too-Tai, but it was Wade, carrying a slim black leather box.

" 'I was going to give you these later.' He tugged at his collar, looking nervous. 'But Too-Tai said I should give them to you now. I hope you like them.'

"I opened the box and found a strand of luminous pearls, heavy and cool as river stones in my hand. 'Oh, Wade,' I said softly. 'They're beautiful.'

" 'So are you. They remind me of your skin.' He blushed. 'Look, I know this is going to be an ordeal. This kind of thing always is for me. When mother has these dos, I used to go out and not come back. She'd get mad as a poked snake, but I'd rather that than get dressed up and have to make polite conversation with these folks. Don't get me wrong—they're all perfectly nice, but there's just too damned many of them.' "

My mother smiles a radiant smile then. "You know, Annie, I think that was when I finally fell in love. Your father was then, as always, the most thoughtful and generous person I'd ever met. Wade fastened the pearls around my neck, and I felt them settle into the hollow of my throat like they'd always been there, a totally different feeling compared to my imitation strand. In that moment I felt as though I could take on anything, as long as Wade was with me."

I put my arm around her thin shoulders. "We'll always miss him," I say softly.

Later, we're back in the kitchen, looking for something to eat, which for once is a productive search since it's Thanksgiving and Myrtistine has cooked up enough food for an army. We sit at the kitchen table with a plate of everything except turkey. I'm probably going to have to get around to cooking it sooner or later, but I urge my mother to keep talking.

"The guests began arriving promptly at three," she says, "the street in front of the Banks mansion filling up with cars so that people had to park and walk from blocks away. By three fifteen, there was a stream of curious guests waiting on the front steps to come into the house to meet me.

"In the entryway, I stood in the receiving line with Mother Banks on one side and Wade on the other, shaking hands and trying to remember to smile while my feet hurt: my new shoes were pinching my toes. Mrs. Banks must have had a sore neck later that night from looking up at all the guests from her wheelchair, but you'd have never known she was anything but delighted to see everyone.

" 'Colleen, I want you to meet one of my oldest friends,' she'd say. I was introduced to all of two hundred people that afternoon, and they were every one of them her oldest friend. Some of the guests brought wedding presents, too, and I had to open them then and there, handing the wrapping paper to Easter Mae to throw away. Wade and I would say how thrilled we were to receive these sumptuous presents, and then Wash would take them to a long table in the parlor so the other guests could inspect our gifts.

"I'd been standing in the receiving line for what seemed like a century when an older couple came in the door with a girl who looked about my age.

" 'Why, how nice of you to come!' Old Mrs. Banks took the other woman's hand. 'And you brought Squeaky, too. Colleen, this is Lydia, but everyone calls her Squeaky. You're sure to be friends—Squeaky's going to be a senior, too. Forgive me, dear, I'm old.' She turned her beaming face up to the girl. 'I forget where you're attending college.'

" 'The W,' Squeaky simpered. 'Where else?' The chubby girl was referring to the exclusive all-girls school, Mississippi State College for Women, where everybody who was anybody went in those days while they were looking for husbands. She was squeezed into a yellow eyelet afternoon dress that clashed horribly with her pink foundation. Her handshake was as limp and clammy as a wet dishrag.

" 'Do you play bridge?' she asked me peremptorily. It was easy to see how she'd gotten her nickname: her voice was a dead ringer for a needle accidentally dragged across a record. '*Everybody* plays bridge and we're starting a club.' Her mother was handing a white paper-wrapped box to Wade, but Mrs. Banks's glittering gaze was fixed on me, waiting for my answer.

" 'I, I've always wanted to learn,' I stammered. In college, I'd never had the time or the inclination. Bridge was for sorority girls, like Tess.

" 'Oh,' Squeaky shrilled, unimpressed.

"Meanwhile, Wade was unwrapping the gift. Thankful for the distraction from my nonexistent bridge skills, I turned to look at the heavy silver object in his hand, a hinged tong-like implement that I'd never seen before. It looked quite a bit like a smaller version of a tool that Wade kept in his alligator doctor bag, so I thoughtlessly exclaimed, 'How wonderful! It's a forceps, isn't it?' Wade looked at the gift in bemusement, while I gushed on about how useful it would be when he had a difficult delivery. 'Wade always says you need the right tool for the job!'

"I felt a sharp poke in my side and looked down to see Mrs. Banks's eyes locked on mine in a terrifying glare of mingled fury and satisfaction. 'It's a *sandwich scissors,* Colleen darling.'

" 'Oh.' I was so shocked and humiliated I couldn't think of any reply other than that. 'Oh.' What in the world was a sandwich scissors?

"Wade came to my rescue. 'Good thing,' he chuckled. 'I already have a brand-new forceps, but no way to pick up my sandwich.' Everybody laughed, but inside I was devastated. Easter Mae appeared to take the paper and ribbon back to the kitchen, and Wash took the damned sandwich scissors to the display table, where a hundred gifts were lined up in shining rows of silver. I tried to turn my attention to meeting the remaining guests in the receiving line, to making polite conversation, but inside I relived that awful moment over and over. After the last people had arrived and been greeted, I knew I had to get away. I told Wade I was going to find the powder room.

" 'Hurry back, darling,' he said. 'I'm going to grab a bite to eat.' Then he disappeared into the crowd of people who were loading up their plates with chicken salad, ambrosia, and pimento cheese sandwiches from the dining table.

"A disorganized gaggle of ladies was waiting to go into the powder room, so I leaned against the wall to take some of the pressure off my aching feet. One by one, they all went inside while I waited my turn. I don't think they even saw me, obscured by another one of those outrageous flower arrangements on the hall table. Finally, the bathroom door opened and Squeaky emerged.

" 'All yours!' she squealed as I came out from behind the flowers. I tried to smile, went inside, and shut the door. It was good to sit down and a relief to be away from the party. I had just finished washing my hands when I heard them outside in the hall.

" 'She didn't know it was a sandwich scissors. She called it a forceps!' It was Squeaky's unmistakable voice. She giggled, a high-pitched, squealing series of snorts. I'd never heard anything like it.

" 'Well, she *is* from some little hick town in Georgia,' some other girl replied. 'I guess I can tell what Wade sees in her, though. She's certainly pretty enough.'

" 'She doesn't know how to play bridge either,' Squeaky grumped. 'Do you think we'll have to ask her to join anyway?' And then their voices faded into the background.

"I stared at my reflection in the mirror and wasn't surprised to find that I was crying, big hopeless tears running down my cheeks in a slow-moving stream. I was always going to be the mill girl from Lannette, never really from Jackson. No one here would ever accept me, no matter what I was wearing. I should go upstairs quietly, pack my bag, and take a cab to the bus station. I should go back to New Orleans.

"I must have stood there in front of the mirror for a long time because finally the tears stopped. Looking at my desperate face, I wiped off their traces but was still unable to open the door. I had to have been in there a while when there was a discreet tapping from the other side.

" 'Collie?' It was Too-Tai. 'You've got to let me in, girl. I need the bathroom right this minute.' I wanted to act like I hadn't heard her, but she kept tapping.

" 'Collie? I'm afraid to try to go upstairs, I need the bathroom that bad. You've *got* to let me in.'

"What could I do then? I opened the door, and Too-Tai pushed her way inside. There was barely room for the two of us in the low-ceilinged powder room. 'Honestly, girl,' she said, sounding exasperated. 'Why are you holed up in here? People are starting to talk.'

"At that, I broke down again. Bless Too-Tai, she dampened one of the linen guest towels and handed it to me. 'Wipe your face,' she said kindly. 'Here.' Handing me a wad of toilet tissue, she said, 'Blow your nose, dear.' I took the tissue and squeezed it into a ball, unwilling to meet her sharp eyes.

" 'You mustn't let yourself be this way, Collie. If you love Wade, and I know you do, then you're going to have to hold your head up in this town. You're going to have to act as though you're good enough for these folks, even if in your heart you're sure you're not. It's all make-believe, anyway. What's real is what's between you and Wade. Now come on out of here and have a chicken salad sandwich, or some cheese straws. Wade's wondering where you are.'

" 'But his mother,' I said tightly, holding back the tears. 'She . . .'

"Too-Tai snorted in contempt. 'Don't you ever forget this, girl. Isabelle Gooch grew up barefoot in a dirt yard on a truck farm that was out from Chunky. Before she married Wade's father, her claim to fame was that she could kill two chickens at the same time, wringing their necks like a field hand. She comes from the same place you come from—not here.' She kissed my cheek and walked out of the powder room.

"Wondering, I touched the pearls at my throat, cool and smooth, sweet to me as Wade's smile. Then I straightened my shoulders, blew my nose, reapplied my lipstick, and went back into that party. I have never cried in a powder room again. That day I learned what make-believe was, but as time passed I also learned how to play bridge, how to entertain, how to pretend that I was as good as anybody, until one day, I realized I wasn't pretending anymore. I'd found a real life, one even better than a seventeen-year-old girl's dream. I'd found your father."

I get up from the table, take our plates to the sink, and run some water over them. "I had no idea," I say. I'm at a loss for words, really. What a valiant bravery she had, how hard she fought for her dream.

My mother gets up and comes to the sink, turns the water off, and turns my shoulders so that I'm looking her square in the eye. She gazes at me searchingly before she says, "And then you, my own child, my only, beautiful child, wanted no part of this life I'd worked so hard for. You wanted . . . oh, I don't know what you want, but this obviously isn't it. You've never wanted this life, you've rebelled against it, fought it to a draw. You're terrible at pretending, dear heart. Find your own dream, no matter where it takes you, Annie. You need to be at peace with who and what you are."

She folds me into her arms and we hold each other tight.

CHAPTER 17

I'm pregnant.

Du came back after a couple of days, ready to be magnanimous and forgive me, but it wasn't any good between us. He wanted me to say I was sorry, but I wasn't, so I couldn't, and as you might expect, this Christmas was a nightmare of unspoken recriminations. (My present from Du was a Bible with the parts about women honoring and obeying their husbands underlined in red.) We lived under one roof for another week until the new year came, sleeping in separate bedrooms, staying out of public life, and making polite noises when we ran into each other in this monstrous house, but as the days wore on, I began throwing up in the mornings. I didn't need an EPT test to tell me I was pregnant at last, and I didn't need a calendar to know it was Ted's baby.

Well, today's New Year's Day, a cold morning possessed of an uncompromising, cut-crystal brilliance. After another night of bourbon-fueled argument, Du's packed and gone for good this time. I'd like to say I've never considered making up with him, letting Du think the baby's his. God knows that was my first thought. I mean, for one thing, I don't know if Ted would even care, and for another, I'm not sure I can raise a child on my own. Finally, though, after a day or two of some serious soul-searching, I know I can't live with myself if I'm not truthful, not even if lying would let me hang onto the old, self-indulgent life of Annie. No, not after that night with Starr last year, not after I've begun to realize that it's way past time I begin to live my life the only way I know how, and not by Jackson's canon.

So since I haven't even a notion as to what Ted's last name might be, much less how I'm supposed to get in touch with him, early this morning after I finish throwing up, I buckle on my big-girl shoes and drive down to the Fair Grounds in New Orleans.

I'm not more than six weeks along, but Bette knows the instant she slams open the Airstream's door in answer to my knock.

"You're pregnant!" she crows, her little brown eyes alight with ursine delight for me.

"You're the first one who knows," I say. "I haven't even told my mother yet."

"Dang." Bette shakes her head and one of her hot rollers falls off onto the Airstream's steps. "But you can't miss it, honey. You're lit up like Grandmaw's birthday cake." I pick up her roller and hand it to her, and she motions me inside her trailer. "C'mon in. What brings you here? I don't see you for years, and this is the second time in a couple of months."

Inside, I look around and notice she's added a swan clock, its wings telling the hour and minute, and a new swan-bracketed paper towel holder. There's a racing saddle propped on the sofa arm and a pair of miniscule, brown-topped boots by the door next to the cement swan, so I gather that her boyfriend Jesús's broken leg has mended and he's come back to the Airstream at last.

"I'm here on a mission," I tell her. "I need to find Ted."

"Ted Clancy?" Bette asks, sounding puzzled. "Honey, he's packing up and headed to Hot Springs this morning. Why d'you want Ted?"

I pause a moment, wondering if I should tell her why I'm looking for him, but then I remember there's not going to be any more hiding from the truth. I say, "He's the father. I thought he should know."

With a gasp, Bette sits on the dinette seat, which responds with a loud creak of distressed plywood. "Oh, Annie." Her eyes go round as one of her snickerdoodles. "Oh, Annie." She gulps. "Does your husband think it's his?"

"I haven't told him yet," I admit. "I wanted to let Ted know before I told anyone else. That way if Du shoots me, at least Ted will have heard it from the horse's mouth."

A silence falls after that. Finally, Bette asks, "Are you going to tell Starr? Are y'all speaking again?"

I make a disgusted noise. "I haven't heard word one from her, not since that night I drove her down here and she repaid me by stealing my car and going back to Jackson the instant 'Mr. Right' called. So as you can imagine, I haven't exactly been keeping up with that particular story, being a little distracted by current events. It's like I've been living underground, so I guess Starr's happy, as happy as anybody could be with that world-class shit head Bobby Shapley."

Bette laughs. "Well, I hope you two get back together one day," she said. "A girl needs her friends. You want some coffee? I just baked a batch of brownies."

Shaking my head, I say, "Brownies, Bette, are one of the reasons I'm in the situation I'm in. Besides, I've given up coffee, wine, and cigarettes—at least until after the baby's born."

Bette laughs again, her big shoulders shaking. "Not *those* kind of brownies, sugar. These are plain fudge brownies."

"You got any of those snickerdoodles?" I ask, feeling hopeful.

Later, I screw up my courage again and walk down the backstretch to find Ted. I find him supervising the grooms in Barn Nine, making sure that the horses' traveling clothes—leg wraps, bell boots, poll caps, tail bandages, antisweat rugs, and light woolen blankets—are all in place. His wide-shouldered back to me, Ted seems to be explaining something to a young man holding onto the same big chestnut horse that's still giving everyone the stink-eye.

"Make sure you load him first, in the front of the van," Ted says. "He's a bad shipper." My heart leaps in my chest in apprehension when he turns away from the groom and notices my silhouette in the barn's entrance. He shades his eyes against the afternoon's bright, cold January sun and begins walking in my direction, his hand outstretched. A step more and then he stops, recognizing me. Ted drops his hand to his side.

"Annie." His voice is flat, without emotion.

So much for that, I think sadly. Still, "Hey," I say. "I'm glad I caught you before you left. Have you got a minute to take a walk with me?"

He seems to think this over, and then he nods, his expression wary. "Okay, I guess so."

We walk in silence beside the barns for a bit before I find the nerve to open my mouth. "So, um, how've you been?" I ask, sounding inane.

Ted keeps walking, long strides I can barely keep up with. "Fine." His voice is short.

"And how're the horses doing?" I pant, practically trotting beside him. Ted is so remote, seems so indifferent, that I can't think of how to bring the baby up. I know I have to tell him before he decides to quit this idiotic conversation and get back to loading the horse van. Instead of getting to the point, though, I babble on. "Has the weather been as cold down here as it's been at home?"

Ted's jaw tightens. He stops suddenly in the middle of the road, turning to look down at me. I've dressed carefully for this meeting, leaving my wedding ring and diamond studs in my jewelry box and the fur parka in the closet. I'd hoped that the old pair of jeans and a brand-new barn jacket would help me appear less Jackson and more backstretch, but the look in Ted's eyes tells me I haven't succeeded. The four-inch suede stilettos, already ruined from the mud and manure on the road between Bette's trailer and Barn Nine, probably weren't the most practical choice, but feeling at a disadvantage, I'd wanted to be as tall as possible for this meeting.

"What are you doing here?" Ted sounds impatient. "Why are you asking me questions about shit you don't care about? The *weather,* Annie? For Christ's sake." He folds his arms across his chest and his gaze goes over my head, looking at nothing.

It's time.

"I'm pregnant."

Now that I've gone on and said it, I feel as though I've flung myself off the roof of the house and haven't hit the ground yet. And Ted, he seems stunned as a lightening-blasted pine, his face pale.

"It's mine," he says softly after a long moment. He's still not looking at me. "It's mine. You wouldn't have driven down here to see me unless I'm the father." Ted runs his fingers through his dark hair and turns away.

"Damn," I hear him whisper. "Damn and damn."

"I brought you your jacket," I say to his back, hopelessly. "I can go to the car and get it." Please, please. Let him turn around. Let him look at me, at least. Please, let him turn around.

And then Ted turns around. He meets my eyes, smiles an

uncertain smile, and that smile grows. Thank you, Lord, Ted smiles that great smile down at me and picks me up, my absurd stilettos leaving the dirt and dangling two feet off the ground. Face to face, he holds me, his eyes searching mine before he folds me close to him. "So, Annie not-from-here—what do we do next?" he says into my hair.

My arms around his neck, I rest my forehead on his shoulder and sigh in pure relief. "I have no earthly idea. I just wanted you to know. By the way, my last name is Banks."

CHAPTER 18

It's a Saturday morning in April, a good day on the backstretch.

Up here in Arkansas, springtime has finally come and there's a sense that the trees are getting ready to pop into achingly green leaf any moment now. The flower beds in front of the grandstand are brilliant, with their banked azaleas and pansies, the rosebushes beginning to bud. Helen Wheels, Ted's sassy little bay mare, won her race last night, and so he was whistling when he left after he kissed me good-bye this morning. The April sun is watery, as though it's shining through a goldfish bowl that needs cleaning, but it's a nice change from all the rain we've had recently. With any luck, the track should dry out and be fast for this afternoon's card, meaning a good race for Triton and a big day for Ray and Stu, his owners. From the excited yelps coming from the distant hay barn, it seems Troy Smoot is engaged in rat removal—an activity that's made him a popular little buzz saw of an exterminator in the barns and tack rooms.

And a few minutes ago, for the first time this morning I felt the baby kick.

I'm sitting on the steps of the trailer, wishing I didn't have to do the laundry today, but if I don't want these jeans to stand up and walk around by themselves, I need to load the Ford and drive into town to the Laundromat. Since my first trimester has passed and with it the god-awful morning sickness that left me leery of even the smell of food, my appetite has come back with a spectacular bang. Now I've got only a couple of pairs of jeans that fit my ever-increasing waistline. No more size zeros for me, but I refuse to go into maternity clothes: all those smocks and elastic panels are so damned dreary that I'm considering wearing Ted's jeans until I outgrow them, too. This morning, one of his shirts—a gray plaid flannel that would have been a circus tent on me back in the days when I didn't eat—is warm on my shoulders in the still-chilly air and smells of Ted's cologne. I smile, thinking that my old saleswoman Dolly would swoon from the shock of it, seeing me dressed like trailer trash and sitting on the steps of a real trailer.

One of the grooms, Old Earl, distinguished from New Earl because he's been working for Ted for ten years, waves at me as he whizzes by on the golf cart with a bale of hay strapped onto the back of it. "Hi, Annie," he calls. I smile and wave back. Yesterday Old Earl asked me when my foaling date was.

"Early August," I said.

"Good," Old Earl said, nodding his approval. "No racing in August." If he and the other grooms actually get around to throwing me a baby shower like they're threatening to, I'll probably end up with a foal halter, a gift certificate to the feed store, and a heavy-duty pair of horse clippers instead of sterling teething rings, cups, and rattles. I'm not concerned since I know my mother and her friends will more than fill the breach.

For the weeks between New Year's and Valentine's Day, the day Troy Smoot and I moved to Hot Springs and into Ted's trailer, I had to have many long, tearful conversations with my mother before she finally agreed that I needed to leave Jackson, to be with the father of my baby. Still, she's determined to come wherever I am for the birth. It's going to be her first grandchild, after all, and I need her with me.

And I filed for divorce, but Du's contesting it like a man who's been made a fool of, and I can hardly blame him. Sometimes, doing what's right hurts innocent bystanders as badly as lying does, so Du's forty-page rant of an Answer to my petition for a no-fault divorce means Ted and I won't be married when the baby comes. I wish things were different, but I've had a lot of time to think it over and have come to the conclusion that I'll have to live with it. Du needs this, I suppose, and besides, life's been good to me. Soon, I'll be rocking my own baby, and not by committee either. For the first time I'm responsible for someone else, responsible for their life.

There's a crow's nest in the top of the pine trees by the clubhouse, and every morning a nesting pair flies across the track to the barns to lay claim to the spilled horse feed. As I lie in the trailer next to Ted in the pale light before dawn, I wake to their cawing, to the mysterious language they speak to each other. I'm told that, like swans, they mate for life. This morning, one of the two is perched on top of the horse van, soaking up the sun just like I am.

"Ock," it says, a bright eye gleaming.

"Ock yourself," I reply.

I'd love to sit here until Ted comes back from the morning workouts, but it's time to get the laundry loaded up. I stretch, get to my feet, and turn to go up the steps inside the trailer when there's a crunch of gravel behind me, the sound of car tires pulling into the lot.

I pause on the steps to see if it's Ray and Stu, Triton's owners, because if it's them I'll need to go tell Ted so he can hustle on over for some serious owner stroking. It's not them. The big white Mercedes with Mississippi plates plows to a stop in the middle of the parking lot like a ship running aground. The crow beats its black wings, taking lazy flight into the sun, and then a woman gets out of the car.

Starr.

We lock eyes, her waiting by the side of the Mercedes with the door open as though she might just jump back into it, me frozen below the metal steps of the trailer. Starr's wearing a gorgeous Arctic fox vest, a cashmere turtleneck the color of her eyes, and a pair of twinkling diamond earrings the size of hubcaps. Even from here, I can tell she's had the baby.

Without taking her eyes from mine, Starr reaches into the car and turns off the engine. "Annie," she says in the sudden stillness. "I found you."

"I didn't know you were looking," I say. "You sure weren't last Thanksgiving."

She smiles wryly. "Okay, so maybe I should have looked harder. I'm sorry."

I nod slowly. "Maybe you should have, but it's all right." It's not: we're neither of us seven years old anymore, and sometimes it isn't about sorry. I know that now.

Starr tosses her hair over her shoulder, that canary-diamond hair, and smiles her big, bright smile. "It wasn't like you think," she says, her voice coaxing. "I know everybody's saying I married him for the money, but we're in love. Really, really in love."

"And your baby?" I ask, raising an eyebrow. "How's Bobby working out as a daddy?"

Starr looks confused for a second, then comprehension smoothes her pretty, wrinkled forehead. "Oh, shoot. You don't know! I didn't marry Bobby Shapley, Annie. I married the Judge."

My knees buckle, and sinking fast as a broken elevator, I have to sit my ass down on the metal treads of the trailer steps. "You *what?*" I ask in disbelief.

With a shrug, Starr walks around the Mercedes and says, "Can I have a sit, too?"

I move over, and carefully she lets herself down, sighing. Her fox vest smells of Giorgio, a fragrance I've never cared for. "I'm still not over havin' the baby," she says with a grimace. "Twenty-one hours of labor. Little Brittany was worth every second of it, though. Yep, I married Otto in Las Vegas last Thanksgiving morning. Of course Bobby wasn't ever going to marry me, but after all, Brittany *is* Otto's baby."

I'm speechless, but somehow I'm able to take this in without my mouth falling open, at least. "You're serious," I finally manage. "You slept with the *Judge* when you were living with Bobby?" At this unlikely point, I don't care too much about sounding holier-than-thou.

Starr sighs and gazes off into the distance. "It wasn't for more than a couple of weeks. Bobby'd begun to have a . . . little problem," she says delicately. "Me and Otto started up when he came over to the condo to talk to Bobby about getting shut of me, but Bobby wasn't home because we'd had a fight. I was upset about that and, well, one thing led to another thing and somehow Otto and me ended up sleeping together. Afterward, he told me he'd never done anything like that before. Me, I was disgusted with myself so I told him we couldn't ever do it again.

"But you did," I say dryly.

Starr smiles a half-smile. "You know how those Shapley men are."

"Don't I just," I say. "They don't let go of anything, not ever, not until they're done with it." I don't need to tell her about my own encounter with the Judge, about his dreadful proposition by the boxwoods at the country club.

Starr looks at her hands, at the enormous diamond solitaire on her wedding finger. "Oh, yeah, they're both tigers in the sack, honey—another family thing, I guess. Remember how I said you can't misunderestimate the power of great sex?"

"It'll make your best intentions into orphan dogs," I say. "How could I forget?"

"Anyhow, after a couple of weeks of sneaking around, I told Otto we had to cut it off. He said okay, but he wouldn't believe the baby was his, not back last fall, not until Bobby told him that night before Thanksgiving how Brittany couldn't be his kid 'cause Bobby hadn't touched me in weeks. That's when Otto called and told me to get back to Jackson lickety-split so we could get married straight off. 'No child of mine is going to be born illegitimate,' he said."

Starr turns those pale eyes to mine, a tentative smile hovering on her lips. "You want to see Brittany? She's only a month old, looking like a three-week-old kitten she was, what with being born so early. My little Pisces."

"Sure." Actually, I'm dying to see her daughter.

Starr hops off the steps and hurries across the gravel to the Mercedes, opens the back door, and unsnaps a tiny, sleeping baby from a stupendously luxe car seat that looks as though it was made for royalty. Knowing the Judge's deep pockets, perhaps it was.

"Isn't she the most precious-est girl? Mommy's little sweetheart," Starr coos as she comes back across the gravel holding the pink-wrapped bundle. I get up to go see.

"If she's lucky, she'll look like you," I say, "and not her daddy." I stroke the seashell fist, and Brittany curls her exquisite little hand around my fingertip. I melt. "She's beautiful," I say simply. "It's good to see her. How did you find me?"

"Bette helped," Starr says. "Otto said we could come on up here for the racing and maybe I'd see you. Your mother told me I should do it."

Remembering my mother's story, the one she didn't tell me until it was almost too late, I can understand why. She and Starr are kindred souls. Of a sort.

"Ted's going to be glad that it's all worked out for you," I say. At least, I think he will. He's the most compassionate man I've ever known, but he's not exactly Starr's biggest fan.

"It's so great you're with Ted," Starr says. "He's one of the good guys, never hitting on me or anything, just acting like a friend whenever I needed one. I think I still owe him fifty dollars. Anyways, I wanted to ask you to be Brittany's godmother. Say yes, Annie. Please? You can stay with us." Starr rocks the baby in her arms and looks at me, her pale eyes begging mine for approval. "Otto and me, we got a big old, brand-new French Provincial house with a ton of bedrooms, and the bathrooms have all got Jacuzzi tubs and cultured marble. Please say you'll come. Those Ladies' Leaguers have to act nice now that I'm Mrs. Otto Shapley, but they're never not gonna call me trash behind my back, no matter they're sweet as pie to my face. I need me a friend for when Brittany gets baptized, there'll be so many high-muckety-mucks hanging around, guzzling champagne, and whispering mean stuff when they think Otto won't hear."

I think it over. Godmother? Then, reflecting on the Judge as this precious child's daddy, I decide she's going to need all the support she can get. So I say yes, Starr throws an arm around my neck, and I'm enveloped in a cloud of Giorgio. The baby wakes up, her eyes the color of star sapphires. My godchild to be.

"I just love you, Annie Banks!"

Disentangling myself, I tell Starr my own news, how perhaps one day our daughters will play with Barbies in the backyard, stand up against second-grade injustice, and vanquish bullies together.

"Jesus take the wheel," Starr breathes, her eyes wide with

surprise. Then we both cry a little, but even though I'm tempted, I don't tell her about the rosebushes and their secret, about the many heartbreaking years I tried to have a child, because that's something between me, Troy Smoot, and my mother.

At last, Starr gets ready to leave after I promise her one more time I'll stand godmother to Brittany, who's good and awake and hungry now. "I've got to go back to the hotel and feed her. Come on, Brittany Anne Shapley."

I raise an eyebrow. "Brittany Anne?"

Starr flashes that big, bright smile. "I named her for you—hopin' you'd say yes. You can't back out now, Mercy Anne Banks." She straps Brittany into the car seat and gets behind the wheel. Leaning out of the window, she says, "You're still my best friend, right?"

I don't even stop to think it over. "Always." I wave until the Mercedes is out of sight.

Morning at the racetrack is done, and it's almost time for lunch. Hoping he's not going to want to share his rat with me, I whistle up Troy Smoot and we head to the barn where Ted will be overseeing the noon feeds, checking to make sure the horses have come through their morning workouts without a strained tendon or a lost shoe. I want to find him, to tell him I'm going back to Jackson one last time to be there for my best friend. She needs me.

It's not a mystery to me any longer. You do the right thing and then live with it, as best you can.

A READING GROUP GUIDE

The Right Thing

Amy Conner

ABOUT THIS GUIDE

The suggested questions are included to enhance your group's reading of Amy Conner's *The Right Thing*!

Discussion Questions

1. Annie is rich, thin, beautiful, and spoiled as a child. Do you find her a sympathetic character? Why or why not?

2. As the story unfolds, do you find parallels between the 1960s and 1970s chapters and the present action in 1990?

3. Responsibility and doing the right thing are dominant themes in the novel. In your opinion, which character best embodies these characteristics?

4. Another theme is the intense relationships shared by small children. Why do you think Annie and Starr's childhood bond survives into their adulthood even though they haven't seen each other in decades?

5. Is this book, in a sense, a coming-of-age novel? If so, when do you see Annie growing up at last after a lifetime of acting like a child?

6. Why do you think Annie stays married to Du for so long, especially since it's obvious that she feels unhappy and stifled in her marriage? Does this give you insight into her character?

7. Do you think *The Right Thing* accurately depicts two different eras—attitudes, prejudices, political realities, etc.—in the American South?